A SELLSWORD'S HOPE

Book Seven
of
The Seven Virtues
by
Jacob Peppers

This book is a work of fiction. Names, characters, places and incidents are either the product of the author's imagination or are used fictitiously. Any resemblance to actual persons, living or dead, or to actual events or locales is entirely coincidental.

A Sellsword's Hope
Book Seven of the Seven Virtues

This book is licensed for your personal enjoyment only. This book may not be re-sold or given away to other people. If you would like to share this book with another person, please purchase an additional copy for each person you share it with. If you're reading this book and did not purchase it, or it was not purchased for your use only, then you should return to the retailer and purchase your own copy. Thank you for respecting the hard work of the author.

Copyright © 2019 Jacob Nathaniel Peppers. All rights reserved, including the right to reproduce this book, or portions thereof, in any form. No part of this text may be reproduced, transmitted, downloaded, decompiled, reverse engineered, or stored in or introduced into any information storage and retrieval system, in any form or by any means, whether electronic or mechanical without the express written permission of the author. The scanning, uploading, and distribution of this book via the Internet or via any other means without the permission of the publisher is illegal and punishable by law. Please purchase only authorized electronic editions, and do not participate in or encourage electronic piracy of copyrighted materials.

The publisher does not have any control over and does not assume any responsibility for author or third-party websites or their content.

Visit the author's website:
www.JacobPeppersAuthor.com

To my wife, Andrea,

Who most certainly possesses the Virtue of Patience,

Even without a mythical creature to help.

And that, I think, is a magic all its own.

Sign up for the author's New Releases mailing list and get a copy of The Silent Blade, the prequel for The Seven Virtues, FREE for a Limited Time!

Go to JacobPeppersAuthor.com to get your free book!

CHAPTER ONE

The house, when they came upon it, looked much like any other in Perennia's poor quarter. A squat, crudely built shack seemingly thrown together by a carpenter with few materials and less skill.

Aaron stifled a yawn and followed the two soldiers to the shack's door. He'd slept little in the last two days. His eyes felt grainy and dry, as if someone had rubbed sand into them while he...well, not slept. Certainly, not that. He found his thoughts drifting to Adina and, particularly, to the bed they shared. Not that she would be in it, of course. As hard as he'd been having to work the last few days, Adina had worked even harder, getting little to no sleep at all as she set about the unenviable task of undoing the damage Grinner had done to the city, excising the results of his treachery like a healer performing a particularly difficult—and time consuming—surgery.

Still, the fact that Adina was suffering even more than he was didn't make Aaron any less tired, for the door on which the soldiers were preparing to knock—or break down, if need be, and it almost certainly would—was not the first, or even the hundredth such door they'd visited over the last few days. Aaron's thoughts were on the princess, on his own exhaustion, so he almost missed the tell-tale warning that rose in his mind as he quested out distractedly with the power of the bond. Almost, but not quite. "Don't," he said.

The soldier's fist was raised to knock, but he froze as if a sword was held at his back. After all, it was not the man's first such door either, and he'd been given occasion to trust Aaron in such situations as this. "General?" he asked, his voice low and uncertain.

Aaron frowned, questing out with the power of the bond, reaching tendrils of it through the door to the two men on the other side. One stood with his back pressed against the wall, a knife in his hand, his thoughts filled with that wild anger few things but fear can engender. But it wasn't him that Aaron was worried about. It was the man who sat in the middle of the room, a crossbow in his hands. This one was angry too, scared just like his comrade, but where the other man's thoughts were frantic and troubled, this one's were ordered, resigned. He knew what awaited him, but he was intent on taking as many with him as he could when it came time to visit the Death God.

Aaron shook his head at the guard, holding up a finger to tell him to wait. Over the last days and weeks, he'd grown considerably in the power he was able to exert with the bond. According to Co, he had mastered it to a degree no one else ever had. But no matter how much power he'd gained, it still had its limits, and the last few days of constant use had stretched those limits to the breaking point. So when he reached out with the bond, it was slow to respond. Where normally he would have been able to get a clear understanding of what the two men felt, of whether or not they would surrender, given the chance, now he only caught bits and pieces, fragments of their thoughts, their emotions, that made little sense on their own.

The frantic one thought of a woman. Or was it a girl? Mary. Or maybe it was Margaret? Certainly, it started with an M. Or...almost certainly. A wife, perhaps, or a daughter. *It doesn't matter,* Aaron scolded himself, rubbing his temples where the headache that had been slowly building over the last few days was rising to a crescendo. *What matters is he might put the blade down—might give up.* The other though...Aaron couldn't read much off the man, but it was enough to know he thought of no one—not even himself. His thoughts were only of the grave, of the cold dark of death that had already begun to seep into his bones, his flesh, and of the certainty that the only way to feel some warmth again was to kill as many of those who came for him as he could.

"Let me," Aaron said quietly, and the guard moved out of the way.

"General, sir," the soldier said, "are you sure?"

No, Aaron thought, *I'm not sure. Maybe the first man won't give up, after all—maybe he'll fight until he's dead. Shit, maybe it's not Margaret or Mary—gods, it could be Mark for all I know. The truth is, I'm too tired to know the truth of it one way or the other. I'm not sure, and that's why I'll go.* He knew what Adina would say to that, had heard the lecture often enough over the last couple of days to recite it word for word. Knew, even, that many of the points she would make would be good ones.

And yet, you'll ignore it, the Virtue said into his mind, and though she tried for anger, what came through her tone was little more than an exhausted resignation, for she had been feeling the stress of the last few days as much as Aaron himself.

Yes, he thought back, standing in front of the door, his own hand hesitating inches from the latch. It was not locked—that much, at least, he had managed to pick up from the thoughts of the two inside.

"Sir?" the second soldier said, holding up the stout length of wood he carried, an efficient, if graceless key for many of the doors they'd visited lately.

"Not this time," Aaron said, and the man gave a gruff nod, offering no argument, as if he trusted the sellsword's decisions without question. *If only I could do as much.*

Aaron frowned, considering. It was a small house, a small room. The door would swing to the left, the man with the knife waited on the right. That would leave any poor fool who entered nowhere to go but forward, directly into the crossbow fire of the second man.

Any poor fool—including a particularly stubborn sellsword, I imagine, the Virtue said.

Aaron sighed. "Yeah, I guess so."

"Sir?"

The guards were looking at him strangely and he realized that, in his exhaustion, he'd spoken out loud. "Nothing. Just thinking."

You know what you should do. Leave some guards on the door—they'll have to come out sooner or later.

And waste even more time and resources? It's not as if we have soldiers lining up to help, is it?

Not that most of the city's soldiers *knew* what they were doing, in any case. After all, there was no telling quite how far Grinner's poison had spread, and Aaron and the others had decided it would be better to rely only on those they could trust—a dishearteningly small number, when they stopped to count it: himself, Darrell, Wendell, Leomin, and, after some debate, the remaining members of the Ghosts, the most elite of Perennia's soldiers who had stood and held the gate against Belgarin's army. There had been well over a hundred of them before that fateful encounter, but unsurprisingly, holding off an army on their own had reduced their numbers significantly, and now there were only perhaps two dozen left.

Aaron drew his sword and one of the knives he carried at his side, then turned back to the two soldiers who gave him a nod to indicate they were ready. "Stay behind me," he said. "On either side of the door."

The soldiers nodded at that, as if it were perfectly reasonable, and that did little to quell the voice inside Aaron's head that told him he was being a fool. He should wait. He knew he should. Yes, it would slow down the search for Grinner's men, further delaying the army's march on Perennia—a march that should have begun days ago—but it would also mean he had a better chance of not ending up with a crossbow bolt sticking out of him, a particularly unpleasant sensation that his bad luck—or, truth to tell, bad choices—had given him cause to experience before.

Over the years, he'd heard countless people—hucksters and traveling showmen, mostly—claim to be able to cut down an arrow in mid-flight. He had even watched a few successfully accomplish such a feat, though more often than not the "show" ended with a visit to the healer's. Yet, even those few who had succeeded had done so by deflecting arrows shot from bows designed for the purpose. Underpowered shots with arrows covered in so much fluffy fletching they looked dressed to attend a nobleman's ball, shot from bows fashioned so that even *had* the shot landed, it would have most likely bounced off, and no harm done.

All pretty enough to watch, he supposed, if the watcher kept his eyes squinted and ignored the fact that the arrows traveled slower than a rock thrown by a particularly timid child. Pretty, fancy, maybe. But not real. In reality, arrows were *fast,* and crossbow bolts—not dependent on the strength of the man holding the bow—were often faster. Still, he had touched the man's mind, if briefly, and had some inkling of his emotions. He thought he might be able to predict, with a reasonable degree of certainty, where the man would aim. Which left a chance—a bigger one than he would have liked—that he'd end the day with an extra hole in him than when he'd started it. It would be better to wait. Smarter.

"It's a damn shame," he said to no one in particular, "but I never have been good at waiting."

With that, he kicked at the flimsy latch on the door with as much strength as he could muster. The house was in the poor quarter of the city—as most of the sanctuaries Grinner's men had chosen were—and, like its counterparts, the wood of its door was weak, rotten. One good kick was enough to shatter the latch and send the door swinging inward.

Aaron didn't hesitate, charging into the darkness of the house. There was a cry of surprise from the man on the side of the door, but from the other, the one with the crossbow, there was only silence. Well, silence, and the particularly ominous *snick* of the crossbow's release. Aaron could see little of the house's interior—vague outlines, no more than that, and it wouldn't have mattered in any case. But he was still holding onto the power of his bond with Co, so even before the crossbow released, he was moving, his hand—and the knife it held—flashing up in front of his neck where he felt the man would aim.

At first, the blade cut through nothing but air, and he had the panicked thought that maybe he'd read the man wrong, that he'd decided to aim for the easier target of his stomach or chest instead, and that he was about to have a new hole in him, a token of his own foolishness. But then the knife struck something and there was a *clatter* as the bolt was deflected to strike the wall beside him. Still cognizant of the man beside him, he brought the blade back and threw it at the shadowy outline further in the house. He was rewarded with a surprised shout of pain, but he was already spinning, his fist lashing out and taking the man at the door—who'd been just about to lunge with the knife he carried—in the chin.

The thug cried out in pain, stumbling backward. Aaron continued his spin, sweeping his leg out to strike his opponent in the back of his knees. The man let out another cry and fell to the ground. Before he could rise, Aaron stepped forward, withdrawing his sword and placing the tip at the criminal's throat. The man froze, his body going stiff, but Aaron could feel him thinking it over, considering going for the blade that had fallen beside him. "Don't," he said. "She wouldn't want you to."

He couldn't see the criminal's face in the darkness, but he saw his body tense as if he'd been slapped. "M-Maisel sent you?"

Maisel. Damn it. "Not exactly, but if you ever want to see her again, you'll stop reaching for that blade and stay still."

The thug did, and Aaron felt as much as saw the fight go out of him. Satisfied there'd be no more trouble from that quarter, he turned to the other man. The chair had been knocked over, and the man himself had fallen to his knees, hissing and cursing in pain. His hands gripped the blade embedded in his shoulder as if he would pull it out. Before he could, the two soldiers rushed in, their own blades drawn, and by the light of the lantern one of them carried, Aaron was able to make out the crossbow bolt the man had dropped when the blade struck him.

The two soldiers set about manacling the criminals. One unceremoniously ripped the knife free of the man's shoulder, eliciting a scream from the criminal, before offering the blade back to Aaron.

The sellsword took it, sheathing it and his sword. Then, suddenly, a rush of dizziness went through him, and the strength seemed to leave his legs. He stumbled and would have fallen had his back not hit the wall behind him.

The two Ghosts were seeing to the prisoners, so they didn't notice, nor did they see him blinking stupidly, shaking his head in a furious effort to banish the spots that danced in his vision. *You've pushed yourself too hard,* Co said admonishingly. *You need rest, Aaron.*

Sure, he thought back as some of the strength returned to his legs, and he pulled himself off the wall. *And starving men need food—that doesn't mean they always get it. You know as well as I do that we have to finish this, and quickly. With each day that passes, Kevlane grows stronger. We're running low on time—might be out of it already.*

And if you get there only to be too tired to stand? I wonder, how effective you will be battling Kevlane and his creatures if two of your men have to carry you around, maybe swing your sword for you, too.

Aaron didn't respond, partly because she was right, and he knew it, but also because the soldiers had finished chaining the two prisoners, and were turning back to him, looking at him with a question in their eyes. "Put them in the dungeons with the others," he said wearily. He gestured to the one with the wound in his shoulder. "Have a healer have a look at that one first, then let Captain Gant know, so his questioners can see to them."

"Of course, General Envelar."

"*General Envelar?*" the fearful man who'd stood behind the door said. "Gods, but...then it's true then. The way you knew I was behind the door...you really can read people's minds."

Sure, Aaron thought sourly, *and for my next trick, I'll fall asleep standing up.* But he didn't bother responding, only motioned for the soldiers to take the prisoners out.

They started toward the door, but one of the Ghosts paused, as Aaron had feared he would. "General...if you don't mind me sayin' so, sir, that was amazing. I've never seen anything like it. Deflecting a crossbow bolt with a knife and throwing the same knife to hit him right in the shoulder of his crossbow arm before he could reload...incredible, sir."

Aaron barely managed to hide his wince. Another story, then, to add to the growing legend of Aaron Envelar, the savior of Perennia, the man who had even bent the demonic Akalians to his will, who had stood—practically alone, if the stories were to be believed—against King Belgarin's army, holding the gate against impossible odds. All bullshit, of course, but legends, he'd come to learn, didn't waste much time on the truth.

He hadn't stood at the gate alone, but with more than a hundred of Perennia's best-trained troops, and still they would have died if not for Ellemont's courageous—and ultimately suicidal—charge into the thick of Belgarin's army. As for the Akalians, they had saved him and the others as surely as Ellemont had. And the knife…well, the truth was that he'd been aiming for the man's heart, and it was only luck that the blade had struck him at all. Still, he didn't think it would do any good to tell the soldiers that. They would just think he was being modest, self-deprecating, and that would only make the stories worse, so instead Aaron only nodded. "Well, go on and get them to the dungeons. There's plenty more work to be done before we're through."

The two men nodded and escorted the prisoners out of the house, but Aaron didn't miss the adoration—bordering on worship—in their gazes as they left. Alone in the house, he took a slow breath, leaning back against the wall, this time not out of physical exhaustion, but surprise and relief that he was still alive. It hadn't been the wisest course, maybe, rushing the two men, but it had worked out, so that was something.

Not the wisest course? Co scolded. *It was beyond stupid, that's what it was. You can leave those soldiers to believe what they will, but you and I both know it's by luck, nothing more, that you're still standing here instead of lying on the floor, hurt or dead. What possessed you to try deflecting an arrow with a knife anyway?*

"It worked, Firefly," he said aloud, since he was now alone in the house. "Isn't that enough? I thought he would aim for my throat, and he did. So relax, would you? Everybody walked away—it's a win."

"And if he hadn't?" she demanded, materializing in front of him, a swirling ball of magenta light. "If he'd aimed for your stomach? Or your heart?"

Aaron grunted. "Then you and I wouldn't be having this conversation, that's all, and I think it would be safe to say you'd have won the argument."

Co made a sniffing sound. "Arguing with you is like arguing with an ox—there's no winning it. Even if there *should* be, the ox is too stupid to know when it's wrong."

Aaron gave a small smile at that. "But if all the oxen in the world suddenly grew smart, started reading books and spending their time in libraries, then who would pull all the carts?"

"I…that's the dumbest thing I've ever heard."

"Well, what do you expect from an ox?" he said, giving a tired laugh that faded as he turned to the door of the house. "I'll rest, alright?" he promised. "Just as soon as this is done."

"Sure," the Virtue said, "what better time to rest than when we're marching to war?" But she said it without much feeling, and Aaron headed for the door, hoping that the others were faring better than him.

CHAPTER TWO

"I can't say as I know why you're both actin' so pissed off. It worked, didn't it?" Wendell said, doing his best to avoid the sullen stares of Darrell and Leomin as they walked down the street. In the early morning hours, the city was crowded, but people made way for them, jumping out of their path as if they were important dignitaries or, maybe, barbarians seeking blood and death. He couldn't be sure, but he thought it had something to do with his companions. Or, more specifically, their smell. He himself could barely stand walking beside them, but he thought it probably best not to say so under the circumstances. After all, they both seemed to hold him personally responsible which, so far as he was concerned, was completely unfair.

Darrell frowned, obviously struggling to keep his patience as he wiped at a suspicious brown stain on his clothes, doing nothing but smearing it in more as far as Wendell could see. But Wendell noticed the idle way the swordmaster's fingers had been playing at the hilt of his sword and thought it best not to say so. "It isn't that we disagree with your method, Sergeant Wendell, and no one can doubt it's...efficacy. The cart *did* knock the door in, just as you thought. Only..." He sighed, apparently at a loss for words.

"*Only,*" Leomin said, scowling as he plucked at something—hay, it looked to Wendell—in his hair. Not for the first time, the sergeant thought a man who took all the time and aggravation to grow his hair out so long and braid it into long strands, even put *bells* in it, for the gods' sake, then the least he could do was keep it clean. "*Only* that maybe it would have been smart to let us know before hand, so that we could get out of the way."

"Seems to me," Wendell said sullenly, "that a man shouldn't need another to tell him to get out of the way, a cart full of hay and shit comes rollin' at him."

Darrell cleared his throat, and Wendell kept a close eye on his hand, in case he went for his sword. "Yes, quite, and I'm sure that we *would* have got out of the way, if given the chance. Foolish of us, I suppose, for thinking to try knocking first."

Wendell grunted. "Well, you said it, not me."

"Still," Leomin said through gritted teeth as the people they passed watched their procession with disgust, several of them coughing as they did and holding their hands to their noses. "Can you explain to me again why it was so important to light the cart—and its...*contents*—on fire?"

"Oh," the sergeant said, nodding. "The hay and the shit, you mean? Well, I saw that fella holdin' the lantern, and I thought, sure, Wendell, the cart ought to break through the door sure enough, but then what if it gets stuck, you know? Or, what if they just keep settin' in there, waitin' on us? Seemed to me, the only thing that'd catch me by more surprise than a cart full of fertilizer breakin' down my door would be if that cart was on fire, and what's the problem anyway?" He grinned, remembering the look on the faces of the three men who'd come running out of the house like they were being chased by the Death God himself. "It got 'em out in the street, didn't it?"

The two men didn't say anything for some time after that, and how could they? He was right, that was all. He'd had an idea, and it had worked. It wasn't his fault if they didn't have sense enough to get out of the way with a cart full of flaming shit rolling at them. They traveled on in silence for a while, and he was starting to hope the whole thing was done, had almost convinced himself that their faces only looked so angry on account of the smoke and...other things...smeared across them. He was even considering striking up a conversation with the three manacled prisoners they were escorting when the swordmaster spoke again. "And the farmer?"

Wendell rolled his eyes. "Ridiculous, the man actin' so put out like that. Here we are, savin' the city and all, and he acts as if the world is endin' on account of one burned-up shit-cart. I ain't ever heard nothin' so ridiculous. Still, once he got calmed down, he was alright, I reckon. Charged a fair enough price for the cart and its contents—leastways, I suppose it was fair, but I tell you if I'd known shit went for so much, I might never have went into soldiering, took up shit-farming instead." He shook his head. "Would have damn near cleaned me out, payin' all that."

"Not that you *did* pay it," Leomin said, and the sergeant figured the man must be coming down with a cold as his words sounded almost like a snarl. "And wait a minute—what do you mean *'would'* have cleaned you out?" His eyes narrowed, and there was no mistaking the violence in his gaze now—one that, to Wendell's discomfort, the swordmaster seemed to share. "You said you didn't have any coin."

"Right," Wendell said, deciding now was as good a time as any to look at the prisoners, make sure they weren't up to anything. "And that's true—I'm as poor as any man walkin' upright can be." Or, at least, he *would* be, just as soon as he visited Salia later in the evening once their work was done. He thought about telling the men what little money he had was set aside to pay on a contract—and he and Salia *had* talked about him visiting again the last time he saw her, so that wasn't a lie—but decided that maybe, with the mood they were in, keeping it simple was the best thing. So instead of talking, he walked on in silence, imagining what the night ahead would be like, and doing his best not to be distracted by the aroma of his two companions.

CHAPTER THREE

Sighing heavily, May let the parchment—a current report on the city's western food stores—fall to her desk to land on top of the ever-increasing pile of such reports that littered the wooden surface. She was glad Grinner was gone, but in the short amount of time he'd been in power, the man had managed to sell or steal nearly everything of value. Armor and weapons had vanished, sold to the gods alone knew who. Food was also missing from the stores they'd so carefully accumulated in preparation for the war, not to mention many of the cavalry's horses. If May didn't figure out where they'd gone soon, the mounted warriors would be riding into battle on mules, or on each other's shoulders. Not exactly an image that inspired confidence.

As far as she was concerned, Silent's answer to Grinner's crimes had been far too easy an escape for the crime boss; true justice would have been forcing him to sit down at the seat May now occupied and figure out some way to solve the host of problems he'd created. Still, she consoled herself, not *everything* could be missing. The man had only had a few *days* for the gods' sake. Perhaps, if she were to send out some troops to the outlying towns around the city she might be able to find some of the goods, and—

Her thoughts were interrupted by a particularly loud snore, one that rose above the steady drone of its fellows that had accompanied her work for the last hour.

She scowled at the big man with his head on the table, and was disgusted and more than a little annoyed to see a line of drool leaking onto the most recent report of troop numbers. After Aaron and the others had taken back the city, Adina had come to May, thanking her for everything she'd done and apologizing for the fact that her sister had very nearly had the club owner killed. When asking May to once more take over the planning of the army's logistics and supplies, she had extolled May's virtues—citing her cleverness, her organizational abilities, and several others. One that she had *not* mentioned—and with good reason, so far as May was concerned—was the club owner's patience.

She gave the sleeping man's chair a hard kick. Urek startled at the noise, jerking up and looking around as if he were being attacked which, given his profession as well as his tendency of drooling on important documents, May understood well enough. "Wha—what in the name of the gods was that?" he said, running a thick arm across his face.

"Hmm?" May said, pretending to study another of the parchments, chosen at random. "Oh, it must have been thunder, I suppose."

The big man turned to her, raising an eyebrow that expressed his doubt clearly enough. "Gods, woma—*May*," he said, clearing his throat and avoiding her scowl. "I'm not one for sittin' at a fancy desk and goin' over reports. I should be out there," he went on, swinging his arm in a sweeping gesture to include the entire city, "helpin' the lads ferret out Grinner's men."

May sighed, pinching her nose in a vain effort to keep the coming headache at bay. "And do you really believe the city would be better served by you stabbing someone than by you using your connections to find where they've gone—not to mention where our *supplies* have gone? Or maybe you enjoy the prospect of eating tree bark on the way to Baresh?"

The big man grunted. "What I believe is that much more of this, and I'm liable to swallow some of Beautiful's fire powder and see what comes of it."

May frowned. After they'd retaken the city, she and the others had spoken in council in the queen's chambers about what each of them had experienced, so she knew well the fire powder of which he spoke, hadn't missed the swordmaster's wince when he told of it, as if even the memory was painful. "If you don't stop your complaining and start helping with these reports, I'm tempted to make you swallow some myself."

The big man sighed, nodding, and grabbing the report nearest him. "Alright then, May. Alright. But the boss was right, you know?"

"Oh?" May said, arching an eyebrow. "About what?"

Urek grunted, giving her a wink. "You're one mean bi—err...lady."

Not everyone believes so, May thought, thinking of Thom, of the morning they'd shared before the work had begun. In the dungeons, she had been convinced she would never see him again. Now that they had both somehow survived, she begrudged every moment without him, just as, she knew, he did without her. He had intended to stay in her office, helping her today, but for all his many qualities, the first mate knew little about supplies and logistics for an army, and he would have only distracted her. Though, it had to be said, he was a most pleasant distraction. Still, she had made him leave, knowing that the army would march before long, just as soon as Aaron and the others managed to track down all of Grinner's men. Not much good, after all, worrying over the thief knocking on your door, only to ignore the one already in your house.

So, though all she wanted was to spend her time with the first mate, she would do what she could to ensure that when the army *did* march, they would have boots to do it in, and swords to draw, when the time came. She gave Urek a small smile. "Mean? Perhaps. And not long ago you were just one more criminal in a city full of them—now, you're the leader of what remains of not one, but two criminal enterprises. Now, you are the man who must sit at a desk and go over reports. In the end, Urek, we are all what we need to be."

CHAPTER FOUR

Adina stood in the doorway of their room, watching Aaron turning restlessly in his sleep, whatever dreams plagued him proving poor company. She didn't need to wonder at what they were, of course, for she, too, was plagued by such dreams. When she slept, that was. Even now, so late in the evening, there was too much to be done and too little time in which to do it. But word had reached her of the sellsword rushing into a room with two men—one holding a loaded crossbow—and besting them both. The guards who'd spoken of it had done so in excited, almost worshipful voices, but Adina didn't feel excitement; she felt only fear. And despite the thousands of things which clamored for her attention, she had needed to see him, to know he was safe.

"He will be fine, Queen Adina."

She turned to look at Gryle, thinking, not for the first time, of how much the past months had changed the chamberlain. Gone was the nervous, anxiety-ridden man she had known, the one who always questioned any decision he made and believed himself of no worth. In his place, stood a man who had seen some of the worst things the world had to offer and come through the other side, a man possessed of a quiet confidence only found in those who had faced terrible odds and lived to tell of them. "Yes," she said. *For now. But soon the war comes and with it, uncountable deaths, slaughter on a scale few can even imagine. Who among us, I wonder, will be fine then?*

Some of her thoughts must have shown on her face, for a look of concern passed across the chamberlain's features. "It will be okay, Majesty. You'll see."

"I wish I had your faith, Gryle."

The chamberlain smiled, giving her a wink. "That's alright, Princess. I have faith enough for the both of us."

Adina nodded, turning back to study the sleeping sellsword. She wished his dreams were good ones, kind ones. The world had enough evil in it already. A person shouldn't have to worry about it following them into their sleep. Yet she knew that, more often than not, it did, and with Aaron it was even worse. His bond with the Virtue of Compassion made him feel things that she could only imagine. Not long ago, he had been plagued with dreams of those poor souls in Baresh who suffered at the hands of Kevlane and his creatures.

He hadn't talked of the dreams lately, but that gave Adina little comfort. Aaron was a man who loathed complaining, and would suffer silently, if given the chance. No, the dreams had not stopped—of that much she was certain. Sometimes, late at night, when he thought she was sleeping, he'd wake from his restless turning and step out to the balcony adjoining their room, staring out at the world beneath him. Adina did not know what he saw when he gazed out from the balcony, but his tense posture and the haunted look on his face told her it was nothing good.

"Princess?" Gryle said, pulling Adina from her thoughts. The chamberlain winced, as if reluctant to speak. "General Yalleck and the others...they wait for you."

She nodded, trying unsuccessfully to banish the image of Aaron standing at the balcony, his shoulders slumped, his chest rising and falling with his uneven, too-fast breaths. "Can we win, Gryle?" she asked, her voice little more than a whisper.

The chamberlain gave her a small, sad smile. "I believe I know what General Envelar would say."

Adina sniffed, wiping at a lone tear that had begun to trace its way down her cheek. "'It doesn't matter if we can win or not—it only matters that we fight.' Something like that, I suppose."

Gryle smiled wider. "Yes, Majesty. Something like that." He stepped forward then, placing a hand gently on her shoulder, a simple act of kindness that would have mortified the old Gryle. "But, for what it's worth, I believe we can."

"Why?" Adina asked, hating the quiet desperation in her voice but unable to hide it.

The chamberlain considered that for a moment. "I once read a study of desert snakes, describing how certain snakes will mistake their own tails for either prey, or another snake—a rival. These snakes, knowing no better, will lash out, attacking their own flesh. Evil, I believe, is much like those creatures. Deadly, certainly, full of venom and dangerous to the unwary but, in the end, like the snakes, it will destroy itself."

Adina nodded slowly. *Perhaps evil does destroy itself,* she thought, *but will any of us be around to see it?* And on the back of that thought came another: *You are enough.*

She stared at the sellsword shifting restlessly in the bed, watched his features twist slightly in anger, as if reacting to the dark phantoms that plagued his dreams. It was strange, she thought, that so much of her hope for Telrear and its people, for winning the coming battle, was wrapped up in the sellsword—a man who, not so very long ago, professed to care nothing for anyone but himself and the coin he earned. But if it *was* a strangeness, then it was not hers alone. She'd seen the way the guards and soldiers studied Aaron, as if he was some god come to set things right. Not just her strangeness, not just her hope, but *everyone's*.

It wasn't fair to put so much of the burden on his shoulders, she knew, yet she could not keep herself from it. The world stood poised before an onrushing landslide, and it would have long since been buried had the sellsword not interposed himself between it and the coming danger. Even now, he strained against that unimaginable weight, felt the pressure of it. And as he shifted in his sleep, the hope of the world and all of its people shifted with him.

He is only one man, she told herself. *How can one man—even one such as Aaron—think to stand up against what is coming?* He couldn't—that was the truth of it. Alone, a man was vulnerable, could be defeated. But *legends,* on the other hand, were more than the men and women from whom they originated. Legends were ideas, and ideas, she knew, were not so easily destroyed. If nothing else, Grinner's treachery had taught her that much. "How many men does Urek now command, Gryle?" she asked, her eyes never leaving the sellsword.

"I...that is, I cannot say for certain, Princess, as I have not seen the latest counts. Every day, it seems, more come to him to offer their...services."

He said the last with a disdain that Adina understood, for those who came to Urek were criminals all, men and women who fed off civilized society like vultures. Men and women who, in a perfect world, would be thrown in the dungeons, forced to answer for their crimes. But the world was what it was, far from perfect, far from ideal, and wishing would not change it. She frowned as a plan crystallized in her mind, one she knew Aaron would not like. But then, he and the others had chosen her as their leader, and lead she would.

"Gryle," she said, turning to the chamberlain. "After the meeting, I wish to speak to Urek. Tell him that I will want an exact count of how many men and women he has under his...command. I have a mission for them."

The heavy-set man raised an eyebrow in surprise. "Forgive me, Princess Adina, for I do not mean to question you but...whatever task you have, are you sure we cannot find those you need somewhere else? From the army, perhaps, or—"

"No," Adina said, shaking her head. "I am sure. This task, I believe, is particularly suited to Urek and his men's...*talents.*"

The chamberlain frowned at that, not bothering to hide his doubt. "Talents, Majesty?"

Adina laughed quietly. "Yes, Gryle. I know you don't appreciate what they do, and I can't blame you. After all, they're criminals. In normal times, I wouldn't trust them either. But then, these are not normal times. In the city's taverns and brothels, in its shops and streets, the people talk of what's coming, and most of that talk is without hope. We cannot blame them, really, for given what has happened recently—Grinner's betrayal—is it any surprise that they have lost some faith in their leaders to see them through the approaching storm?"

"No," Gryle said slowly, "you're right, of course, Majesty. But I'm not sure how criminals will be able to help that."

"Aren't you?" Adina asked. "There is power in belief, Gryle—Grinner's men have taught us that much, if nothing else. But belief must first begin with something to believe in, an *idea*. We cannot stop the whispers, the rumors that are passed among not just the city but the army as well. But what we can do is give them something, *someone* to talk about. A living, breathing legend. Kevlane and his creatures are like monsters out of a child's storybook, an army of evil come to plague the world. And what else do all such story books have in common?"

"A knight," the chamberlain said, his eyes going wide with dawning realization. "I see. But, forgive me, Queen," he continued, his expression growing troubled, "but Mr.—pardon, *General* Envelar—would laugh to be thought of as anyone's knight. I suspect, in such a tale, he would cast himself as the villain before he would the hero."

Adina gave a nod of her own. "Perhaps, you're right, but he would be wrong, and I think we both know it."

"Of course, Majesty," Gryle said slowly, considering. "He won't thank us for it."

"No," Adina said, "he won't." *And when the time comes, I won't ask for his thanks—only his forgiveness.*

"Very well, Majesty. I will tell Urek you will have need of his men. How many should I ask for?"

Adina gave the chamberlain a small, humorless smile. "All of them, Gryle. The army will march soon, and if I have any say, when it does, it will have a legend to lead it." It would be no great trouble, she thought, to turn the man who many already thought of as a hero into a legend, and though she hated how Aaron put himself at risk, such stories would only add to the legend, were food with which to feed it.

"Very good, Majesty. For what it's worth, I believe that—whatever his own thoughts on the matter—Perennia could ask for no better knight than Aaron, the man who saved it not only from an assassination attempt on its queen, but also from Grinner's machinations. As for the meeting…Captain Gant sent word not long before we came here, and the messenger conveyed an unmistakable sense of urgency for your presence."

Adina smiled, surprised as always by the chamberlain's modesty. Aaron had indeed been instrumental in rescuing

Perennia, but Gryle had played no small part himself. She suspected that without him, the city's fate would have been sealed already. Another thought struck her then, and her smile widened. One legend was good, a symbol which the city might gather behind, a light that they might stand with as the darkness approached. But where there was one hero, surely there might be another, and she decided she would have some very particular words with Urek about what stories those in his charge told.

Then she thought of the approaching meeting, of what it might mean that they were assembled in Isabelle's audience chamber without warning, and her smile withered. "Alright—let's find out what's going on."

Gryle led the way, his eyes roaming the castle hallway as if he expected assassins to materialize from the walls, and she didn't miss the way his fists were clenched at his sides. Adina spared one final glance for Aaron, and she let out a soft sigh. "Forgive me," she whispered. "I'm afraid that I have just made the weight you carry a little heavier, but please, hold on. Just for a little while longer."

Her own fears, her own doubts, gathered around her, forcing their way into her thoughts, but she pushed them down as she turned and followed Gryle. The city, the world, had no use for her worries—they needed a leader. And she would be that for them, just as Aaron would be their hope. *You are enough,* she told herself, but the words felt as insubstantial as mist.

***

The meeting had already begun by the time Adina and Gryle arrived, though calling it a "meeting" might have been generous. It didn't seem like a meeting of a council of allies at all, but a shouting match, and the voices of those gathered were so loud she could not even hear the door shutting behind her.

General Yalleck, the commander of Avarest's armies, sat on one side of the room, a vaguely troubled expression on his face. Farther down the table sat a man Adina didn't recognize, an officious-looking sort in silk trousers and shirt that would have cost more than most commoners made in a year. The man was flanked on either side by his servants. Another man sat at the end of the table, the quill and parchment in front of him marking him as a scribe, come to record the proceedings.

Isabelle sat in her throne in the center of the room, and the table opposite Yalleck and the newcomers was taken by Captain Gant alone. Not that he was sitting at it, just then. The captain stood facing the others, his normally calm demeanor nowhere in evidence. His face had gone a deep, angry shade of red. His eyes were locked on the newcomer, and his hands were clenched into fists at his side, trembling as if it was all he could do to keep from attacking the man outright.

"—*Damned fool decision is what it is!*" Brandon roared. "You can pretty it up with whatever words you want, but that doesn't change it!"

He was clearly addressing the finely-dressed man, but if the newcomer was bothered by the captain's anger, he gave no sign. Instead, he favored the captain with an arrogant smile, raising his hands to indicate that whatever decision Brandon spoke of was beyond his control.

"Forgive me, *Captain,*" the man said in a tone that did nothing to hide his evident pleasure at Brandon's outburst, "but the decision has been made already, and I could not change it, even if I wished to."

"Then you doom us all!" the captain shouted. "You would leave us to die on our own, as if it means nothing to you."

The man shook his head, his humoring smile fixed well in place. "Of course not. The Council, after all, holds nothing but the highest esteem for Queen Isabelle and her realms." He paused, taking a moment to give a deferential nod to Adina's sister. For her part, Isabelle didn't even seem to notice—her expression was blank, or nearly so, the only emotions that showed on it a vague sort of confusion mixed with fear, as if she wasn't sure where she was or what was expected of her. She had been in such a state since Adina and the others had returned and taken the city back from Grinner, and neither Adina nor any of Perennia's healers had been able to rouse her from it. She had once been a proud, confident—if vain—queen, but no longer. The woman, the sister Adina knew, was gone. In her place was a sickly creature whose skin hung from her in folds, her eyes sunken pits in her face, and a distinct yellow tinge to her skin Adina didn't like.

"But despite the highest regard in which I—and the rest of Avarest's Council—holds Her Majesty and her domain," the stranger went on, "the choice has been made. Though, if it helps, Captain," he said, turning back to Brandon, "the decision was not made lightly."

The captain turned away from the queen, his disappointment clear in his expression. "Something to carve on your tombstone then," he spat. "A murderer, a coward, but at least he didn't make the decision *lightly*."

The stranger sighed, picking at an invisible piece of dust on his sleeve. "Truly, Captain, there is no need for this melodrama. It is quite crass and demeaning for a man of your station. Take heart for, as ever, our lives are in the hands of the gods. Was it not Platorus, the great scholar, who wrote 'the endeavors of man are like the crafting of sand castles on the shore, and should such ramparts stand it will not be by the labors of those who fashioned them, but by the hands of the gods who ever hold the grim tides at bay'?"

"Actually, it's 'sweeping tides' and that wasn't Platorus," Adina said, "but Ivangian. You were close—only a few centuries off." Those gathered turned, noting her and the chamberlain for the first time. The man who'd spoken frowned, but the captain's face lit up with hope.

"Queen Adina," Brandon said, bowing his head, undisguised relief in his voice. "I am so glad you could make it."

Adina gave the captain a smile and turned back to the other man. "Also, you left out the end of the quote: 'The endeavors of men are like the crafting of sand castles on the shore, and should such ramparts stand, it will not be by the labors of those who fashioned them, but by the hands of the gods who ever hold the sweeping tides at bay. Yet, such truth does not make the works of men without purpose, for such edifices as they create shape the face of the world."

The newcomer fidgeted uncomfortably, his expression looking as if he had swallowed something sour, but it was gone in a moment, replaced with one of affected insouciance. "Queen Adina," he said, bowing his head but not, she noted, bothering to stand which would be proper when addressing a queen. Gryle's sudden tensing at her side showed her that he, too, had noticed the impropriety. "I have heard some tale of your exploits in the past months and even given what were no doubt exaggerations as so often come from stories told and told often, I must commend you on your defense of the city against your brother's armies." The stranger smiled, like a humoring parent praising a particularly clever child. "A feat, I'm sure, of which you are most proud."

"Forgive me," Adina said, holding up a hand to silence the captain who looked as if he would start shouting anew at the man's obvious show of disrespect, "but I'm afraid I didn't get your name."

The newcomer gave a small chuckle, glancing at one of his servants as if amused that anyone should be so far removed from the workings of power as not to know him. "No offense is taken, of course, Majesty. I suspect you have been too busy with your travels and various...exploits, to stay apprised of world events. My name is Faden Arkrest, a councilman of some small influence in Avarest." He paused there, another small, knowing smile coming to his face as if to underline his own humility. "And I have the distinct pleasure of being chosen as the representative of the Council of Avarest and its will, entrusted with the duty of communicating its decisions regarding the disposition of its forces within the city, and, if given just cause, to change them."

The old Adina would have felt fear at the man's words and the news he brought—clear enough, given his purpose for visiting Perennia and Brandon Gant's obvious anger. But she was not the woman she once had been. She was no sheltered princess who understood little of the world, easily given to panic. Like Gryle and all the others, she had been tested over the last few months, forced to grow and become more than that shallow woman she had once been. So, she did not feel fear—only anger. "You say, Councilman, that you have heard some tales of my exploits and those others, is that right?"

"Indeed," the man said. "Quite harrowing experiences, I'm sure, and you must be commended for managing to hold the city against Belgarin's forces—I hope that Avarest's own troops aided you in that. We were pleased, of course, to be of assistance in your time of need."

An unsubtle reminder of the aid Avarest had already given them, and he said the last as if he'd personally held the gates against Belgarin's hordes, as if he had performed some great act of charity for which Adina and all those in Perennia should be grateful. "Of course," Adina said, keeping herself calm and refusing to rise to the man's bait. "I, and all those who have stood and fought with me over these past weeks are not unaware of the help we have thus far received from Avarest, and we are grateful. In fact, I would say that the whole of Telrear is grateful, since it is for them we fight."

The man smiled as if she had told a joke. "The whole of Telrear, is it? Forgive me, Majesty, for I do not mean to question what you have done, but surely it is not so serious as that. Your brother Prince Belgarin is ruthless, it is true, but it seems that a concerted effort was enough to give his army a good whipping, enough to send him and his forces slinking back to Baresh with their tails between their legs."

Adina's anger flared up again, but she forced it down with a will. "My brother is dead, Councilman," she said flatly. "He has been, I suspect, for some time. As for the 'whipping' of which you speak, many men and women—*good* men and women—died defending this city and, by extension, the world. Even now, should you walk the walls, you will see proof of their sacrifice marring the ramparts, for blood, Councilman, does not clean so easily as wine."

"Yes," Faden said, and though he did not visibly roll his eyes, his tone made his thoughts clear enough. "I am quite sure that the warriors of Perennia fought valiantly in this...skirmish."

"Skirmish?" Adina asked, unable to keep all the anger from her voice this time.

"Well," the man said, his tone apologetic, "surely, it must be called that, if we wish to be accurate, Majesty. After all, Belgarin's army was beaten soundly in, what, a matter of days?" He nodded, as if to agree with himself. "Yes, a 'skirmish' seems accurate enough. I am, not to boast, somewhat of a scholar of war, and when this most recent scuffle is compared to some of the great battles of history, well..." He trailed off, smiling and shrugging his shoulders.

"A scholar of war," Adina repeated.

"Quite," the man said, inclining his head as if she'd just offered him a compliment.

"Tell me, Councilman Arkrest," Adina said, "do you know many of history's battles?"

Even the man's laugh struck her as arrogant. "Majesty, such a direct question puts my humility at risk, but yes, I am well-versed in them. I would hazard to say that I am, perhaps, one of the world's foremost scholars on the subject."

"And have you ever fought in one?"

The man frowned, raising an eyebrow in confusion. "Forgive me, Majesty?"

"Perhaps I wasn't clear," Adina said, "my apologies. Let me try again: have you ever taken up your place in line as an army of men ran at you, screaming for your blood? Have you ever stood over the corpses of enemies and friends alike, so many bodies you could nearly swim in them? Have you ever listened to the sounds of the dying as they screamed for mercy, as grown men cried out for their mothers, and you stood by helpless, the smell of blood filling your nose? For blood, Councilman, does have a smell. Many people don't realize just how strong that smell is, just how powerful."

"No," the man said, clearly annoyed, "I have not fought in battles, Majesty, for it is my belief that such endeavors are not well-suited to learned men. No offense, Captain," he said, glancing at the man for a moment before turning back to her. "Still, I would hazard that such martial experience would not be a requirement to be well-learned on the subject, for a man to be a true scholar. After all, historians need not have experienced every event which they record to be masters of their subject matter."

"War is not history, Councilman," Adina said. "It is not words on a page or pages in a book, one that a person might find sitting on a shelf next to a treatise on the different types of flowers, or a study of the stars in the heavens. And if it *is* a book, then it is written in blood, in a language unspoken and unread by any save those who were there to experience it. A scholar of war, Councilman?" She shook her head. "No. No living man might claim as much, for among the truths the past months have shown me is that the only true scholars of war are the dead, and what wisdom they gain they keep to themselves."

"Quite," the councilman said, and this time he did roll his eyes. "In any event, the thing was nobly done. As for your brother being dead, how can this be true? For, among the latest news we of the council have received has been that he is, even now, marshaling his armies in Baresh, intent on attacking Perennia once more.

Though," he said, frowning at General Yalleck who pointedly avoided his gaze, "it must be said that, of late, our communications seem to have been disrupted. Truly, to such an extent that we have yet to receive our regular reports, ones that were agreed upon before Commander Yalleck ever took the army from the city and came to Perennia's aid. It is the reason, after all, why I was forced to come to Perennia in the first place, to ascertain the validity of some of the more...dubious claims."

Instead of responding to the man's obvious reproach, Yalleck met Adina's eyes, and in that stare she saw the truth, and an understanding passed between them. Whatever communication the councilman and his counterparts from Avarest had sent, the commander had clearly decided that it was better if their message had never reached him and decided to act as if such was the case. "My brother *is* dead, Councilman," she said, turning back to the man. "In his place resides an ancient mage who is thousands of years old; indeed, it is the same Boyce Kevlane who, in the histories, stood at Aaron Caltriss's side, who formed the spell that would ultimately lead to Caltriss's death."

The man laughed at that. "Surely, you jest, Majesty. The Aaron Caltriss and Boyce Kevlane of whom you speak are no more than stories—fables told to small children, many of whom, I suspect, are too discerning, even at such a young age, to credit them. Oh, of course, we in Avarest have heard the stories of this fictitious mage supplanting your brother as ruler of Baresh, but they are no more than stories. Why, even the few investigators we have sent to Baresh have discovered nothing more than the king himself, a bit more reclusive than usual, perhaps, but then, that is to be expected after suffering so grievous a defeat as he has. How, I wonder, can your brother be dead, yet those we have sent claim to have seen him, alive and well?"

Adina gritted her teeth. "Boyce Kevlane wears my brother's face, and uses the power this gives him to create for himself an army of monsters. I'm sure—since you are so well informed—that you have heard of the tournament being held in Baresh. Even as we speak, the mage is set about the task of taking these warriors and mutilating them, working his dark art on them and turning them into creatures that are stronger, faster, than any man."

The councilman shook his head in wonder. "An ancient mage wearing your brother's face, making use of magic that does not exist now—if it ever did—to turn men into monsters? Forgive me, Majesty, but if only you could hear yourself...I am sure that it is due, in no small part, to the trials you have faced. Why, it is conceivable that any man or woman, put under such strain, might find themselves taken by such...fancies. With the hardship you have endured, surely such imaginings are expected."

"Majesty?"

Adina turned at the chamberlain's voice, saw him raise his eyebrow in question. She considered for a moment then gave him a nod. With that, Gryle walked to the table at which the councilman and those others with him sat, and the finely-dressed man visibly flinched, as if expecting a blow. The chamberlain paid him no attention, however. Instead, he simply took hold of one end of the table—a table built from solid oak and at least fifteen feet long—and raised it with no more effort than a man might use lifting a glass of wine.

Adina felt a flash of vengeful satisfaction as the councilman, his servants, and the scribe jerked away from the table, shouting in surprise and backing up as if the table—and the chamberlain holding it—were wild beasts that had bared their fangs, preparing to strike.

"Is Gryle truly holding up that table, do you suppose, Councilman?" Adina asked. "Or is it just your fancy? An imagining brought upon, perhaps, by your journey here, by hard days spent on the road?"

"B-b-but this is impossible," the councilman stammered, all his arrogance and self-assurance vanishing in an instant.

"That's a funny word, 'impossible,'" Adina said. "Before a few months ago, I would have told you that all manner of things were impossible—that one man couldn't possess the strength of a hundred, that a woman old enough to be a grandmother couldn't possibly move faster than any galloping horse. And, yes, Councilman Arkrest, that an ancient mage out of legend could have in no way appeared in the world and set about trying to destroy it. Yet all these things—and more, more than you can imagine—have been shown to me during my, what was it you called them? Trials? Yes, Councilman. I have seen the impossible. I have seen evil that belongs in the darkest stories, evil to haunt our dreams and I—and those with me—have fought it. Claims that the knife doesn't exist won't stop it from cutting your throat. I think you would do well to remember that."

"E-even if this is true," the man stammered, regaining some small bit of his equilibrium, "even if this isn't just some trick or...or—"

"Oh, it is no trick, sir," Adina said. "If it would help convince you, I could ask Gryle to lift you, maybe toss you in the air a few times. Would that suffice as proof?"

"N-no," the man said, licking his lips nervously. "I don't believe that...will be necessary. Now," he continued, clearing his throat. "If you would be so kind as to ask your servant to put the table down..."

"Gryle is not my servant—he's my friend," Adina said. "If you would like him to put it down, you can ask him yourself."

The councilman's mouth worked silently for several seconds, and now it was his turn to glance at Queen Isabelle as if in search of some aid, but he was destined to be as disappointed as the captain had been, for Isabelle had the same vacant expression and seemed altogether unaware of the proceedings. Realizing he was on his own, Arkrest turned to Gryle, his features twisting as if he had just eaten something sour. "If you would be so kind, *sir*, would you please put the table down?"

The chamberlain gave him an affable smile and set the table down before walking back to stand beside Adina. The councilman hesitated, then took his seat once more, and the scribe and servants reluctantly followed, casting dubious glances at Gryle and the table itself as if expecting it to float into the air at any moment.

"Now then," Councilman Arkrest went on, regaining his composure and, with it, his arrogance, "that is a nice...trick, I'll grant you, but in the end it changes nothing."

"I imagine," Adina said dryly, "that if Gryle had decided to, for example, swing the table in your direction, it would have changed things a great deal, Councilman."

"Quite," he said in a tone that tried for bored, but was betrayed by a squeak in his voice. "And I must commend your servant—forgive me, *friend*—on his prodigious strength. Yet, it does nothing to prove the veracity of this 'Boyce Kevlane' and these creatures you've mentioned, nothing to show they are anything more than stories produced by frightened commoners."

"They were real enough to try to kill me and my friends," Adina said, unable to keep her anger at the man's willful ignorance out of her tone. "Enough to *kill* some of them. Stories, Councilman, do not sneak upon you in the night and drag a blade across your throat."

"Perhaps not," the man said, nodding, "but in such times as these, Queen Adina, each man and woman must look to themselves. Avarest is a city of great power, but for all her might, even she cannot defend herself without an army. If so much as half of what you are saying is true, then that is all the more reason why I must return to the city with its loyal men to protect it, should the worst come to pass."

"The worst has *already* come to pass," Adina snapped. "As for looking to ourselves, if we fight alone, Councilman, we will have no hope against what's coming, and we will die alone. The only chance we have—the only chance *Telrear* has—is if we face what's coming together."

The man shook his head slowly, his hands held up as if he was helpless. "Forgive me, Majesty. I wish I could help you—truly. But the decision has been made."

Adina was at a loss for words, unable to believe that the man would be so foolish as to not see that his actions would doom them all.

"Councilman," General Yalleck said, clearing his throat and speaking for the first time since she had arrived, "I understand your concerns, and I do not mean to question the Council, but for what it's worth, I think that the queen is right. I have seen the creatures she speaks of myself, and I believe that the only way—"

"Never mind what you *believe,*" the councilman hissed. He took a slow, deep breath. "You, Commander, have not been commissioned to make decisions for the council or to *think*, but to lead our armies in providing the assistance that Perennia required. A task which, it must be said, you have performed admirably."

"But, Councilman," Yalleck tried again, "I really think that if you just—"

"*Enough,*" Faden yelled, then paused for a moment to gather himself. "We will begin the return journey to the city the day after tomorrow, Commander. See that the army is ready to march. And once we return to Avarest, I believe I will meet with my fellow councilmembers on some particular changes that may be overdue. You have a child, do you not?"

The general frowned, clearly caught off guard by the unexpected question. "Two, sir. A boy and a girl."

The councilman nodded. "It must be hard to be away from them for so long, your wife too, I suppose, but I wouldn't worry about that, Commander. After my meeting with the rest of the Council, you may have much more time to spend with them in the future."

The man's threat was clear enough, and General Yalleck's jaw tensed, but he gave a terse nod, saying nothing. The councilman rose from the table, his servants and accompanying scribe following his lead. "Very well," Faden said. "I thank you all for your kind hospitality and for hosting me. It has been...interesting." He bowed to Isabelle and Adina in turn. "Majesty. Majesty. I wish you both the glory of the day, and I hope that, when next our paths cross, they will do so in happier times." And with that, he turned and walked out, his entourage following in his wake.

Adina watched the man go, staring at the door as it closed shut behind him. She was still staring at it, her thoughts in turmoil, when Yalleck approached. "Forgive me, Queen Adina," he said. "I know the importance of what we do—I did what I could to delay the Council, but I'm honor-bound to abide by their decision. You understand?" he asked, meeting her eyes with undisguised need.

"Honor," Adina said, as if it was a word she'd never heard before. "I wonder, General, of how much use is honor to the dead? It will not return murdered husbands to their wives, nor extinguish the flames when they begin to burn. Honor has its place, can serve as a shield against chaos, but without reason to guide it...well, even a shield might be used as a weapon. "

"No," the man grated, turning away from her gaze. "You're right, of course. I...I can only say that I am sorry, Majesty. I was afraid the Council would send a representative, but I...I wish they had not. Better for us all, if he had never come."

Adina nodded slowly, and when she turned to the general her eyes were cold, hard. "And if he hadn't come, General?" she asked. "If this meeting never happened?"

The man shifted uncomfortably, obviously reluctant to speak. "Then...then I would, of course, do what I could to help you and the others, Majesty. But..." he trailed off with a helpless shrug.

"Never mind the rest," Adina said. "Thank you, General. For your time."

The man studied her for a moment, clearly wanting to say more but unsure of what he *should* say, then finally he gave a bow and trudged from the audience chamber. Adina watched him go, thinking thoughts of honor, of what it meant. Was there any honor in the deaths of thousands? Could there *ever* be honor in such a thing?

"Majesty."

Brandon Gant stood beside her, his own anger and worry clear on his guileless features.

"Captain. I apologize for my tardiness, and I thank you for doing what you could before I arrived."

Brandon grunted. "Not that it did any good." He shook his head, anger and disbelief warring on his face. "What are we going to do, Queen Adina? Gods, but if only he'd waited a few more days, we would have been on the march, and it would have been too late. It's the damnedest luck, him showing up now."

"Yes," Adina said, frowning. "Terrible luck for us...and great luck for Kevlane."

For all his gruff exterior, Brandon Gant was no fool, and his eyes widened at that. "Majesty," he said in a low voice, "do you mean to say you suspect the councilman is working for Kevlane?"

Adina shook her head uncertainly. "I don't know, Captain. What I *do* know is that he couldn't have picked a worse time to arrive in the city. Had he waited only a few days, the army would have already marched, and it would have been too late for him to stop it. I find it curious that he should come when he did, on the eve of battle, and even more curious that he was able to arrive at all since, last we knew, Kevlane's creatures were scouring the forest in search of the Akalian barracks."

The captain nodded slowly at that. "He came with a retinue," he said, snorting. "Six armed men, just as pretty as porcelain vases and, if I had my guess, just as fragile. You'd have thought the man were some great king come to visit the city, the way he walked into the castle with them surrounding him, his servants trailing after."

"Six men," Adina mused. "And do you think, Captain, that six men—however skilled—would stand long against Kevlane and his creatures?"

Brandon grunted. "From what I've seen, I don't think six hundred would, Majesty. But, maybe they just got lucky and Kevlane's creatures had already left the forest or..."

"Maybe," Adina agreed. "But in my experience, Brandon, there are few coincidences."

The captain rubbed a hand along his salt and pepper beard. "Forgive me, Majesty, but either way, I don't see how it changes things. It seems pretty clear that Yalleck will do whatever the Council demands." He scowled at the door as if looking past it to where the councilman was no doubt making his way through the castle hallways. "I wonder if that bastard knows what he's done. Because of him, thousands—possibly *hundreds* of thousands—will die."

Adina frowned, thinking. What did it mean to be a leader? Did it mean being willing to save your people, to do what you could to protect them? She had always believed it had, *still* believed it, in fact. But was there another side to that coin? Did being a leader also mean being prepared to take drastic measures, to kill, if need be? "Yes," she said to the captain. "Thousands will die. Or, perhaps, only one."

"Majesty?" Brandon said, turning to her. "What do you—"

"Ask me nothing more, Captain," Adina said. "I beg you."

The older man studied her for several moments then a look of understanding seemed to cross his gaze, and he gave a short nod. "As you say, Majesty." He considered for a moment, as if he would say something more. Finally, he decided, and when he spoke next his tone was filled with memories of the past. "Years ago, when I was a young man with no trace of gray in my hair and had only just received the honor of being in your father's service, an assassin tried to sneak into the castle and murder the king while he was abed."

He paused for several seconds, and Adina was about to ask him if there was more to the story when he finally went on. "It was a long time ago," he said, "and I was a young fool. A fool all puffed up with pride and honor at being given a position as guard in your father's castle, confident as only the young can be. I fancied myself a warrior, well-versed in weapons and combat." He snorted sourly. "Anyway, I was stationed outside your father's bedroom with a man who'd been in the king's service for ten years—it's a thing they used to do back then, pairing a new recruit with one of the older, more experienced guards. I still don't know how the assassin made it so far into the castle—there was an investigation, after the fact, but nothing ever came from it." He waved a dismissive hand. "It doesn't matter. What does is that the assassin made it to your father's quarters. As I said, I was new to the post—a few weeks in, no more than that. I'd been on the training grounds a thousand times, practiced with dull steel and sharpened steel alike, and I fancied myself quite a swordsman, quite a warrior. But when that man walked at us down the hallway, a sword in his hand, the blade slick with blood, I'm ashamed to say that I froze."

Adina frowned, "I...I remember the assassin. I was just a child, but I remember. Still...that isn't how I heard it happened."

"No, I don't imagine it is." He shook his head, his eyes far away. "It's a funny thing—I remember everything about that night. The smell of it, the feel of the sweat-slick handle of my own sword, all of it, but for the life of me I can't remember the man's face. He could have been anyone. Anyone at all."

The captain grew silent then, and Adina waited for several seconds as he relived the memory. "So what happened?" she finally prompted.

Brandon seemed to start as if coming awake, then gave a shrug. "The man attacked, and though I hesitated, the guard with me didn't. He gave a shout and charged the assassin. The guard—Pike, I think his name was, though after so long I couldn't swear to it—was a good man, and a good hand with the blade, too. But within moments of them joining combat, I saw that he was clearly outclassed. I wanted to help, *knew* that I needed to help, yet my feet wouldn't obey my commands, and I watched them fight, watched Pike take one small wound after the other, wanting to help but somehow unable to."

He shook his head, a pained expression crossing his face. "Anyway, it wasn't until Pike gave a loud scream of pain as the other man's blade stabbed through his upper arm that I finally got my feet moving. Somehow, during the fight, the two had switched sides, and the assassin's back was facing me. My sword was in my hand, the opening there for me to take, but I hesitated." He turned to Adina, a quiet desperation on his face, as if praying she would understand. "You see, I was so wrapped up in my own honor, in the *idea* of it, that it felt wrong to strike him when he was unaware. This, after all, wasn't like the dreams I'd had, the imaginings of myself as some great knight, charging into the king's enemies and cutting them down with my skill, winning the day with my courage. For one, the dreams never smelled of blood, not the way that castle hallway did. For another, in such dreams I never cut a man down while he was defenseless. I never…" He trailed off then, clearing his throat.

Adina felt a surge of sympathy for the captain, to have been put in such a position. "So what happened?"

When Brandon went on, his voice was thick with emotion. "I hesitated, and the next time the assassin's blade struck, it went into Pike's stomach, runnin' him through. A mortal wound—even then, I knew that much, and the look on the old guard's face when he turned to meet my eyes said he knew it too. I'll never forget that look, Majesty. It was…anyway. Pike's own blade had fallen from his hands, and he grabbed hold of the assassin's, keeping the man from pulling the sword clear. His hands were shredded to ribbons in the process, and it must have hurt like the curse of the gods, but still the old man held on. Finally, I came to my senses, and I struck the assassin from behind. He never saw it coming; thanks to Pike, he couldn't have got his own blade around to defend even if he had, and the cut was clean. It was over in another moment, and the two men were lying at my feet, dead."

He snorted. "Funny thing. They called me a hero, after that. Said I'd saved the king's life. There were speeches and awards, and far more women batting their eyelashes at me than there ever had been before or since. Everyone talked about my courage, my honor. But in their smiling faces, all I ever saw was Pike's own, covered with his blood, his eyes weighing me, measuring me. In their cries of adulation, in their words of praise, I only ever heard Pike's final scream as the assassin's blade went in." He turned and met Adina's gaze. "See, Majesty, the thing about honor is that it isn't something one man can give to another—no manner of medals or coin can do it. It's something a man has to earn for himself, has to *learn* for himself. I didn't understand, then, what honor meant, and the gods alone know I've only recently discovered it, in truth. But for my lack of knowledge, for my hesitation, Pike died. For my want of honor, another man—a better man—lost his life. And, you ask me, all the pretty eyelashes in the world can't make up for a thing like that."

Adina stared at the man, her own eyes threatening to mist over with tears, and she understood the gift that he had given her, understood, too, what the giving had cost. "Thank you, Captain."

He smiled then, and it was a fragile thing. "Of course, Majesty." He bowed his head, then turned and nodded to Gryle before walking out of the audience chamber.

"I remember that night," the chamberlain said in a soft voice once the captain was gone. "I remember it, but I never knew...I never knew. That wasn't the story we were told."

Adina wasn't surprised. The world, after all, needed its heroes, and why let a little thing like the truth, like a man's suffering, get in the way of a good story? Still, for all the pain she felt for the captain, she felt a certainty fill her, as a thought she had been considering crystallized within her mind. "I think it's time we talked to Urek, Gryle. I may have another job for him after all."

CHAPTER FIVE

Caleb yawned heavily, and gave his head a shake, as if by doing so he might banish the exhaustion creeping over him. He sat in his room in the Akalian barracks. The desk in front of him was covered with parchments—many crumpled into balls, evidence of Caleb's periodic frustrations as he tried and failed to come up with a better way of the Akalians breaching Baresh's walls. He'd spent the last several days in consultation with the Speaker on the matter, and to add to his frustration, the man seemed completely content with a plan that, almost certainly, ended in his death and the death of those other Akalians who followed him.

Caleb, though, was convinced there was another way, a *better* way, and his own anger stemmed in large part from his inability to see it. The answer was there, it *had* to be. With that thought, he snatched up one of the papers from the desk, seemingly at random, but though his Virtue-enhanced intelligence had, so far at least, proven of no use in coming up with a better strategy for the attack on the city, it did let him remember the contents of each parchment scattered haphazardly across the desk's surface. The paper he'd grabbed showed, in detail, the composition of the western wall of Baresh, and Caleb studied it, struggling to think of any means of breaching the walls that wouldn't require a significant amount of time—no doubt more than they would have with Kevlane's creatures bearing down on them—and effort.

He searched for a solution, strove for it and, for what must have been the hundredth time, he came up empty. With a hiss of frustration, he tossed the paper aside, leaning back in his chair and rubbing at his burning eyes. They'd heard news from Perennia a few days ago—good news, as it turned out. Apparently, Aaron and the others had taken the city back from Grinner and his men. Even now, they were busy about setting things right within Perennia's walls. Soon, within the next few days at the latest, they would march on Baresh.

And when they arrive? he thought. *Will we be stuck outside of the city, the Akalians failing at what looks to be an impossible, suicide mission, while we are cut down by Kevlane's creatures?* It was a fate, an outcome, that seemed all too likely, perhaps even inevitable. Caleb hated himself then, with a passion he'd felt few times in his young life. Aaron and the others were counting on him to find some better way into the city, and it looked as if, in the end, he would fail them. Despite the Virtue of Intelligence, he was still as his mother had named him years ago: an idiot. A fool.

Palendesh, the Virtue of Intelligence, appeared floating in the air in front of him, a glowing ball of blue light. "Enough, Caleb," the orb scolded in a voice that belonged to a grandfather. "I will not listen to you criticize yourself any longer. You take on too much, *expect* too much."

Caleb let out a tired, frustrated breath. "They need me, Palendesh. I am not strong like Gryle, I'm not a great warrior like Aaron, or clever like Leomin. *This,*" he said, gesturing with both hands at the stack of papers lying in front of him, "is what I'm supposed to be good at. If I can't do even this then of what use am I?"

The orb floated closer, as if it was studying him. "What use?" he asked. "You have been of much use, Caleb. Thanks to you, the army has tools, such as the caltrops—clever design, by the way—that will help them defend themselves against Kevlane's creatures."

"Thanks to *you,* you mean," Caleb grumbled. "And what difference does it make anyway? Caltrops, trip lines…none of them will do any good if we're never able to get inside the city at all. All the clever gadgets in the world won't save us if we're stuck in the fields and forests outside Baresh."

"And you feel that, if the army is defeated, then it will be you who has failed them? You who is responsible?"

"Well *somebody* has to be!" Caleb screamed, jerking out of his chair and sweeping an arm across the desk, scattering the papers into the air where they fell about the room and onto his small bed. He slumped against the wall then, feeling as if what little energy he'd had left had departed him, and slid down it until he was sitting on the floor, his face buried in his hands. "*Somebody* has to be," he repeated in a voice that was little more than a whisper.

"Yes," the Virtue said in a sad voice. "Somebody has to be, young Caleb. But it is not you, and there is no wisdom in carrying a burden that is not your own. If a man is pricked with another's blade, he might blame himself, might claim that only had he been faster, smarter, it might never have happened at all. But the truth is that the fault lies with the man who grasped it in the first place, and no amount of self-loathing will change that. Just as," he continued, his voice soft, "no amount of intelligence might create a solution that is not there, for the truth is not a beast to be tamed and made to be bent to our will. It is and always will be its own master."

"*Truth,*" Caleb snapped, but with little strength. He shook his head wearily. "I have to save them, Palendesh. I *need* to save them."

"What will come will come, lad," the Virtue said. "We cannot change the equation, or the problem, only because we do not like its answer. The Speaker knows this and, I believe, you do as well."

"But they'll *die,*" Caleb said, his voice desperate.

"Perhaps," the Virtue said. "But all things that live will die someday, young Caleb. All that which has a beginning has an ending."

"It isn't fair," the youth said. "It isn't fair that we have to do this, that Aaron and the others have to. They're my *friends,* Palendesh."

"Yes," the Virtue said, "they are. Now, why don't you go to sleep? Perhaps, in the morning, things will look better."

Caleb *was* tired, there was no denying that. He'd gotten little sleep in the past week, spending his days meeting with the Speaker and discussing their plans, his nights bent over his small desk, searching for an answer that, in all probability, wasn't there to begin with. "I should really check on Tianya," he said uncertainly. Since Aaron and the others had left, Caleb had regularly checked on the woman. She was growing stronger each day, but she was still weak from a long time spent without any food and water but that which the Akalians managed to get down her throat when she was in the grip of her madness. Caleb had made it his personal responsibility to see she got well again.

From brief, once-forgotten memories of his own as well as the stores of knowledge Palendesh had acquired over hundreds of years of bonding one person or another, he had managed to create some tinctures and herbal remedies from plants gathered from the forest to aid her recovery. Although she claimed to be feeling better, growing stronger, Caleb's sense of urgency to get her well grew with each passing day. After all, Kevlane's creatures were still out there, hunting them, and the only thing keeping him and the Akalians from going to the city and meeting up with Aaron and the others was that moving Tianya in her current state would be very dangerous.

So he waited, searching the forest for what herbs it could provide and poring over his parchments, making plans only to discard them, and all the while, what little time they had slipped away.

"You have done everything you can for her," Palendesh said. "You know that as well as I. Now, sleep, Caleb, for exhaustion is the thief of reason, and you will need all your wits about you in the coming days."

"Fine," Caleb agreed, rising and shuffling to his small bed where he lay down. He sank into it, his eyes seeming to close of their own accord. "But only for a moment...and then I need to look at the papers again. Perhaps there is something I've missed."

"Yes," the Virtue said softly, and Caleb could barely hear his words past the fog that settled over his drowsy mind. "Only for a moment."

CHAPTER SIX

Urek was uncomfortable. There were a few reasons for it. For one, being a criminal by trade, he tried to avoid the attention of the guard whenever possible. It was as natural, to his way of thinking, as a mouse avoiding a cat's gaze. It wasn't that the cat would *definitely* eat the mouse, only that it could and, if it chose to, would feel no great emotion one way or the other. All the lessons of his life, all of the commons sense he had, told him that the last place he wanted to be was standing in front of a guard or—as was the case now—several of them, being scrutinized with obvious and, he had to admit, warranted, suspicion.

So it was with some small surprise, then, that he found himself standing at the castle gate, shifting from foot to foot and trying to look as innocent as possible.

Judging by the frowns of the guardsmen stationed at the gate, he wasn't doing a particularly good job. Of course, that could also have been caused, in some degree, by the thickly-muscled woman beside him. Beautiful was a good six inches taller than Urek and the guardsmen, and looked as if she could juggle them, if she took it in her mind to do so. But, just then, she was busy smiling demurely at the guards, as if she were some princess being admitted to a royal ball.

Urek suspected that, considering the fact that she was missing several teeth from the gods alone knew how many street fights, the expression was doing little to help their cause. Not that he would be the one to say so—Urek might be a fool, and he was growing surer of that fact with each passing day, but he wasn't suicidal. At least, not at the moment. He'd accepted the queen's summons quickly enough, happy for the excuse to flee May and her endless reports. Urek had been a criminal for some time—had done quite a few things of which he wasn't proud—but he'd never felt more like murdering someone than when bent over the desk studying reports.

"Well," one of the guards said, and Urek didn't miss the surprise in his voice, "their papers seem to check out. This is Queen Adina's own seal here."

Urek couldn't suppress his sigh of relief. Oh, he'd believed the letter had been legitimate, delivered as it had been by Gryle, the unassuming chamberlain who was known to serve the queen. But he'd had the thought on the way to the castle—more than once, truth to tell—that there were some men and women out there who wouldn't have been all too upset to see him with a few extra holes poked in him, and what better way to do that than sending by a forged letter inviting him to the castle?

"Well, course it is," Urek said, hocking and spitting—always a good way for a man to emphasize his point. The problem, of course, was that he was nervous, and his aim was off, so the spittle didn't go to the side and strike the cobbles, as he'd intended, but instead landed squarely on the boots of one of the guards.

Beautiful made a disgusted sound in her throat, shaking her head as if ashamed. "A deplorable habit, spitting. Don't you think?" she said to the guard who was, even now, staring at his boot in disbelief. The man raised his eyes to look at her, and Beautiful smiled widely at him, an expression Urek suspected was meant to put the man at ease. Judging by the way he recoiled, making a face as if he'd just caught a whiff of something foul—a dead animal, maybe—it didn't work. He grasped the handle of the sword at his side as if reassuring himself it was there.

Urek groaned inwardly, wishing—also, not for the first time—that he had left Beautiful back at May's office or at the tavern he and the rest of the crew had called home for the last week. Not that he'd really had a choice, of course. Beautiful had decided she was going and nothing short of an army—even on that score, Urek thought the issue would have still been in doubt—could have stopped her from visiting the castle. He'd known the volatile woman long enough not to even bother trying to dissuade her. Instead, he'd only sat in impatient silence, pretending to gloss over more of May's papers while Beautiful tried on a variety of dresses and jewels that the club owner offered to let her borrow, doing his best to smile and keep a straight face as she asked him what he thought. Which, mostly, had been varying iterations of *Gods save us*, but he was still breathing anyway, so he consoled himself with the idea that he must have managed to hide his thoughts well enough.

The guards, on the other hand, weren't so circumspect, and they stared at the heavily-muscled woman in the burgundy sleeveless dress, as if she were putting on some joke, one more offensive to their sensibilities than funny, and gods help the first to laugh. Urek himself had done his best to avoid looking at the woman and her attire. Oh, the dress had looked fine enough hanging in May's closet, but the club owner was considerably shorter and not nearly so wide at the shoulders as Beautiful. On someone else, the dress might have contrived to hug the woman's curves, showing them off to best advantage, but on Beautiful, it looked like a tortured, pitiful thing, only one good stretch away from busting at the seams. It didn't help matters that the woman had also insisted on wearing face paint and had kindly rejected May's offers to help, preferring to do it herself.

She'd used too much—even Urek could see that. It looked more like war paint than anything else, and she some insane clown, the kind who told crude jokes, the punch lines of which were always, *And he died horribly.*

"So," one of the other guards said, frowning at Beautiful with a look of disgust usually reserved for when a man found a bug in his ale, "what did you say your business at the castle was?"

Either Beautiful hadn't noticed the man's look yet, or didn't see the open revulsion in it—an easy enough thing to guess, since she hadn't yet taken the man's sword and beaten him to death with it—but Urek did, and he became annoyed despite himself. "I didn't," he growled. "I got the letter, and here I am. Now, why don't you open that gate—if it ain't too much trouble—and we can all go on about our day?"

The man's frown deepened at that, but he turned away from Beautiful to eye Urek now, and that at least was something. "And *what,* exactly, did you say your profession was again?"

"None of your damned business, is what it is. Anyway, you ought to just be glad I ain't in the business of openin' gates that need openin', otherwise I reckon you'd be out of a job. Now, are you gonna let us through, or are we gonna keep standin' here jawin' until we die of old age?"

The guard's jaw clenched, and he turned to look at one of his companions—this one older than the rest and, judging by the way his expressionless face revealed none of the disgust of his fellows, not as inclined to suicide. The older man gave a terse nod. "Alright, let them through."

"Bout damn time," Urek grumbled, and the older man shot him a look that told him he was pushing his luck, so he waited in silence while they swung the gate open.

"This way," the older guard said, motioning for one of the others to follow as he led them into the castle proper.

Urek took a slow, deep breath, savoring it, and reasoning that there were better than even odds that the guards would decide there were a few more spots in the dungeons that needed filling, and he might not get another breath of fresh air for some time. Inside, the castle walls were adorned with portraits and paintings, the floors practically gleaming. Men and women—servants by the harried look of them—hurried past as the two guards led them down the hallway.

"Oh, Urek," Beautiful said beside him in a voice filled with awe as she tried to look at everything at once, "isn't it wonderful?"

"Sure it is, lass," he said. He noted even the servants wore clothes much finer than any he himself owned, and as they followed the guard past paintings and ornate sculptures, he started to feel like nothing so much as a tick clinging to the ass of a particularly expensive horse. His clothes—that had always seemed fine enough for the back rooms of taverns and dark alleys—now felt woefully inadequate, and he felt his shoulders slumping with each step he took. His ears perked as he listened for the inevitable shouts of the guards as they came charging at them, intent on exterminating the pests that had dared to venture into their midst.

Nothing of the sort happened, of course, but instead of putting Urek at ease this served only to increase his anxiety, some part of him thinking they were waiting until he and Beautiful were too far into the castle to have any chance of escape. As they walked, the palms of his hands began to sweat, and while Beautiful stared at everything they passed, remarking on each painting or sculpture as if she were at some art show, Urek's own eyes were roaming the area in search of the guards who must surely be lying in wait.

By the time the one leading them stopped at a door, Urek's nerves were stretched so tight that a bard could have strummed a tune on them, if he had a mind to. The guard looked back, as if to ensure himself that the two criminals were still behind him and also, Urek suspected, to make sure there weren't any new bulges in their pockets to indicate they'd liked some of the things they'd passed so much they'd decided to borrow them. "This way," he said, walking through the door, and leaving the second guard standing outside in the hallway.

Urek swallowed hard, turning to Beautiful. "Well. Ladies first, eh?"

She smiled, taking the offer at face value, and gave him a curtsey. "Thank you, kind sir." And with that, she followed the guard. Urek hesitated, glancing through the door, but he could see little more than Beautiful's wide shoulders and back, and he turned to the remaining guard, giving a laugh he didn't feel. "Ain't no man holdin' an axe and wearin' a black mask in there I should know about, is there?"

The guard only stared at him, not bothering to respond, and Urek sighed. "You oughta learn not to talk so much, fella. Nobody likes a man won't stop waggin' his tongue."

Still the guard said nothing, and Urek grunted. "Well, piss on you anyway," he said. Then he walked inside.

The room was small, looking as if it served as an office, and Urek—used to the tight corners of back alleys—immediately breathed a sigh of relief. Queen Adina sat behind a desk, rising as they entered. Of course, Urek had seen the queen before, though always at a distance, and now, close up, he could see why she was the object of so many drunken fantasies. Not ones that he himself shared, of course. She was Silent's woman, and he figured there were plenty enough ways for a man in his profession to catch his death without deciding to piss that man off.

"Urek, isn't it?" Adina asked.

"Err...yeah," he stammered. "Yeah, that's right."

"And, forgive me, but if I may ask, who is your friend?" she said, turning to Beautiful, and to the queen's credit, her expression betrayed none of the shock or revulsion the guards had shown.

Urek opened his mouth to answer, but Beautiful beat him to it, dropping down into a curtsey so low his own knees ached in sympathy. "Queen Adina, Majesty," the big woman said in a voice filled with an adoration he'd never heard from her before, "it is my distinct pleasure to make your acquaintance. My name is Nallia."

Urek knew that he was staring, but he couldn't help himself. He'd known, deep down, that surely Beautiful *had* a name, but neither he, nor anyone he'd ever met, knew what it was. Still, it wasn't just the name that surprised him, but her manner. Beautiful was many things—fatal not least among them—but never before had he seen the look of worship that now filled her eyes. "A pleasure to meet you as well," the queen said, returning the curtsey and with considerably more grace than Beautiful, if Urek was any judge. "Nallia, is it? A wonderful name."

The thickly-muscled woman blushed, grinning like a child given a treat. "You are too kind, Majesty, and..." She hesitated, nervous for the first time Urek had ever seen. "If it pleases, you, Queen, my friends...they call me 'Beautiful.'" She blushed even more furiously, her face growing a deep shade of red.

The queen smiled pleasantly. "Then 'Beautiful' it shall be," she said, and Urek decided, watching her face betray not a hint of disbelief or doubt, that he could see why the woman was a queen.

"Please," Adina went on, gesturing to the chairs sitting in front of the desk, "have a seat and get comfortable. There are some things I'd like to discuss."

The trip through the castle coupled with Beautiful's uncharacteristic behavior had left Urek unsteady on his feet, and he was thankful for the offer, walking to the nearest chair and sinking into it without preamble. Beautiful did the same, the awe and adoration in her expression as she gazed at the queen so great that a man might have been forgiven for thinking that one of the gods themselves had come down to speak with her.

The queen made her way around the desk to the chair she'd been occupying and waved at the guard. "Thank you, Guardsman Blake. You may leave us."

The guard hesitated. "Majesty?" he asked, glancing at Urek and Beautiful. "Are...that is...are you sure?"

Adina's smile was pleasant enough, but when she spoke it was in a voice that expected to be obeyed. "I am. You may go, and I wish not to be disturbed until my companions and I have finished our meeting."

The guard bowed his head. "Majesty," he said, then he gave a final suspicious glance at the two criminals before walking out of the door.

Once the door closed behind him, the queen turned back to Urek and Beautiful. "Thank you both so much for coming, and I apologize for the urgency of the summons."

"Of course not, Majesty," Beautiful said, "we serve at your pleasure." And Urek suspected that, just then, if the queen's pleasure would have been her boots being cleaned, the big woman wouldn't have wasted the time it would take to get a rag, only would have gone down on all fours and started licking.

"What can we do for you, Majesty?" he asked.

"You are both aware, of course, of the dangers facing the city, and that we've spent the last several days trying to root out all of Grinner's loyalists before we begin our march on Baresh."

Urek was *too* aware, as far as he was concerned. He'd been sitting and staring at reports for so long that he figured the chair he'd used had a permanent imprint of his ass on it, but he didn't think saying such a thing would be proper, so he only nodded. "Yes, Majesty."

"Of course you would be, though, wouldn't you?" Adina said. "After all, it has been in no small part thanks to your efforts that we have been so effective. Thank you for helping to coordinate our men and showing us where we might find Grinner's loyalists. You have been a great help."

Despite his anxiety at being in the castle and Beautiful's uncharacteristic behavior, Urek felt his own face flush in pleasure at the compliment. "Happy to help, Majesty."

"And you're both aware of the damage Grinner caused by spreading rumors of myself and Aaron, as well as the others? Painting us as traitors and turning much of the city against us?"

Urek grunted. "In my experience, folk'll believe just about anythin', you serve it to 'em with an ale or two. They make it a competition of sorts, takin' a story and addin' to it, seein' just how many lies their listener can swallow with his drink."

The queen smiled. "I hope you're right."

There was something about the way she was looking at him that set Urek's nerves on edge. "Majesty," he said, "what is it, you don't mind me askin', that's got you callin' us down here? I got to figure, between the guards and the thousands of soldiers out there, that you'd be able to find plenty of folks as'd be more than happy to do whatever you wanted."

"*Urek!*" Beautiful hissed in a scandalized voice. "How could you talk to her li—"

"It's quite alright," Adina said, raising a hand, and to Urek's astonishment Beautiful stopped talking immediately. The queen studied him for several seconds before speaking. "You're right, of course, to question my motives. After all, as you say, there are plenty available who might perform most any task I would need. But there are certain things that need doing which I believe would be particularly suited to your...talents."

"We'll do whatever you need, of course, Majesty," Beautiful said.

"Well," Urek said, pretending not to notice Beautiful's scowl, "most anythin'. If it's all the same to you, I'd rather not serve as target practice for your executioner, if he's in need of some."

Adina laughed. "No, no, it's nothing like that, I assure you. Only, I thought that, seeing as how effective the rumors Grinner spread about the city were, we might use a similar strategy to our own advantage."

Urek frowned. "Can't say as I see how brandin' you and Envelar traitors all over again'll do us any good." He winced as Beautiful kicked him in the shin. "Err...Majesty."

"I suspect it would do us little good, you're right about that. But, it seems to me, that where rumors might create traitors, they might also create heroes."

"Heroes, is it?" he asked, rubbing at his chin. "Well, I suppose the world likes heroes well enough, Majesty. Though, you don't mind me sayin' so, they like 'em even more when they fall. Anyway, what exactly did you have in mind?"

The two criminals sat in silence as Adina told them of her plan, and as she spoke, Urek's respect for her grew, as did his grin. When she was finished, he barked a laugh. "Make a legend out of Envelar then?" he said, nodding as he thought it through. "Shit, truth to tell he ain't all that far from it now."

"So you believe it might work?" the queen asked.

He frowned, considering. "How long we got?"

"The army will march in two days," Adina said, "three on the outside."

"Not much time then," Urek said. "News travels fast, sure, but I don't know if it'll travel that fast."

Adina nodded, obviously disappointed. "So you don't believe it's possible?"

He glanced to the side at Beautiful who stared at him with a hopeful, almost desperate expression, then turned back to the queen, grinning. "Oh, sure, it's possible. If I can be called to a castle for somethin' other than my own execution, I reckon just about anything is possible. Though, knowin' what I know of Silent, I don't expect he'll thank us for it."

"I'll worry about Aaron," Adina said.

Urek laughed. "Oh, you mistake me, Queen. I'd do it for no other reason, but to see the look on Envelar's face when he realizes he's a livin' legend. I imagine he'll shit, when he finds out." He turned to Beautiful, "Well. I guess we'd better get goin'—a lot to do and not much time to do it in." He started to rise but hesitated as the queen held up a hand.

"There's one more thing," she said, wincing as if the words pained her. "Something else I'd like to talk to you about."

"Oh?" Urek said, sitting back down.

She nodded, taking a slow, deep breath, as if trying to order her thoughts. "Recently, a representative arrived from Avarest. A Councilman Arkrest."

Urek hocked, getting ready to spit before the furious look on Beautiful's face reminded him that he was in a castle, and the thick carpet beneath his feet wouldn't thank him for it. "That bastard, is it?"

"You know of him?" Adina asked, surprised.

"Sure I do," Urek said. "Any man or woman livin' in Avarest knows of that one. A bastard in truth, and as self-serving and cold-blooded as they come. But friendly enough, I guess, if a man's got the coin to buy his favor."

"Do you mean to say that he's known for taking bribes?" Adina asked.

Urek barked a laugh. "Queen, Faden Arkrest don't get out of bed in the mornin', somebody ain't payin' him to do it."

"I see," she said. "Well, Arkrest arrived in the city late last night with an armed escort. He claims to represent Avarest's council, and it's clear that General Yalleck, at least, recognizes him and the authority he bears. He has come to inform us that Avarest's troops are to leave the city and return to their home."

Urek sighed. "Sure, that sounds about right. Damn Council is full of cowards and fools, if you ask me. Not that anyone ever does, mind."

"Yes," she said, hesitating. "But...the thing is, with the war that's coming, we need every soldier we can get to have any chance of defeating Kevlane and his armies."

"Well, sure. But that Arkrest is like a dog with a bone, Queen, and whatever else he is—bastard the least among 'em—the man knows how to get what he wants, and he ain't too keen on changin' his mind, once a deal is done. If he's set his sights on seein' the army returned to Avarest, there ain't much short of killin' him'll keep him from it."

Adina met his eyes then, an intensity to her gaze he hadn't seen there before. "Right."

Urek studied her, waiting for more, then when nothing else came, realization struck, and he leaned forward in his seat. "Queen, bear with me here, as I've got a criminal's mind full of a criminal's thoughts, but it seems to me that you're trying to tell me that the good councilman would be better off—"

"What I am saying," Adina interrupted, her voice low, and he didn't miss the meaningful glance she shot at the door, "is that I find it an unlikely coincidence that Councilman Arkrest decided to visit the city now, of all times, only days before we depart to Baresh."

"Sure, sure," Urek said. "About as coincidental as somebody dyin' with a knife in their throat, I suppose."

"Quite."

They studied each other in silence for several moments then, and when Urek spoke his voice was cold, hard, completely at odds with his normally jovial tone. It was the voice heard only by those who had wronged him or someone he cared about. The voice that was, for most, the *last* thing they heard. "You're sure about this then?"

Adina hesitated then finally gave a brief nod. "For what's coming, there can be no half-measures. Perennia—and all of Telrear—cannot afford to lose thousands of troops on the eve of battle. I would ask," she went on, her voice low, "that you determine whether or not Councilman Arkrest has been 'bought' or if he genuinely represents the will of the Council."

"And if he does?" Urek said. "Represent the will of the Council?"

Adina considered that, and for the first time Urek noticed the dark circles under her eyes, as if she'd gotten little sleep of late. "Then we must pray that he—and the Council through him—might be made to see reason. If not, I think that, sometimes, mistakes happen, do they not? Many have been imprisoned for crimes they did not commit."

"And if he has been bought?"

A coldness entered the woman's gaze. "Then I think it would be best for everyone involved if Councilman Arkrest disappeared. I—and the city too, I believe—have had enough of traitors to last a lifetime."

"And, just to be clear, by 'disappeared' you mean—"

"I mean, Urek," she said in a hard voice, "that if Councilman Arkrest is a traitor in league with Kevlane, then I want him to no longer exist. Find the deepest hole you can and bury him in it."

There was such intensity in her face, her voice, that Urek found himself easing back in his chair, but she wasn't finished. She leaned forward, her eyes flashing. "And Urek? When you bury him—kill him first. Is that clear enough?"

Urek stared at the woman, feeling more than a little awe. The princess was as kind as the rumors said, as pretty too, but what the rumors left out was that she was, in her way, just as cold-blooded as Beautiful, if not more so. "Yes, Majesty," he said after several seconds had passed. "That I can do."

"Good," she said, rising from her chair. "Will there be anything else?"

Sure, he thought. *A new pair of trousers, maybe.* Still, Urek might not have been accustomed to sitting in fancy castles and wearing shirts with as much lace as he could find, but he knew a dismissal when he heard one, and he rose, shaking his head. "No, Majesty. We'll see it done."

"Very well. Thank you. I am in your debt—on both counts."

Urek glanced over to see Beautiful still staring at the queen, and instead of diminishing her clear adoration, Adina's anger and resolve seemed to have only strengthened it, and he didn't think he was imagining the line of drool tracing its way down the muscled woman's open mouth. He cleared his throat, but she didn't so much as turn, and finally he took hold of her shoulder. "Alright then, lass. We've got us a job to do."

"O-of course," Beautiful said, blinking as if she'd just woken from a dream. "Of course. It...it was a pleasure, Majesty," she said, mutilating another perfectly good curtsey. "I hope to have the chance to speak with you again."

The woman flushed at her own boldness, but Adina only smiled. "It would be my pleasure, just as soon as things slow down a bit."

Meaning, of course, never, Urek thought, but Beautiful was beaming as if the sun had just told her it only rose on account of her, so that was alright. As a general rule, Urek himself wasn't much a man for adoration or for bowing, but he made sure to sketch the best one he could—not a particularly fine one, judging by Beautiful's snicker—before heading for the door.

"And Urek?"

He paused, turning back with his hand on the handle. "Majesty?"

"This thing I've asked of you...it needs to be done tonight."

"Sure," he said, nodding. "And why not? I've been sleepin' like shit anyway."

He started out the door, but turned back as she spoke again. "Forgive me, but...I just had a thought. Councilman Arkrest also has two servants, a scribe, and, it appears, six guards within his employ. I cannot say for certain that, even should Arkrest be a traitor, they have any notion of their master's treachery. I would ask that you do not harm them."

Urek blinked. "Majesty, I don't think that the councilman's guards are going to sit by while me and my crew do what needs doin'."

"No," she said, "I don't believe that they will."

Urek grunted. He could have told her that, when you went searching for blood, there was no knowing whose might be spilled. He could have explained that in war, the bodies of the innocent fed the worms just like the guilty, and that when you saw a thing that needed doing, you couldn't rely on half-measures. But he said none of those things. Instead, he only gave a sharp nod. "Alright then."

Her face twisted, her mouth opening and closing, and when she finally spoke, she seemed to have to force the words out. "How...how will you do it?"

"Best you not worry about that, Queen. Killin' is killer's business. When your horse needs shoein', you don't ask the stable hand how he does it—the best thing is to just let him get on with his work. This is our job, and we're good at it...gods help us."

"And the servants?" she asked.

"Well," Urek said, "they aren't slaves, are they, Majesty? They're men paid for a service. What difference to them who's doin' the paying?"

"But...but you do know how you'll do it?"

"'Course I do," Urek said. "Easiest thing in the world."

He walked out then, Beautiful trailing behind him. The older guard was waiting a short distance from the door, and Urek didn't miss the way his hand hovered near the hilt of his sword, as if he'd been prepared to charge in the room should the queen scream for help. The man glanced between the two of them, clearly wanting to go check on the queen but not loving the idea of leaving the two of them in the castle alone. Finally, he came to a decision. "This way," he said, and turned, leading them back the way they'd come.

"So," Beautiful said in a whisper as they followed him, seeming to finally find her voice now that she was no longer in the queen's presence, "let me get this straight. We're supposed to figure out whether this councilman is a traitor or not and, if he is, kill him without anyone *knowing* we've killed him, and, at the same time, without hurting any of his guards—men who get paid to keep exactly that sort of thing from happening—or his servants who will, no doubt, be in the house with him?"

"Yeah," Urek said, scratching his neck. "That sounds just about right."

Beautiful snorted. "What it sounds is impossible."

"Oh?" he said, shooting a glance at the guard to make sure he couldn't hear before turning and scowling at the woman. "Does it? And where were all these objections a few minutes ago, I wonder?"

"She's a *queen,* Urek," she said, as if that explained everything. "And not just *any* queen, but the most beautiful, cleverest queen there's ever been. Still, how does the stable hand change the horse's shoe? How do you plan to do it?"

Urek grunted, suppressing the urge to spit. "I have no fucking idea."

CHAPTER SEVEN

"We're screwed."

Urek sighed, sitting back in his chair. Shits was the one who'd spoken, earning himself the crime boss's best glare, but a quick look around the back room of the tavern showed that the others felt much the same. "I'd think you'd be excited, Shits," he said, spitting on the floor at his feet, and never mind the scowl Beautiful shot in his direction. Sometimes a man needed to spit, was all.

"*Excited?*" the man said. "Why in the name of the gods would I be excited, Urek?"

The big man shrugged. "Well. Seems to me that with that ugly mug of yours, you'd be happy at any chance of gettin' screwed. I can't imagine folks are exactly linin' up to do the job."

Not a great joke, maybe, but the others smiled, some of the dread vanishing from their faces, so that was alright. He wondered, not for the first time, how Hale had done it, how he had managed to lead an empire of criminals, keeping them following orders and doing his bidding. For whatever else they were, men and women who spent their time stealing, mugging, and—when the situation called for it—murdering, had a tendency toward not being particularly dependable.

Shits frowned, but it was Shadow who spoke from where he stood propped against the wall of his room, pausing in using one of his knives to pick his teeth. "Shit's unfortunate face aside, it does seem like a bit of a problem. And, Urek, I have to ask—what are we *doing?*"

Urek frowned. "What do you mean, 'what are we doing'? Seems to me that, right now, we're trying to figure out how we get this job done without getting all of our fool asses killed."

"Right," the hawk-nosed man said. "But *why?*"

"I don't follow you," Urek said, but he thought maybe he did all too well.

The other man glanced up from his blade, meeting the crime boss's eyes. "Look, boss, you know I'll follow wherever you lead, but this needs sayin' and since nobody else seems to want to, I guess I will. We're *criminals,* remember? We ain't soldiers or knights in some queen's army—we're pickpockets and thieves."

"I know what we are, damnit."

Shadow nodded slowly. "Of course you do, boss. Thing is, we haven't been acting much like criminals lately. People always call us 'vultures,' or 'scavengers', and maybe that's not far off, but I've never taken offense at it. After all, vultures have to eat too, don't they? But lately, it seems to me that we haven't been acting much like vultures or criminals but like soldiers in some queen's army. For starters, we've been hunting down our own kind. Don't get me wrong, those bastards who followed Grinner deserve what's coming to them, sure. For what they did, for what they *tried* to do, they're in need of some bloodletting...but then, that's not what we're doing, is it? We're tracking them down and letting the soldiers throw them in the dungeons."

"You got a point, Shadow?"

The smaller man shrugged. "I guess what I'm saying is that it just seems strange, is all. Trying to rescue May and the boss from being executed, sure, it made sense, for we look after our own. Always have. Even this here, lately, tracking down those poor dumb bastards who followed Grinner, I can kind of understand. After all, less competition for us, right? But now, you're talking about a whole different thing. Now, you're talking about following a queen's orders on a job that'll most likely get us all killed, to take care of a man who, if anything, has been good for us in the past. After all, Faden Arkrest is a man with a price, and as long as you can pay it, he isn't a problem. Seems to me I recall Hale doing exactly that, a time or two."

Urek grunted, glancing around at the others in the room. Beautiful standing by the door, Osirn, beside her. Shits and

Shadow and a few others. Ten in all, and all of them looking at him, waiting for what he would say. "You all feel this way, then?"

Osirn, flinched as if struck when Urek's gaze fell on him. Shits was still frowning sullenly, looking as if he wanted to say something, but it was Beautiful who finally spoke in a hesitant voice completely at odds with her normally assertive tone. "It is…a little strange, boss. You have to admit that much."

Urek tried to remember the last time Beautiful had called him 'boss' and came up empty. She was serious then, and that made him really start to think on Shadow's questions himself. The truth was, he'd been so caught up in events since trying to save Hale from execution that he really hadn't stopped to consider the matter. Now that he did, he had to admit they were right. It *was* strange. They were criminals, in the business of crime, and lately they'd been coming perilously close to acting like soldiers.

As he thought it through, the others only waited in silence, watching him, but Urek barely noticed. He was too busy considering his actions over the last week. Why *had* he been so quick to take up the queen's task? Gods, he'd barely asked any questions at all, had even went so far as to walk *willingly* into the castle, putting himself completely in the power of its guards, a thing he would have never done a few months ago. He sat that way for several minutes, wondering. When he finally did speak, he did so slowly. "You're right," he said. "You're all right. We have been actin' against our natures. Standing and fighting when we'd normally run and hide, defending the innocent instead of takin' what we can and gettin' out before the guards come."

They all nodded at that, and Urek nodded along with them. "I could argue that everythin' I've done, everythin' *we've* done, is on account of, with that bastard Kevlane and his monsters out there, we've only been actin' in our own self-interest. After all, it seems to me that if he has his way, there won't be a hole deep enough to escape what's comin'. I could tell you that's the reason—but I'd be lyin'. I could tell you that I'm only tryin' to do what I think the boss, Hale, would have done in the same circumstances, but even that ain't the truth. I knew that man for years, and even I wouldn't ever think to hazard a guess at what he might do from one minute to the next."

There were mutters of agreement at that. "Though," Urek went on, "I think it has to be said that, when it came down to it, Hale stood. He didn't run or hide, didn't try to buy his way out. He stood and because he did, May Tanarest is still walkin' around breathin'."

"And he died," Beautiful said, her voice little more than a whisper.

Urek grunted. "Yeah, and he died. And what Hale would think of this here, I can't begin to guess. All I can tell you," he said, realizing the truth of his own feelings even as he spoke, "is that it feels right. What we did—what we're doin'. As for Silent and the word we're to spread," he added, finally looking back at Shadow, "well, like you said, we take care of our own. And whatever else he is, whatever else he's become, Silent is one of us. Anybody gonna argue that?"

No one seemed inclined to disagree, so Urek went on. "Plus," he said, grinning, "I can't wait to see that bastard's face, he finds out he's been turned into a hero while he's sleepin'."

"Sure," Shadow agreed. "The Blade is one of us, boss. But...what about the other thing?"

"Oh," Urek said, "you mean the 'assassinatin' a councilman without harmin' any of his servants and doing our level-best to keep our own heads attached to our shoulders' thing?"

The hawk-nosed man grinned. "That'd be the one."

Urek scratched at his chin, considering that. "Ain't a very criminal thing to do, is it? Oh, sure, we'll stab a man quick enough, if he's got somethin' worth takin', but this...this is something altogether different."

"S-s-seems that way, b-b-boss," Osirn said, flushing as everyone turned to look at him and cringing as if trying to disappear into the wall.

"Yeah, lad," Urek agreed. "It does. But you know what?" he said, taking the time to meet each of their eyes in turn. "I'm gonna do it anyway. More likely than not, I'll get my fool ass killed, but I'll do what I can. And why?" He shrugged. "I can't really say. Maybe it's because I believe if this Kevlane fella gets his way, we'll all be dead soon regardless. Maybe it's because that bastard Arkrest has had it comin' for some time now, and I'd just as soon be the one who gave it to him. Might even be the queen struck me as a woman worthy of such a risk, or that I'm tired of runnin' and hidin', tired of lurkin' in alleyways."

"Or maybe it's that you're a stubborn bastard who doesn't know when to let something go," Beautiful observed, but she was grinning as she said it.

"Maybe," Urek agreed, grinning back. "But I'm gonna do it, either way. I don't expect none of you to come with me, and I won't hold it against ya if you don't. But I'm gonna see this thing through, one way or the other."

They were silent then, absorbing his words, which was just as well. Urek couldn't remember the last time he'd talked as much. He never had been one for speeches, and he was out of breath. They all glanced at each other after a few minutes, and an understanding seemed to pass between them. Finally, Shadow shrugged. "Alright, boss. So...when are we leavin'?"

Urek grunted, surprised at the response and even more surprised at his profound sense of not just relief, but gratitude. "We, is it?"

Shadow nodded, and the rest of those in the room nodded along with him. "Sure. We can't let you go alone, now can we? The gods know you'd be dead inside of five minutes, and it's really more trouble than it's worth, finding a new boss and all."

"That your reason then?"

"Well," the other man said, grinning, "let's say it's one of 'em."

"Alright then," Urek said, glancing around at each of them. "You're all a bunch of fools, you know that? Well, come on. Let's go see if we can't save ourselves a kingdom. Osirn, Shadow, Beautiful, and Shits, you're with me. The rest of you lot, go on out there and spread the word. By tomorrow mornin', I want folks thinkin' Envelar can sprout wings and shit gold, you understand?"

"Yes sir, boss," one of the men said, his eyes dancing with amusement. "Sprout gold and shit wings."

Urek grunted. "Close enough. Now go on, you bastards." They did, walking out the door with pleased expressions on their faces, and he shook his head in aggravation mixed with disbelief as he turned back to the others. "Well. Anybody got a plan doesn't end with us seein' what our insides look like?"

CHAPTER EIGHT

Can you explain to me, again, why we're doing this? And alone no less?

Seline didn't bother answering the Virtue, just as she hadn't the last dozen times he'd asked the question. She couldn't deny that the incredible speed which her bond with the Virtue gave her was useful, but, most days, it seemed like a bad trade when she considered how much the Virtue—Davin, as he liked to be called—second-guessed every decision she made, worrying more than an old maid.

Instead of answering, though, she only shot a quick glance over her shoulder, trusting the shadows of the alleyway to hide the movement from the two men following her. Grinner's men, she was certain, just as she was sure that the others—one, perhaps two—who were no doubt approaching the alley from the opposite side, were also loyalists of the dead crime boss.

I'm not arguing with the necessity of it, you understand, Davin went on in her mind, *only with your methods. After all, General Envelar and the others have teams hunting down Grinner's men every day. You could just join with one of those groups, instead of insisting on setting out alone each night. There's just no reason to take the risk.*

And she couldn't argue with that, even if she'd been of a mind to, which she wasn't. The Virtue was right, of course—Seline could have easily taken up Leomin's offer to accompany him and the others on their hunt for Grinner's men, spending her days helping to track them down. But when he'd asked, she'd found herself coming up with excuses—empty ones, even she had to admit that—and the Parnen had noticed it as well, the hurt clear in his eyes. She'd told him she needed time to work through her feelings about her father, about her life, and he had nodded and agreed, saying all the right things and, in so doing, increasing the guilt she felt. Yet she had persisted.

She was still confused about her father, still trying to reconcile the fact that the monster she'd chased all her life wasn't a monster at all, but a man. But the real reason she'd declined the offer, the real reason she spent her nights moving from one tavern to the other, hunting Grinner's men down on her own, was far more complicated, and she wasn't even sure she fully understood it.

She had spent so much of her life alone, had built up so many walls around herself to protect her from the world and everyone in it. Now, it was difficult for her to let anyone too close. And so she made excuses, she hesitated and, yes, she lied.

You could just tell him the truth, the Virtue said, able to hear her thoughts as easily as if she'd spoken them aloud. Leomin cares for you, and you care for him. You don't have to lie to him.

The men were close now; she could hear their footsteps behind her and thought that she could also detect the faint sound of those ahead, from the alley's mouth. In a minute, maybe less, the men would appear there, springing their trap, only to discover that where one trap might be laid so, too, might another. Maybe, she thought back, but he wouldn't understand.

How could you know? You haven't even given him a chance to try.

She knew Leomin wouldn't understand her nightly outings because, in truth, she hardly understood them herself. She knew only that here, in the darkness, she felt more at peace than anywhere else. Perhaps it was because she had spent so much of her life hunting monsters, surrounded by them, that she had grown accustomed to it. Had, in some strange way, become dependent on it. Perhaps by vanquishing the monsters of the world, some part of her thought that she might somehow vanquish those demons—fear, shame, and anger chief among them—that warred within her own soul. All she knew for sure was that here, in the darkness, with the monsters gathered around her, the questions that plagued her in the daylight, the voices that asked, demanded to know who she was, what she was, grew silent. For whatever else it was, the world of monsters was a simple one—kill or be killed—and the one who walked away was the one with the sharpest teeth, the quickest claws.

She heard the footsteps a moment before she saw the two shadowy figures emerge from the end of the alley. "Well, hi there," one said, and though Seline couldn't see his face, she could hear the pleasure in his tone.

A quick glance behind showed that the two following her had stopped no more than a dozen paces away. Four men in all, each of them ready for violence. Another person might have felt fear, perhaps even terror, but Seline felt only relief as all her uncertainties and worries vanished at the approach of the impending fight. "Hello."

"Someone told me," the man who'd spoken went on, "that you've been asking after those as followed Grinner. That right?"

"Everybody's asking after them," Seline said in what she hoped was a fearful tone. "They're wanted by the guard for conspiring against the city."

"That right?" the man asked, laughing. "And what are you then, some loyal citizen trying to help out?"

"Yes," Seline answered, drawing the blade hidden inside her tunic. "Something like that."

The man laughed again. "What do you mean to do with that then? Butter my bread for me? Well," he said in a voice full of feigned regret, "you should have stayed inside tonight, lass, and you should have kept your questions to yourself. Don't you know bad men come out in the darkness?"

Seline smiled as she glanced over her shoulder where the two from behind her were creeping closer. "Yes. I was counting on it."

***

She emerged from the alleyway minutes later, replacing the blade in its hidden sheath and glancing around the street. Normally, there would have been at least a few people about, even at this hour, but the recent troubles had apparently made the city's citizens decide to stay inside, and she couldn't blame them. Had she not known better, Seline would have thought she journeyed through some ghost city, a place in which all the inhabitants had left or, more likely, died.

No merchants shouted out their wares, no prostitutes hung out the windows of the brothels she passed. Even the beggars, it seemed, had found some place to shelter—or more correctly, perhaps, hide—for the evening. She was alone with herself and the silence, and the bodies littering the alley behind her. And in that silence, her thoughts began to drift once more, the questions and uncertainties that the encounter with Grinner's men had quelled coming back, slowly at first, in little more than whispers, but growing in volume and insistence with each passing moment.

Frustrated and looking for anything to distract herself, she caught sight of a slight movement disappearing down an alleyway far along the street ahead of her. Grateful for the distraction, Seline called on the power of her Virtue and traveled the few hundred feet in a blur, standing in the alley mouth a moment later and watching the figure hurrying away.

You should leave it, Davin said. *I'm sure it's nothing and, even if it isn't, don't you think you've pushed your luck enough for one evening? Besides, you need to get some rest—you're tired. You know it as well as I.*

Seline was tired, exhausted really, for tonight was not the first one she'd spent out in the darkness, searching for Grinner's men. But she also knew that if she tried to sleep, the questions and uncertainties rolling around in her head—*Who am I? Without my father to hunt down, who am I?*—demanding an answer, louder and louder until she could scream, would keep her from it.

You can't go on like this, the Virtue said. *You must talk to someone—to Leomin, at least. No matter what your fears are—and do not pretend you do not have them—he will understand. However tall you have built the walls that surround you, Seline, they* can *be knocked down and he, I think, would love nothing more than to help you do it. If only you would let him.*

And I will let him, damn you, she thought back. *Only...not tonight.* Tonight, she would follow the figure moving through the darkness. After all, the questions would still be there, waiting, come the morning.

Yes, the Virtue said, *but if you continue the way you have been, sooner or later, you won't be.*

Seline ignored that, following after the figure, ready to draw her blade once more should he—or she, for in the darkness there was no way to tell for certain—turn and accost her. But the figure only walked on, and so she trailed after for nearly fifteen minutes. She had just begun to convince herself that the figure's errand must surely be nothing of note—an unsatisfied husband visiting his mistress, likelier than not—when she followed the figure around a corner and saw him walk up to a group of three or four others huddled in the dark mouth of an alley.

They're probably just meeting for a hand of cards, the Virtue said, though from his tone Seline could tell even he wasn't wholly convinced. *Or, maybe, they plan to go to a tavern and have a drink. There's nothing to say that they're criminals.*

Nothing, of course, except that even in the darkness, Seline was able to make out the knife one of them held.

And even if they are *criminals,* Davin went on, a desperation to his tone now, *we have more important things to be about. It's not as if you can kill every criminal in the city. What you need to be doing is preparing for the march to Baresh. You'll do no one any good—including Leomin, mind—if when we go there you are too exhausted to be of any use.*

Well, Seline thought back, *call it practice, if you like, but I'm going to see what they're up to.*

Practice? the Virtue asked. *How in the name of the gods is this practice?*

You're always telling me I need to work on growing the power of the bond, Davin. It seems to me there's no better teacher than experience. The Virtue said something in response, but she wasn't listening, and she started down the street, a grim smile on her face.

***

"I'm just saying it's a dumb idea, that's all."

"So you've mentioned once or twice," Urek said, narrowing his eyes at Beautiful. "And while we've spent hours standin' out here jawin' times been wastin'. Light's only a few hours away, so unless someone has a better idea?"

"Sure," the woman responded, and if she noticed Urek's frayed patience, she apparently wasn't concerned. "Why not just have Shadow here cut your throat with one of those knives he carries? I doubt it would hurt as much as what those guards are going to do to you, and either way it'll save you the walk."

Urek scowled at the thickly-muscled woman. "I *mean* does anybody have any ideas that don't start with me dyin'?"

"Funny," she said, folding her arms across her chest and glaring back at him, "that's the only sort of ideas my mind keeps comin' up with, just now."

"Boss, no offense," Shadow said, pausing in trimming his nails with one of his blades to glance up, "but the plan's shit."

"Damnit," Urek growled, "am I the boss or not?"

"Of course you are," the man said.

"T-that's right," Osirn blurted. "Y-you're the boss, err...boss."

"At least for now," Beautiful said. "I imagine once you've tried your plan out, we'll be having to elect a new one quickly enough. But don't worry, Urek, I don't think you'll mind—you'll be *dead*, after all."

Urek gritted his teeth. "And what about you, Shits? What's your thoughts on the matter?"

"My thoughts?" the man asked, blinking. "Well, it's damned cold out here, that's my thoughts. Gods, but how these northerners choose to live here, I'll never know."

Urek stared at the man, giving some serious consideration to what he'd look like with a black eye and what the most enjoyable way of finding that out might be, when Shadow let out a hiss of surprise and warning, hefting his blade as if preparing to throw it.

Urek spun, his hand going for the sword at his side, sure the guards had decided maybe they had room in the dungeons, after all, and was surprised to see a lone figure walking up. She was cloaked in the shadows of the night, and he could make out none of her features, but there was no doubt she was a woman. "Act natural," he hissed in a voice low enough for only the others to hear.

"Hi there," he said, trying on his best grin.

"Funny," the woman said, drawing closer, and as she did Urek saw that she was smiling. "That's the second time someone's said that to me tonight. I wonder, is there a manual all you criminals read?"

"Criminals?" he asked, incredulous. "Oh, no ma'am. Not criminals, us. Only some friends having a late night is all." He tried a laugh, and immediately regretted it once he heard how forced it sounded. "Leastways, we ain't criminals unless there's a new law bannin' fun."

She only continued to stare at him, and he cleared his throat. "What uh...if you don't mind me askin', what would make you think a thing like that? You know, crazy as it is."

"Well," the woman drawled, "there are a few things, really. First, there's the fellow standing behind you there holding a knife, and he looks a mite too comfortable with it, if you ask me."

Urek frowned, turning around to see that Shadow had gone back to trimming his nails with his blade. The hawk-nosed man glanced up at him questioningly, as if he had no idea what he'd done to merit such a scowl.

"I told you to act natural," Urek mouthed.

"T-to be fair, boss," Osirn volunteered, "that is p-p-pretty natural. I mean...that is...for Shadow."

"Hmm," the woman said. "A knife, a man referred to as 'boss,' and another called 'Shadow.' Sure do sound like criminals."

Urek stared at the woman, suddenly unable to think of anything to say. She only stared back in silence, the small grin still in place. After a moment, he gave a grunt of recognition. "Hey, wait a minute. Ain't you the Parnen's?"

The woman's grin faded in an instant. "I'm not a cow or a sheep, criminal, nor am I a porcelain vase to be set on a shelf and admired. Nobody *owns* me. Now, why don't you tell me what you and your...*companions* are doing out here so late at night? Or should I call the guards and see if you'll be able to come up with a better story for Queen Adina?"

Urek sputtered at the ridiculousness of it all. Here he was, standing in the middle of the street, being accosted for a crime he hadn't even *committed* yet, when the gods knew he'd gotten away with plenty in his time. What's more, the woman was threatening him with the very same person who had sent him out here to begin with.

"O-oh, we don't want to make the queen mad, lady," Osirn blurted. "That's the last thing we want to do. After all, it was her as sent us. Tell her, Urek."

"What the fuck, boy?" Urek said, turning and staring at the youth who wilted under his glare. Wincing, he turned back to the woman. "I wouldn't pay him no mind—the boy ain't completely right in the head. A born liar, and not a good one."

"Not as bad as you at any rate...Urek, is it?" She frowned. "Wait a minute—I've heard that name before." Her eyes widened. "You're the one who took over for Hale, aren't you?"

Urek considered lying, but thought they were past such conveniences now, so he only sighed. "I reckon so, gods help me."

The woman nodded slowly, glancing around the street. "Alright. I think you'd best tell me what you all are doing out here, and what mission the queen's given you."

Urek spared another glare for the youth, then he told her about his meeting with the queen, about councilman Arkrest, and his plan. The woman listened in silence until he was finished, and he breathed a sigh of relief, glad to be done with telling the story at any rate. If somebody would have told him that becoming the boss meant he would have to do so much talking, he would have stabbed the first bastard who suggested it.

"So the queen believes this councilman Arkrest is a traitor then?" the woman asked.

"That's right," Urek said. Nodding at a house a few hundred feet down the street, he added, "That's his there." *Well, in for a penny and all that,* he thought, and proceeded to tell her his plan to deal with the councilman.

She nodded. "I see. Well, if what you said is true, and Queen Adina wants it done before the morning, what are all of you doing standing around out here?"

He grunted. "Had a bit of a disagreement about the plan, is all."

"The plan's shit," she said distractedly, turning to study the house, and Urek did his best not to notice the smug looks on the faces of the others. "Still...there are six guards, you say?"

"That's right," he muttered. "And two servants and a scribe."

"Anyone else?"

"How the fuck should I know?" he asked, still sore about the way she'd dismissed his plan so quickly. "Might be the bastard has a dog."

She turned back to him. "Fine. I'll help you."

Urek raised an eyebrow. "Beggin' your pardon, miss, but we didn't exactly ask for your help, and we don't rightly need it. No offense meant, but this sort of thing is what we do, you understand?"

"Sure I do," she said. "Just as I understand that, had I not come along, you, at the least, would have been dead before morning, and the queen's problem would have remained."

"*Thank* you," Beautiful said. "I mean...knockin' on the door, Urek? Seriously?"

He avoided meeting the gazes of the others, staring instead at his feet. "Well. He wouldn't have expected it, that's all," he grumbled.

"No, he wouldn't have, I'm sure," the other woman said. "Because, of course, no one would be stupid enough to try it. But that's okay—I've got a better idea."

"Probably a bad one," Urek muttered.

"What's that?" Beautiful asked. "Couldn't quite hear you." But judging by the amusement dancing in her eyes, Urek thought she'd heard well enough.

He sighed. "So what's the idea?"

"Well," the newcomer said, smiling, "I'll be the one doing the knocking."

He grunted. "Look, lady, no disrespect meant, and all, but if knockin' is a sure way to get dead—somethin' I still ain't completely sold on, mind—then it seems to me that I'll have a better chance of survivin' it than you. Oh, you're brave enough, sure, walkin' up on a group of what you took to be criminals like you done, but back when I was a soldier, my sergeant was fond of sayin' that courage alone is only enough to get a man killed. He was a bastard through and through, that one, but it seems to me he was right enough about that."

"You're correct, of course," she said, smiling wider. "But, then, I have more than just courage, I think. Now, all of you just wait here, and be ready when I give the signal."

With that, she turned and walked away, headed directly toward the councilman's house. "But b-b-boss," Osirn said, "what's the signal?"

Urek sighed again. "Couldn't say, lad. Her screamin' in agony, maybe."

CHAPTER NINE

Councilman Faden Arkrest awoke to the sound of thunder only to realize, after a few confused moments, that it wasn't thunder at all, but someone knocking at his door as if they intended to break it down. He frowned, waiting impatiently for Ianden, his servant, to get rid of whoever was foolish enough to come calling in the middle of the night.

He waited, but the knocking only grew louder, so loud that it seemed to be coming from inside his own head. An ache began to form in his temple, a promise of pain to come. Cursing, he tossed the silk covers aside and climbed from his bed, deciding that whoever was so impolite as to accost him this late at night would answer for it, as would Ianden.

He moved to the door of his bedroom, his anger building with each resounding *thump* at the front door, and threw the latch back, slinging it open. The main room of the house was dark, without so much as a lantern or candle to give any light. He cried out as he stubbed his toe on something, hissing in pain and reaffirming his promise that whoever was behind waking him up at so indecent an hour would regret it. He made his way across the dark room, groping with his hands extended to keep from running into anything else. The knocking grew louder, so that he half-thought the door would come crashing down at any moment. It wouldn't, of course. He had made sure it was reinforced before making use of the house—a man of Faden Arkrest's prominent position could never be too careful when protecting himself from the disreputable side of society. Which, as far as he was concerned, included nearly everyone.

Another security measure upon which he had insisted was the small peep hole in the door, the cover of which he now slid open to gaze outside. Faden had a moment of intense fear when he noted the figure standing on the other side of the door, for if any human form had been contrived by the gods to do violence, then surely the one that was even now knocking without surcease on his door was it. He couldn't make out too much with the small view afforded by the peep hole, but it was enough to see the impossibly wide shoulders, and the blunted features of a face which served as evidence of a life spent fighting, or proof that the gods could, at times, be particularly cruel.

The figure seemed to realize he was staring through the small hole, bending down and smiling widely back. Faden was shocked to realize that the stranger was the ugliest woman he'd ever seen and was missing more teeth than she had.

"Councilman Arkrest," she said, her voice muffled by the thick door, "I have a question."

"Yes," he said, low enough for his ears only, "as do I. One you will answer, alright, but to my guards." Then he frowned as he realized for the first time that he hadn't seen any of them. *Probably all sleeping, the worthless bastards.* He would have a talk with them as well, once all this was sorted. Faden Arkrest was a man who knew well the power of coin, and he had paid plenty to have the guards accompany him.

"Guards!" he yelled, moving away from the door and the continuous knocking and further into the room. "Ianden!"

No answer, save for the resounding thumps on the door. He frowned at the surreality of it all, beginning to believe that he must surely be dreaming. Then there was the sound of a flint being struck and a moment later a light bloomed in the hallway, leading to the rooms his servant and the guards occupied. The light was dazzling after being in darkness for so long, and Faden held up a hand, wincing. "Ianden, is that you?" he said, unable to make out anything of the figure holding the light. There was no answer, and his worry gave way to anger. "You listen to me, you worthless commoner scum, I pay you good coin—the gods know more than you deserve—and in return, I expect you to do your *job*. And where are all those worthless guards? What's the point of paying for guards that don't actually *guard* anything?"

"Oh, they're all tied up, at the moment."

Faden frowned. That voice hadn't sounded like his servant's. Not at all. It was a coarse, uncultured voice. Little more than a growl, really, and he felt his heart speed up in his chest. "Ianden?"

"Not quite," the voice answered, and the light rose, revealing the grim expression of a man Faden didn't recognize. All thoughts of punishing his servant vanished as he was abruptly covered in a cold sweat.

"W-who are you?" Faden sputtered.

"Doesn't matter who I am," the big man said. "What matters is who sent me."

Faden swallowed hard. "And who...that is, what can I do for you?"

"You can tell me, Councilman, about Avarest's troops. Why are they still here, in Perennia?"

Faden scowled, trying to order his confused thoughts, then realization struck, and he breathed a heavy sigh of relief. "Oh, *he* sent you. Well, why didn't you just say as much?" More confident now that he knew what he was dealing with, he walked toward a small cabinet against the wall, retrieved a glass, and began to pour himself a drink. "I hope you didn't hurt my servant," he said, inwardly outraged that these men should dare to come into his house in the middle of the night. "It is no small thing, training a servant to be even halfway acceptable. If you have done him any harm, I will be adding it to my fee."

"I have a question, Councilman Arkrest," the man said, echoing the words of the woman outside the door.

"Oh do you?" Faden sneered, turning and taking a drink of the liquor. "So do I. For instance, I wonder how pleased your master will be when I send a letter telling him, in detail, how you accosted me within my own house. As for the troops, they will leave the day after tomorrow—that is the soonest it can be done. Unless, of course, I have many more interruptions such as this one, in which case I will make my aggravation known in my fee. You may tell your master as much, the next time you speak with him. I am Councilman Faden Arkrest, and I am no man to be trifled with, do you understand me?"

"My master?" the man said, as if he'd never heard the word before.

"Oh, do not be any more ignorant than you need to be," Faden snapped. "You know well of whom I speak, and you tell your master, also, that for all his ancient powers, it is not *he* who can remove Avarest's troops from Perennia, only I can. And the price of me doing so has just doubled."

"You mean Kevlane."

"Of *course* I mean Kevlane," Faden growled, out of patience. "Who else, in the name of the gods, *could* I mean, you fool?"

The man nodded, his visage shadowed in the darkness, but he said nothing, and Faden was just about to ask him what he was about when he heard the door opening. He spun to see the woman—if the term could be applied to one such as she—stepping inside his house as if she owned it, closing the door softly behind her. "I have a question, Councilman Arkrest," the woman said.

"Oh, you will pay for these theatrics, I promise you," Faden hissed.

"How much," a voice said, and this one came from directly beside him, so close that he could feel the touch of breath on his neck, "was the price of your betrayal? How much is your soul worth?"

"What is the *meaning* of this?" Faden demanded, stumbling away from this third, shadowed figure, fear making it past the anger now.

The big man sighed. "I never said I worked for Kevlane."

The councilman frowned, confused, and he was still trying to order his jumbled thoughts when the knife slid across his throat, taking his life, and his questions with it.

***

"How much is your soul worth?" Urek said, echoing Shadow's words as he regarded the hawk-nosed man standing over the corpse.

The other man shrugged, the gesture just visible in the poor light, and if he felt any sort of emotion at just having killed a man, he showed no sign. "Seemed like the right thing to say at the time."

Sure, Urek thought, *just the right thing, if you want two people in the crew called Shits.* He grunted and lifted the lantern higher, illuminating the councilman's dead form. "You're one cold-hearted bastard, you know that? And what about you?" he said to Beautiful. With all this 'I have a question' nonsense?"

The woman grinned. "Shadow's idea. Still, you have to admit, it was a bit theatric, wasn't it?"

"Sure," Urek said. "If you two ever decide to leave the streets, you can always find work in some actors' troupe."

"Shame about the rug, though," Shadow said.

Urek glanced at where the councilman's blood pooled on a rug that, he suspected, cost more than most people made in a year. *Cold-blooded bastard is right.*

"Just grab him—the job's only half done. Now, we've got to make the fella disappear before the guards come back. Shits, get his shoulders, Shadow his legs, and Beautiful, grab the fuckin' rug, would you?"

"Aw, boss," Shits said, "why do I have to grab his shoulders? Why, he's leakin' all over the place."

"Just do it, you bastard," Urek growled. "That Seline woman seemed to know what she's about, leadin' the guards away, but they'll be back sooner or later, you can count on that."

"I-I ain't never seen nobody move so fast," the youth said from the corner of the room, pointedly keeping his gaze away from the body. Osirn had done well enough for unlocking the door, but the lad wasn't cut out for the bloody parts of the business. But, then, Urek was beginning to grow certain that he wasn't cut out for it himself.

"Neither have I," he admitted, still a little sour that they hadn't gone with his plan. "Now, come on. Let's get this thing done."

CHAPTER TEN

A full night's sleep had done Aaron good, and as he walked toward May's office in the castle, he felt better than anytime in recent memory. Which was to say almost human. He nodded to the guard stationed outside May's door—Adina's precaution against any further treachery, and one the club owner complained about incessantly. "Good morning. Is May in?"

"Y-yes sir, General sir," the young guard said, sketching an awkward bow, his eyes wide with surprise as if Aaron hadn't been coming to May for the last several days to hear the latest information on Grinner's men.

"Well," Aaron said after a minute, glancing over the man's shoulder at the door. "can I see her?"

The guard's face reddened, and he practically jumped out of the way. "O-of course, sir. Forgive me, sir."

Aaron frowned. "I got something on my face, is that it?"

The man blinked, apparently only just realizing he'd been ogling Aaron like a bar of gold had just fallen from the heavens to land at his feet. "N-no sir," he said, giving a nervous, breathy laugh. "And, that is...General, if you don't mind me sayin' so...I sure am glad you're on our side, sir. If there's anything me or the other lads can do, anything we can help you with, all you have to do is ask."

Aaron grunted. *What in the name of the gods is going on?* "Sure," he said, giving the man a grin, "got any answers for a headache?"

The guard considered, a panicked desperation on his face. "Sir, forgive me, I don't know much about headaches, but I can run and get a healer if—"

"I'm joking, man," Aaron said. "Everything's good. I uh...I appreciate it, though."

The guard breathed an audible sigh of relief. "Of course, General. Sorry, sir."

Aaron nodded to the man, doing his best not to break into a run as he went to the door, eager to escape the strange encounter. As he shut it behind him, May looked up from her desk. "Ah, Silent. It's good to see you."

"Thanks," he said, sighing. "Hey, have you noticed anything strange about the guard out there?"

"Sure," May said, frowning, "such as, maybe, the fact that he's there at all. I'm no child in need of a babysitter, Silent, and no matter what *Queen Adina* seems to think, I can take care of myself well enough."

"No," Aaron said, shaking his head and sinking into the chair in front of her desk. "It's not that, it's...forget it. I just wanted to come by and get the latest on Grinner's men."

"The latest," May said, "is that it's done."

He frowned. "Done?"

"That's right," the club owner answered. "Leomin and Darrell are rounding up the last of them now. I tried to send Sergeant Wendell with them, but for some reason neither of them wanted him to come." She frowned, shrugging. "Anyway, if there are any more of Grinner's men left in the city, they've got their heads buried so far in the dirt they won't be able to come up in time for air, let alone give us any trouble."

Aaron grunted. "Well. That's good then. What else do you need from me?"

"Nothing," she said. "Unless,"—a pause as she smiled wickedly—"you want to help me go through some of these reports." She gestured at the stacks of papers on her desk. "Help me find out where some of these missing items are."

Aaron cleared his throat, rising. "I'd love to, May, but I think I'd better go check on the army, see how things are coming along. If Grinner's men have all been accounted for then we'll need to be prepared to march as quickly as possible."

"Mmhmm," May said. "Right. Well, off with you then—I've got enough work to do without having you in here distracting me."

Aaron grinned, giving her a wink. "Well, if you insist."

***

He stopped to ask one of the guards where Captain Gant was, since he'd been in charge of the preparations of the armies, and in between his nervous sputtering—as if Aaron wasn't a man at all but some god come to visit him personally—the guard finally managed to direct him toward the eastern wall of the city where the captain was overseeing preparation of the three armies.

Feeling as if everyone must have surely gone mad, Aaron left the bowing, scraping guard and hurried out of the castle, suddenly feeling claustrophobic. He ventured into the crowded city street, and had barely taken a step when men and women turned from where they were studying the merchants' wares to stare at him, whispering excitedly to each other.

What in the name of the gods is going on with everyone? he thought.

I'm sure I couldn't guess, Co said, but he didn't miss the amusement in the Virtue's tone.

He started walking faster, but a heavy-set woman stepped in front of him, holding a bundle in both hands and thrusting it toward him. Aaron only just managed to stop himself from reaching for his sword. "General Envelar," the woman gasped, her face red as if she'd been running, "please, sir. Bless my baby."

Aaron frowned, and a quick look around him showed others in the street watching. "Uh...sure," he managed, looking at the baby who appeared moments away from breaking into tears. "So...bless you?"

The woman shouted in joy, seeming nearly to swoon, then rushed off into the street, people gathering around her to hear what had happened. *What is going on?* Aaron thought as he turned, hurrying toward the walls and barely restraining the urge to break into a run.

It seems, Co said in his mind, the amusement clear in her tone, *that they have come to look at you as something of a hero.*

Aaron shook his head in disbelief. He'd hoped that, given time, his suicidal stand at the castle gates when Belgarin and his men had attacked would be forgotten, but, it seemed, that if anything, the adoration had only gotten worse. "I'm just a sellsword, Firefly, that's all. I'm not some knight or hero with statues made after me, and thank the gods for that."

It seems, Aaron, that they disagree.

Aaron did his best to ignore the adoring, almost worshipful gazes of those he passed, breathing a heavy sigh of relief when he finally made it to the base of the city wall. Here, at least, there were few people, only the guards posted along the wall, keeping watch in case Kevlane or any of his creatures should come in view of the city. He saw Captain Gant and started up the stairs toward him.

He'd barely made it halfway up when the guards stationed along the wall begin chanting his name. *"En-ve-lar! En-ve-lar!"*

They were still chanting when he made it to the top of the wall, and he hurried to Brandon Gant who watched him approach with a wide grin on his face. *The bastard.* "How do you make them stop?" Aaron said, desperate now.

The captain raised a hand and the shouting cut off. "Alright, that's enough out of you—you've all got jobs to do so get to them!" The guards who'd begun to gather around the wall broke off and went on about their business, and Aaron heaved a heavy sigh of relief.

"Thanks for that. I don't know what's gotten into everybody today, but I'm starting to think maybe I'm losing my mind."

"Ain't easy, I reckon," Brandon said, still grinning, "bein' a living legend."

Aaron frowned at something in the man's tone. "What do you know, you bastard?"

The captain shrugged, his face full of feigned innocence. "Not much more than you do, I'd guess. Tell me, Aaron, you been to any taverns lately, maybe stopped in to have a drink?"

"No. I've been too busy helping round up Grinner's men to relax and have a drink. All I did was go back to the castle and go to sleep, then woke up to a world that has apparently decided to go fucking crazy."

Brandon nodded. "Of course. Well, I'd avoid them in the near future, if I were you. Unless, that is, you like the prospect of being mauled by people trying to buy you a drink. See, from what I heard, there's been some stories circulating around about you."

"Stories?" Aaron demanded. "What kind of stories?"

The captain grinned at the sellsword's obvious discomfort. "Well, all kinds I guess. The latest I heard was you killed a few dozen of Kevlane's creatures all with your bare hands." He frowned in thought, scratching at his beard. "Seems to me there was a bit in there about you savin' a small child or somethin'. Can't say I remember exactly. There's another about you goin' into the forest alone and rescuing a bunch of folks—Leomin and Queen Adina among them—who had been captured."

"*What?*" Aaron said, incredulous. "That's bullshit."

"Oh?" Brandon said, raising an eyebrow. "Didn't go into the woods alone then?"

Aaron rubbed at his temples where a headache was beginning to form. "Yes, I went into the woods alone, and it was a fool thing to do but I was…well, I was angry. Anyway, I didn't save them, I—"

"Didn't happen to kill a few of Kevlane's creatures, while you were on your little jaunt then?"

The sellsword grunted. "Yeah, I did, damnit, but I wasn't the one who saved them. We all would have been dead, if it hadn't been for the Akalians—they were the ones that did the saving."

Brandon nodded. "Oh, right, yeah that's another one. Folks are sayin' you've even managed to bend those demons, the Akalians, to your will."

"They're not *demons* for the gods' sake," Aaron hissed. "They're just men like you and me, and they're also the only reason why I'm breathing right now. Everybody's got it all wrong."

"Yeah? I'd say you could tell 'em that," he continued, leaning in close, "but I don't think they'll listen, lad."

Aaron followed his gaze around the wall and saw all the guards stationed along its length had turned to watch him, as if at any moment he might do something heroic, and they didn't want to miss it. "This is damned ridiculous," he said, turning back to frown at the captain, "and when I find the person responsible for it, I'm going to have some words for him. We've got more important things to worry about than this."

"Do we?" Brandon asked in the humoring tone usually reserved for someone that was being particularly dense.

"Well," he said, "considering we've got an ancient mage working to build an army of creatures out of nightmare, bent on destroying the world, yeah. Yeah, I'd say so."

"And you don't think they know that?" the captain asked softly. "Sure they are. And what better time, Aaron, when things look so bleak, for men and women to have someone to look to for guidance, someone to trust in? Better they believe the stories than think there's no chance of them coming out the other side of this thing. Better for them to have some hope, don't you agree?"

"But they're all lies," Aaron said, grunting as the other man met his gaze. "Fine, they're not *all* lies, but most of them are."

"I'm no philosopher, Aaron, and the gods know I'm just about as far from a priest as a man can be, but it seems to me that that's mostly what hope is—lies. Stories we tell ourselves so we can go to bed at night, so we can get up each day and take on whatever shit the world's cooked up for us while we were sleepin'. People breathe air, they eat food, and they drink water, but they *live* on hope. They hope tomorrow will be better than today, they hope even the worst storm will pass. It's a good thing, hope."

"And if it's false hope?"

Brandon shrugged. "To be honest with you, I don't even know what that means. All hope is false, ain't it? If it weren't, well, it wouldn't be called hope, it'd be called knowledge, truth, maybe. Hope is a single lantern shining in the darkness, believing—true or not—that its light is enough to chase away the shadows. And, if you ask me, considerin' what we're going to be marching against, hope is something we need right now. If the price of those men,"—he paused, gesturing to the guards whispering excitedly—"being able to laugh and face what's coming with courage and smiles on their faces is you being a bit uncomfortable, well, that's a trade I'd make any day."

Aaron sighed. "You're a real bastard, you know that?"

The captain grinned. "I've been told as much. Don't exactly change the facts though, does it?"

"No," Aaron muttered. "No, it doesn't. Anyway, how's the army coming?"

"Going alright, so far. I received word from Lady Tanarest that all of Grinner's men have been dealt with, leastways all those we know about, and as per Queen Adina's order, we've been getting everything prepared. I reckon we'll be ready to march by tomorrow mornin'."

Aaron gazed out over the wall at the gathered armies, even now setting about the tasks of loading materials onto supply carts prepared for the purpose. Hundreds, thousands of men and women, all of them come to fight against an enemy out of legend, ready to stand against an army of unnatural creatures, ones which they had, at best, heard stories of but had never actually seen. Even from this distance, he could feel their emotions through the bond, a storm of them. There was fear, of course, not just for themselves but for the families they left behind, those who were counting on them. But there was also courage, and a willingness to see the thing through, whatever came. "One day," he said. "Then it begins, in truth."

"Yes," the captain said, following his gaze. "Then it begins in truth. And we will show that ancient bastard of a mage that the world is not so easily destroyed as he might think, that its people are not so easily broken."

"Another lie, Captain?"

Brandon grinned. "Call it hope."

CHAPTER ELEVEN

Adina stared into the looking glass of the room she and Aaron shared. She'd woken early or, perhaps, it was more accurate to say that she had risen from where she lay in bed shifting restlessly, and had begun dressing for the day ahead.

It had taken her longer than it would have on a normal day, for whatever else it was, today was far from normal. Today, they would march on Baresh, would set their feet on the path that would inevitably lead to a battle with Kevlane and his creatures. Despite the earliness of the hour, she could hear the sounds of the army preparing for the journey ahead, soldiers hastily packing their tents and belongings, finishing the final touches before marching to war.

A war in which they expected *her* to lead them. Adina frowned at her reflection. She had discovered something in the last few hours. Her upbringing within her father's castle had afforded her many opportunities, and her tutors had taught her much of the world, her nursemaid educating her on the proper way a lady of her rank should act and conduct herself, what fork to use at dinner, how to address noblemen and noblewomen of all stations and backgrounds.

All useful lessons serving to teach her how to comport herself, how to lead the life of a princess. The problem, of course, was that she was no longer a princess but a queen and, what's more, a queen preparing to lead not just one army to war, but three. She knew, from her childhood lessons, what dress or gown she would wear for occasions ranging anywhere from a formal dinner to a ball to meeting with visiting dignitaries, yet none of her lessons had covered the proper attire for marching to war.

It doesn't matter, a part of her thought, *no one will care about your clothes.*

But of course they would. Another of the lessons her nursemaid had taught her at a young age, had *instilled* in her, was that people had certain expectations of their rulers, were guided by their actions, their words and, yes, their dress. Wearing a lacy, colorful dress would project the idea that she did not take the war—and therefore, the lives of the soldiers following her—seriously. On the other hand, something more somber might seem far too much like funeral attire and would inspire fear when it was her job to inspire confidence.

This, then, was the reason she had spent the last several hours trying on and discarding one outfit after another until finally she had settled on what she now wore—simple well-made tunic and trousers and boots, clothes she would have worn for a long day's ride on horseback. Her nursemaid, she knew, would have been scandalized. She could picture the woman now, scolding her, explaining that princesses wore dresses, not trousers. But, then, the woman had never led an army to battle. *If only I were as lucky.*

There was a knock on the door, and she was so engrossed in her own thoughts, in studying her reflection in the mirror, that she jumped, nearly crying out in her surprise. *And wouldn't that be just perfect?* she thought. *After all, what projects more confidence than a queen who screams at every sound?*

Of course, the people of Perennia had another queen, her sister Isabelle, but since Adina and the others had returned, wresting power of the city back from the crime boss, her sister had said little. Now, she spent her days flinching at every raised voice. When she spoke, she did so in a weak, timid tone, barely audible at all. It was up to Adina, then, to be brave where her sister was scared, to stand tall while her sister cowered. Or, at least, to appear so. The truth was she was terrified, for the coming battle would decide not just her fate, but the fate of every man, woman, and child in Telrear.

"Yes?"

"It's Gryle, Queen Adina."

"Please, come in."

The chamberlain stepped inside, closing the door shut behind him. "Forgive me for disturbing you, Majesty, but General Envelar sent me to inform you that your escort is prepared."

Adina nodded, not trusting herself to speak. It was really happening, then. They were about to march to war against an army of creatures from nightmares. A war that she herself had insisted on, had fought for. How many men and women would die because of it? How many children would be left without fathers, without mothers? "Thank you, Gryle," she said.

She considered asking the chamberlain's thoughts on her attire, but decided against it, for if he had another suggestion there was no time to change now. She took a slow, deep breath, forcing her eyes away from the mirror to Gryle. "Any word from Urek?"

"Sorry, Majesty, but so far at least, there has been no news."

Which meant that it was possible she would walk out into the city only to find Councilman Arkrest, and Avarest's army, marching not toward the war, but away from it. She swallowed, forcing a calm into her voice she did not feel. "Very well. I'm sure that we will know whether he was successful or not soon." *If he wasn't, your army will lose thousands before the battle has even begun. And if he was? If he was, then you are a murderer, and never mind that it wasn't your blade that spilled blood.*

The chamberlain studied her with a compassionate expression as if he could see the direction of her thoughts. "Of course, Majesty. And, Majesty...if you'll forgive me for saying so...about Councilman Arkrest. You had no other choice."

And how many murderers, how many tyrants, have told themselves as much? she thought. But the time for doubt, for uncertainty, had passed. Now, she had to be strong, to be the queen the world needed her to be. "Thank you, Gryle," she said. "You are a true friend." She took one last glance at the mirror, at the woman staring back at her. *You are enough.* But the woman in the mirror seemed uncertain, and she turned away quickly.

She took a deep breath and nodded. "Okay. I'm ready."

***

Wendell sat his horse, along with the twelve other soldiers—all members of Envelar's Ghosts—chosen as Queen Adina's honor guard. They waited outside the castle gate for the queen's appearance, all of them looking regal in their fine armor, each of the soldiers obviously proud to be part of the queen's escort. For his part, Wendell was too busy trying not to ruin the image by puking all over himself or his horse to feel much pride at all.

News had come the day before that they would be leaving the city in the morning, marching to Baresh, and Wendell had done what—under the circumstances—had seemed the only reasonable thing *to* do. He'd gotten drunk. Hopelessly, terribly, drunk. It had seemed sensible enough at the time, but now, sitting his horse with the sun shining directly in his eyes no matter which way he turned, with his stomach roiling unpleasantly, up to a bit of mischief that promised to show itself soon, he thought that, just maybe, a good night's sleep would have been better.

The noise from the crowd lining the street did little to improve his headache. It looked to him as if everyone in the city had come out to witness the army's departure, to see their queen escorted to the head of that army, and Wendell couldn't help but remember that the last time such a crowd had gathered it had been to see Hale and May executed. His stomach gave a kick, and Wendell brought a hand to his mouth, covering a belch that promised more—and worse—to come.

"Everything alright, Sergeant Wendell?"

He turned to scowl at the swordmaster, Darrell. The man was also part of the queen's escort, and though he'd been at the same tavern Wendell had, along with Leomin, the older man seemed none the worse for wear. He'd seen the Parnen earlier and he, too, had seemed unaffected by their night spent drinking. Wendell was beginning to suspect that the bastards had tricked him somehow, seeking revenge for the shit cart as if it was somehow *his* fault they'd been too big of fools to get out of the way.

"Just fine," Wendell said. *You bastard.* But the swordmaster's answering grin seemed to indicate he knew well enough the issues plaguing the sergeant, and was getting some pleasure at his discomfort. "Ain't never felt better."

"You're certain?" the swordmaster asked, his smile widening. "Forgive me for saying so, but you look a little...green. Almost as if you might be sick. I'd hate to think you weren't feeling well."

Wendell opened his mouth to tell the man his mind, but abruptly the castle doors opened, and the crowd erupted in cheers so loud, so piercing, that all of his attention was pulled to the sharp, pounding in his head, growing worse by the second. Abruptly, he was too busy concentrating on not showing the gathered people last night's dinner to care about the smug swordmaster.

After a moment, the worst of the pain subsided, and Wendell noted the queen and the chamberlain moving toward the gate. Despite his discomfort, Wendell couldn't help but be impressed. He'd seen and spoken to the queen plenty of times, of course—more than a man like him had any right to, in truth—but he was still impressed by the figure she struck. She sat tall in her saddle, her long hair falling across her shoulders, and on her face was a confidence, an assurance, that did nearly as much to set Wendell's mind at ease about the coming battle as the drink had done and, he suspected, with none of the more unfortunate side effects.

The crowd must have been impressed as well, for they cheered all the louder as she drew close to the gate. The guards stationed there swung it open, bowing low as she and the chamberlain made their way past. "We couldn't have asked for a nobler queen to lead us," Darrell said, his eyes dancing with what Wendell took to be amusement. Then, he gave a pull on his reins and started toward the queen and the chamberlain.

Bastard, Wendell thought again, but he gave his own horse a kick and followed.

***

"They seem excited enough," a voice said beside him, but Aaron was barely listening. He was too busy watching Adina approach, surrounded by her honor guard. If ever a woman looked the part of a queen, it was she. She sat her saddle proudly, waving at the people she passed and projecting a confidence that Aaron knew she didn't feel.

Gods, she's beautiful. Whenever he considered it, he was still shocked a woman like her—a *queen* like her—would want anything to do with a man such as himself. What could a woman like that see in him? How could such a one love a man who had spent his life skittering along Avarest's underbelly, caring only for himself? Yet, for reasons beyond his understanding, she did.

You are not that man any longer, Co said. *You have changed, Aaron.*

"We've all changed," he muttered.

"Mr. Envelar?"

Aaron started, pulled from his thoughts by the voice, and turned to Leomin. The Parnen sat his horse on the sellsword's left while Captain Brandon Gant waited on his right. General Yalleck sat atop his own horse on the other side of the captain. Beside Leomin, Urek, squatted uncomfortably on his own mount, obviously embarrassed to be included in the spectacle. Not that Aaron blamed him—he was embarrassed himself, had been made even more so by the chanting that had arisen in the crowd when he'd arrived. *A ship captain, a criminal, a sellsword, and a general. This is who the city must rely on to lead them. Gods save us.* "I'm sorry, Leomin," he said, turning to the Parnen. "What did you say?"

"Nothing of any consequence, Mr. Envelar. I only remarked that the crowd seems excited enough. They seem...brave."

Sure, they do, Aaron thought. *It's an easy enough thing to be brave when the monsters are still miles away, and the journey not yet begun. I wonder, how many of those shouts of adoration will turn to screams of fear before long? How many of those faces, smiling like the army's departure was some Fairday celebration, will be frozen in death before the month is out?* "Yes," he said. "They do seem brave."

Adina and the chamberlain finally arrived, their honor guard spreading out to surround Aaron and the others while Adina rode up beside Aaron, the chamberlain—perhaps unsurprisingly—taking a spot on the end, as far away from the center of things as possible. An even greater cheer went up from the multitude of people at their gathered leaders.

What do they see, when they look at us, I wonder? he thought. *Is it salvation? Do they see a group of men and women who will lead them against what's coming? A group capable of defeating a legendary evil, of driving it back into the shadows? And, if they do...how?*

They see hope, *Aaron Envelar,* Co said into his mind. *And hope, in such dark times, is a thing well worth celebrating.*

Aaron grunted. Hope. He wondered if maybe any of those in the crowd had some to spare, some he could borrow for a time, for his own thoughts were dark, shadowy things, and there was no hope within them. Leomin cleared his throat, looking at him expectantly. The sellsword frowned, beginning to ask what he wanted, but then he realized it wasn't just the Parnen that was studying him, but all of those gathered. Adina, General Yalleck, Brandon with a grin on his face, and even Urek, his own malicious smile doing little to hide the obvious relief he felt at not being the center of attention. And, of course, the thousands lining the street, all staring at him and waiting for something.

Gods, what do they want of me? he thought.

You know, Aaron, the Virtue said.

Aaron did his best to hide his wince as he cleared his throat and gave his reins a tug, relieved when his horse didn't decide to spill him on his ass in front of all the people—and wouldn't *that* be the perfect way to begin the thing?—but took a few steps forward, as he'd wished. A fresh roar went up from the crowd at that, and once again the chanting began. *En-ve-lar. En-ve-lar.* The sound of his name thundered in the morning air, echoing through the city streets, and Aaron reflected, for a moment, that he had never thought to hear his name called by the voices of so many, with so much passion. At least, that was, unless they were attending his execution, demanding his head. But one look at the hopeful, almost worshipful faces of those gathered showed that it wasn't his head they were after, but something much more difficult, something he feared he could not give them.

Good men try, he told himself, deciding to forget, for the moment, that though they tried, good men often failed as well. He cleared his throat again. He held his hand up for silence—feeling all the while like the worst kind of impostor, feeling certain that, any second now, someone would step forward and call him down: *You are not the man we want. You are just a sellsword, a thug for hire. A man who has murdered dozens of people—not a hero at all but a villain.* And if someone did step forward and say such things, what could he say in return?

To his surprise, though, no one challenged him. The cheering subsided as if by magic, and they only stood watching him expectantly. Aaron took a slow, deep breath, feeling as if he were dreaming. "People of Perennia," he began, raising his voice to be heard, but he needn't have bothered, for an almost supernatural silence had fallen on the city as virtually all its inhabitants waited on what he would say. He winced, rubbing at his chin. "Maybe, it's better to say 'people of all Telrear.' For what we do now, we do not just for ourselves, and when we march it will not be for the glory of any one city, any one kingdom. Instead, we'll march—we'll fight—for all of Telrear and its people."

The crowd roared in approval, clapping and cheering, shouting his name as if he were some great king instead of a fool well and truly out of his element and trying his best not to make an ass of himself. Wincing, he raised his hand again, and once more the crowd quieted. "I want to thank you all, for your support," *Never mind that, barely more than a week ago, many of you were going to execute one of my closest friends and would have been all too thrilled to do the same to me.* "*We* thank you," he said, gesturing back to where Adina and the others sat atop their horses. "The coming days won't be easy—the gods know the truth of that. We have all had to sacrifice in these past weeks; we have all lost something or someone." And that, too, was true. Few in the city had not lost a loved one when Belgarin and his army had attacked—one needed only to look at the city walls, still stained with the blood of its defenders, to know it. "And we will have to sacrifice more yet," he added, taking in the somber faces of the crowd.

I think you misunderstood me, Aaron, Co said, her own voice tense. *I meant for you to give them hope. Not make them all feel as if they've already lost.*

Aaron ignored the Virtue, pressing on. "But I'll promise you all one thing—whatever we have lost, we will take from our enemies tenfold, and they will pay for every drop of blood they've spilled, every tear shed for the loved ones we have lost." He paused then, his thoughts going to Beth, and to Hale, and he had to clear his throat before going on. "I have lost people I cared about, just as you all have. Good people...and some of them maybe not so good." There was some laughter from the crowd at that but most, at least, still watched him with those solemn expressions, waiting to hear what he would say. He shrugged. "But either way, they were *my* people. And I don't intend to let such a crime go unanswered. I will fight—will make as many of the creatures we face know my anger as I can before I'm through—but what of you, Perennia? What of you, Telrear?" he asked, his eyes scanning the crowd. "I'll march on Baresh alone, if I have to," he paused to grin. "But I'd just as soon not."

There was more laughter in the crowd then, and he went on. "Kevlane and his armies have asked us a question, Telrear. With their swords and their knives, they have asked it. I go now to give answer. *We*," he said, gesturing once more to the others and beyond them to the armies camped outside the city, "go to give answer. Will you go with us?"

"*Yes!*" The answer came in a roar so powerful that Aaron fancied he could feel his ribs shake, and he smiled. "Alright then." He turned his horse, meaning to go back to the others, when a voice called out of the crowd.

"But will we win?"

Aaron winced. *Almost made it away, didn't you?* he thought. He turned back, searching the crowd for the owner of the voice, and saw that an old man, his gray hair thin atop his head, had stepped out from the crowd.

"Will we win, General?" the man asked again, and in that question Aaron could hear fear and hope both, could hear how desperately the man wanted him to say yes.

Aaron considered that for a moment, looking around at the people lining the streets, seeing the question in their gazes too, now. "I could lie to you," he said. "I could tell you that we'll hunt Kevlane and his monstrosities down like animals and be back here before dinner. The gods know I've lied before and for much less." Some more scattered laughter from the crowd.

"But I won't do that. It seems to me this city has had its fill of lies lately." There were grim nods as people remembered Grinner, all of them convinced since his defeat that they'd known the truth all along, that it was only *others* who had been foolish enough to listen to the crime boss, and his rumors. "But I'll make you a promise," Aaron said. "I promise that so long as you stand against the darkness, I'll be there beside you. I promise you that those deaths—those losses we have all suffered—will not go unanswered. Kevlane, a mage out of storybooks, out of legends, sits in Baresh even now, believing himself invincible, thinking he has crafted an army great enough to send all of us scurrying into corners and huddling under our beds like frightened children. He believes he has won already."

He saw anger now in the faces of those watching him, anger matching his own. "I intend to prove him wrong," Aaron said, his voice hard and cold. "And before the month's out, I intend to show that bastard that even legends can bleed."

They erupted into cheers at that, taking up the chant once more, and Aaron rode back to Adina and the others, accompanied by the sound of *En-ve-lar! En-ve-lar!*

Adina grinned when he drew close, and the mounted leaders of Avarest turned and began to lead their horses toward the city gate and the fields beyond, where the army waited. "Pretty good, for a sellsword," Adina said to him as they rode.

"Gods, but give me an army of monsters to face any day."

She laughed, looking out at the crowd, but the amusement didn't touch her eyes. There was a worried, almost haunted look there. "You're their hero, Aaron. Speeches, I think, come with the territory."

He grunted. "A hero. And I wonder if someone might have had something to do with that, with all the stories and rumors that have been circulating throughout the city."

Adina put on an expression of mock-innocence. "I'm sure I have no idea what you mean."

Aaron sighed. "We've really got some talking to do after all this is done. Now," he said, leaning close, "will you tell me what's bothering you?"

She started as if surprised. "What...what do you mean?"

"Adina," he said, "for the last few months, I've been dealing with a Virtue which sometimes sends me into an uncontrollable rage, one in which I have killed more people than I care to count. Safe to say, I know what guilt looks like. Shame, too. And it seems to me that you're feeling both right now. So, what's bothering you?"

She smiled, but it was a weak, fragile thing, one that looked like it might change into tears at any moment. "Nothing, Aaron. I'm fine."

He studied her for several seconds before sighing. "Okay. But just know, Adina, I'm here, if you need me. I always will be."

"Thank you, Aaron. It's just a lot, that's all. Everything...the city, the army, what we're going to do. I guess maybe I just got overwhelmed for a minute."

"Only for a minute?" he said, smiling. "I can't remember the last time I wasn't."

She started to answer, but just then Captain Gant rode up beside them. "Excuse me, Majesty. General." He gave Aaron a grin. "Nice speech, by the way."

Aaron scowled, and the captain barked a laugh. "Anyway, I thought you might want to go over some final things about the army and marching order before we set out, if, that is,"—he paused, his grin widening—"you don't have anything heroic planned in the next few minutes."

The sellsword glanced to Adina, and she smiled as if everything was fine, but he didn't need the power of his bond with Co to see the lie in it. "Go ahead," she said, "I'll be fine."

"You're sure?"

"Of course," she said.

Aaron waited a moment longer then nodded. "Okay," he said, turning back to the captain. "Lead on."

***

Adina watched the two men go, the smile fading as soon as their backs were turned. She hated lying to Aaron, but reasoned with herself that he had enough to worry about already. There was no need to bother him with the issue of Councilman Arkrest's visit. It would just add another worry on top of a pile of them, and he wouldn't be able to do anything anyway. Either Urek had managed to get rid of the councilman or he had not. Either she was a murderer, or they would be marching on Baresh with several thousand fewer troops than they had planned, turning an already difficult battle into an impossible one.

As if her thoughts had summoned him, the crime boss rode up beside her, clearly uneasy in the saddle and doing his best to keep his horse under control. "Queen Adina," he said, not turning to look at her but staring ahead as the procession made its way through the crowded city streets. Thankfully, there was no chance of being overheard, for the people that lined either side were shouting and cheering as the group passed.

"Urek," she said, her mouth suddenly dry. "A wild day, isn't it?"

"Wild enough, Majesty," the crime boss agreed. "But, then, I'm a criminal. We're used to wild days. Nights too, so far as that goes."

Adina studied him then, feeling as if he were trying to tell her something, but she forced herself to calm down, to control her expression. "I imagine you're correct," she said. "Of course, we have all had wild nights lately."

The big man grunted, nodding. "Sure, sure. But I doubt there's been too many to top last night, for me at least."

"Oh?" Adina asked, suddenly breathless. "I hope everything is alright, of course."

"Sure," the crime boss said. "Had a problem or two come up, but they've been dealt with now, and I'd say it's safe to say they won't be an issue anymore."

Murderer then, she thought, feeling at once relieved and ashamed. "That is good," she said, fighting back the tears that threatened to come to her eyes. "I am glad to hear that you have...resolved our problem."

He turned to her then for the first time, studying her with an intelligence that belied his thick, blunted features. "Are you?"

For a moment, Adina was at a loss of what to say. *Are you?* she thought. *Are you glad?* "I am...relieved," she said, blinking away the tears that were beginning to gather despite her best efforts.

The crime boss watched her for several seconds, then his features softened. "Not always easy, dealing with the sort of problems that come up, Majesty," he said, "but, if you ask me, it's better to deal with them just the same. After all, the solution might not always be a good one, but it's usually a damn sight better than leavin' the problem alone to fester. Just ask me about Beautiful's fire powder sometime." With that, he gave his reins a pull, and rode forward, bouncing awkwardly in his saddle.

Adina watched him go and was still trying to compose herself, to get her ragged breathing under control, when a voice spoke from beside her. "Good morning, Majesty."

She turned to see General Yalleck, commander of Avarest's army. The last person she would have chosen to talk to just then. *Did he hear?* she thought, and she took a slow, deep breath, forcing her panic down before answering. "General."

He must have seen something of her thoughts on her expression, for he leaned forward in his saddle, studying her. "Forgive me for asking, Majesty," he said, glancing once at the departing crime boss before turning back to her, "but is everything alright?"

"Of course," Adina said, "it has just been an emotional day, General, that's all. Forgive me."

"There is nothing to forgive, Majesty," Yalleck said, watching her with a penetrating stare. *He knows,* she thought. *Gods, he knows.* The general glanced around them, frowning. "Tell me, Queen Adina, have you seen Councilman Arkrest this morning?"

Adina forced a calm into her expression, into her voice, that she did not feel. "I'm afraid I haven't," she said, meeting the general's gaze.

The man nodded. "Curious, that. I had expected to hear from the councilman early this morning with some word of what he wished regarding the disposition of Avarest's forces. When I did not, I sent a messenger to his house. Do you know, Majesty, what they found there?"

Adina shook her head slowly. "I cannot imagine, General but, then, I have been busy attending to other matters."

"Of course," the general said, "of course. Well, I will tell you. The messenger, upon arriving at the councilman's residence, found that Arkrest and his staff—including the six men he had hired to protect him on his journey—were gone."

"Gone?" Adina asked.

"That's right," Yalleck said. "Gone. And, what's more, without a single word about where he was going or when he would return. Strange, don't you think, considering we are marching to war today, and he had expressed, in no uncertain terms, his intention of returning to Avarest with its troops?"

"Yes," she said, keeping her features composed. "That is quite strange. But, then, General, we are marching to battle with the armies of several kingdoms who—until recently—have been at war. We march against a foe who—also until recently—was thought to be nothing more than a legend, a myth. A foe who, even now, is creating monsters out of nightmares that we will face in the coming battle. These, it seems, Commander Yalleck, are strange times."

The man nodded. "That is true enough. And without any further word from the Councilman to verify his wishes, I will continue, of course, on the path I had originally intended, marching Avarest's armies with the rest to defeat this threat."

"And we thank you for that, General. The people of Telrear, I am certain, are grateful."

"Yes, Majesty," the general said. "As am I, for I, too, wish to see this enemy defeated." He met her eyes then, his own expression hard. "After all, when we are victorious, there will always be time to launch an investigation into the whereabouts of Councilman Arkrest and his retinue. I do not doubt that such an investigation will discover the truth of what happened and—should any party be behind the councilman's abrupt disappearance—I'm sure that, in time, they will be found out, and will be held accountable for their crimes. For though his absence is fortuitous, still any crime against a representative of Avarest is tantamount to a crime against the city itself. A city I have sworn to protect."

Adina's heart quickened in her chest, but she nodded. "Of course. It is your duty, after all. Still, perhaps there are simpler, less menacing reasons for the councilman's absence, General. Not everything, after all, is a conspiracy."

"True, Majesty. Either way, once this battle is won, we will discover the truth of it. I will be sure to let you know the results of the investigation."

"*If* the battle is won, General," Adina said, meeting the man's eyes, "then I look forward to hearing the results of such an investigation. Until then, I think we both have greater concerns than if Councilman Arkrest has decided—perhaps not all that surprisingly—to leave a city marching to war."

"Quite," Yalleck said. "As you say, we have more pressing concerns, Majesty. We will talk again—once this is finished."

"I look forward to it." Adina watched the general ride toward the front of the column, and looked down at her hands where they held her reins in a white-knuckled grip. When she wiped at the sweat beading on her forehead despite the cool air, she did so with a trembling hand.

CHAPTER TWELVE

Caleb woke to someone grabbing his shoulder. He jerked upright and, for a moment, had no idea where he was until he realized that he had fallen asleep sitting at the small desk in his room. He looked up to see an Akalian regarding him silently, his expression hidden by the black cloth he wore. "What is it?" Caleb asked, swallowing and rubbing at his weary eyes. "What's happened?"

The Akalian didn't answer, but then, he didn't need to, for a moment later Caleb noted the bared steel in one hand, the blade slick with blood. He noticed, too, that the Akalian's free arm hung loosely, a bloody slash across it, his sleeve stained crimson. "Oh gods, they're here, aren't they?" he said. "I had thought...but...we need more time. Tianya isn't ready to travel yet it...we need more time."

The Akalian only watched him, but his eyes held a cold truth, the answer to Caleb's desperate pleas. Perhaps they did need more time, but they did not have it, and whatever shape she was in, it would be better for Tianya to risk death traveling with her wounds than to stay and let the matter be certain. "O-okay," he said, glancing at the papers on his desk, "but I need to get my papers, my—"

The Akalian grabbed his arm, shaking his head. Only a single, simple gesture, but it was enough to tell Caleb just how much trouble they were in. So instead of trying to sort through the pages and notes, he only grabbed as much as he could, hugging them

A Sellsword's Hope

against his chest. "At least we can see to your arm," he said, "surely, there is time enough for stitches or—" He cut off as the Akalian shook his head once more. "O-okay," he said.

The Akalian moved toward the door, and if his wound pained him, he gave no sign. He eased the door open slowly, looking down one end of the hall, then the other, and Caleb heard the sounds of fighting from inside the barracks, the unmistakable sound of steel striking steel. The Akalian beckoned him, and then they were in the hallway and running, Caleb's heart hammering in his chest as he followed after the swiftly darting figure.

As they traveled the hallways, Caleb quickly realized the Akalian was leading him to Tianya's room. There was no sign of Kevlane's creatures here, no blood or battle being fought, but as they ran the sounds of fighting grew louder, seeming to come from all around them, and his bond with the Virtue of Intelligence separated those sounds, analyzed them, until he was sure that there were at least six separate skirmishes going on in the barracks.

He felt exposed, vulnerable, in the open, and when they finally came to Tianya's room, he breathed a sigh of relief as he followed the Akalian inside. He had thought they would find the woman sleeping, for she had done little else since Aaron had rescued her from her madness. But she was awake and clutching a blade in her hand, staring at the doorway with a grim expression on her face.

"I-it's me," Caleb stammered. "B-but the creatures, they're here."

Tianya sank down onto the bed, as if it had taken all of what little reserves of strength she had left to stand and be ready to fight. "I know. I heard them nearly fifteen minutes ago." She sighed. "It took me that long to get up out of bed. You had best go, boy. Run as fast as you can—I'm sure this one here will do what he can to keep you safe."

"W-what about you?" Caleb asked.

She smiled a slow, sad smile. "I owe the world a death, I think. It is only by luck and chance I have survived this long. Now, do not worry about me—go and live. If you can."

He studied her for several seconds, his thoughts racing. Then, finally, he shook his head. "No. I won't leave without you."

"Please," she said, her voice desperate and wretched, "don't do this. I cannot be responsible for any more deaths. I can't..." She shook her head. "Just...please. Go."

"Not without you," Caleb said, surprised by the strength in his own voice. "I can help you. Now, come on." He rushed to her bedside, draping one of her arms over his shoulder, and lifted. He was shocked by how light she felt, as if she were hardly real at all. "We're going to get out of here," he said, "and we're going to do it together."

She winced with pain, but nodded grimly. "Very...well. It seems there is no end to the debt I will owe. Lead on, young man. I will come with you as best as I may."

Caleb nodded to the Akalian who had watched the proceedings in silence, then the black garbed man moved to the door, again checking the hallway before stepping outside and starting down the corridor, pausing when Tianya spoke. "No. Not that way," she said, rubbing at her temple weakly, as if she had a headache. "They block the path."

Caleb started to ask her how she could know that, but then remembered that she possessed the Virtue of Perception and only nodded, following after the Akalian who didn't argue but started in the other direction, blood dripping from his wounded arm and leaving a crimson trail behind him. "H-how many are there?" he asked.

"Too many," Tianya hissed through gritted teeth as she shuffled after the Akalian. "Our only chance...is to...get out. While they're distracted."

"But what about the Speaker and the others?"

"They'll be fine," she said, but Caleb didn't need the Virtue of Intelligence to hear the uncertainty in her voice.

"Are you sure?"

She heaved a breath. "No, child, I am not sure. But what I *am* sure about is if we remain or try to help them, we will die. We are neither of us warriors, and at the very least we would only get in their way. Either they will escape, or they will not. There is nothing we can do to help them and dying here will be of no use to your friends in Perennia."

Caleb winced, but didn't argue. For a time they walked in silence save for when Tianya guided the Akalian around the fights raging in the barracks. Yet for all the powers the bond gave her, a few of their turns took them terribly close to the fighting, and more than once Caleb could see figures locked in combat at the ends of the hallways they passed.

At such times, they did their best to hurry past, taking the corners as quickly as they could, but Caleb knew one glance would be all it would take for the creatures to find them. And if one did decide to come at them, it didn't take a genius to know what would happen. He was a kid, Tianya a wasted woman who could barely stand, and over the last few minutes, the Akalian's steps had grown less and less sure as blood loss took its inevitable toll.

All these thoughts, these worries, crowded his mind, along with a thousand others, as they made their way through the barracks, taking hallways seemingly at random, always at Tianya's direction, but eventually they arrived at the main door. "A-are they out there?" he asked.

"A moment," the woman said, closing her eyes. Several tense seconds passed, and Caleb, his nerves frayed, was just about to ask her what she was doing when she opened them once more. "I can't be sure," she said. "But I don't hear any of them close. We'd best hurry."

The Akalian eased the door open and scanned the darkness before stepping out of the barracks, Caleb and Tianya following. He motioned them toward the shadowy tree line, barely visible at all in the pale light of the moon. They crossed the open area as quickly as they could, Caleb's heart hammering in his chest.

He was just beginning to think they were going to make it, when he heard a rush of displaced air behind them.

The Akalian reacted instantly, spinning and gliding in front of Caleb and the woman with a grace completely at odds with the stumbling walk he'd shown thus far. "Wha—" Caleb began, but then he saw. One of Kevlane's creatures stood not far away, and the sound he'd heard had been it taking advantage of its impossible speed, rushing forward. Its skin was pale, almost translucent in the moonlight, and the shadows contrived to make its scarred face look ghastly, its cruel, twisted features suited for no living man. It had the slender, too-long arms Caleb had come to associate with Kevlane's swiftest creatures, but it wasn't just its appearance—or its unnaturalness—that made a gasp erupt from the youth's throat, but the blood-slicked sword, almost black in the moonlight, it held in one limp hand.

The creature studied them with its head cocked, as if trying to determine what or who they were. There was a confused, almost pitiable quality to it, but one that vanished quickly enough as the Akalian raised his sword. The creature's attention turned away from Caleb and Tianya, eyeing the blade and the man who held it.

"*Damnit,*" Tianya wheezed between her ragged breaths. She'd moved better than Caleb would have thought possible, given her malnourished state, but it had clearly cost her, and he felt her trembling where her arm was draped over his shoulder, though whether from fear, pain, or simple exhaustion, he could not have said for sure.

"W-what do we do now?" Caleb asked, hating the naked terror in his voice.

The question—and its attendant possibilities—were driven out of his mind a moment later as there was an audible *pop*, and the creature launched itself forward in a blur. If the Akalian shared Caleb's fear, he didn't show it. Instead, he was already moving before the creature started forward, whipping his sword around so it stuck directly out in front of him.

The creature, moving at such a great speed, was apparently unable to stop its momentum, and an instant later it impaled itself on the Akalian's blade. Caleb felt a great sense of relief, one that quickly vanished as he realized that, though it was stuck through by the Akalian's blade, its own had found its mark, burying itself deep in the shoulder of the black-garbed man's sword arm.

For a frozen moment, the two stood without moving, seeming to regard each other, then they collapsed to the ground where they both lay unmoving. Caleb overcame his own shock an instant later and started toward the Akalian. "We have to help him, we have to—" He cut off as Tianya's hand latched around his arm with surprising strength, her fingers digging into him.

"Don't be a fool, boy," she hissed. "He's dead, and if not, he will be soon enough. Anyone with eyes can see that."

"B-but," Caleb stammered, suddenly very close to tears, "I-I can help him. Maybe I can find some herbs to make a poultice and—"

"And maybe," she said, "that creature's fellows will just sit back and relax while you see to him, is that it? Is that what you think, boy?"

He turned back to her then, desperate, his words coming out in a plea. "But he saved us. He...we have to help him."

"The only ones who can help him now are the gods," the woman said, her voice softer than it had been. "He gave his life for us, lad, a trade he chose. Now, I know you want to help, but we'll do no one any good if we stay here to die."

"N-no," Caleb said, "I won't. I won't leave him."

"*Think*, boy," she growled, shaking him. "Kevlane, the great enemy, has only one of the Seven now, yet with it he has managed to create an army great enough to threaten the world. What, then, do you think he will be able to do once his creatures have finished with us, and he has *two more* Virtues to enhance his power? What horrors will he be able to create with your intelligence and my perception to guide his workings?"

Caleb glanced helplessly between her and the Akalian. Had he only imagined the man moving the smallest amount? Or was he, even now, bleeding out, *dying* while they stood and argued. "I-I can't," he said, the tears that had been threatening spilling from his eyes now. "I can't leave him. We...we can't—"

"Then you'll die," the woman said flatly, no mercy or understanding in her tone now, only cold, hard truth. "And I will die as well, and your compassion, your *mercy* will doom not just us, but the entire world to a cruel and terrible end. Do you want that on your conscience, boy? *Do you?*"

She grabbed both of Caleb's shoulders as she said the last, giving him a rough shake, her fingers digging into him so hard that it was all he could do to keep from crying out in pain. "N-no, of course no—"

"What about Aaron?" the woman went on. "What about Adina? I've heard something about how they saved you, how they've cared for you. Is this, then, how you repay them? By dooming them all with wasted heroics, by giving their foe the exact thing he needs to ensure their slaughter? *Is it?*"

Caleb's shoulders slumped, his head hanging as he stared at the ground, blurry from the darkness and his tears, anything to keep from meeting the woman's cold, unforgiving eyes. A second passed, then another, and when he finally looked up, whatever innocence, whatever childish faith in the world he'd still held was gone. In its place was a grim understanding, an *adult's* understanding. "Okay," he said, his voice weak, barely more than a whisper. "Okay. What do you want me to do?"

"Can you find our way back to the city?"

"I...I think..." *You are a child no longer,* he thought. *Never again.* "Yes. But Aaron and the others won't be there, not now. They'll be marching toward Baresh—the Speaker received news earlier tonight." And it said something of the death that had occurred within him, that he did not so much as even glance at the barracks as he was reminded of the Speaker, the man who had saved him and the others, did not allow himself to think that, even now, the man might be fighting, might be *dying* along with the rest of the Akalians.

"Fine," Tianya hissed. "And can you lead us to them?"

"I...I can."

"Good," she said, nodding sharply. "Then let's go." She started into the forest, shuffling and using the trees as support, and Caleb watched her.

He gave one last look behind him at the barracks, perhaps to mark the death of those Akalians who were battling within its walls, perhaps to mark the death of his own innocence and saw that the large wooden building was in flames. Small now but growing by the second. Soon, they would reach far into the night, a funeral pyre on which burned the bodies of men who had sacrificed everything for the world, the only thanks the world seemed to have for its heroes. He could see figures moving around in the distance, vague, indistinct, and there was no telling if they were Akalians or, more likely, Kevlane's own creatures.

He looked for another moment. Then, without saying a word, Caleb turned and followed the woman away from the light and into the darkness.

CHAPTER THIRTEEN

Boyce Kevlane was weeks away from getting everything he wanted. With each day that passed, the tournament went on and men and women who'd spent their lives training in combat battled for a chance at the purse of gold they'd been promised. And each night, Kevlane worked his Art, adding more and more troops to his army. He worked without sleep, without rest, stretching the power of his bond with the Virtue of Adaptation to its limits. And all the while he imagined Aaron Envelar and his companions laid low beneath him.

He should have been pleased, should have been eager for the victory to come, but he wasn't. Instead, he was angry.

He growled, crumpling the letter he'd been reading and tossing it to the ground in disgust. The members of Baresh's council, seated around him on the stage in the tournament ground, recoiled at his obvious anger, turning away from the current match—a tall, muscular man who fought a thin, wiry one almost half his size—to glance warily at their king.

Kevlane knew their suspicions of him grew with each day, knew he should say something to console them, to reassure them he was the same Belgarin he'd always been. But he couldn't find it in him to care. They could believe what they would—soon, they would die like all the rest. They watched him from their seats even now—the old High Priest, a pompous fool, convinced of his own importance, his own sacredness; the general, his back stiff and straight in a manner he thought noble, a military man who wanted everyone to know it. And then there was the woman, Maladine, representative of the Golden Oars bank. Of all of them, she alone presented any real danger, and if one of them discovered the truth of his identity, Kevlane did not doubt that it would be her.

It doesn't matter. Their fear, their suspicions, were irrelevant. They would all be dealt with, soon enough. Frustrated, unable to stand their gazes any longer, he stalked away from the crowded platform, feeling the almost irrepressible urge to unmask his true self, to show these fools that they sat before a god.

Caldwell followed at his heels, as Kevlane had known he would. "It seems," Kevlane said, once they'd gotten out of ear shot of the others, "that the good councilman has failed."

The advisor nodded. "Yes, Master."

"Too many failures, Caldwell," Kevlane hissed. "Far, far too many. This Aaron Envelar and his friends have proven to be a nuisance."

"Forgive me, Master," the advisor said, "but, in the end, it matters little. Our armies will crush them just the same, and they will soon learn the futility of opposing you."

"*Our* armies?" Kevlane asked softly, and Caldwell's eyes went wide.

"*Your* armies, of course, Master. I meant no offense, I only intended to say—"

"Forget it." Kevlane turned and looked in the direction of Perennia, where, even now, an army marched toward him, and he was reminded of a time, long ago, when another army marched toward the city he called home, an army bent on destroying everything he had come to call his own. "They are too confident, Caldwell. Send some of the experiments out—let each step they take toward us be bathed in blood, until they learn the true meaning of fear."

"Master," the man said, "are you sure that's wise? With the creatures we lost to the failed ambush, the numbers have been diminished and—"

"*Do not question me!*" Kevlane roared, and the advisor recoiled as if struck. The mage turned to see the council members watching him from their seats and sneered before turning back to the thin man. "They think to challenge their god, Caldwell, and they will suffer for it."

"O-of course, Master," the man said, bowing his head and starting away.

"And Caldwell?" The man turned, and Kevlane bared his teeth in a grin without humor. "If you ever think to question me again, I'll rip you apart from the inside out. Do you understand?"

The thin man nodded, his face pale and waxy in the sunlight. "Y-yes, Master. F-forgive me."

CHAPTER FOURTEEN

Gryle couldn't sleep. He knew he *should,* knew that he would need rest in the days and weeks to come, yet try as he might, he couldn't quiet his troubled thoughts, and so the peace of sleep eluded him. A condition which, judging by the number of campfires burning in the darkness, was shared by many of the army's soldiers.

He knew he had changed, knew that the past months had made him a different man than he once was but here, in the darkness of the woods, great sentinels of trees all around, he felt once more like the overweight, middle-aged chamberlain who had felt absolute terror at something so simple as a stain on his clothes. He thought that, while people changed, they never did so completely, always keeping some of their old selves, snakes who, try as they might, could never fully shed their skin and become something—or some*one*—new.

He wished, not for the first time, that he had Aaron's courage, or Adina's. They, at least, always seemed so sure, so confident, as if they knew how to handle any problem that might arise. *Or,* he thought, *perhaps your sleeplessness isn't caused from worry at all, at least not from worry of Kevlane. You have the Virtue of Strength, after all, and you do remember what it did to Aster Kalen, don't you?*

Yes. He remembered. The Virtue had driven the man insane, and although he wasn't ready to start gnawing on his own hands or laughing maniacally while he rocked in a dark corner, Gryle sometimes wondered how much of the change in him was due to

A Sellsword's Hope

his experiences and how much to the Virtue inhabiting him. Unlike the others, his Virtue did not speak—had, perhaps, lost the ability to do so in its madness. From time to time, Gryle thought he detected what *might* have been the Virtue: unintelligible, animalistic sounds that could have as easily been his imagination, but such sounds were rare and, when he quested inside himself, seeking out their source, he inevitably found nothing.

"Chamberlain Gryle, 'ello there!"

Gryle jerked in surprise at the sound of his name and turned to see a soldier approaching him from a nearby campfire. He realized with a start that he had wandered to the edge of the camp; the torches that burned at regular intervals, marking the army's perimeter and serving as a means of keeping anyone from creeping up on them in the darkness, were close, the nearest less than a dozen feet away.

As the man walked closer, Gryle promised himself that, should the man offer him a drink, he would not accept it. The last time he'd taken an offered drink, he had woken to find himself in a clearing with a battle raging around him. "H-hello," he said.

The man's grin was visible as he drew near. "Thought that was you, sir. I hope you don't mind me botherin' you. I was just over there, havin' a bit of a drink as I can't sleep."

Gryle tried a smile of his own. "It's going around, I think."

The soldier laughed at that, slapping his knee as if the chamberlain had told the world's funniest joke. "So it is, so it is. Well, sir, I won't keep you, as I'm sure you've got important things to be about. I just wanted to shake the hand of one of Perennia's heroes, if you don't mind, that is."

Gryle stared at the man's offered hand in surprise. *I'm sure you've got important things to be about. Hero.* For a moment, he couldn't understand what the man could possibly mean, then he realized with a shock that the soldier was talking about *him*. "I uh...I'm not a hero, but thank you just the same," he said, giving the man's hand a shake.

"No?" the soldier asked, grinning. "I got the wrong man, have I? You ain't the same chamberlain as helped take back Queen Adina's kingdom single-handedly? Not the fella who helped stop the execution of the good Lady May, and Councilman Hale, the gods keep 'em? Ain't the one is said to possess the strength of a thousand men?"

"Well," Gryle said, feeling his face flush, "a thousand? I...it's unlikely. As for the rest...well, there were other people with me during all those events. In truth, I'm afraid, I did little more than get in the way, but I thank you for your kindness just the same."

"That right?" the man said, as if he didn't believe a word of it. "Well, that ain't how I heard it. Rumors goin' around seem to all agree that you're one tough son of a bitch."

Gryle frowned at that until he realized that the man was giving him a compliment. "I...well...thank you."

"No, thank you," the man laughed. "I ain't never met a hero before, and I just want you to know, it does me and the other boys good to have you with us. That bastard of a mage ain't got a chance so long as—"

There was a flash of something in the darkness, and the man cut off abruptly, his body stiffening. Gryle gave a shout of surprise and confusion as something wet struck his face, and immediately felt a fool. *Overreacting again, jumping at every sound, screaming at the rain. Some hero, alright.* "Sorry I..." He frowned, looking closer at the man. His features were hard to make out in the darkness, but there was something strange about them. Something...wrong.

At first, Gryle couldn't put his finger on what it was. Something about the way the man was standing, perhaps, or the way his neck sat strangely on his shoulders...then, abruptly, the man's neck wasn't sitting on his shoulders at all but it—and the head attached to it—were sliding off and falling to the ground, his body following a moment later.

Gryle's eyes grew wide, and wider still as he saw the figure standing behind the man, a thin figure with a bloody sword in his hand, the crimson looking black in the moonlight. "Wha—I don't—" The newcomer stalked toward him, a shadow in the darkness, but had barely taken a step when something whistled through the air, lodging itself in the approaching figure's throat. Kevlane's creature—some part of Gryle's confused mind recognized it as such—took another stumbling step toward him before collapsing at his feet. Gryle stared down at its form, and the thing sticking out of its neck, in stunned surprise. *An arrow. Oh, by the gods that's an arrow.*

He spun in the direction from which the arrow had come and saw one of the army's sentries stumble into the light of the perimeter torches, one of his legs dragging noticeably, covered in blood. "*Bastard,*" the man spat, lowering the bow he held and turning to the chamberlain, wobbling drunkenly. "S...sound. The...alarm."

"A-alarm?" Gryle asked, his thoughts confused and jumbled at the sudden violence. "I...I don't—" But the man abruptly collapsed on the ground and did not rise.

Gryle heard something, what sounded like the rustle of dry leaves, and spun to see other figures emerging in the torchlight, their too-slender forms marking them as more of Kevlane's creatures. *Sound the alarm. Sound the alarm.* "A-alarm," he said, his voice little more than a whisper, and he spun. *Do not be a coward now,* he told himself, *not now.* "Alarm!" he bellowed at the top of his lungs. "*We're under attack!*"

Soldiers began to rouse themselves from the nearest tents, poking their heads out groggily to see what all the fuss was about. The creatures moved forward slowly, like wolves stalking their prey in the darkness, apparently unconcerned with the soldiers beginning to form up against them.

Gryle had been backing up without being aware of it, and the creatures were past the torches now, less than a few dozen feet away from the camp itself. He was still backing up when a hand grabbed his shoulder from behind, and he nearly screamed. He spun to see a soldier looking at him with wide eyes, along with at least twenty others. "C-chamberlain?" the soldier asked. "Oh gods, they're here. What do we do? What do we do?"

Why are you asking me? Gryle thought wildly. *Gods, where's Aaron? Or Adina? Someone else, anyone else.* They were all looking to him, all watching him and waiting for what he would say, as if he was some hero that could save him. *I'm no hero,* he wanted to scream, *I'm a chamberlain, and a coward. That's all.* But there was no one else, not yet at least, and by the time someone else arrived, there was no telling what damage the creatures could have caused, so Gryle took a deep breath, turning back to the approaching monsters. "Go and send for help," he said, and he was surprised by how confident his voice sounded. "Look for General Envelar." *He'll know what to do,* he thought. *He'll know what to say. I only pray that we're still alive to hear it.*

"The rest of you," he said, swallowing hard. "Follow me." He started toward the creatures then, and was stopped by another hand on his shoulder.

"Sir?" He turned to see the man offering him a sword. "You'll need this."

Gryle took the offered blade, feeling awkward and stupid, like a cow who has fastened wings to itself and suddenly decided it could fly. *I'm no hero,* he thought. The problem, of course, was that all of the heroes were sleeping or unaware of what was happening—either way, they weren't *here*. He nodded his thanks to the man. "Come on."

He had seen how fast the creatures could move, when they wanted to, so he approached them warily, the sword feeling clumsy and alien in his hand. *And just what do you think you're doing?* a little voice, a hold-over from his old self, whispered into his ear. *What do you know of sword fighting? They're all laughing at you behind your back, you can see that can't you? All just waiting for you to fail, for the foolish chamberlain who tried to rise above himself to be knocked back down again. It's what the world does, you know. Knock you back down when you get out of your place. So what,* exactly, *do you think you're doing?*

Gryle took a deep breath, forcing the fear away. *What I can,* he told the voice, remembering the words Aaron Envelar had told him only weeks before. *It's all any man can do.* The creatures watched Gryle and the makeshift defensive force of soldiers walk toward them with their heads cocked to the side, as if surprised that any of the men would be foolish enough to stand against them. They watched, they waited, and when Gryle and the others were less than a dozen feet away, they *moved*.

There were several *pops* of displaced air, as the creatures launched themselves forward in a blur toward the overmatched defenders, kicking dried leaves in the air as they did. Gryle tensed in expectation of being cut down for his foolishness—*who was he to wield a sword against such creatures?*—when, at the same moment the creatures started forward, he saw something fly over his head from behind. Or, more accurately, a bunch of somethings,

A Sellsword's Hope

tiny, metallic somethings that glittered in the pale moonlight and scattered in front of the defenders on the forest floor.

The onrushing blurs of the creatures moved over the covered area an instant later, and instead of the death that he'd so expected, Gryle watched in surprise as they stumbled and fell, rolling and tumbling to a stop only feet away from the chamberlain and his companions.

"What?" Gryle asked in confusion, but the soldiers didn't hesitate, moving forward and taking advantage of whatever miracle had transpired to cut the creatures down before they could get their feet under them. Just like that, the attackers were dead.

"I don't..." Gryle began, but hesitated as he looked closely at the nearest creature, saw that his feet were bloody and mangled, and not from one of the soldier's blades. Instead, the chamberlain could make out the tiny metallic shapes embedded in the creature's booted feet. *The caltrops,* he thought surprised, *the ones Caleb had the smiths working on before.*

Of course, these weren't normal caltrops, built to stop cavalry charges. At the youth's instruction, the smiths had made them smaller, with more hooked metal edges than their larger counterparts, and where they'd entered the creature's feet, the metal had torn and ripped at the flesh, opening great bloody furrows. *But how,* Gryle thought, *how did they get here?*

There was a satisfied grunt from behind him, and he saw Sergeant Wendell standing a short distance away, a bag in one hand, the other covered in an absurdly thick glove. "That'll serve you bastards right," the sergeant said, spitting.

"Sergeant Wendell?"

"Ah, Chamberlain," he said, grinning as he walked up. "I'd shake your hand, but..." He glanced down meaningfully at the glove he wore, and Gryle saw that several of the metallic devices had embedded themselves in the thick material.

"Um...t-that's quite alright," Gryle said, imagining what the caltrops would do to his hand, tearing it to shreds as easily as they had the feet of the creatures. "B-but thank you, Sergeant Wendell, for showing up. Were...were you on guard duty, then? I had thought you were with the honor guard around Queen Adina's tent."

"And so I was," the sergeant said, his expression souring. "But that bastard Darrell either has the gods' own luck, or he's a cheater at cards, and when faced with either, a wise man walks away from the game while he's still got some coins in his pocket." He scowled. "Not that I did, mind. If I'd hung around any longer, I would've been marchin' to Baresh in my bare feet."

Gryle nodded slowly, his panicked mind—he'd been sure, only moments ago, that he was going to die—struggling to understand the other man's rambling words. "Well...in any case, I thank you for showing up when you did. I had thought..." He glanced around, making sure none of the other soldiers were within earshot, and saw that they were even now finishing up the creatures, making sure they were dead. "I thought we were going to die."

"Well," the sergeant said grimly, staring over the chamberlain's shoulder as his gloved hand reached into the bag he carried, "you might still get the chance."

Gryle frowned, and his heart leapt in his chest as he saw a dozen more of the creatures only now emerging from the woods, the flickering torchlight making of their already cruel, twisted features nightmare visages that would have been more at home on the faces of demons. "Oh gods."

"Not quite," Wendell said, "but they ain't human, that's for sure."

Gryle looked around him and was relieved to see that more soldiers had gathered, the news of an attack spreading. It appeared as if at least a hundred armed men waited for the creatures now. He breathed a sigh of relief. There looked to be only ten of the creatures, if that, and with such numbers against them, even they would be cut down in short order. It was then that he heard the roar.

If, he thought, *such a noise can be called a roar at all.* It was not the angry shout a man might make, not even the deep, resonant sound—somewhere between a bark and a cough—that was said to be made by some of Telrear's largest jungle cats. Instead, this sound was what might be made if some great, angry mountain were given lungs and a mouth. It was a sound unlike anything he'd ever heard, one that seemed to crash like thunder, and he had a vague idea that the ground beneath his feet trembled. The soldiers, too, must have felt some of the panic racing through Gryle, for they began to look around frantically, casting their gazes about for the source of the great cry.

Surely, everyone in the army heard that, the chamberlain thought. *They'll be here in a few minutes, Aaron and the others, and they'll handle whoever—or whatever—could make such a sound.* A moment later, a massive shape—eight or nine feet tall at the least—lumbered out of the shadows of the trees, and Gryle stared in shock at the impossibly thick shoulders, the grossly muscled chest and arms of the giant. He'd seen one of Kevlane's strong creatures before, of course, when Aaron and the others brought the corpse of one back to Perennia to prove to the council what the ancient mage was creating. But seeing it in real life, standing before him, its scarred, thick features twisted with an insane rage, was very different, and his breath caught in his throat.

"Well, shit," Wendell muttered beside him. "Reckon I should have kept playin' cards, after all. A man can survive without boots."

The smaller, faster creatures drew closer to the giant as he emerged, their small frames making them look like nothing so much as ticks swarming around a dog. The sergeant glanced at the big creature, then down at the handful of caltrops he was holding, a dubious expression on his face. "Don't think the same trick's goin' to work twice, Chamberlain. Unless, maybe, we can convince that big bastard to swallow a few of these, that is. What's the plan?"

Why are you asking me? Gryle thought wildly. But he took a deep, shuddering breath in a vain attempt to still his galloping heart, and turned back to the creatures where they were making their way past the perimeter torches. "I think...I think we'd better kill them."

Wendell grunted. "Sound plan, I reckon, if a bit vague on the particulars." He turned to regard the soldiers around them. "Well, you heard the man, lads. Let's kill 'em then, aye? And while you're at it, maybe do your best to keep all your insides where they belong."

There was some nervous laughter at that, but a moment later the giant gave another roar, and the sound—if such an all-encompassing, earth-shaking thing could be *called* a sound—drowned out any answer they might have given. Then the giant and the creatures milling around him started forward, the large creature's long strides eating up the ground with a deceptive quickness.

What are you doing here? Gryle thought. *You're no hero.*

Kill.

Not his own voice, his own thoughts, but another's, and in that one word was a rage that was nearly unfathomable, and not just rage—madness. The Virtue of Strength had spoken at last, and for all his efforts at communicating with it in the past, Gryle wished that it had not. *Hello?*

Kill, the voice said again, and suddenly Gryle's mind was filled with thoughts of Beth, with the way she'd died, of how she'd looked lying there in the tavern, bloody and unmoving, her normally kind, slightly cynical expression slack in death. *Kill,* the voice said. Had anyone who knew him seen the snarl that rose on the chamberlain's face, they would not have recognized him, for he was that man no longer.

"Yes," he hissed, "kill." Then he let out a roar of his own, quieter than the creature's, but no less full of hate and rage, and he rushed forward, some small, still sane part of his mind guiding his feet around the shining pieces of metal littering the ground between him and the creatures. *These creatures killed Beth. They killed her and took from Michael his grandmother. Now, I will take from them. I will take.*

***

Wendell recoiled at the chamberlain's roar, saw the man's face twist with a rage he would not have thought him capable of, then he watched, stunned, as the normally quiet-spoken, polite man charged toward the creatures, his chubby hands balled into fists. In another place, at another time, such a thing might have seemed ludicrous, funny even, but there was nothing funny about it now, and the bestial, guttural sounds the chamberlain made as he charged were, in their own way, even more unnerving than the giant's.

"Well, alright lads," Wendell said, clearing his throat as he turned to the soldiers who watched the chamberlain with shocked expressions. "Let's not let him have all the fun."

With that, they rushed forward. It wasn't until he was standing directly in front of one of the small, thin creatures—its sword held up and at an angle behind it—that Wendell realized he hadn't drawn his sword, that, in fact, he still held the bag of caltrops in one hand, the other covered by the thick glove that did well enough to protect his skin against the caltrops, but that he doubted very much would help stop a blade.

The creature seemed as surprised as he was himself, staring at the sergeant as if trying to decide what sort of weapon he carried. Wendell was telling himself, once again, that he should have stayed at the card table with the swordmaster and never mind how the man cheated, when one of the soldiers gave a shout, charging the creature from the side.

It reacted instantly, its sword lashing out with the incredible speed Wendell had seen its kind use before, and the soldier screamed as the blade traced a bloody line across his chest, stumbling away. The creature's head spun back to Wendell, no doubt intending to take him out next, and doing the sergeant the favor of adding its unnatural momentum to his strike as his gloved hand—and the many, jagged caltrops embedded in it—struck it in the side of the face.

Blood spurted from the creature's already ruined features as the metal tore into it, and it stumbled, though if it felt any pain, it showed no sign. It straightened a second later, regarding him through a crimson mask. Staring at it, the blood pouring down its face, one eye gone, Wendell promised he'd take the first opportunity to puke his guts out—assuming he survived—then dropped the bag he was carrying, drawing his sword. "Come on then, you ugly bastard," he growled.

The creature appeared intent on doing just that, when a soldier separated himself from the melee going on all around the sergeant and charged the creature from behind. The creature spun, its blade impaling its attacker, but that did nothing to stop the man's forward momentum, and the wounded soldier bowled into it. Wendell felt an instant of relief at being saved, but it was short-lived as, a moment later, the soldier—and the creature—toppled into him, all three sprawling on the ground.

The soldier lay unmoving—clearly dead—but the creature somehow managed to get on top of the sergeant, and he grabbed its too-thin wrist, hissing as he struggled to keep it from bringing its blade down. Despite its frail form, the creature was possessed of a wiry, frantic strength, and it was all Wendell could do to keep it away. His own sword had gone flying when the two struck him, and so he lashed out with his free hand—the one that happened to still be wearing the glove, now soaked with blood—hitting the creature in the face again.

More blood spurted, but the creature fought on, seemingly not inconvenienced in the slightest that half its face was little more than mash. "Just *die,* you bastard," Wendell growled, struggling desperately now as, to his shock and dismay, the creature's squirming thrashes were bringing the edge of its sword closer and closer to his throat.

He cast his eyes about him, desperate for any weapon that he might use, and was surprised to see the bag of caltrops within reach. He lashed out with his gloved hand, and at first he couldn't get a grip on it past the thick material of the glove then, finally, he did. "Try this on, you son of a bitch," he growled as he slipped the bag over his attacker's head. The creature reacted instantly, thrashing wildly now, and Wendell pulled the bag tight, keeping as many of the caltrops from spilling out as he could.

In seconds, the bag was soaked through with blood, dripping onto Wendell's face, but he held on grimly until the creature's struggles finally ceased, and it collapsed on top of him, unmoving. Sucking in deep, ragged breaths, the sergeant pushed the creature off with a grunt and rose unsteadily to his feet, careful not to step on the caltrops scattered around him.

He stared down at the creature, the blood-soaked bag covering its head like some particularly terrible hat. For the moment at least, he was safe. Dozens of soldiers were engaging the creatures all around him, but it was the giant that caught his eye and the chamberlain that stood, small, yet defiant, in front of it. A pocket of space had opened around the two, and Wendell watched as the massive creature bellowed, its insane eyes falling on the pudgy man who dared stand in its way.

The giant raised one massive fist, and Wendell started forward, knowing he would be too late, and would arrive only in time for the chamberlain to be smashed to bits. "*Look out, you crazy bastard!*" he shouted, but if the overweight man heard, he gave no sign, and the giant's fist descended with inevitable finality. But instead of being crushed beneath the blow—as Wendell had expected—the pudgy man caught the fist in both hands in an impossible display of strength. The giant must have been as surprised as the sergeant, for he stared down at the smaller man in front of him with something like disbelief in his twisted, strange features.

The creature's unnatural muscles strained as it tried to force its fist down on the pest in front of it, meaning to crush him. The chamberlain's feet slid across the grass under the force of the blow, yet still he held the creature at bay. Then, with a roar of his own, the chamberlain strained, heaving against the fist and—it seemed it was a day for impossibilities—the creature was forced back a step, then another, until the chamberlain gave another shout, thrusting his arms forward, and the creature stumbled away.

"Well I'll be damned," Wendell said. There was a hesitation then, as if the creature was trying to figure out how such a puny opponent had managed to stand against it, but Gryle didn't wait. He charged forward, landing a punch on the creature's midsection. The creature let out a grunt, the air exploding from its lungs in a *whoosh*. It stumbled back into the torchlight, remaining standing only because it slammed up against a tree with a *crash*.

Gryle followed, but before he could close with it, the creature made use of its much greater reach, sweeping an arm out and hitting the chamberlain. The smaller man hurtled through the air, striking a tree, and Wendell winced as he heard the thick oak—one that had no doubt stood for centuries—*crack* at the impact. A moment later, the tree wobbled and crashed to the ground, and the chamberlain was hidden from view in a shower of limbs and leaves.

Oh gods. Wendell hurried forward, his expression grim, expecting to find a bloody mass that had once been the chamberlain pooled at the trunk which was all that remained of the once massive tree.

The creature, too, seemed confident that whatever threat the chamberlain had presented was no longer an issue, for his mad eyes locked on Wendell, freezing the sergeant in his tracks. Wendell glanced down at the glove still on his hand, remembering that—fool that he was—he'd forgotten to pick up his sword from where he'd dropped it. "Well, shit," he said, facing the creature.

Suddenly, several soldiers rushed beside him, and a quick glance showed him that they'd apparently managed to finish off the remaining creatures by weight of numbers, but the corpses littering the ground—most of which weren't the too-thin forms but ones he recognized all too clearly as some of the army's soldiers—showed they had paid for what victory they'd achieved.

"Sergeant," one of the soldiers said as him and the others gathered around Wendell, eyeing the giant with a naked fear not unlike the terror Wendell felt seizing his own heart. "What do we do?"

Die, like as not, Wendell thought, but didn't think it would be inspiring to say so. He was still trying to come up with something better—die fighting, maybe—when movement in the corner of his eye caught his attention. The pile of branches obscuring the chamberlain's form began to stir. "No fucking way," he said.

"Sir?" the soldier asked, confused, and Wendell, suddenly unable to find his voice for the first time he could remember, pointed to where the chamberlain was knocking the branches aside and slowly rising to his feet.

The chamberlain was bloody, battered, his clothes torn in dozens of places, as if the force of the impact had nearly ripped the clothing from him, but still he was standing, regarding the creature with a hate and anger visible even in the poor light of the torches. *Can't be,* Wendell thought. *Ain't no damn way.* The man ought to be dead, not standing up looking pissed off, yet there he was, bloody, true, but damn sure not broken, and looking just about as ready to fight as any man Wendell had ever seen. Then the man wasn't just standing, but stalking toward the giant creature, his bloody lip turned into a snarl.

The giant, however, didn't seem to notice, still studying Wendell and the others, walking toward them, apparently unaware of the chamberlain stalking closer, assuming—rightfully so, as far as the sergeant was concerned—that he was out of the fight. He wasn't though, and the massive creature discovered that a moment later when the chamberlain latched on to one of his massive wrists, dragging it to a halt.

The creature turned, and the chamberlain gave a mighty tug, pulling the giant down so that they were eye to eye. He said something Wendell couldn't hear then, with a massive heave, Gryle spun, still holding onto the creature's wrist, and someone beside Wendell gasped as the creature flew through the air, striking a tree much like the chamberlain had, its greater mass not stopping but plowing through it to strike a second tree which cracked in a shower of splinters.

The chamberlain stalked toward the creature, his hands balled into fists at his sides, and the giant was only beginning to rise when Gryle grabbed hold of him again, jerking him to his feet. He punched the giant in the stomach once, then again, and the creature bent over, its breath clearly knocked from it once more. But for all the punishment he was dealing out, the chamberlain wasn't invincible, and striking the tree as he had had clearly taken its toll. So instead of following up the attack, he stood trembling, heaving as he drew in ragged, gasping breaths. The creature, then, had a moment to recover, and it rose up to its full height once more, towering over the middle-aged, overweight man standing before it.

It swung one of its massive fists, and Wendell winced in anticipation, but to his surprise Gryle called on whatever last reserves of strength he had, bringing his arm up and catching the fist in his hand, stopping a blow of so much force that once again his feet slid back across the ground. Still, the chamberlain held on, letting out a growl that was somehow angry and exhausted all at once, then he gave the hand holding the creature's fist a savage twist, and its wrist broke with a *snap*.

The giant bellowed in rage and pain as it tore free of the chamberlain's grip and took a lumbering step back. Gryle followed it, and the creature struck out with its other hand. The chamberlain grabbed this one too, shouting as he gave another jerk, and the creature's forearm *snapped,* the bone ripping out of the skin in a shower of blood. The noise that issued from the giant's throat this time held no rage, only pain and the unmistakable sound of fear.

"You killed her!" Gryle shouted, his voice breaking with emotion, and he waded into the creature, his fists striking it in the midsection with a mechanical regularity, each blow punctuated by

what sounded like ribs snapping. Finally, the creature fell to its knees at the chamberlain's feet, and the pudgy man left it wobbling there uncertainly, moving to a nearby tree and ripping a limb as thick as Wendell's waist free with no more effort than a normal man might show snapping a twig in his hands.

Gryle stalked back to the creature and unceremoniously rammed the makeshift weapon through its chest. The wood exploded out of the creature's back, burying itself in the forest floor. That done, the chamberlain stepped back, watching the creature, his back to Wendell and the others. The giant struggled weakly, as if it might somehow tear itself free of the limb impaling it, but it was stuck fast and, in another moment, it slumped over the bloody limb, dead.

Silence descended over Wendell and the gathered soldiers then, a silence of shock and awe at the chamberlain, at the feat he had accomplished, but a silence, the sergeant thought, that also held more than a little fear. The chamberlain had won, but there had been something in the man's face, something in his shouts, that Wendell didn't like, that seemed somehow...inhuman.

Then, the moment passed, and with an abruptness that nearly made Wendell scream, the soldiers all around him erupted into cheers, clapping and shouting in approval. Wendell, too, felt a great relief to still be breathing, great relief at the chamberlain still being alive. But such relief as he felt was tempered by the reality of the impossible violence he had just witnessed, violence of which no man should be capable. Such power, he thought, should not exist, would be better if it had never existed at all, for men, being men, were not to be trusted with it.

Being a sergeant in the army, Wendell had a good understanding of what most weapons cost—swords and bows, and no matter how crude or how magnificent, there was always a price. Weapons, power, neither was ever free. He thought, looking at the chamberlain's slumped shoulders, his fists still clenched at his sides, that the price for such power as the man now carried was more than any should have to bear.

Gryle finally turned to look at the soldiers applauding him, and Wendell felt a surge of fear, as he saw the man's features twisted with an insane rage, a hate so great that it had not been extinguished when he vanquished his foe. The man visibly shook, as if barely able to contain the murderous need he felt, but the soldiers seemed not to notice, clapping and cheering, and Wendell tensed as the chamberlain stalked closer, to within feet of where he and the others stood. Finally, and to Wendell's great relief, the chamberlain seemed to win whatever battle waged inside him, and the snarl of hate left his face, and he no longer looked angry, only tired.

Abruptly, he collapsed to his knees on the ground, his head hanging as if in shame. The shouts, the cheers, went on, and with each yell of victory, the chamberlain flinched as if he'd been struck. "Shut the fuck up, will ya?" Wendell yelled, and the soldiers turned to him.

"B-but sir," one of the nearest said, "he saved us…it…I've never seen anything like that in all my life."

"Course you hadn't," Wendell spat. "Just leave off it and go see to the wounded—see if any of ours are still alive." The men hesitated, glancing between the sergeant and the chamberlain, and Wendell let out a growl. "Now, damnit. Unless each of you fancies being sent out on deep scoutin' duty with those fuckers." He waved a hand at the corpses of the creatures littering the ground.

That got them moving, at least. "Alright then," he said, turning back to the chamberlain who was staring at a headless body, his features twisted in unmistakable grief. Combined with the blood from a cut on his forehead and what dribbled from his lips, it gave the man a terrifying visage, and Wendell cleared his throat, remembering all too well the anger and insensate rage that had possessed the man only a few minutes ago. "Everything uh…everything alright, Chamberlain? Not plannin' on, I don't know, goin' crazy and killing anybody or anything are you?"

The chamberlain spun on him with a surprising swiftness, and the sergeant took an involuntary step back, thinking again about how his coin wasn't the only thing—or the worst—that a man could lose. *"I'm not crazy,"* Gryle yelled. "I'm *not!*" He turned back to the corpse as abruptly as he had looked at Wendell, and when he spoke again his voice was low, little more than whisper. *"He's* crazy. Sure. Just about as crazy as anyone—or any*thing*—can be. All he wants to do is kill. It's all he cares about, all he *thinks* about. But not me, I…I'm not crazy."

"Well, 'course not," Wendell said warily, glancing around to see how far away the nearest soldiers were. "I was just uh...just foolin' with you, that's all. And I'm sure he *is* crazy. Whoever he is. Ain't no fault of yours, no sir. Certainly not somethin' to, you know, get pissed off over, maybe kill a certain sergeant as talks too much."

The chamberlain turned back to him, slowly this time, studying him with an expression Wendell couldn't quite identify, and the sergeant waited tensely. "I wouldn't kill you, Sergeant Wendell," Gryle said in a whisper, but his voice held no real conviction, no real emotion at all. "I wouldn't...I wouldn't do that. You're a friend. My friend."

Wendell nodded, the man's empty tone doing little to reassure him. "Sure I am. Bad business, killin' your friends. After all, who are you gonna borrow money from then, am I right?"

If the overweight man heard, he gave no sign. Instead, he began studying the corpse once more. "Anyway," Wendell went on, after pausing to clear his throat, "I think a 'thank you' is in order."

"You're right, of course," the chamberlain said, still in that dull, uninflected voice. "Thank you, Sergeant Wendell. I appreciate all of your help."

"What? No, gods, man, I mean *I* should be thanking *you*."

"Thank *me?*" he said, not turning from the corpse he studied.

"That's right," Wendell said, in the most reasonable voice he could muster, the same one he'd used when trying to convince Leomin and Darrell that it hadn't been his plan to get them both covered in shit when he'd pushed the cart. A voice that, to anyone that knew him, might normally serve as an indicator that he was getting ready to tell the biggest lie he thought the listener could swallow. But not this time. This time, he meant every word. "Well, you're a hero, ain't you?" he went on. "Saved us all from that big bastard...well..." He paused, looking grimly at the dead around them. "Maybe not all. But I gotta tell you, Gryle, if I hadn't been here to see it, I don't know I ever could have believed it. The most incredible thing I ever saw, and I once seen a three-legged mongrel chase down a cat and...well, it ain't important. Just say by the time the day was over, they were both wishin' it had gone a different way."

"I'm no hero," Gryle whispered. "Just a fat, foolish old chamberlain with more curiosity than sense."

Wendell frowned. "I ain't tryin' to argue with you, but it seems to me that killin' monsters is pretty damn heroic. Anyway, so what if you are fat? I know a wh—that is, a woman, just as big as you please, but she don't let it slow her down in her occupation none, I can tell you that. Havin' some meat on her don't make her—or you—any less." He grunted a laugh. "Makes you a bit more, in fact."

"You're making fun of me."

"Gods, no I ain't," the sergeant blurted, all too aware of the blood coating the chamberlain's fists and how it had gotten there. He took a slow, deep breath, gathering his thoughts before continuing. "Look, Chamberlain, so you got a bit more on you than some, what of it? You're fat, and I'm ugly, and the sun'll still rise tomorrow. There's worse things than carryin' some extra pounds or havin' a face looks like a pissed-off cat took after you, and that's the truth."

"Like what?" the man asked distractedly.

Well, being dead, for one, Wendell thought, but figured maybe it wasn't the best thing to say at the time. "Shit, plenty. I knew a man, once, a rich bastard, he was. Had enough gold, I reckon he could've bought the sun and the moon both, he was of the mind. Good lookin' fella, the type women always swoon over whenever he walks into a room, the kind'll get an ugly bastard like me feelin' sorry for himself and fingerin' his blade, if he's carryin' one. Not that I'd have ever had the balls to try anything. The man could fight too, you see, his da had paid to have him trained in the sword from a young age, and I don't reckon I've met many—save General Envelar and those Akalian fellas—who could've bested him, but I suppose a tutor can't teach you some things. There's some lessons a fella only learns once someone comes at him with steel in his hand and blood on his mind."

"Forgive me, Sergeant Wendell," the chamberlain said, "but I fail to see your point."

Wendell grunted. "What I'm sayin' is, this man, he had just about anything anyone could ask for, had all the things a fella like me spends his nights dreamin' on. Women. Coin. Skill with the blade. Women."

"You said that one already."

"Sure, but I figured it needed sayin' twice. Anyhow, you know what this fella *didn't* have?"

The chamberlain turned to him then, a dubious expression on his face. "In a story, I suppose he would be cruel, lacking compassion."

"Shit no. He was a nice guy, this one, though I'll admit I hated him all the more for it. Seemed to me then that if a fella has everything he did, he ought to at least be a bastard, so folks like me could hate him and feel good doin' it. But he wasn't. Like I said, a nice guy. Used to buy drinks for everyone in the tavern, whenever he happened in, and that was most nights. Type of guy that'd be willin' to give you his last coin, shit, the shirt off his back, if you asked it of him, and smile all the while. Nice to nobles and commoners too, leastways, I never heard of him so much as whisperin' an unkind word about anyone. But you know what, Chamberlain? As nice as this fella was—as downright *blessed* as he was—my ugly ass is still lingerin' like a pockmark on the face of the earth while he's buried in some lonely graveyard, the dirt and the worms seein' to whatever looks he had long ago."

"So...what? You're saying that you're...vindicated somehow, because he's dead and you're alive?"

Wendell frowned. "I ain't real sure what 'vindicated' means, but what I'm tryin' to say is that, while he was nice to everybody he ever met, he weren't nice to himself. Oh, this guy, he'd smile and wave, say all the right things to anybody walked up on 'em—and he'd mean 'em too, I reckon, 'less he's a better liar than I've ever seen. But there was a sadness in him anyway, one I caught a peek of, sometimes, when he thought no one was lookin'. When the rounds had been bought, the women had come and the women had gone, and it was just him sittin' alone, I saw somethin' in him, and it wasn't just sadness, Chamberlain. It was hate. Not for the world or for us unworthy bastards sharin' it with him, but for himself. Every once and a while, I caught a glimpse of that hate, and I tell you it was enough to make me figure that, if given the choice, I'd let him keep his life and me mine, for whatever problems I've got—and the gods and my ma knew there were plenty—they're problems I can set down from time to time, troubles I can forget about."

"But...he couldn't?"

"Naw, he couldn't," Wendell said, clearing his throat and wiping at eyes that had suddenly grown misty. *Damned allergies. Damned forest.* "See, I watched this fella, watched him kinda, shrink in on himself, as the weeks and the months passed. Most times, he was fine, seemed just as happy as ever, but I could see it there, in his eyes, whatever it was, see it gettin' worse. It was like he had some kind of sickness eatin' him up from the inside, one that was all but invisible. And so the days went on—like they'll do—and this fella got worse and worse until, in the end, even some others started to notice, started to ask him what was wrong. To which, of course, he always said nothin', smilin' and sayin' whatever needed said to make the questions go away."

"So what happened?"

"He died," Wendell said, surprised at the pain that waited for him as he ventured back into the memory of that day. "Nobody knew, at first, though. We showed up—the usual tavern crowd, whores and drunks, mostly—and he just wasn't there, the chair he usually used empty. We didn't remark on it much, 'cept one fella mentioned it looked like we'd have to pay for our own drinks for a change. There was some laughin' at that, but not so much as you'd think. After all, the man was about always there, close to the end, and him bein' gone, well, it was almost like walkin' in and findin' the bar and the barkeep both nowhere to be seen. Strange. Off-puttin'."

Wendell paused, sniffling, then hocked and spat. *Damned forest. Damned allergies.* He looked at the chamberlain and saw the man watching him now. "We found out the next day the man'd died. He'd been walkin' around that big old house of his, leavin' a fine lookin' woman in the bed waitin' on him, mind, when he fell off his balcony with pretty predictable results."

"Gods," Gryle said. "A terrible accident."

The sergeant nodded slowly. "Some folks say so, figure maybe he wanted a breath of fresh night air, maybe just to take a breather before he got back to business with his lady friend, and tripped and fell. But you know what, Chamberlain?" he said, meeting the man's eyes. "I don't think so. You ask me, I think that whatever disease was eatin' that man up got to be more'n he could bear, and he did the only thing he could think of to make it stop. Say whatever you want to about throwin' yourself off a balcony, there's one thing for sure—it'd make a man's worries seem small enough."

There was silence for a time, then finally the chamberlain spoke. "I'm very sorry to hear that, Sergeant Wendell. A terrible, sad story. But I'm not sure—"

"We're all broken, Chamberlain," Wendell interrupted. "All of us. I don't know whether we're born broken, or we end up that way once the world's taken its hammer to us a few times, and I don't think it matters much in any case. All of us are vases with cracks in 'em. Some of us—shit, *most* of us—wear our flaws on the outside, easy for anyone to see. But not all of us do—that don't mean we ain't cracked, understand, that we ain't broken. Just means that the hammer hit us different, that's all. You're fat, I'm ugly, he's dead, and the world'll keep right on doin' what it does."

"It's the world then?" the chamberlain asked, raising his eyes to look at the field still littered with corpses, the soldiers going about the work of tending to what few wounded there were—the mage's creatures didn't tend to leave many—and dragging the bodies away. "It's evil?"

Wendell grunted. "I don't reckon the world's any more evil than good, Chamberlain. It just *is,* that's all. I don't think it's got no malice in it, when it takes the hammer to us. It's just doin' what it does, same as the way you like to eat more'n other folks or your body likes to hold on to it more, whatever the case is. You—and I, and the dead man—we're just doin' what we do. Maybe not doin' it the best way, but the only way we know how. And as for you bein' fat—seems to me that's proof that you got some learnin' to ya."

"Oh?" Gryle asked, surprised.

"Sure," the sergeant said. "Tells me you—or your body, either one—know a truth few folks do. That, sometimes, the world brings a man a feast, and sometimes it brings him a famine. A smart man—a wise one—eats while he can, knowing that, any day now, he might find himself starvin'. A smart man takes what happiness he can find where he can find it because, who knows, sooner or later he might just open his eyes and see that he's standin' on his balcony, the ground a long way below him."

The chamberlain nodded slowly, turning back to the corpse at his feet. "This man, here...he called me a hero. Said he just wanted to shake my hand. Then before we were done talking, one of those things came out of the darkness and killed him."

Wendell grunted. "I see. And did you shake it?"

Gryle turned to him, a confused expression on his face, as if the sergeant had just spoken in another language. "I'm sorry?"

"His hand. Did you shake it?"

"I...yes, but—"

"Well, that's alright then. We're all gonna die one day, Chamberlain—the world's got our spot all picked out for us, even if we don't know it. You ask me, there's worse ways to go than dyin' as you're shaking the hand of a man you admire. Better ways maybe—there's a brothel, comes to mind—but that sure ain't the worst."

"But...I'm no hero."

Wendell laughed, slapping the chamberlain on the shoulder. "Naw?" he asked. "Well, might be these fellas here think otherwise."

Gryle followed his gaze to the soldiers around them, studying him with expressions that could be nothing but awe and admiration. "The world needs its heroes, Gryle," Wendell went on. "Folks need someone to be strong when they can't, someone to give 'em hope when their own pockets turn up empty."

The chamberlain seemed to slump even further, shrinking in on himself. "It...it is a heavy weight to carry, Sergeant."

"Sure it is," Wendell agreed, "but that's alright. Just carry it as far as you can, for as long as you can, Chamberlain, and know that every man breathin' has his own load on his shoulders. Only the dead get a pass."

Gryle took a slow, deep breath. "Thank you, Sergeant Wendell. I...it's remarkable, but I feel better."

Wendell grinned, giving him a wink. "Well, that's something then, ain't it?"

CHAPTER FIFTEEN

Balen stood on the deck of Festa's ship, breathing in the cool sea air and reveling in the feel of the wind against his face. For the first time in recent memory, he wasn't running for his life or doing his level best to defend it. At least, mostly. Captain Festa was not a patient man at the best of times, and these were far from the best of times. Thom, unwilling to be separated from May again after her recent imprisonment, had marched out with the army when they left Perennia nearly a week ago, and no matter of threats—of which there had been many—from Captain Festa had been able to sway him. And, since Balen served as first mate on Leomin's ship, and the Parnen captain also marched with the army, serving as Festa's first mate until Thom returned to take his place had seemed like fate.

If, that was, fate was a cruel joke the gods played on mortals for their entertainment—something Balen was becoming more and more sure of as the days went on. Still, the ships had left the same day as the army, and Balen had not loved the prospect of staying in the city, thinking that, judging by recent history, it was only a matter of time before someone else tried to kill him if he did.

So, despite his own misgivings—namely, not wanting to find himself the target of one of Captain Festa's common, and always violent, rages—Balen had reluctantly agreed to accompany Festa and the armada of other ships, manned with sailors and soldiers both, as they journeyed on the task General Envelar had set them.

A Sellsword's Hope

Namely, traveling to Baresh and encircling the port in order to cut off any possible retreat for Kevlane or his inner circle. That, of course, as far as Balen was concerned, was a particularly optimistic bit of fancy, but at least it had gotten him out of a city that seemed bent on killing him, and put him back on the sea again.

So even though he'd felt like the type of fool that put his head in a lion's mouth expecting it not to bite when he initially agreed to be the first mate on Festa's ship, *Gorgeous*, Balen was enjoying himself. Its appearance aside—which, it had to be said, held nothing in common with its name—*Gorgeous* sailed the water well, skimming atop it with a grace he hadn't expected. Of course, it wasn't any match for the *Clandestine*, the ship upon which he normally served as Captain Leomin's first mate, but as far as Balen was concerned, there wasn't a ship in the water that was.

Even taking on the role of Captain Festa's first mate had—so far at least—not been nearly as terrible as Balen had imagined. In fact, he had come to almost enjoy the captain's company, and found himself having to suppress a grin as the heavy-set man, wearing even *more* clothes and furs than normal now that they were out at sea, launched into one of his many inevitable tirades. Humor, he'd found when once the captain had seen him smiling and decided to change the target of his ire to Balen, was sometimes best kept to oneself. Particularly if, said one, wanted to keep his self—and all his parts—intact.

And the truth of it was, Balen felt lighter, *freer,* than he had in weeks. Some men were made to be farmers, born with the dirt of the land on their hands. Others were made to be clerks, their shirts always stained with the ink of their trade, blinking myopically through thick-rimmed glasses at reports all day...but Balen, he was made for the sea, the wide open ocean, stretching out in all directions. Out here, with the feel of the sun on his face, the cool breeze on his skin, Balen's worries melted away until they seemed—*almost* but not quite—laughable in retrospect.

It was as close to paradise as he ever thought a man like him would get, and most of the time it felt like more than he deserved. It was beautiful, and it was peaceful, just so long as he stayed on his toes, prepared to dodge whatever was near the captain's hands when he grew angry.

As if the thought had summoned him, Balen heard the loud, unmistakable footfalls—even *they* somehow contrived to sound furious—on the deck behind him. "How's things treatin' you then, Your Lordship?"

Balen turned away from the view of the sea reluctantly, removing his hands from the deck railing to look at the heavy-set man, bundled in so many furs it was a miracle he could stand at all. "Captain?" he asked curiously.

"Why do you look confused, Balen? You are a *lord,* ain't you? A man with gold and mistresses aplenty, hired my *humble* ship and crew to cart him around so he could see the ocean in all its glory?"

"Um...no sir, Captain. I don't—"

"*No?*" Festa interrupted as if surprised. "Huh. Then why, I wonder, are you standin' here like a damned tourist, gawkin' at everything we pass instead of doing your damn *job?*"

The last was said in a roar, and Balen winced. "Forgive me, Captain. I...only, it's good to be at sea again."

"Well, course it is," Festa answered as if Balen had just said something incredibly stupid. "Where the fuck else would we be?" He shook his head. "I swear but the gods have taken it in mind to test my patience of late. First, that fool Thom goes marchin' off to war, chasin' after that red-head's skirts and playing at being a soldier. The gods know the bastard's too old to be wearin' armor and swinging a sword. Only thing he ought to be concerned about wavin' around is a hand for someone to help him up, if'n he falls. Then, if that ain't enough to make a man weep for a world gone mad, my new first mate is more concerned with feelin' the wind in his hair than seein' to his duties!"

Balen nodded, doing his best to look properly chastised—there was a hope, however small, that if he did so, the captain's annoyance wouldn't turn into an outright tantrum. Still, he found it difficult to look properly ashamed. After all, it wasn't the first time he'd heard such a speech—he'd long since lost count of the exact number—and for all his gruff, brash exterior, it was obvious that Festa was worried about Thom. Not that Balen could blame him. He figured there were enough ways for a man to catch his death in the world without him marching with an army that, so far as he could see, was pretty much courting it.

But for all his own worry, he was happy for Thom. There'd been a time—barely more than a week ago—when it looked as if the first mate would never see his lady love again, and only a lot of dying and a lot of luck had managed to change that. He couldn't blame the man for wanting to hold on to what happiness he could in a world that looked intent on finding the tallest cliff it could and jumping off it. "He'll be okay, Captain," Balen said.

Festa, who'd just paused to take a deep breath, no doubt preparing for his next recrimination, hesitated. "What's that?"

"I said he'll be okay. Thom, I mean. I know you're worried about him, marching with the army like he is, but if I know one thing, it's that May won't let him get anywhere close to the front line, when the battle starts."

Festa sputtered in disbelief. "You...you think I'm *worried* about that...that...fool? If he wants to go off playin' soldier, that's on him. His choice, and the gods never let one pass without makin' sure a man pays for it." He sniffed. "*Worried* about him. Like I'm some old hag sittin' and rubbin' her hands together, wishin' her son'd visit more." He frowned, leaning close to Balen. "I'll tell you what I'm worried about, Blunderfoot. I'm worried about my ship falling apart while my new—and temporary, thank the gods—first mate gazes out at the horizon like a poet gettin' ready to write somethin' nobody'll read. And I'll tell you now, Blunderfoot, the first rhymin' words I hear out of your mouth, I'm throwin' your ass overboard, and you can appreciate the view as much as you want while you're thrashin' in the water with sharks circlin'. You hear me?"

"Yes sir, Captain," Balen said, schooling his features to hide the grin that threatened to come to his face. "I hear you."

Festa studied him suspiciously, as if he were picking up some of Balen's amusement despite his efforts. "Well. Good," the captain said, as if he'd been expecting an argument and, now that Balen hadn't offered one, he wasn't sure what direction to take the conversation in. He snorted. "Actin' as if I'm missing that ornery old bastard. Ridiculous. Since he's got with that woman, he ain't done nothin' much but test out the beds in the cabins anyway. It'll serve him right, somebody comes along and caves his head in for him. Seamen belong on the sea, Blunderfoot. The Sea Goddess might be a cruel bitch, but she's ours, and it don't do a man any good to go lookin' for somethin' else, once the goddess has picked him. You understand?"

"Yes, Captain," he said, nodding dutifully. "I understand."

Festa frowned. "Ah, get out of here, you bastard, before I take it in mind to throw your ass overboard just for the fun of it. Go talk to Emer. Tell that surgeon that once he gets done sewin' up those fools as nearly got themselves killed savin' Thom's woman, I got a table in my cabin I need him to see to fixin' up." He grunted. "And tell him I don't want to hear none of his complainin' neither—if that bastard was as bad of a surgeon as he was a carpenter every one of those bloody bastards he's workin' on would be doomed."

Maybe he seems like a bad carpenter because you're always picking up the things he makes and throwing them, Balen thought, but he only nodded again. "Of course, Captain. I'll go at once." He started away, headed below decks, but paused when the captain spoke.

"Blunderfoot," Festa said quietly. "Did you hear as much?"

"What's that, Captain?"

"About the woman, May, keepin' that old wrinkly bastard out of trouble? Keepin' him off the frontline. She tell you as much?"

"Aye, Captain," he said. "She did."

Festa grunted. Then, seeing Balen was still watching him, gave a scowl. "Well? What the fuck you waitin' on? Ain't you got work to do?"

"Of course, sir," Balen said, hurrying away so that the captain wouldn't see his grin.

CHAPTER SIXTEEN

Caleb had long since lost track of the times he and Tianya had almost died. They had spent the last three days slinking through the woods, starting at every sound. Every rustle of leaves in the wind or call of a bird sent a shiver of fear through him, and each time he was certain their luck had finally run out, that Kevlane's creatures had found them. But, so far at least, they remained undiscovered.

Of course, without the help of the Virtue of Perception Tianya carried, they would have been dead days ago, but with the power of the bond she could discern sounds from much farther away than any normal person, and had been able to give advance warning when one of the creatures—or what they took to be one of the creatures—drew too close.

In such times, they would look for somewhere to hide, a big tree to put their backs against, an overhang under which they would huddle quietly, waiting to see if this would be the time the creatures would find them and finish the work they had begun at the Akalians' barracks. They'd spent the last night in a small cave, one Caleb would never have seen but that Tianya, her vision aided by her Virtue's gifts, was able to make out clearly, despite the undergrowth covering its entrance.

Caleb's own Virtue had also proved of use, allowing him to know—from half-remembered conversations and books, many of which were memories from one of the Virtue's previous bond mates—which plants and berries were edible and which would kill them or make them violently sick. Still, despite their foraging, they had not stopped to hunt for hardier fare—knowing that to do so would be as good as signing their own death warrants. Each day, the patrolling creatures seemed to draw closer and closer around them, and the plants they'd managed to scavenge only kept the worst of the hunger pains at bay.

He was thinner, he knew, and there was a slight tremble to his hands that spoke of malnourishment, but it wasn't himself he was concerned about. Despite all of her assurances that she felt fine, that she *was* fine, Caleb knew that Tianya's condition was growing worse. Whatever good the few days spent resting at the Akalians' barracks had done her was quickly being reversed as her already weakened body was forced to endure hardships that would have been difficult even for those in peak physical condition. She was tired, malnourished, and the signs of their exertions were beginning to become impossible to ignore, never mind her assurances.

Caleb suspected it was simple will, more than anything else, that kept her upright and putting one foot in front of the other. But even such a strong will could not last forever, and if they didn't find succor soon, neither her will nor their Virtue-enhanced senses would save them.

Thankfully, they were close to where he suspected Aaron and the others were, now. Using the increased intelligence his bond afforded him, Caleb had predicted with what he considered an acceptable margin of error where Perennia's army would be. Assuming, that was, that they hadn't run in to trouble. If they had, there was really no telling where they were, and he and Tianya—who trusted in his deductions about which direction they should travel without complaint or question—might simply pass by them without ever knowing it. And if that happened...well, such a thing didn't bear thinking about.

And even if the army *hadn't* run into trouble, still he and the woman might miss them, for though Caleb thought he had accounted for everything—the speed at which the army would move, considering their size and the necessary supplies they would be forced to bring—he couldn't shake the feeling he had missed something. Even a small error in his calculations could result in adding another day, even two, to their journey, and he was painfully aware that either would be more than the woman could handle in her weakened state.

Relax, young Caleb, Palendesh said into his mind. *Your calculations are good. You will find the army soon. You are less than a day's travel from them.*

He wished he shared the Virtue's—and apparently the woman's—unquestioning confidence, but he couldn't. All he could think about was how, not so very long ago, he had been a dim-witted servant in a tavern most people wouldn't have been caught dead in, a young boy whose own mother had known to be a fool.

Your mother's recriminations, Caleb, had nothing to do with you and everything to do with her. You know this.

And he did. At least, intellectually. Logically. But not everything a person felt *was* logical, and he couldn't shake the feeling of being an impostor, a failure. A fool. He couldn't rid himself of the idea that the woman was trusting him and that he would, inevitably, disappoint that trust. That he was a child playing at intelligence, wisdom, and that even now they were walking past the army, had, perhaps, done so already, and they would remain lost in the woods until malnutrition or Kevlane's creatures did for them both. He had thought of telling the woman as much, over the last few days and nights, but had not. His worries were for him and him alone—she had enough to concentrate on just to put one foot in front of the other, and he had no wish to trouble her with his own doubts.

"Which way?"

He started at the rasping sound of the woman's whisper, and looked up to see her slumped against a tree. Despite the cool evening air, she was covered in sweat. Another sign—had one been needed—that her body was on its last reserves of strength.

He looked around, his Virtue-enhanced mind taking in a thousand things at once, signs of where they were—moss on one side of the trees and not on the other, the sun only just beginning to set, lowering in what he knew would be the western part of the sky. Then, with that knowledge, he quickly examined their course for the thousandth time, looking for any mistakes or errors he may have made. "This way," he said, pointing in the direction that—he hoped—was right. "But listen, Tianya, it will be dark soon. Maybe we should..."

"We press on," the woman wheezed. "I'm fine, boy, so stop looking at me like I'm a corpse that stood up and decided to talk."

Caleb felt his face flush at that. "Yes, ma'am."

She grunted what might have been a laugh. "Ma'am, is it? Well, as you will."

With that, she rose from her place against the tree, unable to completely hide her wince of pain and exhaustion, and started out once more. Caleb did his best to silence the voices of doubt in his head and followed. After all, there was little else to do.

***

They'd been walking for a few hours and dark had come on in full, when Tianya's shuffling steps slowed, and she froze, her hand going up. It was a gesture that Caleb had come to fear over the last few days, as it signaled that Kevlane's creatures—or *something*, at least—was close. More than once, the woman's heightened senses had picked up sounds of movement, and they had rushed to the nearest cover only to find after several tense minutes that it had been nothing more than a squirrel or a deer going about its business.

She closed her fist, then held up two hands, displaying seven fingers in all, and Caleb's breath caught in his throat. This time, it seemed, wouldn't be a false alarm. Unless, that was, squirrels had suddenly decided to band together in large groups, roaming the forest like a street gang looking for trouble. *Seven.* So far, when Tianya had picked up on movement, it had almost always been from only one or two sources and—on one particularly frightening occasion—it had been three. The fact that she now heard seven, seven of Kevlane's creatures who were close enough for her to make out the sounds of their movement, sent a shiver of terror running down his spine.

He stood frozen, fearing even to breathe too deeply, lest the creatures somehow pick up the sound. When the woman started back to him, she did so carefully, slowly, taking great care in raising her feet and placing them on the forest ground, avoiding any dry leaves or twigs that might crinkle or snap underfoot and give away their position. The creatures didn't possess Tianya's own incredibly powerful senses, but Caleb knew they could still see and hear better than a normal man.

He waited tensely, sweat gathering on his brow, and it seemed to take an eternity for her to make it the dozen feet back to where he stood. "Seven?" he asked, "are you su—"

He cut off at a sharp, negating gesture from her, and she spun to stare off into the forest, her muscles tense and rigid. After a while, she let out a breath she'd been holding slowly, turning back to him. "Seven, maybe more," she said, her voice so low that he could barely hear her despite the fact that she was standing right in front of him. "The bastards are fast, and it's hard to tell for certain."

"What...what do we do?"

"I think," the woman said, her eyes roaming the forest, "that they've all wandered off for—" She paused abruptly, her eyes going wide. "*Hide!*" she hissed. "And be *quiet.*"

Heart hammering in his chest, Caleb cast his gaze around the surrounding woods, searching for anywhere to go, but there were no overhangs now, no caves in which they might shelter. Only trees and more of them. The woman seemed to see as much too, for she grabbed his arm, pulling him roughly toward the nearest one, a towering oak that looked as if it might have stood for thousands of years. "*Up,*" she snapped, cupping her hands, and it took Caleb's terrified mind several seconds to realize what she wanted. Swallowing hard, he planted his boot in the bowl she'd made of her hands. She groaned, and he could feel her trembling, but she lifted him high enough to reach the lowest limb of the tree. He flailed at it, barely managing to grasp it with one hand before her strength failed her.

For a moment, he was sure he would fall. It was only eight feet, yet it would kill him as surely as a sword thrust, for it would alert the creatures to their position. But then he managed to get his other hand around the limb, and he strained, pulling himself up.

That done, he reached a hand down, and the woman grabbed it. She was thin from the days spent in the grip of her madness— far too thin—and his fear lent him strength. His teeth gritted with the effort, his breath hissing between them, he pulled for all he was worth and, a moment later, the woman was in the tree beside him. Caleb had a second to notice that her face was sickly pale now, her skin almost translucent, before there was a *snap* of something below them. He looked down, and nearly screamed in surprise as he saw one of Kevlane's creatures standing only feet away from where they had been seconds before.

Like the others he'd seen, the creature's face was twisted and scarred, its features barely recognizable as human, but Caleb felt a stab of pity make it through his fear as he realized that what he could make out of the figure's face showed it to be a young woman, perhaps only a few years older than he. But whatever the woman had once been, whatever hopes and dreams she may have had, they were gone now, and what remained in her gaze was hardly human at all.

The creature cocked its head, as if listening for something, turning slowly to gaze around the forest. Caleb watched it, not even daring to so much as breathe. There was little cover in the tree in which they squatted. If the creature happened to look up, there was no way it could miss the boy and woman crouched in its branches.

He glanced at Tianya, more for comfort than anything, and saw that she was swaying drunkenly on the branch, her eyes closed, her face slack. *Oh gods,* he thought wildly. *Just hang on, Tianya. Just for a little while longer.* He reached out tentatively, aware that even the slightest sound would doom them both, and touched the woman on the arm, nearly recoiling at the fevered heat of her skin. Her eyes opened slowly, and she stared at him with a vague confusion, as if she couldn't remember where she was or how she'd come to be there. She opened her mouth as if she would speak, and Caleb's other hand shot up, bringing a finger to his lips.

She frowned as if she'd never seen the gesture before, then, suddenly, her eyes rolled up in her head, and her chin drooped to her chest. Slowly, she started to tip to one side, and Caleb caught her, straining with the effort of holding her upright. With only one arm able to balance her, the other holding on to the tree itself for support, he struggled to keep her from falling off the limb where she would land practically at the creature's feet.

He risked a glance down at the creature, sure that they must have made some sound that had warned it of their presence and that, even now, it was preparing to kill them both, but the creature didn't seem to have noticed them. It looked around the forest for a few seconds more, its head still cocked, and if it was capable of any human thought at all then no evidence of it showed on its face.

Caleb's arm began to shake, and he knew that he wouldn't be able to hold her in such an awkward position for long. Just when he thought he had no more strength left in him, the creature abruptly spun, as if hearing something off in the woods, and there was a blur of movement and a rustle of dry leaves. Then the creature was gone, vanished into the woods. *Thank the gods,* Caleb thought. *But now what do I do?*

CHAPTER SEVENTEEN

Aaron was exhausted. He'd gotten little sleep since the army began its march. He spent his days consulting with Brandon Gant and the other officers, his nights scanning the woods for any signs of life, any tell-tale indicators that might warn him of another impending attack. There'd been many such since they started out, and it seemed that each time he closed his eyes to steal even a few hours of rest, the creatures would come. He'd long since lost count—*a hundred, two?*—of the number of soldiers that had died. Deaths which, he believed, would have been largely avoidable had the soldiers been alerted of the attack before it came.

So instead of giving in to his body's demands for sleep—demands starting first as suggestions, then as declarations, and now approaching uncompromising shouts—he spent his nights sweeping the surrounding woods with the power of his bond, searching for any sign of the creatures.

He walked the camp's perimeter now while those soldiers not chosen for sentry duty slept. Bastion, the giant youth who was a member of the Ghosts, and Seline, the Speaker's daughter who was also in possession of the Virtue of Speed, walked with him. With her and Aaron's Virtue-gifted powers, they'd set up a sort of a relay system over the past several nights: Aaron seeing where the attack was coming from, and Seline using her unnatural swiftness to warn the soldiers before it came. It wasn't perfect, for the creatures were fast too—if not as fast as Seline—and she wasn't

A Sellsword's Hope

always able to arrive in time, but it was the best they had been able to come up with.

If the woman felt any exhaustion at the last several nights spent patrolling the camp, she didn't show it, but Aaron supposed she could make up some of that lack of sleep during the day while he was bogged down with all manner of reports. He was beginning to think the bastards were just making up things to send him as a sort of competition to see who could drive him insane first.

He glanced over at Bastion and only just managed to repress a sigh as he noted the big man watching him with the unblinking, almost worshipful gaze with which nearly all of the army's soldiers viewed him, as if he was a god that might at any moment perform some miracle, and they didn't want to chance missing it.

"Eyes on the tree line, Bastion," he said for what must have been at least the hundredth time since they'd started their patrol a little over an hour ago.

"Of course, General, sir," the youth said, nodding and obediently looking past the torches ringing the camp and into the shadowed darkness of the forest.

Aaron rubbed at his eyes, studying the woman who didn't so much as turn. She hadn't spoken since they'd set out, and seemed almost unaware of the two men walking beside her. He wondered, not for the first time, what thoughts plagued her. Did she think about her father, the Speaker of the Akalians? About hardships she had endured in her life, the quest for vengeance now abandoned? Or was the vaguely troubled expression on her face a sign of the worry anyone might feel after nights spent fighting creatures out of nightmares?

You could stop wondering altogether, you know? Co said into his mind. *You could figure out what is bothering her quickly enough.*

By using the bond? Aaron thought, then slowly shook his head. *No, Firefly. Some thoughts, some feelings, should remain one's own, and I've no right to go digging into her mind without asking. I don't think she'd thank me for it. Besides, you know as well as I that it's more difficult to use the bond on another Virtue-bearer. Odds are it wouldn't even work.*

I meant, Co said, as if he were a fool, *that you could* ask *her.*

Oh. Right. "Eh...how's things, Seline?"

The woman started as if surprised to hear her name. "What's that?"

"I said, how are things? Everything good?"

She stared at him for a moment. "You mean besides the fact that, until recently, I'd spent most my life searching for my father so I could kill him? Or that I'm currently sharing my body with an ancient Virtue out of myth, one who—despite my best efforts to dissuade him of it—insists on scolding and fussing over me like a nursemaid after a particularly unruly child? Or, instead, are you referring to the fact that I am currently patrolling an army camp, searching for creatures that should never have existed, marching to a city full of them with the intention of defeating not just them, but also the ancient mage who created them?"

Aaron cleared his throat. "Eh. All of it?"

She shrugged, turning back to the forest. "Things are fine, I suppose."

"Good. That's good. And how's Leomin?"

She smiled at the mention of the Parnen, an expression that looked alien on her normally dour features, but one that was pleasant for all that. "Leomin is...Leomin. I find he can be rather difficult to describe in words."

"Yeah," Aaron grunted, smiling himself at thoughts of the talkative Parnen. "I find that cursing helps."

She laughed. "Leomin is certainly...interesting. But he is refreshing, too. I have never met anyone else like him."

"Me neither," Aaron agreed. *And thank the gods for that. One Leomin is more than enough.* Still, despite the thought, he knew that the Parnen had become one of his closest friends, and he found himself wanting to talk to the man, if for nothing else but the dubious reassurance he always offered. "He's a strange man," Aaron said. "But he's also a good one."

"The best," she agreed.

They walked on for some time in silence after that, and Aaron felt better. He realized the conversation had been the longest he'd had with the woman since they'd started their nightly patrols. She was not normally very talkative—in the same way that a rock could be said not to be talkative—and she, at least, didn't seem impressed by the stories and rumors about him. A fact for which he was extremely grateful. It was nice to have at least a few people who didn't look at him as if he were about to shit a brick of gold any minute.

That brought his thoughts to Gryle, the chamberlain, and he grinned to himself, remembering the man's visit two nights past. Aaron wasn't the only one, it seemed, who was struggling with newfound fame. The short, pudgy man who, in another world, another time, would have spent his days educating princes and princesses about which fork to use at dinner and fussing over their clothes like a mother hen. Now, he had become revered as a hero to the army at large. His deeds before they'd left the city—and tales of his impossible strength—had circulated throughout the army, and the fact that he'd bested one of Kevlane's giant monstrosities single-handedly had done nothing to dissuade the people of his status as a living, breathing hero.

A situation with which the chamberlain was supremely uncomfortable, and he had come asking Aaron how to deal with it, as if the sellsword had any idea. Which, of course, he didn't, just as he didn't have any idea how to deal with the fury that the chamberlain said overcame him during the fight, an unthinking, mindless need to kill that sounded similar to what Aaron had experienced on the occasions when his own Virtue's power had gone out of control. He had met Aster Kalen, after all, the last to bear the Virtue of Strength, and the man had clearly been insane.

Melan was not always so... Co said. *Once...once, he was a good man. A good friend. If a bit vain.*

I'm sure he was, Firefly, Aaron thought back, *but whoever he was, he is that man no longer. You told me as much.*

Yes.

Aaron wondered at that. If they won the coming war, it would be in large part due to the gifts the Virtues provided their bearers, enhancing their abilities and making them something more than human. The problem, of course, was that such power always had a price. For him, the price came in the form of an uncontrollable rage. For Beth, the Virtue had granted her great speed, but had, at the same time, stolen years from her life, making her old before her time. A side-effect that was no doubt working on the woman walking beside him even now.

He glanced at Seline, seeing if he could detect any signs of premature aging. The problem, of course, was that he didn't know her well enough, and he resolved to ask Leomin if he'd noticed anything the next time he saw him.

Nor was Gryle immune to the double-edged blade which was the power of the bond with the Virtues, and Aaron hadn't missed the strange facial tics the chamberlain had displayed when last they spoke. Holdovers from a night spent fighting Kevlane's abominations, or the first indication that the Virtue was doing its dark work? Aaron thought he knew the answer all too well.

Tianya, the former leader of the Tenders, and possessor of the Virtue of Perception, had also suffered for her Virtue's sake. When Aaron had first met her, she'd been forced to live in a dark, soundproof basement that had seemed more like a cave than part of a house within the city. Leomin, too, had spoken to Aaron on more than one occasion of the cost of bearing a Virtue, reckoning it to a battle that the bearer would, inevitably, lose. The Speaker, the possessor of the eighth Virtue, had told Aaron that the Virtue's power could be controlled, its damaging side effects mitigated, but the man had also been willing to sacrifice his life and the life of his companions to open the gates of Baresh. Simple, heroic sacrifice, or an indicator of his own Virtue's power working on him, changing him?

There was no way to know for sure, and that uncertainty raised another question. Was Kevlane evil, truly? Or was his mad need to see the world destroyed simply a product of carrying the Virtue of Adaptation for so long? Had his mind been twisted and warped by the Virtue's influence after so many years?

It is...possible, Co said slowly, clearly reluctant to add weight to Aaron's worries. *But, even if it is, does it matter?*

Aaron considered that. *No. No, it doesn't.* Whether the mage was evil by himself, or had been made so, he was a threat to be dealt with. And in the end, if they did somehow manage to defeat him? How long before Aaron gave into the rage, how long before Gryle went insane from the Virtue's power, or Leomin? Would he, would *they*, become just another monster, threatening the very world they had sacrificed so much to save?

The thought was not a reassuring one, and Aaron walked on in silence, his mood growing darker with each step he took. Another worry then, to add to the growing list. Not the least of which was that they had still received no word from the Speaker and the other Akalians. They should have joined the the army by now, and with each night that passed without hearing news, a sense of hopelessness rose in him, one that was becoming more and more difficult to force back down. Had Kevlane's creatures found the barracks hidden away in the woods? *Or did Tianya or Caleb succumb to the Virtue's power?*

The woman hadn't *seemed* crazy the last time they'd spoken—at least not any crazier than usual. Or, maybe, that wasn't exactly true. After all, Aaron had been forced to delve into her mind, a mind overcome with madness, and help her escape it, had he not? Still, he thought the woman was probably alright. She had appeared well enough when he'd left the barracks, but he'd been in such a hurry to make it back to the city and help Adina and the others fight Grinner that he'd paid little attention. What was worse, he hadn't even taken a moment to speak to Caleb before leaving, couldn't say for sure how he was doing at all, or in what manner the darker side of the Virtue of Intelligence might present itself. The woman, he thought, was alright. But what of the boy? For reasons he couldn't understand, this thought, more than any other, clouded his mind and would not leave. *What of the boy?*

CHAPTER EIGHTEEN

Caleb sat huddled underneath a small earthen overhang in the forest. The nook had been carved out when some large tree in years past had fallen, succumbing, perhaps, to a particularly cold winter or to simple age. He was covered in sweat and dirt, and was just now managing to get his breathing back under control. He was the possessor of the Virtue of Intelligence and, as such, was arguably the smartest person in the world, having answers for which most people, in their limited understanding of the world around them, didn't even know there were questions.

Yet, for all his knowledge, if there was an answer to the problem before him, he could not find it, and he stared at the unconscious woman lying a few feet away from him in the small bit of covered space the overhang provided, struggling against a hopelessness that threatened to overcome him.

It had not been easy, getting her out of the tree without hurting her or himself or making so much noise that they would alert one of their hunters, but he had managed it. Had managed, too, to half-carry, half-drag the unconscious woman to this small shelter, hoping it would be enough to hide them from the view of any of Kevlane's creatures that might pass. Upon first arriving here, he had felt a great sense of victory of a challenge overcome, but he did not feel so now. Now, he felt only despair.

How long before one of the creatures managed to find them? He'd done his best to hide their small shelter, covering it with limbs and shrubs in the hopes of keeping them from view, but for all that, he knew that the creatures, possessed of uncanny senses, would find them sooner or later. He could not even console himself with the fact that he might hear them, should they approach, for despite their speed, the creatures were quiet and, what was worse, it had begun to rain only shortly after he had brought the woman here.

A hard, driving rain, the sound of which would certainly mask the approach of any of the creatures. Yet even that wasn't the worst of it. He had done what he could to push Tianya further back, into the driest part of the overhang, yet still the water reached her, winding its way through the hastily-constructed shelter he'd made, adding the risk of her catching a bad cold to their troubles, a cold which, in her weakened state, might well be enough to kill her.

Caleb himself was soaked through, had been so for some time, and in the cool northern night, his hands had begun to tremble with a chill, one that was growing worse with each passing minute. He wished, not for the first time, that he could light a fire, but he dared not. Such a blaze would serve as a beacon for the creatures roaming the woods and would draw them to him and the unconscious woman like moths to a flame.

His thoughts troubled, he crawled toward the woman—the overhang not allowing enough room for him to stand—and pressed a hand against her forehead, wincing at the fever he felt there. Frowning, he reached into his pocket, withdrawing some elderberries that he'd happened across while dragging Tianya to the shelter. He mashed them up and stuck them into her mouth. It would have been better, he knew, to have boiled the herb and made it into a tea for consumption—knowledge gained from the Virtue he possessed—but such niceties were beyond them now. The berries would, he hoped, help with her fever and the cold she'd no doubt be fighting. Of course, they were mildly toxic in themselves, but he thought that, given their current situation, they could worry about unfortunate symptoms they might cause when—and if—they survived the next few hours.

The woman didn't open her eyes, but he was relieved when she swallowed on reflex, taking the berries he offered without rousing from unconsciousness. When that was finished, Caleb hurried back to the entrance, putting his back to it and blocking most—but not all—of the driving rain from reaching the woman.

The small task complete, his thoughts went back to their situation. Tianya needed rest, proper food and care, none of which he could give her here. They needed to reach the army where they would find the supplies and medicines that her weakened body needed so badly. The problem, of course, was that for all his Virtue-gifted intelligence, Caleb was still a thirteen-year-old boy, and even if the woman was far too thin, she was heavier than he could manage for long. His muscles still ached from the short trip getting her here, to this small hidden sanctuary. Her body was weakening, and to grow stronger she needed the healing that only sleep could provide, but if he waited long enough for her to get the rest she required, the army would only get further away. And rest or not, he knew that the woman would not last long in the cold and wet of the woods without proper food or medicine.

They couldn't stay, for to stay meant a slow, cruel death as her frail body eventually succumbed to the elements and the fever, yet neither could they leave, for even if he *did* somehow find a way to move her, still there were Kevlane's creatures to think about. They were out there in the dark woods, he knew, gliding along the shadows of the trees and searching for him and the woman. The thought sent a shiver through him, but he told himself, knowing it was a lie even as he did, that it was just the cold and the damp.

The creatures *were* out there, and without the woman's heightened senses to warn of their approach, what chance did he have? Particularly when he would be struggling under the weight of carrying her, and he doubted he would even realize they were upon him before they were both cut down. He thought that, had he been in the forest alone, he could have made it to the army. By his calculations, they were only three, perhaps four hours away now. He had even considered leaving her for long enough to get help and coming back, but had quickly dismissed the idea.

Even if she somehow survived that length of time alone and unconscious—unlikely to say the least—there was a good chance Caleb wouldn't be able to find where she was again. For the dark and the rain made it all but impossible to find any landmarks—he'd looked already—and even in broad daylight the small overhang would be all but invisible to the naked eye unless someone stumbled upon it. It was, after all, why he had chosen it in the first place.

No, going on without her in the hopes of coming back with help would be nothing more than a death sentence, slower, perhaps, than if they braved the woods with him trying to carry her to what he *hoped* was the army's location, but no less certain for all that.

Leave her. The voice came out of nowhere. It wasn't Palendesh's voice, nor was it his own, and Caleb jumped in surprise.

He spun, looking behind him, half-expecting to find one of Kevlane's creatures crouching there, shadowed in the darkness. Foolishness, of course. The poor souls upon which the mage practiced his Art were no longer capable of speech, and had they found him and the woman in their hiding place, they would have no doubt let their blades do the talking for them in any case. Caleb frowned. *Palendesh?*

Leave her. The voice came again, and though the voice was not his own nor the Virtue's, there was something vaguely familiar about it, as if he had heard it before, in a dream, perhaps.

Who are you? he thought back.

The voice didn't respond to the question, and when it spoke again it went on as if he had never asked it. *She is dead either way. Whether here or with you dragging her to the army, the woman will die. Alone, you will have some chance. Small, but some. It is the only thing to do—the only* intelligent *thing.*

No, Caleb thought back, shaking his head in furious denial, as if by doing so he might banish the voice and its cold logic. *I won't leave her. I can't.*

Then you will die, and the others, left without your mind to guide them, will die too. You alone will bring on the destruction of the world and those you would call friends.

"Who *are* you?" Caleb hissed, his voice shaking from the cold and his fear both.

You know.

He frowned at that, opening his mouth to speak a denial, but then stopped, realizing what it was about the voice that sounded so familiar to him. It was *his* voice. Not the voice of the thirteen-year-old he was now, but the voice of himself as a grown man. A man who understood the ways of the world, who knew well its dark truths. His voice. His words. *Leave her.*

"*I won't,*" he rasped. "*I can't.*"

Yes, you can, the voice said, *he* said. *You must. A thousand things you might wish for—soldiers to guard you, the medicines you need to save her, warmth and comfort, yet none of those you have, nor will you. The woman will die—that is certain. The only choice is whether you will die with her or not. The problem is not unsolvable. It has a solution. It is only that you have not wished to see it. You cannot save her. You never could.*

Caleb glanced at the shadowy form of the unconscious woman, watched her breath rise and fall slowly. Too slowly. The voice might sound cruel, but there was a cold truth to its words, one that was undeniable. A cold, dark truth, but a truth just the same. Had he really thought that he could save her? Had he really believed that, somehow, he would be a hero, would rescue her and not *just* her, but the entire world, that he might somehow save them all?

A child's hope, a child's wish, and he heard his mother's voice in his head then, the way she had spoken what felt like a lifetime ago, before she'd left him at the tavern and gone on to live her life with her new, better family. *Foolish boy. Useless, foolish boy.* Cruel words, maybe, for a woman to say to her son, but that didn't make them a lie, did it? However much pain even the memory caused him, that did not mean they were untrue.

It was a simple equation—he was no hero. The woman would die. *Tianya,* some small part of his mind thought, *her name's Tianya,* would die regardless of his efforts. There was nothing he could do to save her. Even without her, there was a chance that he would die before reaching the army; with her, it was a certainty. And if he died, then Perennia's army would be without two Virtue bearers when they fought Kevlane and his own twisted army.

Leave her, the voice said again, and this time it didn't sound cruel at all. In a way, it was almost comforting. It wasn't as if he had a choice, was it? What use would there be in him throwing his life away to no purpose? If he had a *chance* to save her, well, that would be a different thing. But he didn't, and he couldn't be blamed for that, could he? None of the others would blame him, he knew. They would just be glad that he, at least, had survived the attack on the barracks. They would understand. Surely, they would understand.

But would you understand? Would you blame yourself? This thought came not in Palendesh's voice, nor in the adult version of himself, but his own. "Palendesh?" Caleb asked, his voice weak and afraid, hoping that the Virtue might somehow help, might guide him to the right decision.

But there was no answer, only the sound of the rain pattering outside their makeshift shelter. The Virtue either would not or *could not* answer, and it seemed that whatever decision he made, Caleb would have to make it on his own, for he could not delay it any longer. Even doing nothing, he knew, was making a choice in itself, a choice that would only serve to have them both die when they were inevitably discovered by one of the creatures, an outcome that became all the more likely with each moment he wasted on indecision.

There was no time, then, to wait on the Virtue to answer, no time to mull over his decision. He had to act. And now.

Leave.

"*Fine*," he grated, barely recognizing the sound of his own voice. "I will leave." He rose to his hands and knees again, glancing at the entrance to his shelter for a moment before turning back to the unconscious woman. "But she is leaving with me." The last he said with confidence, not a confidence born of a belief that they would both survive the coming journey, for it seemed all too certain that they would not. Instead, the confidence in his voice, in his *heart,* came from the fact that what he was doing felt right. Either they would both survive, or neither of them would. There would be no compromise.

The voice, either disgusted at his choice or losing whatever power it had possessed, did not speak again, and with his decision made, Caleb began to think about how he would bring it to pass. He would have to make a stretcher to drag her on, for over such distances as they would travel, he would not be able to carry her for long, and they could not afford the delays that would inevitably result each time he was forced to stop and rest.

And what of the sounds the stretcher will make? This thought, he heard with relief, was only the worry of a thirteen-year-old boy. Frightened, true, but his. Yes, the sound of the carrier sliding across the ground would inevitably make some noise, and he would only have to hope that whatever sound it did make as it slid across the forest floor would be masked by the rain or the other assorted sounds of the forest.

"Sometimes," he said, looking at the woman's form, but speaking, he knew, to himself more than anyone else, "logic isn't enough. Sometimes, hope is what is called for." He crawled out of the shelter and into the driving rain, setting about gathering the materials he would need. He would try. And he would hope. That, at least, he could do.

CHAPTER NINETEEN

The rain did not abate as Caleb set about gathering the materials he would need to craft the litter, and as the night went on, the temperature continued to drop. By the time he had two sturdy, equally-sized limbs of sufficient strength and the vines he would use to lash the poles together, he was shivering uncontrollably. The task took him longer than it normally would have as he paused often to look over his shoulder, certain that one of the creature's had snuck up behind him, its approach masked by the driving rain. But there was nothing—only the darkness and the shadows that clung to the trunks of the surrounding trees, only the chill rain, and a wind nearly cold enough to steal his breath.

He had entertained some small hope that Tianya would wake on her own, but it was a vain hope, he knew, and when he checked on her within the small shelter the overhang afforded he saw that she was still unconscious, her chest rising and falling in weak, almost imperceptible breaths. He would have to carry her then, and pray that Kevlane's creatures would not detect the sounds the litter made. Another thought struck him, and he frowned, turning back to his work.

The poles were lashed together cleanly, a skill the Virtue had known from one of its previous bearers, but there was no support in the center on which he would lay the woman. In some areas of the world, he might have been able to find large, thick leaves that could serve the purpose, but there were none such around him here, and he didn't dare waste any more time in a vain search for them. Morning, after all, was on the way, and once the sun rose, the army would march again, growing further and further away. The image of him dragging the woman through the forest, stumbling and struggling under the stretcher's weight while the army marched in the opposite direction was a powerful one, and one he dared not contemplate for long.

He considered using his own shirt—it wasn't as if the sodden fabric was doing much to keep the cold at bay anyway—but then his gaze fell on the piles of vines that were left from where he'd used them to lash the poles together, and he shook his head at his own foolishness. *It's the cold, stealing your wits,* he thought, *it must be.*

He set about his task, and in a few minutes, he'd used the vines to craft a support that he believed would hold the woman's weight. Then, he examined his work before adding two more small poles that stood upright where the woman's head would lie. That done, he stripped off his soaked shirt and propped it on the poles—he couldn't keep the rain off all of her, but the makeshift canopy would, at least, do something to keep the worst of the elements at bay. Or so he hoped.

Ca...leb?

The voice in his head was weak, little more than a faint whisper, but he recognized it just the same, and he breathed a heavy sigh of relief. "Palendesh?"

It...is I, young one.

"W-where did you go?" he asked, ducking under the shelter and rubbing his hands together in a vain effort to warm fingers that felt as if they had turned to ice.

I...went away? the Virtue asked in a confused voice completely at odds with his normal self-assurance. *Yes. I went...away, for a time.*

"Someone else was here, Palendesh," Caleb said, ashamed at the memory, ashamed that he had almost left the woman to die in order to save himself. And that, he realized, would have been the truth of it, and never mind the justifications and rationalizations that he would have used.

I know, young Caleb.

Caleb nodded, swallowing. "It was me, Palendesh. My voice. But...older."

No, Caleb, the Virtue said, and he jumped at the unexpected intensity of the Virtue's normally calm voice. *Whatever it is, whatever he is, he is not you. Do not ever forget that. Do you understand?*

"But, Palendesh," he said, taken aback at the Virtue's tone, one he'd never heard it use before. "Who—"

Tell me you understand.

Not a question at all, this time, but a demand, and in it Caleb thought he could detect a hint of anger, and not *just* anger, but fear. "I understand," he said, swallowing and suddenly more nervous about the Virtue than he had been since first meeting it in an alleyway what felt like a lifetime ago. "Palendesh," he went on, his voice weak, "are...are you mad at me? Did I do something wrong?"

The Virtue let out a sigh. *No, Caleb. You did nothing wrong. Forgive me, only, it is important that you know that the voice you heard is not your own.*

"Then what was it?"

Several silent seconds passed, and he was beginning to think the Virtue wasn't going to answer at all. When it did, it did so in a voice that somehow sounded haunted. *Every rose has a thorn, child, and even those things which man most covets might be turned into weapons to destroy him. A man who marries a young, beautiful wife, but in treating her like a possession instead of a person turns her heart against him. Another who spends his life lusting for coin, trying to fill a hole within him, might lose friends and family, even his own life, in his quest for fortune. We Virtues are no different. For though we might bestow on our bearer great gifts, there is always a cost. The quest for knowledge is a worthy cause, the possession of it a noble goal, yet even knowledge has its dangers. For not all knowledge, not all intelligence is kind, and many of the world's truths are cold ones, indeed, truths cold enough to freeze a man's soul within him, to make of him a monster.*

Caleb frowned, thinking over the Virtue's words. "So...are you saying that the voice was right? That, in trying to save the woman, I doom us both?"

Forgive me, Caleb, but I must answer your question with one of my own. If you knew it to be true, if you knew that by attempting to save the woman's life, you would doom yourself, would it change your decision?

Caleb thought about that, glancing back at the woman's form. Then, finally, he shook his head. "No. I have to try to save her, Palendesh. I have to."

Good, the Virtue said, a clear note of relief in his voice. *Then let us be about it—our time grows short.*

CHAPTER TWENTY

It started with a feeling, one of being hunted. Stalked. Some distant part of Aaron's mind knew that he was asleep in his tent in the army camp, that he was dreaming, but that did not change the *feeling*, the primal fear, that something—or someone—was after him. The *things* had not found him yet, but they were searching for him, their unnatural senses listening, looking for any sign of his passing.

Something wet struck him in the face, then again. It was raining, the water coating his slender frame which was wracked with shivers from the cold. He tried to look down at himself, knowing that there was something different about him, that he felt smaller, but the eyes that gazed out into the night were not his own, nor were the ragged, panting gasps of exertion, the breath that plumed out in a fog in front of him as he half-ran, half-stumbled forward.

They're close. The thought was not his, but that did not stop him from feeling a surge of dread. Three times already, he had managed to evade them, more by luck than design, the darkness and the driving rain covering his movements even from their heightened senses. But they were getting closer. One of his feet struck a rock that had been obscured by the shadows, and he cried out as a litter he hadn't realized he'd been holding slipped from his hands, landing on the sodden forest floor with an audible *thump*.

He froze at the sound, as loud as thunder in his ears, and spun, looking around the darkness for any sign that one of his hunters had heard, that they were coming. Aaron wanted to reach for the sword that was always strapped at his back, but his hands would not obey his commands, for they were not his at all, and he realized that he did not feel the reassuring weight of the scabbard in its accustomed place. Shadows moved in the darkness, his mind—the mind of the person he inhabited—turning each of their shifting forms into creatures grinning lurid, bloody grins, each creaking sway of the branches the sound of them drawing their blades.

But a moment later the forms resolved themselves into the shadows of trees and foliage instead of the blood thirsty creatures he had imagined. Not his hunters then. Not this time. There was a soft groan from behind him, and he looked back at the form lying on the makeshift stretcher he had dropped. She was a wretched, pitiful-looking thing, her body shrunken, her face so white as to almost appear translucent in the darkness, shining with a fey, sickly quality. *Have I killed her?* a thought came. *Have I killed us both?*

But there was no time for such worries, and the chance to second-guess himself had long since passed. He was set on his course, and could not turn away even should he wish to. So, his breath hitching in his lungs from the exertion and the cold, he made his way to the stretcher and grabbed its poles once more, giving one final glance at the woman. *Tianya, I'm sorry.* This thought, too, was not Aaron's own. *So sorry.*

Then he was running again. He was close now, he thought, an hour away, no more than that. But the creatures were closer, and though he couldn't be sure, he thought that most of them were in front of him now, between him and the army, for each of the three he had seen as he waited, huddled protectively over the woman's form, sure that they would notice him, had paused only long enough to glance around the woods before hurrying in the direction which he now traveled.

The sound of a twig snapping, a sound loud enough to be heard even over his ragged breaths, jerked him from his thoughts, and he spun, seeing a shadow not far away, standing near the trunk of a tree. *Oh gods. Oh gods, they've found me.* And it was then that Aaron realized that he recognized that inner voice. It was the voice of the youth, Caleb. And it was afraid.

***

He jerked awake with a shout, his eyes casting about for his attacker, his hand reaching for the sword at his back only to find that it wasn't there. Then he saw it, sitting propped against the desk—*why in the name of the gods is there a desk in a forest?*—and snatched it up, ripping the blade from its sheath, spinning to face his attacker, to study the tree where the creature stood.

But there was no tree, and there was no attacker, not here, at least. He stood not in the forest, but in his tent. The small collapsible desk sat before him, as did the chair he'd fallen asleep in, now lying on the ground where he'd knocked it over in his haste. Slowly, lucidity returned, and he remembered that he'd been going over reports for the army when his lack of sleep had finally caught up with him.

There was a sound of the tent flap opening, and Aaron spun, the feeling of being hunted he'd felt in the dream not yet dissipated. He brought his sword up with a snarl, and the guard who'd entered recoiled, his eyes going wide. "F-forgive me, General Envelar," he stammered. "I thought I heard a shout and…" He trailed off, swallowing as he stared down at the length of steel aimed in his direction.

Aaron recognized the man as one of the two guards stationed outside of his tent—a precaution upon which Brandon and May had insisted, but one that he left him feeling ridiculous nonetheless—and let his sword fall. "Sorry, Brenson. Just a bad dream, is all." *But was it? Was it really?*

Unlike a dream, the images, the feelings of the experience were not fading upon waking as a dream would. What's more, he had never felt a dream so powerful, so *real.* No. Whatever the vision had been, it had not been a dream but, he suspected, something brought on by the power of his bond working while he slept.

Caleb was out there somewhere, he and the woman, Tianya, and they were being stalked by Kevlane's creatures. Never mind that the two of them should have been safe in the barracks of the Akalians or, at least, traveling with the black-garbed warriors. Something must have happened, something to force them to venture into the woods alone, and whatever it had been, that was a worry for another day. For now, it was enough to know that the boy was in danger.

Aaron called on the power of his bond and quested out in the direction he thought Caleb would be coming from. At first, there was nothing, then, straining with the effort of stretching the bond to its limits, he began to make out signs of life. A lot of it. If this *was* an attack, then it was going to be the biggest one yet. And were the boy and the woman out there too? Were they one of the dozens of life sources he felt in the distance? He couldn't be sure, but he believed so. And if that was true, they were walking right into dozens of the creatures.

"Brenson," he said, turning back to the guard, "do you know where the others are? Leomin, Gryle, Seline and all the rest?"

"I-I'm not sure, sir," the guard said, clearly confused by the unexpected question. "But I'll be happy to find them, if you nee—"

"I do," Aaron said, sheathing his sword and fastening the scabbard in place over his back. "Gather them and as many others as you can as quickly as you can, and have them meet me at the southwest corner of the camp."

"Of course, General," the man said, then he turned and started to walk out of the tent.

"And Brenson?" Aaron said.

"Sir?"

"Tell them to come armed and ready to fight. And hurry—we don't have much time."

"Yes, General."

Aaron emerged from the tent at a run. This late in the evening, most of the soldiers and camp followers would be sleeping. He considered rousing as many as he could but decided it would take too much time, and settled for shouting at those few he passed, ordering them to gather as many others as possible and make their way to the southwest corner of the camp.

He'd been running for ten minutes when he caught sight of a campfire around which a group of soldiers sat. Among them was one Aaron recognized, and he hurried forward. "Wendell."

The sergeant looked up, surprised, and when he saw Aaron standing there he looked more than a little guilty. "Ah, General, sir, we weren't gamblin' understand, but—"

"Gamble all you want," Aaron said, aware that they were running out of time. "But later. Now, grab your sword and come on."

"Sir?" the sergeant asked, dropping the cards he'd been holding, and Aaron noted one of the nearby soldiers taking the opportunity afforded by Wendell's distraction to lift a few coins from the sergeant's stack and pocket them. "Has something happened?"

"Not yet," Aaron said, "but it's going to—soon."

Wendell grunted, grabbing his sword and rising. "I was losing anyway," he grumbled, scowling at the others gathered around the campfire. "Don't none of you bastards touch my coins."

The man who'd filched several grinned widely. "We wouldn't dream of it, Sergeant."

Wendell's sigh made it clear what he thought of that, but he turned back to Aaron. "I'm ready."

Aaron gave a sharp nod. "You others, gather as many as you can and meet us—there's little time." And then they were off and running, and with each step they took, Aaron tried to shake the feeling that they were already too late.

CHAPTER TWENTY-ONE

Caleb hissed with the effort of dragging the stretcher forward. His jaw ached from keeping it clenched against the cold, but it was nothing compared to the burning in his arms and legs. He thought it a cruel jest of the gods that he should be freezing and burning all at once. He'd started sniffling not long ago, and he was dizzy. He'd attributed it to his exhaustion at first, but the dizziness had grown steadily worse, and he didn't need a healer to know he had a fever.

Tianya stirred from time to time, groaning in obvious discomfort, but there was nothing he could do for her, so he only pushed on. And as he half-walked, half-stumbled forward under the weight of his burden, a thought troubled him.

Why had all the creatures been heading in this direction, the direction of the army? Was a battle going on there? Had Kevlane perhaps decided to meet Perennia's troops in the field, and would Caleb arrive at the army encampment only to find that they had already been defeated? Such thoughts, such worries nagged him as he forced one weary foot in front of the other, demanding strength from arms that had long since run out of it.

And there were other worries, other fears. A few minutes ago, he'd had a strange sensation, as if someone had been sharing his head, his thoughts, with him. This one had been different than the Virtue's presence, or even the presence of the older "him" he'd experienced before. It had seemed alive and, somehow, vaguely familiar. Had it really been there at all? Or was it only an imagining brought on by his own exhaustion and rising fever? He didn't know, and couldn't spare it a thought, all of his energy concentrated on driving deeper into the forest, toward the army and whatever fate awaited him there.

Soon, he was going uphill, and as hard as pulling the makeshift litter on even ground had been, this was worse. Much worse. He was less than halfway up the increasingly steep incline when one of his legs suddenly gave out, and he collapsed to one knee. The stretcher slipped from his hands, and he spun just in time to catch it with one hand before it—and the woman strapped to it—went sliding back down the hill to crash to the forest floor.

The joint of his shoulder, already tight and swollen from having his arms bent back behind him for so long, screamed in protest, and a sound somewhere between a hiss and a whimper escaped him as he fought to control the stretcher. Whether from the rain-slicked ground or just the incline, the stretcher began to slide down the hill, dragging him along with it, and he lashed out desperately with his free hand, grasping the trunk of a small nearby tree.

Let go, a voice said, and he recognized it as the thing which had spoken to him hours ago, trying to convince him to leave the woman behind. *You tried. No one would blame you. No one would even have to know. There is darkness here and darkness only, and it is long practiced at keeping secrets.*

"I would know," Caleb snapped. Shaking from the effort, he gave a tug, and was rewarded by the stretcher sliding up the hillside a few, almost imperceptible inches.

You fight a battle already lost, the voice said. *There is no wisdom in what you do, no intelligence. The woman will die, is dying even now. Leave her and save yourself. If you can.*

Caleb shook his head, tears of effort and exhaustion gliding down his face and mingling with the rain so that one could not be told from the other. "No," he said. "I won't. Go...a...way."

Truth, young one, cannot be so easily banished. Your choice is a simple one. Let her go and live, or continue your doomed quest and die.

"Then I'll die!" Caleb hissed, his voice a harsh whisper, and he gave another mighty pull, his anger and desperation giving him strength, and the stretcher slid up over a foot, coming even with him, close enough so that he could grab it with his other arm. He breathed a ragged sigh of relief, as he held it there for a moment, bracing against the tree to give his weary muscles a rest.

Then he rose, concentrating on keeping his grip on the poles, slick now with rain and mud. His shoulders felt numb, loose in their sockets, and he didn't dare try to drag the stretcher behind him as he had before. Instead, he began backing up the hill, pulling the litter after him. He moved slowly methodically, all too aware that it would take no more than a badly-placed stone or root to trip him up and prove the mysterious voice right.

After minutes or hours—in his exhausted, tortured state he couldn't tell for sure—the ground slowly began to level out, and soon he crested the ridge, leaving the incline behind. He paused, gasping for breath, and wiping an arm uselessly at the rain and tears intermingled on his face.

He looked down the ridge, and the breath caught in his throat as he saw the campfires in the distance, hundreds, maybe thousands of them, their flames flickering in the darkness reassuringly, as if all of those fires had been lit for him and him alone, to guide him to sanctuary. A great sense of relief overcame him then, and he fell to his knees. They were close now, so close. He jerked his gaze up again to the flames, suddenly afraid they would somehow vanish should he look away, and it was then that he saw figures moving in the darkness.

At first, he took them to be no more than shadows, thought it his fevered mind playing tricks on him. But then he saw it: a huge, hulking shadow, far away still, but standing between him and the sanctuary the flames promised. It seemed as large as a mountain to his weary mind. And when it moved toward the distant flames, he almost fancied he could hear the earth shake beneath its feet. And now that he had noticed it, Caleb saw two more of the hulking figures, each seemingly bigger than the last, and around their feet, scurrying like ants, what might have been as many as fifty, even a hundred of what he was sure were Kevlane's faster creatures.

He stared at the sight of what amounted to a small army marching in the direction of those fires and, for a time, was at a loss for what to do. His first instinct was to wait them out, to let whatever was going to happen occur and then follow after, but he dismissed the idea nearly as quickly as it had come. For one, just because so many of the creatures were ahead of him didn't mean there weren't any behind and, if there *were*, they were undoubtedly heading in this direction even now, making it all too likely they would stumble upon him and the woman. But even aside from that, he didn't think that Tianya could survive anymore time in the cold air and the rain than she already had. Glancing at her, he saw that her breath was fluttering and weak, her face sunken and sallow. He couldn't go back, he couldn't wait here. The only choice—bad choice though it was—was forward.

As for the creatures, he would worry about that when he came to it. For now, the steep downward slope that lay ahead was of more immediate concern. As hard as going up the hill had been, going down would be even more difficult.

Groaning, he lifted the stretcher again and started down the hill. Despite his own misgivings, he made it to the foot of the hill without losing hold of the litter, though he was covered in sweat and panting for air. His weary muscles begged him to slow down, to stop and rest, but Caleb pushed on, not knowing for certain that his legs would be able to take another step until they did.

He knew that, had he the time, the smart thing would be to skirt the creatures altogether minimizing, at least, the risk that one of them would hear him or the scraping of the litter as it dragged across the forest floor. The problem, of course, was that time was one of the many things he didn't have. If he was going to have any hope of saving the woman, any hope of saving *himself,* then the only way forward was forward, and that as quickly as he could manage it.

So he pressed on into the darkness, his eyes scanning the shadowed trees around him, listening for any sound of the creatures' presence

Careful now, Caleb, the Virtue said, *you must be so very careful.*

And even if I am? Caleb demanded, his fear and exhaustion making him temperamental. *There's next to no chance we'll make it to the army either way.*

Perhaps not, the Virtue agreed, *but when there are no good choices, no intelligent ones, a man must make the best one he can and where intelligence fails, where planning fails, still hope is there to take its place.*

Hope, Caleb thought bitterly. He'd learned long ago that hoping was a fool's game. He'd hoped for his mother to love him, had spent much of his life doing what he could to please her in the *hopes* that she would thank him, would pull him close and tell him she loved him. But his childish fancies had done nothing to replace the loathing she felt for him.

I'm cold, Palendesh. Outside and inside too. I've never been so cold. And, what's more, he wasn't just cold. He was sleepy. Even as he stood gazing out into the night, his eyes tried to drift closed of their own accord. He shook his head in an effort to dispel the fog gathering over his thoughts. It would be such an easy thing, to lie down. He *had* tried, after all, hadn't he? The voice had been right about that much, at least. He had tried, had done his best, and would it be any real surprise if he failed? After all, he was only a thirteen-year-old boy, little more than a child, in truth. What chance did he have against the cold and the rain, and the creatures that shared the darkness with him? He could stop now, could rest. But it would be more than rest; he was not so foolish as to think otherwise. To lie down now, to give in to the exhaustion that pulled at him like weights, would mean his death, and not *just* his, but the woman's as well.

Grunting, Caleb started forward again, the litter in tow. He set off at an angle from where he'd seen the creatures walking, reasoning that, if his past experiences with the creatures were any indication, they would think nothing of strategy or flanking tactics, but would only drive forward into the army, killing as many as they could. It would delay his arrival at the camp, but to follow directly in the creature's footsteps wouldn't be to risk death but to guarantee it. Still, all too aware of the woman who was slowly dying, her life leaching out of her with each moment, he pushed his weary body on as fast as he could.

He walked for what felt like days, his mind ragged from constant stress and fear, his thoughts muddy and unfocused. And despite his efforts, it seemed as if the fires never got any closer. Perhaps, they never *would* get any closer. Perhaps, he would spend the rest of his life walking through this cold, dark forest, until finally one of the shadows he passed separated itself from the others and finished what the cold and the wet had started.

And if no creature *did* come? If the campfires were just a hallucination or, perhaps, some sick joke, yet another way to torment him? To bring him low and make of his efforts a parody, a farce? Then he would walk on anyway, until his feet were nubs of bone and bloody flesh beneath him, until the tremors wracking his body became so great that his bones began to snap from the force of them. And eventually he would fall, a twisted, misshapen thing born of pain and sorrow, not so unlike those creatures which hunted him.

He wanted to check on the woman, to assure himself that she was still alive, but even so simple an action as that was beyond him now, and he knew that should he stop to examine her, he would never be able to start again. So he walked, just another shadow in a world of them.

He wasn't sure when things first started to change, his exhausted thoughts focused completely on his forward motion, but eventually they *did* change. The vague glow of the flames in the darkness slowly became more distinct. Not campfires as he'd thought but torches. *Has it all been for nothing then?* Were these torches not the army at all, but instead carried by those creatures he had tried so hard to avoid?

He wanted to ask Palendesh his thoughts on the matter, but the Virtue had been silent for the last several hours, as if, in his exhaustion, Caleb had lost some vital part of himself, the part that allowed him to access the power of the bond and communicate with the Virtue. And his thoughts then—such as they were—were not the clever, informed musings of the most intelligent person in the world, but only the scared, vulnerable thoughts of a child lost and alone in the darkness.

No. Not the creatures. He had seen them on several occasions, and none yet had carried torches or any other source of light, their unnatural senses apparently making such things unnecessary. Still, there was something about the sources that struck him as odd and, at first, he couldn't place what it was.

Finally, he realized what was bothering him and felt a vague sense of relief. The flames of the torches were low to the ground, no more than four feet up, their flames not nearly as high as they would be had a man—or creature—held them aloft. *Perimeter torches. They have to be.* At another time, he might have been overcome with joy at the realization that, finally, he had reached the army, that his journey was almost at an end, but even that was beyond him now.

Another thought followed on the end of that: if he *had* reached the army, then it was certain the creatures he'd seen were coming too. Which meant that his chances of being detected were greater now than ever they had been. But he walked on—he could do little else. Either the creatures would find him, or they would not. Either way, his journey would end. Soon. And so he walked.

As he drew closer, he began to make out the vague outlines of the poles on which the torches sat and was just beginning to believe he would make it, after all. It was then that several shadows separated themselves from the trees, gliding out from behind the large trunks like phantoms to stand in front of him, blocking his way. At first, they were only vague shapes, but soon he could make out the too-long arms, the skinny frames, and distorted features of Kevlane's creatures.

There was a sound behind him, the snap of a twig underfoot, and he knew that, had he the energy, the will to look, he would see yet more standing there, surrounding him. Caleb did not look, could not, but his plodding steps grew slower, then slower still, until he was less than ten feet away from those in front. Then, finally, he stopped.

He wanted to rail at his plight, to scream and shout and rave that he had come so close, that he had suffered so much only to be cut down minutes away from sanctuary, but that thought was a distant thing, its voice buried under piles of exhaustion. And so he stood silently, waiting for what would come. The creatures studied him silently, their heads cocked in their strange, alien way, as if trying to determine what manner of thing he was, and how best to kill him. Then there was a flash of silver in the darkness as each of them drew their blades.

"*Palendesh?*" Caleb asked, his voice breaking with the tremors that even now wracked his small frame.

The Virtue, however, did not answer, and Caleb felt a vague sadness at that. He would have liked to have spoken to the Virtue once more, to have heard a friendly voice, before the end. He watched the creatures move closer, wanting to look away but unable to do so.

The creatures were only a few feet away when he heard a sound even over the driving rain. *Snick.* One of the figures approaching him stumbled, as if it had tripped, and Caleb blinked at a thin wooden shaft sticking out of its neck. *What? How*—There were shouts from off to his right and suddenly a dozen soldiers erupted from the shadows, rushing toward the creatures, several of them carrying torches that seemed to blaze impossibly bright in the darkness.

And running at their front was Aaron Envelar, his sword lashing out with a speed and surety that was hard to follow, cutting the nearest creature down. Its companions turned to face the new threat, but Caleb barely noticed. He was busy watching the sellsword with something like disbelief. The man's face looked haggard, but his strikes were purposeful and graceful, like a master artist at his work, never missing a stroke, and where his sword quested, creatures fell dead or wounded around him. The soldiers followed him, guarding his flanks, a few pausing to finish off those left alive in the sellsword's wake.

Caleb's grip on time slipped then, and the next thing he knew, the sellsword was standing in front of him, his form blurry and wavering, as if he was rocking from side to side. "Caleb?" he asked, his gaze taking in the youth and the litter behind him.

Caleb wanted to ask him how the woman was, if she was still alive, but the words would not come and, in another moment, his hold on time didn't just slip, but fell away altogether, and then he was falling, falling into the darkness through which he had traveled for so long.

***

Aaron stared down at the youth in disbelief. The boy's small, naked chest bore dozens of scratches and small abrasions. He was pale, too pale, and when the sellsword reached down to lift him, his skin was hot to the touch. Aaron looked up, saw the soldiers standing around him, staring at the youth with wide eyes. "What of the woman?" he asked.

One of the men looked up from where he knelt beside the litter. "She's breathing," he said, "but barely. Sir, I'm not sure if…"

"Never mind that," Aaron said, struggling against the emotions—a mixture of rage and grief—roaring inside him. "They've made it this far, somehow. We'll carry them the rest of the way. Grab her and let's go."

As they did as he'd ordered, Aaron stared down at the youth in his arms, at his face, his features slack with unconsciousness, yet on them he thought he saw a hint of the ordeal the boy had gone through. Whatever had happened back at the Akalian barracks, it was clear the youth had been traveling through the forest for some time. How he'd made it this far while carrying Tianya, Aaron couldn't imagine.

"You did good, Caleb," he said, his voice little more than a choked whisper. "Now rest. We'll finish this."

The soldiers were waiting on his order, two of them holding either end of the stretcher on which the woman rested. He glanced around at the half dozen creatures scattered dead on the ground, as well as a soldier who also lay unmoving among them, the blade that had taken his life still impaling him. There was no time to bury him, no time to put his body to rest.

He gave a grim nod, and then they were running again. After all, the night's work had only just begun, and there would be more blood before the thing was through.

CHAPTER TWENTY-TWO

With a shout that was more a scream than a battle cry, Leomin gripped his sword in both hands and swung it with all the strength he possessed. His intended target had three arrows protruding from its chest and could barely stand—which was just as well as, of the many names and titles Leomin had been called by over the years, "swordsman" was not among them. Still, the blade did its work well enough, chopping deeply into the creature's neck. Blood fountained out in a spray, and the creature collapsed to the ground, dead.

Give me jealous husbands and angry fathers any day, he thought, panting for breath.

All around him, soldiers and the mage's creatures fought a desperate, bloody struggle. Leomin and those with him would have been overwhelmed nearly as soon as the fight began, if not for Gryle and Seline. The chamberlain was even now facing off against one of the giant creatures, while Seline flew through the enemy ranks, reaping a bloody harvest, her Virtue-enhanced speed proving greater than the dark sorcery that had twisted her opponents. Yet for all his strength, Gryle could not hold an entire army on his shoulders, and for all her speed, Seline couldn't be everywhere at once. The creatures, however, seemed to be in every direction Leomin looked, moving with that unnatural swiftness they possessed, their faces eerily vacant as they fought and killed and died.

Leomin stood in a cluster of twenty soldiers who would have long since been reduced to a pile of corpses, had they not been steadily reinforced by others rushing forward from the camp to join the fray. He'd thought, some time ago—it could have been minutes or hours—that he had seen Sergeant Wendell, but he couldn't be sure, and it was impossible to pick the man out among the hundreds of soldiers spread in a ragged line, fighting for their lives. Another creature appeared out of the chaotic melee taking place to one side of them, coming directly toward Leomin, but its sprint turned to a halting stumble as several crossbow bolts appeared in its chest as if by magic. Yet still it came forward. The soldiers surged to meet it, and despite its wounds, the creature killed two of their number before finally being cut down.

Gods, what am I doing here? Leomin thought.

Ah, but how many wives, how many daughters have woken to see you lying in bed beside them and asked themselves the same question, I wonder? Aliandra asked into his mind. For all the flippancy of her words, Leomin could hear the fear in the Virtue's voice, and for some reason he didn't understand, the sound of it made him feel courage.

None, he answered, drawing himself upright and walking to the front of the line. *You know as well as I that I depart far before the day breaks—nighttime lovers should be that and that alone.*

What I know, Leomin, is that anyone who says the phrase "nighttime lovers" has no business on a battlefield.

And maybe that was true; he didn't belong on a battlefield. But, as far as he could see, no one did. No one, except, perhaps, for the dead, their still faces, frozen in the pain and disbelief of their final moments, a mute testament to the tragedy that occurred when words failed, when men chose the easier path instead. And dying *was* easy. Leomin needed only to look around to see the truth of that.

Suddenly, something *hissed* past him, perilously close, and he cried out before he saw an arrow strike the back of one of the creatures that had become visible in the melee. Swallowing hard, he risked a glance behind him at the dozens of crossbowmen and regular bowmen standing behind the ragged line of infantry, and wondered how he had been so foolish as to not ask for a bow. True, he knew nothing of its use but, then, he knew nothing of how to use the sword which he held either, and if he were back there, he wouldn't have to worry about being stuck with an arrow from one of his frightened allies.

The arrows the men fired were helping, slowing the creatures, but their effectiveness, just then was a dubious comfort, and the space between his shoulder blades itched as he imagined it all too likely that one of the men would miss his mark and strike him instead. And despite all the archers' efforts, the creatures' unnatural speed meant that more than one made it to the line of infantry without any wounds, the proof of which could be seen in the bodies scattered around, most of which belonged to Perennia's army.

He was pulled from his thoughts as someone shouted nearby. He spun, and saw three of the creatures coming at his small group, scything through the men in front like they were so much wheat despite the arrows that soared past Leomin and the others, finding their marks in the attackers' flesh. But the creatures didn't have it all their own way, and one fell, then another. The final one that made it to Leomin bled from dozens of cuts, and when it swung its sword at him, it displayed none of the characteristic speed of its kind. Leomin parried the blade, nearly dropping his own, then with a sound somewhere between a growl and a whimper, he lunged forward, plunging his blade through the creature's stomach and just managing to avoid tripping as he did.

The creature went rigid as the blade entered, but its free hand gripped the sharp edge, and Leomin watched in horror as it began pulling itself along the length of his sword, oblivious of the sharpened steel shredding its hand to the bone. Leomin grunted, trying to wrestle the blade free, but the creature refused to allow it, edging closer inch by inch despite his efforts, raising its sword in preparation of a strike. Just when Leomin was sure he was going to die, a sword flashed out, taking the creature's head from its shoulder. With a scream of relief and fear, Leomin planted his foot in the creature, kicking it free of the blade and stumbling backward.

Hands caught him, and he turned to see a young soldier, at least a decade younger than Leomin himself, standing there, his eyes wide as he stared at the headless corpse. "Thanks," Leomin gasped.

"D-don't mention it," the soldier answered, his eyes still studying the corpse.

Leomin looked around and saw to his surprise that he and the soldier stood surrounded by dozens of dead on the ground, their blood mixing with the rain that puddled at his feet. All along the lines, hundreds of soldiers engaged in bloody battle. The young soldier hissed, and Leomin looked in the direction the man indicated with a shaking finger to see more of the creatures emerging from the forest. Leomin was not a man to despair—such an emotion was far too close to the cynical, passionless outlook his people had on the world—but he despaired then.

"W-what do we do?" the soldier asked.

Leomin gazed at the creatures and, somehow, in watching his inevitable death approach, he found courage. Yes, he would die, but then there were worse things than death. Better to die fighting for something he believed in, with his friends around him, than to live a lifeless, passionless existence like the one chosen by his people. "What do we do?" he said, echoing the soldier's words, though whether he asked the question of himself or the youth with him, he could not have said for sure. And when next he spoke, there was no fear in his voice, only determination. "We go and meet them, lad."

What? Aliandra sputtered. You can't go and meet them. Damnit, Leomin, you are not a fighter!

When faced with evil such as this, Aliandra, he thought back, *a man can be nothing else.*

Not a fighter, but a fool certainly!

"Perhaps," Leomin said, "and, most times, a coward too. But not today. Today, I am a soldier." And then he was running, his sword raised awkwardly over his head, stumbling on the wet ground but running for all that.

Three of the creatures stood and watched his approach, and despite their expressionless gazes, he couldn't help but think he saw something like the incredulity he felt as they waited for him. He was nearly on them, still screaming and never mind the harsh rasp of his throat, when his foot caught on something—a body or part of one—and he tumbled to the ground, rolling in the mud to flop almost directly beneath the foremost creature's feet.

Not the way I thought it would go, he thought, watching the creature raise its blade and knowing he would be too late to defend himself. Then something blurred across his vision, and the next thing he knew, the three creatures collapsed, their heads sliding off their necks as they did.

Leomin was still blinking in shock when someone grabbed him, pulling him to his feet. He turned to see Seline standing beside him, a sword held in her other hand. She was coated in blood as if she had bathed in it, but she was smiling a fierce, confident smile, and Leomin thought that, even here, in this place, a man might find beauty.

"You don't get off that easy, Parnen."

"I...that is...I wouldn't think of i—" He cut off as a roar louder than any thunder reverberated in the air, and they both spun to see one of the giant creatures, nine feet tall at least, stalking toward them and the soldiers that had now formed up on either side.

"Hmm," Seline said, glancing at Leomin and raising one eyebrow. "Well, what will it be, Leomin?"

He looked between her and the approaching giant then sighed. "I suppose we'd best not leave him waiting."

She flashed him a grin, tossing her sword away and drawing two knives from her waist. "Oh, Leomin, but you really know how to show a lady a good time."

CHAPTER TWENTY-THREE

Dark shadows rose all around him, rose and rose until they blocked out the sky itself. They were coming for him. No. Not coming. They were here. Hundreds, thousands of shadows, birthed from darkness, looming over him. Though they were silent, he could feel the menace coming off them in waves. There was no light to be found no matter where he looked, only the darkness, only a perpetual night that seemed to have swallowed the entire world and everything in it. And cold. A cold that seeped into his bones, into his heart.

They had come for him, these shadows, this cold. The world was covered in darkness, all those he had grown to care for, come to love, swallowed by it. Gone. Only he was left, alone and afraid, and any second the darkness would surge forward, bringing with it not just death, but oblivion. He knew this, just as he knew there was no one left to aid him, no one left who he might look to for help. There was no one. Nothing. Only him and the darkness.

I told you this would happen. The voice was like an intruder in his thoughts.

Caleb spun to see a man he didn't recognize watching him with cold, calculating eyes, illuminated by a fey light that seemed not to banish the darkness but enhance it, define it. "W-what? I don't...I don't understand."

"Yes, you do," the man said, and this time he spoke aloud. "You have doomed them, Caleb. Doomed them all."

"N-no," Caleb said, realizing even as he shook his head in furious denial that there was something familiar about the man. "No, I couldn't have."

"But you did," the man said, his voice merciless and without compassion.

"What...what has happened?"

"*You* happened, Caleb. You killed them, all of them."

"No," he rasped. "No, I wouldn't have done that...I wouldn't. You can't know—"

"But I can," the man said, leaning down so his face was only inches from Caleb's own. "I know, young Caleb, because I *am* you." He gestured at the towering figures of darkness and shadow surrounding them. "They come for you now, these things you have brought upon the world." His voice was dry and without inflection, but it was all the more terrible for that, and Caleb screamed.

He screamed, and he screamed, and the darkness surged forward, swallowing even the sounds of it until there was nothing left.

"... *okay*. You're okay."

Caleb gasped like a drowning man finding air where he had expected none. Something warm and damp touched his forehead, and he opened his eyes to see Adina leaning over him, realized that the sensation he had felt had been the warm rag which she held.

"Q-Queen Adina?" he asked, struggling to order his thoughts.

"I'm here," she said, and those simple words, so heartfelt and reassuring, were enough to make tears gather in Caleb's eyes.

He swallowed, and tensed as he remembered what had happened. "We've got to warn the army," he blurted. "There's an attack coming—the creatures are massing and—"

He started to rise from the bed, but she pushed him back down, at once both gentle and firm. "Relax, Caleb. You're safe."

You're safe. "But...I don't understand. The creatures..."

"The attack did come," Adina said, her own expression growing grim. "The creatures came in mass, as you said. But thanks to Aaron—thanks to *you*—we were not caught completely unaware. There were losses," she said, her own eyes filled with sadness, "but...it could have been much worse."

"Thanks to me? But I didn't—"

"He said he dreamed of you," Adina said. "He said that, because of that, he knew the creatures were coming, and we were able to prepare."

Caleb swallowed at that, and another thought struck him. "Tianya. I was carrying her on a litter, when Aaron found me and—"

"She has been seen to," Adina interrupted. "The healers tell me they believe she will recover. She has been awake for two days now, and though she is weak, she is lucid enough. She is *alive*, Caleb, and she has you to thank for it." She shook her head, as if amazed. "You are so brave."

Caleb didn't feel brave. He felt like just about the biggest coward anyone could be, but he didn't dare question the queen, so he only nodded. After a moment, something she had said made its way past his own troubled thoughts, and he frowned. "You said she's been awake for two days? But...but that can't be. It was only a few hours ago that..."

"Aaron and the Ghosts found you in the woods four nights ago," Adina said. "You have been unconscious since then." She stared down at him, and Caleb was shocked to see tears gathered in her eyes. "We feared that you would not awaken. You had a terrible fever and..." She cut off, shaking her head and putting on a smile, the effort of which obviously cost her. "But you're okay. Thank the gods, you're okay."

"Four days," Caleb said in wonder. *I've been asleep for four days.* He did a quick calculation. Based on the army's rate of travel—proven accurate by the fact that he had found their camp at all—and how many miles they had left to travel to reach the city of Baresh...his eyes went wide. "But...but that means that we'll reach the city in..."

Adina nodded. "Two days. Our scouts report we'll be within sight of the city walls by mid-afternoon the day after tomorrow."

Less than two days. Caleb's heart quickened at the thought. Two days, and then they would discover what the mage, Kevlane, had been up to and that, at least, was knowledge he thought he could do without, never mind that Palendesh said every bit of knowledge a man could find was of incalculable value. For such knowledge as that would not be free, and the learning of it would be paid for in hundreds, almost certainly thousands, of lives.

"I...so soon?" A stupid question, but it was all he could think to say, all he could force past the lump that had gathered in his throat like a stone.

"Yes," she said, and Caleb thought he could detect a fear similar to his own in her troubled gaze. "Oh, speaking of which..." She rose from her chair and offered him a glass of cool water, which he took gratefully. "Aaron and the others will no doubt wish to know you're awake. They have been asking after you, and it will do them good to know you're okay."

Caleb paused in taking a drink of the water—he'd never tasted anything so good—to blink in surprise. "They...asked after me?"

"Of course," she said, putting her hand on his where it sat atop the blanket, and Caleb felt his face heat. "We all care about you, Caleb. You have to know that. And when we return to Perennia victorious, the people of the city will owe much of their thanks to you."

"If we return," Caleb said, unable to stop the words from coming, and wincing, sure she would scream at him now, would demand to know how a tavern boy would *dare* question a queen.

She didn't though. Instead, she only smiled, patting his hand. "*When* we return, I expect Michael will be very glad to see you. He has missed you, you know."

Something about the way she said it, so sure, so confident, made some of the worry and fear that had nestled in Caleb's heart dissipate. Foolish, perhaps, for he knew the truth of what they faced, knew the odds of victory more than he wished, yet he believed her anyway. And this time, thinking of Michael, he didn't have to fake the smile that came to his face. "I miss him too. Do you think I'll see him again...soon?"

She winked. "I know you will. Now, the others will be waiting to see you, when you're ready. And, if you can, we'd love to know anything you can tell us about what happened at the barracks." She must have seen something of his reluctance in his face, for she shook her head, holding up a finger. "Only when you're ready, Caleb. Unfortunately, speaking takes a lot out of Tianya, and we have been able to get little from her. But you take your time. I'll be back to check on you soon."

Caleb watched her go, blinking furiously in a vain effort to banish the unshed tears in his eyes. *We all care about you, Caleb. You have to know that.*

Some rulers are made so by design, others by circumstance, but that one, I think, was born to lead.

"Palendesh, you're okay!" Caleb shouted, unable to keep the grin from his face as the Virtue appeared in front of him, a floating ball of blue light hovering above his bed.

"Well, of course I am," the Virtue said, but Caleb could hear the pleasure in his tone. "Still—and I do not mean to be alarming, young Caleb, but...I seem to have misplaced a few body parts. You haven't seen any lying around by chance, have you?"

Caleb blinked. "Palendesh...did you just make a joke?"

"I...yes?"

Caleb laughed. "We're going to have to work on your humor, sometime."

"Some believe," the Virtue went on defensively, "that humor, at its basest form, is a perversion of intellect, a maligning of the truth to make the improbable conceivable."

Caleb laughed again, but he quickly sobered when he remembered Adina's words. The others were waiting—Aaron, Gryle, and all the rest. They would want to hear of what had transpired at the barracks, would want to know what happened to the Speaker and the other Akalians. After all, they were counting on them to open the gates of the city, and without the Akalians there to do it...*It will be a blood bath.*

"Leave tomorrow's troubles for tomorrow, Caleb," the Virtue said, "for today has worries enough. I would not count the Akalians out and, even should they not make it to the city in time, we will still find a way. But not now. For now, I wish for you to know that I am proud of you. Because of you, Tianya is alive. Thanks to your efforts, all of the Virtues, save for Adaptation itself, will be brought to bear against Kevlane and his twisted creations."

Caleb winced, the Virtue's words causing him an almost physical pain, and he felt his face heat with shame. "I almost left her, Palendesh," he said, his voice breaking with emotion. "You weren't there or weren't answering, and the other...*he* was there." He looked at the Virtue, tears streaming from his eyes. "I almost left her."

"Yes. You almost left her. But you didn't. All are tempted in such situations, Caleb. It is not a crime to be tempted, just as it is not a brave man's shame to feel fear. Without temptation, one cannot overcome it, just as without fear there can be no courage. And you, young one, have shown much courage."

Caleb wiped furiously at his eyes, shaking his head. "It wasn't courage, Palendesh. I was terrified. I...part of me *wanted* to leave her."

"Not courage, you say," the Virtue answered, his tone thoughtful, as if he were a scholar considering a particularly complex problem. "Very well, then if it was not courage that made you carry her when most would have left her behind, if it was not courage that sent you into the dark and the cold, dragging your burden behind you...then what, Caleb, was it?"

"I..." His shoulders slumped, and he stared down at his hands which sported dozens of scratches from his time in the woods. "I don't know."

Don't you?

Caleb shifted uncomfortably. "He was...persuasive, Palendesh." He shook his head slowly, remembering the voice. "He was so sure so...confident. I've never been like that. My ma...my *mother,* she used to say I was a coward, that I was scared of my own shadow."

"And why shouldn't you be?" the Virtue asked. Though the question was simple enough, Caleb thought he could detect anger in his tone. "It is not cowardice to fear the shadows, young one. For you, unlike most, know well what they might hold, what waits, hidden, in the darkness. As for the other," he went on, his voice full of disdain, "yes, he is always sure of himself, always confident. But such surety is not gained from wisdom or from intelligence, Caleb. The servant of King Belgarin with whom I shared the bond was an example of one such as this. It is not knowledge which lends their words weight, only the pretense of it, and the tower upon which they sit and judge the world is built of nothing but artifice and illusion. For in such confidence, men show their beliefs—a belief that they are wiser than others, possessed of more knowledge, more understanding, and that they, alone, know the inner workings of the world. Beware of anyone, young one, who claims the possession of absolute truth."

"But there *are* absolute truths, Palendesh. Aren't there? The sun rises in the morning, the moon rises in the night..."

"Yes," the Virtue said, "until they don't. But as you say, there are such things as absolute truths, rules by which the world is governed. Yet such truths cannot be found in a book, or taught by a tutor; instead, a man—or a boy—must find them himself. And even in finding them, he must understand that he will never see the whole truth, not as it really is, for between it and him is a great fog, one that might be dispersed in part, but never in full, for complete viewing of the world's design is for the gods and the gods alone."

"Then what's the *point?*" Caleb demanded, suddenly angry. "Why bother learning anything at all, if we're bound to get it wrong? Why bother, if nothing can be gained from it?"

"Is that all there is to the world then, young one?" the Virtue asked. Though his voice was little more than a whisper, Caleb heard the reprimand in it. "Seeking to gain, to hoard your knowledge, your wisdom like some miser who refuses to leave his plunters and so will die atop a pile of them? Is that why you risked yourself carrying the woman through the forest?"

"I don't *know* why I did it," Caleb said, and even he could hear the wretched desperation in his voice. "I don't *know.*"

"Ah, but I think you do. You see, Caleb, the virtue, the treasure, is not in the outcome but in the quest itself, in a course set and a course followed. You did what you believed was right not because it was easy or because you stood to gain from it, and in doing so you displayed a wisdom few possess. And if the worst had come to pass, then still you would not have been wrong to do so, for it is a fool who expects to predict the world, to make of it a servant to do his bidding. A wise man does not try to master the world, but endeavors to master himself."

Caleb frowned, thinking the Virtue's words over, and several minutes passed before he spoke again. "So...he was wrong, then? The voice?"

"Yes," Palendesh responded instantly. "And even had every word he spoken been true, yet still he would have been wrong. For that...one...he would make of knowledge a whip, one with which you might be bent and broken and become a cruel, twisted thing not so unlike those creatures which we fight. I have seen it before, young one. Too many times."

The last was spoken in a haunted voice, and Caleb thought to ask the Virtue what he meant but decided against it. He thought he'd had enough of truth for one week. "They will want to know what happened at the barracks," he said. "The others. I will have to tell them."

Yes.

"They won't be happy."

"No, I suspect they will not. But, young one, unlike yourself after your own trial, they will, at least, be dry."

Caleb sighed, rising from the bed. He didn't want to, but he did it anyway. "Alright. Then let's go tell them."

CHAPTER TWENTY-FOUR

"*Damn,* but that is dark news," Brandon Gant growled, rubbing wearily at his eyes. Not that Aaron could blame him—they'd all got little enough rest over the past few weeks, the random attacks of Kevlane's creatures making sleep all but impossible.

Now, they stood in the tent that served as Aaron's command post. General Yalleck was busily frowning at nothing and no one in particular, and to his left stood Adina and Gryle, the chamberlain obviously uncomfortable about being included in the proceedings at all. Leomin and Seline stood a short distance away from the table at which the others were gathered, so close that their shoulders touched.

The two hadn't spoken yet, clearly feeling out of place, and that was fine, so far as Aaron was concerned. If Leomin started speaking, they'd no doubt pass another sleepless night listening to his stories of sexual conquest. *Or maybe not,* Aaron thought, eyeing the woman standing beside the Parnen. He'd seen, first-hand, that the woman knew how to use the knives she carried, and he didn't doubt Leomin had learned as much too—would, Aaron suspected, learn it more than he would like, should he say the wrong thing. Aaron grinned at that.

Still, regardless of how annoying Leomin was at even the best of times, given the recent attacks and the critical roles they would play in the coming battle, Aaron had thought it best to include all of the bearers of a Virtue in their strategy meetings. Brandon Gant and Adina had both agreed readily enough, though whether that

A Sellsword's Hope

was because they thought the decision wise, or that they were beginning to believe—wrongly—that Aaron knew what he was doing, he couldn't have said for sure.

"I'm sorry," Caleb said, avoiding the eyes of those gathered.

Aaron grunted. "It's not your fault, lad. Start apologizing for all the wrongs in the world now, and you'll still be doing it when you're gray-headed and lying on your death-bed."

"Agreed," the captain said. "Sorry, Caleb," he said, turning to the youth. "I didn't mean to imply anything by it, just worried is all."

And rightly so, as far as Aaron could see, but he didn't think saying so would help. Without the Akalians to open the western gate of Baresh, the army would be forced to employ more traditional siege tactics—battering rams, catapults, and more. Given that the walls would no doubt be manned by creatures that were stronger and faster than any living man, there was no telling what cruel surprises Kevlane would show them while they were stuck in the field outside the city. How many would die before they even breached the city gates? A quarter of the army? Half? All of them? It was a worrying question, but an unavoidable one, and Aaron could see in the eyes of the others gathered in the tent that they were asking it of themselves as well.

"The Akalians may yet show up," Adina said, though her voice held little hope for it. "The Speaker and his brothers will not be easily beaten, I think."

"But do we *want* them to show up?" General Yalleck asked. "I did not meet with these *Akalians* as you all did, but I have heard stories of them, of their...*exploits*." His tone made the last a condemnation. "They are not known for their kindness." He held up a hand to silence any objection. "Understand, I am aware of our situation, of the risk we take. Breaching the city will be no easy feat—many will die to see it accomplished. But I cannot help but wonder if it is wise to ally ourselves with these...*men*. After all, when a farmer finds a coyote in his henhouse, he does not invite a wolf inside as well. True, the coyote and the wolf might destroy each other, but it seems all too clear that whichever is left will feast on chicken flesh."

Brandon Gant's jaw clamped together, and he spun to Aaron, who held his hand up to tell the man to relax. "So what would you have us do, General?" he asked, his voice little more than a whisper, yet Yalleck flinched, as if he'd yelled the words.

The general cleared his throat, looking around at the eyes studying him, and shifting uncomfortably. "Well, I'd have us fight this Kevlane, of course. I'd have us fight him and beat him. I only argue that we don't need those...those *demons* to do it."

Aaron nodded slowly. "Tell me, General Yalleck, is a swordsman immune to the edge of his own blade? Will it, being his, refuse to turn in his hands, should he be careless, and teach him what I have heard some of the army refer to as a 'red lesson'?"

"Of course not," the other man said, frowning. "But I don't see—"

"And what of an archer's bow?" Aaron went on. "Is it impossible the string will snap in battle, or that, should another hold it, the arrow it shoots will find its owner as easily as any other target?"

"You know it would," Yalleck said, "but what does this have to do with anything?"

"And knowing this," Aaron went on, ignoring the man's question, "is it wiser, then, to go into battle without sword or bow and in doing so avoid the risk of your own weapon being turned against you?"

Yalleck grunted. "Any fool knows better than that."

"Yes," Aaron said pointedly, meeting the man's eyes. "Any fool does. A carpenter must have his chisel and hammer, General, a clerk his pen and parchment, for they are the tools of his profession, and without these he can't do his job. Just as a sword, a bow, armor and all the rest, are tools of a soldier's profession, and only a fool, as you say, would go into battle without either."

"I assume," Yalleck said, "you have some point, General Envelar?"

"My point is simple. The Akalians are tools—weapons we might wield against Kevlane and his army. That is not an insult but a simple fact. All of us here are also weapons, ones we hope will be great enough to strike down this bastard and whatever monstrosities he's created. As for the Akalians themselves, you have already heard the story, General: they saved not just my life, but the lives of a lot of people I care about, when they could have done nothing. They put themselves at great risk, sacrificed many of their own, to see that we survived Grinner's ambush. And the truth, General?" he said, meeting the man's eyes, "The truth is I trust them more than I trust you."

The other man hissed in a sharp intake of breath, and Adina spoke before he could. "What General Envelar is saying, Commander Yalleck," she said, and Aaron didn't miss the sharp, reprimanding look she gave him, "is that the Akalians helped us when they didn't need to, even when helping us cost them greatly. We here," she said, gesturing to the others, "are only able to stand with you against this threat *because* of the Akalians and their sacrifice. No one here doubts your courage or your resolve, but I ask that, in this, you trust me, you trust *us*."

Yalleck frowned, glancing between her and Aaron, then finally he sighed. "I suppose we have no other option. Still, if what the boy says is true, it may not matter in any case. If the creatures really did find the barracks—something I don't doubt—then it's possible whatever help they might have given us will no longer be available. What is our plan then, if they don't show up?"

Aaron shrugged. "Then we bleed, General. We bleed, Baresh bleeds, and so does that bastard Kevlane, and we can only hope he bleeds out before us."

Yalleck frowned, nodding slowly. "Yes. But, then, given what is at stake, should we not delay, in case your friends, the Akalians, do show?"

"Because of what is at stake, General, we can't afford to." He glanced around at the others, waited for them to nod their agreement before turning back to Yalleck. "We are not without weapons of our own, after all. One way or the other, we will reach Baresh the day after tomorrow, and we will end this." A silence descended on the tent then as each of them thought of the coming days, and of what end that might be.

They are scared, Co said.

Of course they are, Firefly. And they've a right to be. Shit, I'd be worried, if they weren't.

And you? she asked. *Are you scared?*

Me? he thought, gazing at the tent flap where, in the distance, the city of Baresh lay, ruled by the ancient mage whose twisted workings had haunted Aaron's dreams for months as he subjected the city's citizens to unspeakable torments to feed his lust for destruction. *Scared? Not so much, Co. Me? I'm angry.*

"They will come."

They all turned, pulled from their dark thoughts, to look at Caleb, and the youth squirmed under the weight of their gazes, clearly uncomfortable being the center of attention.

"What's that, lad?" Brandon Gant asked.

"The Akalians," Caleb said, meeting Aaron's eyes. "They'll come."

Aaron nodded slowly, watching the youth, the same boy who blanched under the attention of the others, who had traveled alone through a dark forest, through freezing rain, to carry a woman to safety. "Your Virtue has said as much?"

The youth shook his head, a small smile on his face. "Not directly. Neither Palendesh nor I has any knowledge of what happened to the Akalians."

"Then how can you sound so certain?" Leomin asked, his voice not accusing but simply curious.

Caleb's grin grew wider, and he looked around at all the others. "Because of hope, Leomin. When you have done all that you can do, all that can be done, all that is left is hope."

Aaron met the eyes of the others in the tent. No one spoke, and though their worry still showed in their faces, it was not as prevalent, as noticeable, as it had been before. He studied Caleb then, the youth once more staring at his feet as if wishing he were invisible, and smiled. For all that bastard Kevlane's power, neither he nor the Virtues were the only magic the world had to offer. "Alright then," he said, surprised to find he was feeling better himself. "If no one else has anything, we'd best get some rest. I think we're going to need it."

CHAPTER TWENTY-FIVE

"Good," Darrell said, stepping back and allowing his sword to point toward the ground. "You're getting a lot better."

Thom scowled at his empty hand and at his sword lying on the ground a few feet away as if they'd betrayed him. "Thanks, swordmaster, but it seems to me that a fella might want to keep hold of his blade, in a fight."

"True," Darrell said, grinning, "but you are much improved. Only, you do not wish to hold the sword so tightly—doing so makes of your blade a stone, where you want it to be the wind. Stones, after all, can be broken."

"And wind can dispel the stench of my shit swordplay," Thom muttered.

Darrell laughed. "It is a common mistake, Thom. Don't be so hard on yourself."

"Two weeks we been at this, and I'm just as terrible now as when we started." The first mate stalked to where his sword lay and, with a growl, he hefted it once more, turning back to the swordmaster. "Let's go again."

And they did. Again, and again, and again. And when Thom picked himself up from the ground for the seventh time, it was all he could do to keep from throwing the sword as far as he could just for the satisfaction of watching it fly. If the thing landed in a pile of deer shit, it'd only serve it right, so far as he was concerned. "*Damnit.*" The swordmaster watched him with one eyebrow raised, a small smile on his face. Thom took a slow, deep breath, fighting down his anger. "Sorry, swordmaster. Tell me, is it true what they say, that you taught the general? I mean, how to use the sword and all?"

Darrell's small smile broke into a wide grin at that. "You could say that. Though it might be more accurate to say I spent those years trying to teach Aaron how to control his anger more than anything. And, I suspect, it was a test by the gods—wishing to know the full extent of my patience, perhaps."

Thom grunted a laugh. "You passed, I suppose?"

"Well, he's still alive for now but...I'll let you know."

Thom grinned back, stretching his back in a vain effort to rid it of the ache beginning to form there. *Gods, but what do you think you're doing, old man? It's far too late to pick up a new trade. And if you're looking for one, why not try basket weaving? Nobody's ever been killed by a basket.* Despite the thought, he made his way back to the small practice area and raised his sword. "Again?"

"Certainly," Darrell agreed, but he'd barely taken a step when a shout drew their attention.

"Thomas Eugene Belan!"

Thom winced as May stalked toward them with a purposeful stride that he suspected wouldn't have been slowed in the slightest should a brick wall have been foolish enough to get in her way. Her mouth was set, her expression grim, and Thom got a suddenly wild urge to go for a run, one which he was able to resist only by the barest of margins.

"Eugene, is it?"

He risked a glance at the swordmaster—not a long one, for fear that May, like some nightmare creature, might gain speed when he wasn't looking—and saw that the other man was grinning widely. He scowled. "It's a strong name."

"Of course," the man answered, but Thom was barely listening. He was too busy watching May's approach. He'd been a sailor for a long time, had seen all sorts of tempests and hurricanes, and had survived more than his share, truth be told, but even a blind man could see the clouds gathering around the club owner.

"Hi, May," he said as she drew close.

"Hi?" she demanded. "*Hi?* Is that all you've got to say to me?"

Suddenly unsure, Thom glanced at the swordmaster but saw that the man had found something interesting on the ground that demanded his full attention. *Sure,* he thought sourly, *the man might be brave enough to take on Kevlane's monstrosities, but not a clearly pissed-off club owner.* Not that Thom could blame him. "How's your morning, May?" he ventured.

He could see the muscles of her jaw clench, could see her taking a deep breath, no doubt in an effort to keep from strangling him, for which Thom was grateful. "I heard an interesting story," she said. "You see, I heard tale from one of the soldiers who came to me looking for a new pair of boots. While I was preparing the writ for the quartermaster, he happened to mention he'd seen a certain old *fool* playing at swords. Oh, he thought it was good—and it just goes to show the world has its share of imbeciles and then some—said he'd seen this old man out here training every morning, had even been *inspired* to train more himself, if you can believe that."

"May—"

"The thing is," she went on as if he hadn't spoken, "I *know* the man must *surely* have been lying, wouldn't you say? No, I told him, Thom couldn't be out playing with swords each morning because, according to what he told me, he left early each morning to check on the stores, feeling like he had to double check them despite me telling him there were others whose job it was to look after their safety."

Thom winced. "Look, May, I knew you'd be upset and—"

"You're *right,* Thom. I *am* upset. First, that you lied to me—oh, the gods know I've told my share in the past, and I suppose I'd be willing to overlook such a thing in normal circumstances, but these *aren't* normal circumstances, are they? In fact, I'd say they're just about as abnormal as you can get—creatures that shouldn't exist attacking us near every day, and us marching to a war against a mage out of a storybook. But on top of lying, you are *here,* practicing with a sword. As if you mean to fight. Ridiculous, of course. You're a sailor, not a warrior, and—"

"I do mean to fight, May."

She stared at him in shock, as if he'd just claimed that dogs could fly. "*What?*"

Thom shrugged, dreading her anger but not willing to give in. "I'm going to fight, May. You said it yourself—we're at war. I'm not going to sit back and let others do the fighting for me, not when I can hold a sword."

"Oh, is that right? You're some great warrior now, is that it? A couple of weeks of practice, and you're ready to take on those, those *things?* Things, by the way, which even the Akalians, the best warriors in the *world,* can't beat in a one-on-one match, according to Silent. But you, a first mate, a man who has spent his life on a ship and doesn't know the first thing about battle or swordplay, you're going to fight them. Is that what you're telling me, Thom?"

"Yes. And...I know where the handle's at. So that's something."

She scowled. "Don't you try to pass this off as some joke with me, Thom. You dying isn't something to laugh at."

He sighed. "I don't plan on dyin', May."

"Says the man jumping in front of a run-away horse cart." She shook her head. "No. You'll stay and help me with the supplies. The gods know I could use the help, and you'll be better suited for that than swinging a sword and pretending to be a warrior."

Thom took a slow breath and met her eyes. "No, May. I won't. Fighting needs doin', and I aim to do it."

"*Dying* needs doing, you mean."

He set his jaw. "If that's what's called for, then that's what I'll do."

"But *why?*" she demanded, her voice coming out in a yell. "Why in the name of the gods would you be such a fool?"

"Because I love you, damnit!" he shouted back, then glanced at the swordmaster to see that the man had apparently seen something particularly interesting in the distance and was staring off at it as if his life depended on it. Which, judging by May's anger, might not be that far from the truth. Thom cleared his throat, turning back to the red-haired woman and taking her hands. "Look, May. It ain't right, me askin' folks to die to protect what I care about, and me not bein' willing to do it myself. I'm a lot of things, and you're right, a fool's probably not the worst of 'em, but I won't be a coward."

She snatched her hands away from his grip. "Then we're through, Thom. I won't be with a man who's got a death wish—the gods know I've seen enough of it without attaching myself to a man doing his level best to seek it out."

"May," Thom said, aware of the hurt in his own voice but unable to repress it. "You don't mean that. You're just angry and—"

"Damn right I mean it!" she screamed. "You want to die, then you go on ahead and die, but don't expect me to be waiting to bury you, to weep all over your grave. I won't, Thom. I just won't."

Thom stared at her, wanting to say something, wanting more than anything to make her understand, but her face was set, her eyes challenging, and he knew that anything he said would be the wrong thing. So he only nodded, doing his best to keep his hurt from his expression. "If that's your will, lady." He cleared his throat again, turning to the swordmaster. "Tomorrow, same time? I reckon we got one more day left, I'd best get what practice in as I can."

"Of course," the swordmaster said, and the compassion in his face made Thom's own sadness well up all the greater, as if in answer. "I'll see you in the morning, Thom."

The first mate nodded. "Until then, swordmaster." He turned back to May, and bowed his head. "Whatever comes, May, whatever you want, just know I love you, alright? Never thought I'd say that to another person in my life, and I don't expect I'll ever say it again, no matter how the next few days go. But I love you." And with that, he started away, back toward the army camp and to his own small tent. Suddenly, he was tired. So very, very tired.

***

May watched the first mate shuffle away, saw the slump in his shoulders, a slump *she* had put there, and at once she felt ashamed, heartbroken, and angry. But more than anything, she was afraid. She wanted to yell at him, to call him a fool, wanted to scream for him to come back, to tell him she didn't mean it, to tell him she loved him too. She wanted to beg and plead and be reassured, but she did none of those things. Instead, she only watched in silence as he stalked back into the camp. And she felt it when she could no longer see him, felt it in her bones like a presentiment of doom, an echo of a tragedy that had not yet happened but seemed, just then, inevitable.

"You are wrong, you know."

She turned to see the swordmaster staring at her, and for all the expression his face showed, he might as well have been talking about the weather. "What?" she said, taken aback.

"I said, you're wrong," he repeated, a simple observation, one said without anger or malice.

May took a deep breath, preparing to tell the swordmaster that her and Thom's business was theirs alone, and that he'd do well to keep out of it. But for some reason, the words wouldn't come, and she only sighed, feeling deflated and tired, her shoulders slumping much like Thom's. "Why do you say that?"

"It's simple enough, isn't it?" Darrell said calmly. "At their core, every man or woman must have things for which they stand, principles on which they refuse to compromise. It is these principles that make us who we are. And should any of us be willing—or even able—to do what it is you ask of Thom, to abandon those principles at a moment's notice for the sake of pleasing another or ourselves—perhaps *most* of all, ourselves—then they mean nothing. And if *they* mean nothing, then *we* mean nothing. Do you understand?"

"So what, then?" May demanded. "I'm supposed to allow him to march off to war like a fool, knowing full well he'll die?"

The swordmaster gave a small thoughtful smile, turning away from her to gaze back into the camp. "I am not from Avarest—not originally—and it has been many years since I have last seen the city. But even I, little more than a stranger to its winding ways and busy streets, have heard of May Tanarest. The woman who would spit in the face of the gods themselves, should they attempt to bar her path. A woman who criminals, both great and small, have learned to fear. Even Avarest's Council, I suspect, steps warily around such a woman."

May, who'd been preparing herself for a shouting match, frowned instead. "Not that I'm normally opposed to flattery, swordmaster, but is there a point to all this? After all, I know well the life I've led. Its goods and its evils sing me to sleep every night like two birds perched on my shoulders."

"Strong-willed, they say," he went on as if she hadn't spoken, "a woman who could argue the rain down from the clouds. I wonder if a woman such as that would ever let another tell her what she was 'allowed' to do."

May scowled. "If I was about to do something foolish that ended with pain and a cold grave, I'd hope they would."

He nodded. "Of course." Then he turned to her, meeting her eyes. "And would you listen, do you suppose? To such advice?"

She grunted. "What are you driving at, Darrell? Time's wasting, and I've a thousand things to do before the day's done."

"Clever too, the rumors tell," he went on. "So, I suspect you know well enough my point, but I will say it just the same. Thom is not a man to be ordered about, to be told when to sit and when to come and when to heel. People have dogs for such purposes. And even if Thom *were* such a man, would you be satisfied with that? Forgive me, but I find it difficult to believe that *the* May Tanarest, the fiery-haired she-devil who vexed even Avarest's most powerful crime bosses, would believe such a man her equal."

May frowned, mostly because he was right. It was one of the things that had first attracted her to Thom—his courage, and a directness, so different from the sort of people she'd spent her life associating with. Even Captain Festa, a man known for losing his temper, incited no fear in Thom. He was a rock, *her* rock. Or...at least...he had been. *Gods, I am a fool. What have I done?* Another thought struck her then and she let out a soft, ragged sigh. "But he'll die, Darrell. Surely, you see that."

"Perhaps," Darrell agreed. "But then, all men die, May. It is the way of the world, after all. We are born, we live, and we die."

"Sure," she said sarcastically, "but not all of us die with a sword buried in our guts."

"That's true," the swordmaster agreed. "Perhaps you're right. Maybe it would be better to keep him away from the battle. Of course, he might still be attacked when walking around the camp. It *is* full of soldiers, after all. Maybe it would be better if you didn't allow him to leave your quarters—that, I think, would be safest. Although," he continued, frowning, "even that is no guarantee, for walking about your rooms, he might slip and fall, break his neck. I've known men it has happened to. Maybe, then, the answer is to find a cage—not too large, of course. You wouldn't want him to get any ideas and start moving around more than is strictly necessary. A dangerous thing, moving. So many things could happen." He scratched his chin where a thin scruff of white hair had begun to grow. "You could tie him down, I suppose, but—"

"Alright, alright," May huffed. "I get your point, damnit. Has anyone ever told you, Darrell, that you're a bit of a bastard?"

The swordmaster laughed. "Aaron has told me on more than one occasion, and lately Sergeant Wendell has taken it in his mind to remind me, lest I forget." He met her eyes, and when he continued his voice was serious, but kind. "Have you ever seen an exotic bird in a cage, May? I have. I have walked city squares where all manner of animal and beast sat caged, and one thing that I have noticed is that, without fail, those majestic creatures shrink to their cages. The feathers of the birds lose their luster, and the once muscled, graceful bodies of great cats become too thin or too fat, and they lose, in the caging, all they once were. And the worst of it? If you look deeply into their eyes, you can see the memory there of the greatness they once had, the greatness they lost."

Unexpectedly, tears began to gather in May's eyes, and she wiped them away furiously. "I've really screwed things up, haven't I?"

Darrell smiled reassuringly. "He loves you, May. No damage has been done that cannot be undone, so long as you both continue to draw breath."

She gave a weak snort. "I guess I'd better hurry then."

The swordmaster shook his head, looking out into the woods, toward the city of Baresh. "I'm an old man, May. Old and tired, and I've long since lost count of the number of battles I've survived that should have been my last." He turned back to her. "As long as we draw breath, there is hope."

"Hope," May repeated dubiously. "It hasn't been on any of my supply lists, swordmaster, I can tell you that much." She sighed heavily. "I love him, too."

"I know. And he loves you. For love, you would save him. For love, he would save you, if he could. Speak with him, May. While there is still time."

"Doesn't sound much like hope, Swordmaster."

Darrell smiled, but there was no humor in it. "I'm an old man," he repeated.

CHAPTER TWENTY-SIX

Aaron crouched on the same hill upon which he'd stood what felt like months ago, gazing at the distant walls of Baresh. He remembered feeling afraid then, afraid he would fail, afraid he, and those who followed him—Wendell, Darrell, and Leomin—would suffer, would die, because of his failure. Now, there were thousands in the nearby camp, tens of thousands of men and women who had come to fight Kevlane and his creations. Should he fail now, he would be responsible not just for the deaths of his friends, but of everyone, and thousands would go to their graves with him to thank.

You are not alone, Aaron, Co said. *Not anymore. You have friends here to help you—this is not a burden you must carry alone.*

If not, then why is it so damned heavy?

The Virtue didn't respond, and he thought that just as well, for any answer she might have given would have rung false. Staring at the fields spread out before the city, at the city itself, Aaron was troubled. Kevlane knew the army was coming—almost every night, they had been attacked by his creations, and the cost of their journey had risen—the last time he'd checked with May—to over a thousand dead. The mage knew, and yet the fields in front of the city walls were empty, the city itself some great, slumbering beast in the darkness. It would awaken, sooner or later, and when it did, it would be hungry.

"Where's his *army?*" Aaron hissed, frustrated. After all, from everything Caleb had said—and on such matters, he'd long since learned to trust the youth—Kevlane should still have thousands of regular troops at his command, soldiers remaining from the force that had attempted the attack on Perennia only a short time ago. Yet, no campfires burned in the plains in front of the city, no great host stood ready to meet them. There was only the stillness and the silence that were more unnerving than if an army *had* been there.

Tomorrow, they would reach the city, and he suspected whatever surprises the mage had in store would be revealed quickly enough. And without the Akalians to open the gate, they would pay in blood for each step they took toward the city. Aaron frowned. "What are you planning, you bastard?"

His bond with the Virtue alerted him to a presence behind him. *Foolish,* he scolded himself as he spun, *wandering off on your own.* The blade was in his hand before he'd finished turning. What looked like a dozen shadows separated themselves from the trees, gliding forward. "Come on then," he hissed, and found that he was almost eager for the fight to come. This, at least, was something he understood, something he could control.

"The magi, for all his cruelty, for all his malice, is no fool."

Aaron frowned at the familiar voice, but then the Speaker of the Akalians stepped out of the shadows of the trees, and the pale moonlight illuminated him and the dozen black-garbed figures standing with him.

"You're alive," he said. After hearing Caleb's tale and seeing no sign of the Akalians for days, he'd felt sure they had all been killed at the barracks. Relief flooded him, banishing the feeling of doom that had plagued him for days. Still, it was clear their survival had been a near thing. The Akalians looked bruised and battered, their black clothes were stained with blood and ripped and torn in several places. The Speaker looked little better. His left forearm was bandaged, and he held himself stiffly, the way a man did when he was in pain.

"Gods, how many did the bastard send after you?"

The Akalian shook his head slowly, his gaze far away as if in memory. "Not enough. Not quite. Aaron Envelar," he said, his voice reluctant. "I regret to inform you that we lost Caleb and the woman, Tianya. During the fighting—"

"They made it back," Aaron said, wanting to alleviate some of the pain he heard in the other man's voice. "The boy made a stretcher and dragged her back here, if you could believe that."

The Akalian's relief was visible, and he breathed out a heavy sigh. "Thank the gods for that, at least. And they are well?"

"As well as could be expected. Better, actually. The healers tell me Tianya has made a full recovery. As for Caleb..." He wasn't sure what to say about the youth. His body had healed well enough, but Aaron hadn't missed the haunted look in the youth's eyes, when he thought no one was watching. He'd tried to talk to Caleb about it, but, so far at least, he had refused to tell him what was wrong. "Well...something's troubling him," he said finally.

The Akalian nodded thoughtfully. "It is a miracle that he made it through the woods with the woman. A miracle, I suspect, aided in large part to the Virtue he bears—though I do not underestimate the boy himself. A remarkable youth, one who will one day become a remarkable man."

"If given time enough," Aaron said.

"Yes. If given time enough. But what I mean to say, Aaron Envelar, is that in such an extremity, Caleb would have called deeply on the power of the bond, and in such callings...there is danger."

Aaron frowned. He'd thought as much, but he'd hoped he'd been wrong. To hear it from the Akalian's own mouth did nothing to reassure him. "You mean something like the rages I feel? But I thought you said I could control those."

"Yes," the Speaker said. "It was what you needed to hear, at the time, and it was not a lie. You—or any bearer of a Virtue—can control its side effects. For a time."

Aaron sighed. "But not forever."

"No," the other man said, shaking his head. "Not forever. Man was not meant for such power, Aaron Envelar, as the Virtues bestow upon him. And while the...*repercussions* of your own Virtue mean that your anger is given life and breath, they are all different." His eyes got a faraway look again, and Aaron didn't need the bond with Co to realize the man was thinking of a certain desert, and the woman and child he knew there. "For every gift, a curse."

"You say his is different," Aaron said. "How?"

"With your rage, you burn, Aaron Envelar," the Speaker said, meeting his eyes. "But knowledge is different—the truth, I need not tell you, can oft times be a cold thing. Cold and terrible."

Aaron thought of Caleb, and all the others, Leomin and Gryle, Seline. Each of them battling their own demons, their own curses. And would they be able to hold those demons off long enough to do what must be done? "Come on," he said. "Let's get you back to camp. I imagine you and your men would like a hot meal and some rest."

The Akalian gave him a small smile. "A rest would be good, I think."

CHAPTER TWENTY-SEVEN

The day, when it came, came like any other. The sun rose slowly into the sky, once more chasing the moon and the shadows away. Animals of the forest scurried through the trees, and birds sang their morning song. But this day, Aaron knew, would not be like those that had come before it. Today, the fate of the world would be decided, for good or ill.

He passed dozens of tents where soldiers were doing last-minute checks on their gear and weapons, preparing for the final march, the one that would lead them to Baresh.

Seeing them all as he walked, feeling the nervousness that covered the army camp like a shroud, Aaron had to resist the urge to bring his own sword out again, to test its edge. He'd done so at least a dozen times already during the sleepless night just passed. He had more important things to do just now.

The Speaker of the Akalians walked beside him, and despite the dangers they faced, soldiers paused in their preparations to stare at him warily as if some wild, ferocious beast had been brought among them, displaying a distrust that had been bred into them since childhood. But if the black-garbed man noticed, he gave no sign, seemingly lost in his own thoughts.

The command tent was bustling with activity when they arrived, a flurry of messengers and scouts coming and going with reports. Aaron stepped inside to see a harried-looking Brandon Gant speaking with a messenger. He said something, and the man nodded before hurrying past the sellsword and the Speaker without a word. "Any news?" Aaron said.

"Oh, there's all kinds of it," Brandon said. "Just none that's of any use."

Aaron nodded. "Still no sign of Baresh's army?"

Brandon grunted, shaking his head. "None. It's as if the bastards just up and vanished."

"I doubt we're that lucky," Aaron said.

He glanced at Adina where she stood at the table with General Yalleck, watching him. They'd spoken little the night before. There had been a thousand things Aaron wanted to say, things he needed to tell her, but somehow every time he'd opened his mouth, nothing had come out. So instead they had lain in the small bed they shared, holding each other, and taking comfort in that. Some things, after all, didn't need to be said to be known.

"Well, I'll show you what we've got so far," Brandon said, motioning to the table where a map of the area surrounding the city had been laid out, spotted with small pieces representing the separate sections of the army.

As he followed the captain to the table, Aaron noted the suspicious glare Yalleck shot the Speaker, fingering the hilt of the sword sheathed at his waist. "Good morning, everyone," Aaron said. "I apologize for the earliness of the hour, but now that the Speaker and his brothers are here, we need to discuss strategy."

Brandon grunted. "Wasn't sleepin' anyway."

"Right. Now, we need to gather the bulk of our forces at the gate." He glanced at the Speaker who nodded. "Once the Akalians open the gate, we'll need to drive through as quickly as we can. That should—"

"*If.*"

General Yalleck was looking at the Speaker, his lip curled with distaste. "You have something to add, General?"

"Yes, I do." He glanced around at the others. "Oh, come now. You have heard as well as I—these *Akalians* don't even number twenty men. And somehow, we're supposed to believe that they are going to manage to sneak into the gatehouse and get the gate open? I doubt that Baresh's soldiers will just sit back and let that happen. And even if they *could* open the gate, I would not feel comfortable trusting such a scheme."

What he meant, Aaron suspected, was he didn't feel comfortable trusting the Akalians themselves. "Well, then that's good news, General. It's a war, after all—you're not supposed to be comfortable. As for the Akalians being able to open the gate..." He turned once more to look at the Speaker, and again the man answered him with a nod. "If the Speaker says they can, I believe it. We will march on the city today. Tonight, the Akalians will make their move, and so we'll need to bring the army close to the gate. Now, we will need all of the Virtue-bearers waiting near the gate and—" He cut off as Yalleck made a sound that was something between a laugh and a growl. "Is something else bothering you, General?"

Yalleck looked around the tent incredulously. "Gods, but you've got to be kidding, right? Not only does our strategy rely on these"—he gestured at the Speaker—"these...*men* to do what is essentially impossible, but we intend to keep all the Virtue-bearers in the same place? And what if they are needed elsewhere? Would it not be wiser to conduct a slow siege operation? If the fleet of ships we sent manages to take the docks, then we can starve out our enemy. There is no need—"

"Yes, there is," Aaron said. "Understand, General, this is no normal war, and our enemy is no normal man. We march against a mage from ancient times, one who has had weeks to prepare for our coming. He has spent that time growing stronger and terrorizing the innocents inside the city's walls with his abominations. We will not, on top of all of that, starve them. As for the Virtue-bearers, it is necessary they be close to the walls, along with the Ghosts, and the best troops that Captain Gant has already picked from the other armies. Once the gate opens, we must push through as hard as we can, as fast as we can. As you say, I doubt Kevlane will sit back and let us walk in without a fight."

Yalleck shook his head. "Madness. And if the gate doesn't open? If they fail? Then what?"

"It will open." They all turned to look at the Speaker, even Yalleck seeming taken back by the certainty in his voice. "My brothers and I," the Speaker went on in a soft voice, "have been fighting this evil for longer than you can imagine, General Yalleck. We have been here since the beginning, doing what we could to stop the harm that he would cause. We have dedicated our lives to this, to protecting the world from the magi and his evil. We will not fail."

They were all silent then, even the general who seemed to have no words to answer the conviction with which the Akalian spoke. Aaron glanced around and gave a final nod. "Alright then. We all have things to do—let's get them done."

***

"Do you really believe they can do it?"

Aaron looked up from the map of Baresh to see Adina standing beside him. The others were gone, seeing to their own tasks so, for the moment, the two of them were alone. The Akalians?" he asked. "Yes, I believe they can. I have to believe it, Adina. It's the best way. If they don't..." He trailed off, shaking his head.

"I know," she said, coming close and putting a hand on his shoulder. "I believe you. Where is the Speaker now?"

"He's meeting with Caleb," Aaron said. "They're going over the gate mechanism one more time, making sure everything is in order."

Adina nodded. "Aaron, there was something else about what you said. If the Virtue-bearers are stationed at the gate to help force the army's way through, then you'll be among the first into the city."

"Yes," Aaron said. "I know, Adina, it's dangerous, but it has to be done."

She opened her mouth to say something else, but suddenly the tent flap was thrown open and the young giant, Bastion, peered inside. "Forgive me, General, Queen. But Captain Gant says to tell you the army will begin marching within the hour."

Adina nodded. "Thank you, Bastion. We will be ready." The man left, and she turned back to the sellsword. "Aaron," she began, then paused, swallowing hard.

"I know, Adina," he said. "Me too. But everything's going to be okay." She gave a nod and walked out of the tent. Aaron watched her go, surprised by how easily the lie had come. Whatever else happened, things were just about as far away from okay as they could get.

CHAPTER TWENTY-EIGHT

Simon lay in his bed, pretending to be asleep while his mother opened the door of his room and peered inside to check on him. She did so every night, as if he were still a kid like his little brother, Everett, as if *he* were the one who woke up crying from nightmares about monsters under his bed. Ridiculous, of course. Simon was eleven years old—practically a man grown—and everyone knew monsters didn't hide under the bed. What would they even *eat?*

Still, he made sure none of his annoyance showed as he waited impatiently, his eyes squeezed shut, until his mother finally left. Once she was gone, he remained unmoving, listening to the hushed, frightened sounds of his mother and father speaking in the hallway outside his door. Though he couldn't make out their words, he thought he knew well enough what they would be. Something about the army camped outside the city walls, *that* was sure—it was all they seemed to want to talk about since news had arrived early in the morning.

The army *this* and the army *that* all in hushed, frightened tones. It was the same reason Simon's father had refused to let him play outside with his friends and, when Simon had argued, had sent him up to his room. It wasn't fair but, then, parents were *never* fair. Simon's eleven years had taught him that much, just as it had taught him that monsters didn't hide under beds, but in dark alleys where they might chomp on anybody that walked by. But

Simon wasn't scared of them, just as he wasn't scared of the army outside the city walls.

Simon considered himself a risk-taker, a warrior. He had long since lost the count of the bandits and monsters he'd slain over his eleven years of life, but he was confident it was in the thousands. Big or small, scaly or slimy, they had all succumbed to his sword—a sword that, at the moment, was a long stick with the twigs trimmed away, hidden carefully under his bed. Yet it was a sword for all that, just as the monsters he fought were dangerous even though they didn't, strictly, exist.

He heard the door to his parents' room shut and risked opening his eyes to look around. Satisfied they wouldn't be back, he pulled the coverlet aside and crept to his room's small window, careful to avoid the parts of the floor that might creak and give him away. The moon was high in the sky, bathing the dark city in its pale light, and Simon was reminded of a story his father had once told him. The story claimed the moon was alive, that it was a man who had been trapped up there, tricked or lied to by some goddess—Simon forgot which—and left to spend all eternity looking upon the world but never again allowed to be a part of it.

He didn't believe a word of it, of course, and thought it all too likely the story had just been his father's way of trying to scare him away from his nightly excursions. It hadn't worked. Nor had the stories about strange creatures roaming the city—his best friend, Blake, had even claimed to have *seen* one of the things—dissuaded him. Blake said the thing had looked like a man, but with its face all cut up, its arms far too long and far too thin. Ridiculous, of course. Simon had imagined—had *seen*—a lot of different monsters in his time. There were big ones with claws, hairy ones with sharp teeth and thick muscles. A thousand different ones, but none of them with arms so small. How could such a skinny monster be dangerous at all?

The truth was, and though it hurt Simon to admit it about his best friend, Blake was a bit of a coward. Simon used to try to get the other boy to go on his nightly monster hunts with him, but his friend had always refused, claiming his parents would be angry if they found out. So Simon had long since stopped trying to convince him. And what kind of silly reason was that to keep from having fun, anyway? Parents were *always* angry, always complaining about kids sneaking out or tracking mud through the house, torturing you with lessons from an old tutor whose breath smelled of garlic, and then getting mad when you ran out on the lesson—as if anybody could be blamed for doing such a thing.

Still, Simon felt good. The night was clear, without rain. Perfect weather for fighting monsters. So he crept out of his room and down their house's small hallway to stand outside his parents' door. He was rewarded with the sound of his father's snoring, a sound that had, on more than one occasion, represented the angry growls of a monster or wild beast that had somehow managed to sneak into Simon's house, and that had quickly been defeated by Simon's skill. Simon the Swordmaster. It was what they called him. Or, at least, it was what they *would* call him, when he got older and was able to get himself a *real* sword and fight *real* bandits.

For now, make-believe monsters were good enough—and no real bandit or thief was ever as scary as the creatures Simon fought. He waited another moment then, satisfied that his mother and father would be asleep for hours yet, he crept back to his room and grabbed his sword before easing the window open and climbing out. He no longer had to look for the handholds on their two-story house, he had memorized each long ago and could have done it with his eyes closed.

Seconds later, he was in the street, his trusty sword in his hand. He'd just finished killing the last of the monsters waiting for him there and was taking a minute to catch his breath when a girl ran up to him. She was pretty—he'd seen her in the market a few days ago, but this time instead of the long blonde hair she'd had before, she had short, dark hair. Because, after all, it was *his* imagination, and he could change things however he wanted.

"Sir Simon," the woman said, "we need your help."

"Oh?" he said, in a voice not high and squeaking like in real life, but brave and sure and deep. The voice of a hero. "What is it, fair maiden?"

They were always saying that, in the stories. Fair maiden this and fair maiden that.

"Monsters," she said, her eyes wide and adoring as she gazed at him, taking in his shining white armor. "There are monsters, Sir Simon, climbing over the walls. Please help us."

"Of course, fair maiden," he said, taking her hand and kissing it gracefully, and the real Simon, the boy who stood in the street holding the invisible woman's hand in one of his own while the other held the long stick, felt himself blushing as he did so.

He'd lived in Baresh all his life, and their house was close to the western wall of the city. Usually, the monsters didn't go up that far—no doubt scared of being caught by the guards and having them tell his parents again. Simon didn't think his father would *actually* put bars on the windows, but he didn't really want to test him. But the night was still young and his parents had gone to bed earlier than normal after a long day at the market. He thought he could probably slay the monsters and be back long before they woke up.

So, glancing down the street both ways, Simon hurried toward the nearest staircase leading to the top of the wall. He waited at the corner of a building, studying the area near the staircase for any hint of monsters or—more dangerous still—guards. He waited, patiently, for about three seconds, then decided he was clear and sprinted for the staircase.

He took the steps two at a time, staying as low as he could, sure that at any moment he'd hear a shout from a guard. But there was nothing, no one. Except, of course, the monster waiting for him at the top of the stairs. It swiped at him with a cruel, taloned claw, but one quick strike of his sword sent the offending limb spiraling into the darkness. His next sword stroke took the monster's head from its shoulders.

When he reached the landing at the top of the wall, he crouched, shoulders tense, as he waited for one of the guards to give a shout. Never before had he made it all the way up the steps without being caught. No matter how much he looked, how long he spent watching their patrols, the guards always seemed to notice him. He usually escaped without getting caught—Simon the Swordmaster was fast, like, *really* fast—but sometimes the guards, who outnumbered him, managed it. His father had promised him the next time they did, Simon would be sleeping on his stomach for a week. So Simon waited, struggling to contain his excitement about making it this far as he scanned the battlements carefully for any sign of the guards.

It was for this reason he noticed something hanging over the edge of the wall, caught the barest glint of metal in the moonlight. Frowning, he looked around once more, assuring himself no guards were near, then crept closer to see what it was. Not a make-believe monster, not this. *This* was real. Though, it had to be said, it did share some similarities with the monster claws he imagined. But where he always envisaged sharp, cruel talons of bone, the hooks on this device were metal. Three in all, each as sharp as the last, and two of which appeared to have caught on the stones of the wall. Simon's heart began to gallop in his chest as he realized Blake might have been right after all.

Fighting monsters was one thing—something any champion swordsman was sworn to do, but this was different. He'd read enough stories (most snuck behind his father and mother's back) to know this was a grappling hook, the kind used by thieves and ...and *assassins*. His mouth suddenly incredibly dry, Simon scanned the wall, and soon saw other grappling hooks along its length.

He was counting them—had reached six—when he heard what sounded like the beginning of a shout, quickly silenced, and spun to look at the corner of the battlements less than thirty feet away. At first, he thought that he must have imagined the sound the same way that his younger brother imagined monsters under his bed. After all, everyone knew the night played tricks on you, if you weren't careful and...Simon's breath caught in his throat as what he'd taken to be no more than shadows at the corner of the battlements *moved*.

There were two shadows outlined vaguely in the pale moonlight, moving oddly, as if they were hugging. No, that wasn't quite right. Their feet were moving too, and it didn't look like they were hugging, not really. It looked as if they were dancing. Then one of the figures stumbled away from the other, collapsing to the ground. He sprawled in the light, and Simon saw that he wore the uniform of a city guardsman.

Simon had never seen a dead body before—at least, not a real one—but there was something *wrong* about the figure on the ground. It took him several confused seconds to figure out what it was, and when he did a shiver of terror ran up his spine. The figure's neck was bent at an impossible angle, one no living man could ever bear. Simon scrambled back to the stairs and huddled behind the stone railing, his heart hammering in his chest.

He knew he should leave, should run home as fast as his legs could carry him, but he found that the thought of turning his back on whatever or whoever—the shadows made it impossible to tell for sure—had killed the guard was even worse than staying where he was. At least here, he could see the bandit, if that was what it was. Even as he had the thought, half a dozen other figures joined the first, and the group began to make their way along the battlements, in his direction. *Oh gods.*

As they drew closer, Simon saw that they were only men after all, but the realization didn't give him as much relief as he would have liked. Men, maybe, but that didn't make the city guardsman any less dead.

Simon the Brave would have stood up then and said something tough, would have fought and beaten them all. But, cowering behind the wall, he realized that he *wasn't* Simon the Brave. He never had been. Simon the Small, maybe. Simon the Scared. But certainly not Simon the Brave. Movement on the battlements caught his eye, and he looked further down the wall where three figures were making their way up the steps. They wore heavy robes, but even in the near darkness he could see that their arms were too long and too thin, just like Blake had described.

The bogeymen. They were real. Just as the long swords they carried were real. Barely daring to breathe, Simon turned back to look at the bandits and saw that one seemed to be staring right at him. He prepared himself to run, but the figure made no move toward him, and a moment later it turned back to the three bogeymen. Then there was a *pop* in the air, and the robed figures charged forward, impossibly fast, their swords leading.

***

The Speaker and his brothers watched the three abominations as they stepped off the stairs and onto the battlements. A quick look at the other side of the wall showed that his brothers there had finished off the regular guardsmen and were even now sprinting toward him and the others. He wondered at the child crouched by the top of the stairs, but dismissed it immediately. Whatever poor luck had brought the child to the walls on such an ill-fated night, it was clear he was no threat.

He turned back to the three figures in time to see them rush forward with their unnatural speed. The first was on them in seconds, the narrow battlements making it impossible for more than two to wield their long blades at once. Its sword flashed toward the nearest Akalian, and the black-garbed figure responded with a perfect parry. Or, at least, what would have been perfect, had the magi's dark arts not invested the creature with a speed far beyond that of normal mortals. So instead of turning the creature's blow, the Akalian's sword arrived too late to keep the slender blade from slicing a deep, bloody furrow across his left arm. The creature tried to pull the blade back, but didn't manage it before the wounded Akalian dropped his own blade and grasped the creature's, keeping it in place, the sharp edge cutting into his hand and his arm deeply where he held it.

The creature had time to cock its head in the vaguely confused way of its kind, then two more of the Speaker's brothers lunged forward, their swords impaling it before it could pull its own blade free. The creature collapsed, and the wounded Akalian's blood soaked left arm hung limply at his side now. The Akalian bent to retrieve his sword, but his fingers wouldn't obey his commands, and he stood a moment later, weaponless.

He met the Speaker's eyes then, and though his wounds made him incapable of communicating using the intricate hand-language which belonged to them and them alone, his eyes spoke well enough. And so the Speaker wasn't surprised when the next creature rushed forward, and his wounded brother charged. A slender blade flashed out, tearing through the Akalian's stomach, but his momentum sent him stumbling into the sword's wielder, and they both fell to the ground.

The Akalians didn't hesitate, their own blades flashing out, and if some of the blades seeking the struggling creature found their brother, then he and they took it as no more than a kindness.

In another second, the thing was done, and two more corpses lay on the battlements. *And now there are eleven of us,* the Speaker thought, as he and his remaining brothers turned to face the last of the creatures.

***

"Hold the fucking line!"

The bellow came from somewhere off to Darrell's right. He couldn't be sure over the din of battle, but he thought he recognized the voice as that of Sergeant Wendell, and he spared a thought to hope the man made it through the next few hours as he waited for the next of the creatures to come upon him. The swordmaster stood in a line hundreds of soldiers across, a line that buckled as the creatures attacked.

Harsh breaths from beside him drew his attention. A young soldier stood there, his eyes wide and wild. "D-demons," he rasped. "They're demons."

Darrell could understand the man's fears, for whatever they were, the creatures were not human, not any longer. And when they'd appeared on the western side of the army, fifty of them at least, they had done so silently, with none of the shouts and horn blasts that usually accompanied an attack. They'd raced toward the army like wraiths come to harvest the souls of the damned, and though he had fought them before, even the swordmaster had felt a surge of panic at their silent approach.

"Not demons," he said, as much to himself as to the other soldier. "And whatever they are, they still bleed. They still die. Remember that, lad."

If the soldier meant to answer, he didn't have a chance, for a second later another one of the creatures charged Darrell's spot in the line, and he and those to either side of him were too busy trying to keep from dying to talk. Normally, such an attack against an established line would have been suicide, but the creatures' great speed meant they could attack and retreat with little chance of falling victim to a counter stroke. Not that they did retreat. Whatever else the mage's dark workings did, it seemed to make his victims care nothing for their own survival. Each appeared intent only on taking as many soldiers with them into death as they could.

And take they did, their long slender blades reaping a bloody harvest on Perennia's army, and for every creature that was brought down, half a dozen defenders fell with him. As if summoned by his thoughts, a creature charged Darrell's part of the line. Its blade flashed out, lightning-quick, and it was only his long years of experience that allowed the swordmaster to anticipate the strike and duck under it. The sword passed inches over his head, embedding itself in the heavy shield of the man on Darrell's left. The creature tried to jerk the blade free, but before it could, several blades lashed out, and though they were panicked, uncoordinated strikes, the combined blows proved enough to bring the creature down.

"See?" he said, turning back to the young soldier. "They..." He cut off as he saw two others dragging the young soldier back to the line of healers stationed behind the army. Darrell only got a glance at the young soldier before he was hidden from view by others stepping forward to fill the gap he'd left, but it was enough to see the deep gash in his neck, the blood almost black in the ruddy glow of the torches spaced out behind the battle line.

Dead then. Suddenly feeling very tired, Darrell swept his gaze around the area behind the line and saw what appeared to be hundreds of the dead and wounded, the army's healers shuffling around the bodies, doing what they could to mend them or, as more often was the case, to ease the agony of their passing into Salen's Fields. How many were there? he wondered. Two hundred? A thousand? There was no way to tell for sure. Too many, that much was certain, far too many for the hour or two that had passed since battle was joined.

And even those terrible losses were nowhere near as bad as they could have been. As they would have been, had Caleb not prepared the army with the caltrops that were even now being thrown over the shoulders of the defenders to litter the ground between them and the creatures who moved wraith-like in the darkness. Thanks to the devices of the youth's design, many of the creatures were wounded, their feet torn to ribbons by the time they made it to the line, but still they fought, as if such wounds meant nothing to them. Still they killed.

There was a shout nearby, and Darrell pulled his gaze away from the dead and dying to where more creatures were rushing forward. He forced down the bitter ache of exhaustion and sadness that threatened to overcome him and raised his sword, preparing to meet the charge. There would be time, later, to grieve for the wounded. If, that was, any of them survived.

***

Captain Gant scanned the latest casualty report, his jaw muscles working furiously. "This just from the southern side?" he asked the sweaty, panting messenger in front of him.

"Yes sir," the man said. "Sergeant Biladen wished for me to tell you that he's in need of reinforcements."

Of course he is, Brandon thought, *who isn't?* But he gave a sharp nod. "Very well—go back to the sergeant and tell him that he'll have the men he needs. Hurry now." The messenger nodded and left the tent at a run, leaping into his horse's saddle and speeding away, but Brandon noticed the way the man slumped in his seat, clearly exhausted. He sympathized. He, too, was tired, weary from coordinating the army's troops and healers, exhausted from report after report—all of them bad, it seemed—of casualties, of reinforcements, and of the healers running low on string or gut.

He glanced at May. The club owner had proved invaluable since the battle had started, seeming to know exactly how much of each supply they had and where the quickest place to get it would be. Still, he could see his own worries, his own fears etched on her features. Battle had only been joined a few hours before, and already nearly a thousand troops lay dead or wounded. For at least the fifth time since the fighting began, Brandon fought down the urge to send a messenger to Aaron, asking for the Virtue-bearers to reinforce the army's flagging line.

After all, he knew the importance of what they planned, knew that, should the Akalians manage to get the gate open, the Virtue-bearers would be needed to push through the troops inevitably waiting on the other side. Aaron had said that he *would* split the bearers up, if needed, but only in the greatest extremity, for to do so would be risk losing their one chance at a quick victory. And Brandon didn't believe they were at that point—not yet. But they were getting closer by the minute, and if the Akalians didn't manage to get the gate open soon...well, better not to think of that.

"Celad."

"Sir?" the messenger said, stepping forward from where he waited against the tent's wall along with three others.

"Go see that Sergeant Senler's squad is sent to Biladen's aid. You know where?"

"Yes sir," the man said, which was just as well as they'd spent the hours of the night before going over where each commander would be.

"Good, and Celad?"

"Sir?"

"The healer's on the southwestern side are running low on gut and bandages. See they're sent some."

"Of course, sir."

Then the man was gone, and Brandon took the spare moment—there had been few enough in the last hours—to glance once again at the map of the terrain around Baresh. All along it, markers denoted each squad's deployment. Beside the map, a pile of quickly-depleting markers waited, and he grabbed the one representing Senler's troops, moving it onto the map. On the other side of the table sat several other markers, and he did his best not to look at the pile that had been rapidly growing in the last hours, for those markers represented squads that had been crippled in the fighting or—in a few cases—slaughtered outright.

All this slaughter already, and when the sun rose in a few hours' time, it would do so on a field covered in the dead and dying, yet still there had been no sign of Baresh's army. *Where are they, damnit?*

He saw May looking at the tent flap with a mixture of fear and anxiety. "I'm sure he's fine, May."

"How can you be sure?" she said. She didn't sound angry, only tired and scared.

"We would have heard news. Besides, I placed him near Aaron and the others—if there's a safer place to be during the battle, I don't know of it."

She didn't press him further, which was just as well. He'd done what he could, but the truth was, Brandon's own thoughts were dark and growing darker, and he had little comfort to give. Still, none of the fear had left her face, and he was just opening his mouth to try again, when another messenger rushed in. "Commander," he said, bowing low to Brandon.

Brandon waved a hand dismissively. "No time for that, lad. Tell me, what news do you bring?"

"A behemoth and twenty speedies, sir, on the north-eastern flank, third quadrant."

"Third quadrant," Brandon said, rubbing at the scruff on his chin, glancing at the map. "That's Sergeant Tenal's section isn't it?"

"Not anymore, Commander," the messenger said. "Tenal's dead, sir—one of the speedies done for him."

Brandon grunted. He hadn't been close to Tenal—the man had been with Cardayum's army—but Brandon had made a point of meeting with each of the squad leaders before they'd left Perennia, spending as much time with each as possible, getting a feel for their strengths and weaknesses. Tenal had been one of the best.

Shit. Behemoths and speedies—they were the names the soldiers had given to Kevlane's creatures, and he supposed they were as good as any other. "Very well," he said, his mind going over the troops still held in reserve, and a moment later the messenger departed with orders to bring two squads to aid the quadrant he'd indicated.

No sooner had the messenger left than the tent flap was thrown open, and one of the guards poked his head in. "Forgive me, Commander, but you're needed out here."

Brandon shared a troubled glance with May before heading out of the tent. As he stepped outside, he was immediately struck with the smell of blood, and he cleared his throat, glancing around at the army spread out around him, at the corpses—gods, but he'd never thought to see so many—scattered behind the line. A groan from nearby drew his attention, and he turned to see a man sitting slumped across a horse.

The rider was swaying drunkenly and his horse's flanks were covered in several deep cuts, running with blood. The man, too, looked no better, one of his hands clamped around the shaft of an arrow buried in his gut. "Help him," Brandon said, motioning to one of the guards, but before they could reach him, the man let out another groan and toppled from his saddle.

Brandon hurried forward and knelt in front of the man. He recognized him as one of the scouts they'd sent to watch the army's flanks. Uner, he thought was the man's name, and looking at the wounded scout, a feeling of dread began to build in Brandon. "What is it, man? What's happened?"

"T-the commander," the man hissed, blood bubbling from his mouth as he spoke. "I need to...speak to...Commander Gant."

"I'm he, lad. Now, what's happened?"

The scout blinked, looking at Brandon as if seeing him for the first time. "It's...the woods, sir. I...they're coming."

Brandon's heart began to gallop in his chest, but he forced himself to remain calm, all too aware of the healers and messengers watching him. "Who's coming, Uner?"

The man's gaze was unfocused, distant, as if staring at something only he could see. "My wife's gonna...be so mad that I...hurt myself. Again." He grasped Brandon's hand with a desperate strength. "Can I see her, Commander? I'm tired and...I'd like...I'd like to explain what happened, before I sleep. So...so she won't be mad."

Brandon clenched his jaw, swallowing the emotion that suddenly welled up in him. The man's wife was miles and miles away in Perennia, but Brandon nodded. "Of course, lad," he said, his own voice haggard and coming out in little more than a whisper. "We'll get her, just as soon as we're done talking. Now, why don't you just tell me what you meant—who's coming?"

"B-behind me," the man said. "They..." Then he trailed off, took one last, hitching breath, and was still. Brandon recognized that stillness, for he had seen it far too many times in the last few hours.

He crouched there for several seconds, his jaw working, until one of the guards spoke. "General? What do you want us to do, sir?"

Brandon cleared his throat, rising from the body. "Get one of the stablemen to see to his horse." He turned to the guard. "Which direction did this man ride in from?"

"West, sir."

West. But how? Brandon turned, looking off into the darkness of the distant trees. There'd been no signs of troops to the west, and it didn't make sense at any rate. For one, if there *had* been troops there, the army would have passed by them during their march to the city. *Unless they were hiding, lying in wait.* He looked back at the scout's corpse. Not killed with a sword, this one, but an arrow. And for all the many dangers they presented, Kevlane's creatures did not use such weapons, and that could only mean one thing.

It could have been a single enemy scout, perhaps, but the man hadn't said "he" or "she" but *them.* Not one man then, but from the way the scout had spoken, many of them. *Gods watch over us.* "Send runners," Brandon said. "We need all of the reserve companies ready to support our western flank."

"Commander?" the guard asked. "The western—"

"You heard me," he snapped. "Do it now, lad."

As the guard departed, Brandon turned back to the east where the western gate of Baresh still remained stubbornly closed. Had the Akalians run into more trouble than they could handle? Were they, even now, lying dead along the battlements? Had they even managed to reach the top of the wall at all? Questions that would be answered all too soon, and he feared the only answers would be dark ones indeed.

He felt a presence beside him and turned to see May standing there, the club owner's sharp, intelligent eyes meeting his own with a fear that meant she too had understood. "Should we send for Aaron and the others?"

Brandon considered, then finally shook his head. "Not yet." He gazed once more at the dark forest in the distance where, if he was right, thousands of soldiers marched toward them, ready to crush Perennia's army between Kevlane's creatures and the wall. They would be surrounded, with nowhere to flee, no position to which they could withdraw. "Not yet," he said again.

Aaron, whatever your friends have planned, they had better do it and soon. We are running out of time.

CHAPTER TWENTY-NINE

Simon stared in shock at the abrupt violence, clapping a hand over his mouth to keep the sound—whimper or scream, he wasn't sure which— from escaping and giving away his position. It had all happened in an instant, and now four bodies lay on the battlements, their blood pooling around them like oil in the moonlight.

If the five bandits that remained were at all affected by the deaths, including one of their own, they didn't show it. Instead, they turned and started down the wall once more, moving closer to Simon, and he balled up as tightly as he could, hoping against hope that they would somehow miss him as tears of terror streamed down his face. He squeezed his eyes shut, wishing more than anything that he were at home in bed. *I should have listened to my parents,* he thought, *I should have listened.* Repeating the words in his head again and again, as if the admission were some oath of protection that might keep him safe.

A slight rustle alerted him to something or someone close, and he cringed, looking up to see someone standing over him. The figure's face was twisted and scarred terribly, and the eyes looked like they belonged on some feral beast instead of a person. The figure cocked its head at him, studying him. Then Simon saw the blade in its hand. Looking at that dark visage, possessed of no human kindness or compassion, Simon was no longer able to stay the sound he'd been holding and, as it turned out, it was a scream after all.

He was still screaming when the creature's blade plunged toward him, and he squeezed his eyes shut once more, sure that he was about to die. But instead of feeling the bite of steel on his neck, Simon heard a metallic ringing, and his eyes snapped open. The creature's blade was inches away from him, but another blade had interposed itself between him and certain death, stopping the bogeyman's strike.

The creature started to turn to the newcomer, but spasmed as several lengths of steel appeared out of nowhere, impaling it. A second later, the blades ripped free and warm blood splattered over Simon's face as the creature fell, toppling down the stairs. Several of the black-garbed figures stood over him. Their faces were covered except for one, the man whose blade had saved him. The stranger gave him a small, comforting smile, offering him his hand.

Simon stared at the bloody hand with wide eyes, unsure what was expected of him.

"Quiet, lad. Lest more of them come."

Simon realized that he was still screaming, and he clamped his mouth shut, his teeth chattering with fright.

"Good," the man said, "that's good. You're alive, boy. Everything's alright."

Simon blinked in shock at the dark, bloody streaks the creature had left as it tumbled down the stairs, and thought that the man was wrong. Nothing was right. Nothing would ever be right again. "A-are you going to kill me?"

The man knelt, shaking his head. "No, lad. We're not going to kill you."

"T-then...what do you want of me?"

"I want you to run. Run just as fast as you can. For there are others, like that one," he said, motioning to the dead thing lying broken at the bottom of the steps. "And they will be coming."

"M-m-monsters aren't real," Simon managed.

"You're wrong, boy," the stranger said, his voice not unkind. "Perhaps, sometimes, that would be true but not here, not now. Tonight, for this night of all nights, the monsters *are* real. Now go—run and do not look back."

Simon nodded, allowing the man to pull him to his feet. Then, without another word, Simon did one of the things he had rarely done in all of his life—he listened to an adult. He took the steps two at a time, running as fast as his legs could carry him. Maybe not Simon the Brave, after all. But Simon the Safe. Simon the Alive. And that, he decided, was good enough.

***

The Speaker watched the child go, saying a quick prayer to the Shadow God to look after him, then turned back to the others. Eleven in all now, one of their number having already fallen to the magi's abominations. Only eleven, when once there had been thousands. And with so much left to do. *Witness,* he thought, *the end of the Akalians. And alas, it is I who have brought us to it.* But when he spoke, his voice was sure, confident. "Come," he said. "There is little time."

They made their way across the wall, seeming to glide like phantoms, their steps silent as they moved with one purpose, one will, to their objective. They stalked down the stairs, eleven shadows in the darkness. The streets were quiet, empty, and had the Speaker not been able to hear the sounds of fighting—and dying—going on outside the city, he might have thought he had died already, and had awoken to find himself in his god's realm.

He led his brothers toward the gatehouse, unable to keep from marveling at the accuracies of the maps Caleb had sketched from memory. Each building, each side street or alleyway, was in exactly the place he'd said it would be.

As they walked the streets toward the gatehouse, the Speaker was reminded of a time long ago, in another city, one smelling of rotting meat and blood, the odors of a charnel pit. He remembered the rage he'd felt, the righteous anger that had demanded the city be razed to the ground, its buildings, shelters to cannibals or cages for its victims, burned to so much ash. And he had. They all had. And should the magi have his way, he would make the evil of that long-dead city no more than a prelude of things to come.

They were nearly upon the corner of the street, about to take the turn that would lead them to the gatehouse, when an alarm went off in his mind as if some great bell had been struck. He froze, and his brothers reacted immediately, stopping and raising their swords, their eyes scanning the darkness. For a moment, the

Speaker couldn't figure out what had warned him of danger, but then he knew. The streets were too quiet, too silent. The magi was no fool. He knew the army was outside the city and, after his ambush in the forests outside Perennia had failed, he would know also that the Akalians had arisen once more to stand against him.

They wait. Just around the corner.

The voice of the dead king held no emotion save for a cold, lonely sadness.

"Yes," the Speaker of the Akalians said, realizing that some part of him had known they would be there all along. There was no escape for him and the others now but, then, there never had been, and he found that some part of him was glad at the thought. His only regret would be that he would not get the chance to know his daughter.

You might still leave, the ancient king said into his mind, his tone without emotion, showing nothing of his own feelings on the matter. *There is still time. You could live.*

"Yes." But, then, living was not enough. That, at least, was a lesson he had learned long ago. He'd learned it among the swirling sands of the desert, as his feet guided him out of that wasteland, away from the only family he'd ever had, the winds of that place shifting the dunes beneath his feet so that, in moments, even the marks of his passage disappeared behind him.

He turned to the other Akalians, saw them watching him. There was no fear in those eyes, no worry or anger, only purpose. "They wait for us, brothers," he said. "Around this corner, our death waits for us. It has been searching for us our whole lives, just as we have, whether we knew it or not, been traveling to meet it. I would journey on, would see it, face to face. Will you come with me?"

They did not speak, but the metallic hiss of their drawn swords was answer enough, and he gave a sharp nod. "Very well. You all know what must be done—the lives that depend upon it. We will do what is required of us, just as we always have. We will not fail. Now," he said, smiling, "our god awaits us, brothers. Let us go and meet him together."

They were waiting around the corner. Two dozen of the abominations gifted with speed. But the Speaker of the Akalians barely saw them at all. Instead, he saw a woman, smiling and cooing softly in a tent while the wind of the desert night rustled the fabric around them. Nor did he hear the sounds of fighting from outside the city, for his ears heard only the soft snores of the baby in the woman's arms, so young and innocent and full of promise. And, with a smile still on his face, the Speaker of the Akalians led his brothers into battle for the last time.

CHAPTER THIRTY

Aaron watched Baresh's army march down the hill, closing the door on the trap Kevlane had set for them. At once, he felt despair, anger, and more than a little relief. For good or ill, the thing was begun in truth now. The mage's creatures continued to appear out of the forest, attacking Perennia's troops from either side, and now that Baresh's army had appeared at their backs, Perennia's soldiers had nowhere to run, even had they wanted to. The time for second-guessing, the time for deliberating, was over.

They could not turn or flee—now, the only way out was forward. All complications, all complexities had come down, as they always did, to one single truth, one single question, and the question was one of flesh and bone, of blade and blood. And its answer? Death. It was the only answer, the only one there ever had been, and never mind that men and women spent their lives searching desperately for another, *any* other.

Still, there was something to be said for that. Death, after all, was simple enough—anybody could do it. But what little relief he felt was tainted by the smell of blood and offal in the air, by the screams of the men and women around him as they died fighting Kevlane's creatures. He glanced around him at the other Virtue bearers. Gryle rubbed his hands together anxiously, though whether that anxiety was because he was ready to get started or afraid to, Aaron doubted the man himself knew. Leomin and Seline stood on the other side of the chamberlain, holding hands, as if each other's touch gave them strength to endure the bloody spectacle playing out all around them. Caleb was on Aaron's other side, looking small and scared and alone despite Tianya standing beside him.

They stood as a part of the army, yet apart from it, for those Ghosts which remained after Belgarin's attack on Perennia stood in a protective circle around them, together with the Virtue bearers forming the blade which would drive deep into the city, questing for its corrupted heart, in the hopes of being fast enough to avoid its opponent's parry. A parry which, in this case, would come in the form of the gate being forced closed once more. Half a dozen times since the battle had started, Aaron had fought down the urge to separate the bearers, spreading them out among the army to aid those soldiers who fought—and died—so bravely.

But resist he did. They wouldn't have long, he knew, once the gate was open, and it was too much to hope that the mage had neglected defenders at the weakest point of Baresh's defenses. It would be bloody then—a bloody struggle in a day filled with them, and if they did not manage to break through into the city, the soldiers' sacrifices would mean nothing. Even with all of the Virtue-bearers gathered together, accompanied by the Ghosts, the most elite of the army's soldiers, still it was a nearly impossible task. Without them, it would have been impossible in truth. Of course, the gate had to be opened first—without that, all of it meant nothing.

So Aaron and the others waited as men and women—men and women who had chosen to follow *him*—died around them, buying the Akalians time with their blood and their lives.

And yet here we stand, doing nothing.

There is no choice, Aaron, Co said into his mind, though even her voice sounded strained, tense, and it was clear that the gravity of the situation had not been lost on her. *You know that.*

Maybe, Aaron thought. But the idea was no comfort, did not change the cost of each unanswered atrocity occurring around them as he only stood, watching it unfold, the soldiers waiting for a response, an answer to all that was taken from them, for all that they gave.

Kevlane will answer, Co said, her voice full of anger and sadness. *He will be held accountable for what he has done—we will make sure of it.*

Maybe, Aaron thought again. *But if the only answer to blood is more of it, Firefly, then what kind of world do we fight for?*

For a world that can be better, Aaron. We fight for hope.

A better world. Aaron had walked the streets of the Downs, had seen the priests of one god or another always assuring those poor wretches to whom they ministered that theirs' was the right way, the only way, and always within those speeches was talk of a better world. The priests took their donations, took the new acolytes who volunteered, yet the world remained what it was, what it always had been, refusing to bow to, or even acknowledge the efforts—real or imagined—of those wandering its surface.

"Mr. Envelar? Is everything okay?"

Leomin was watching him with a wary gaze. A ridiculous question on the whole, of course, but he followed the dusky-skinned man's gaze down to his hand and realized he had drawn his sword, and now held it in a white-knuckled grip. He glanced around and saw the others watching him, their expressions carefully controlled.

Not that he could blame them. After all, had they not all seen him lose his mind with the rage brought on by the Virtue, and that more than once? He forced a weak smile, refusing to let his hurt show on his face, for though there was worry in those gazes, so, too, was there a certain desperation, a need to be reassured the way a child might look to his parents in the darkness, wanting, *needing* them to explain away the monsters and bogeymen.

"The gate will open," he said. That much, at least, he could give them, never mind that it felt like a lie as it slid out of his throat.

"Shouldn't it have opened already?" Gryle asked.

"Yeah, it should have," Seline said, frowning at the gate as if it were an enemy she could conquer, a foe she could slay. "Something's wrong. Something's happened."

Aaron hesitated, not knowing what to say, for his own thoughts had been colored with the same worry, one that he hadn't dared voice. Now that she had, though, he saw her thought reflected in the eyes of all the Virtue-bearers around them, save for Caleb who shook his head slowly.

"Not necessarily. Given the length of the wall, and the rate at which they scaled it before I lost sight of them in the darkness, the

Akalians would have crested the top only a little more than an hour ago."

"An hour," Seline said. "An hour to travel from the wall to the gatehouse. Tell me, Caleb, how long would such a trip take at walking speed?"

The youth winced, shifting uncomfortably. "Ten minutes, no more."

She nodded, as if some thought had been confirmed. "Which means that fifty minutes are left unexplained—fifty minutes at the least, and still we have seen or heard nothing."

"But, anything could have happened once they reached the wall," the youth said, his tone sounding desperate, as if he would make the others understand. "There would be guards, certainly, and who knows what things might wait on the other side of the gate. It would be no small task to reach it."

"As you say," the woman said, turning to stare at the massive gate in the distance. "Who knows what might wait on the other side? Forgive me, boy, but I don't find that very comforting. They're *dying* out there," she growled, sweeping an arm around to indicate the army. "And we're just standing here doing nothing!"

She finished the last in a scream, drawing the attention of several nearby soldiers who, Aaron saw, looked at them with eyes full of fear. For his part, Caleb recoiled as if slapped. He opened his mouth to speak but hesitated, and it was Tianya who answered. "I understand your worry," she said, loud enough for the soldiers around her to hear, for apparently she, too, had noticed their reaction. She spoke as if each word pained her, and Aaron realized for the first time that being here, among the terrible sights, sounds, and smells of battle, must be an incredible trial for her, since her Virtue enhanced all her senses far beyond any normal human's. "I had much the same worry," she went on, "when I was weak in the woods, barely able to walk and then not even that, hunted by these...these *things*."

"And?" Seline asked.

Tianya gave a smile. "And I'm alive. Thanks to this one here," she said, putting a reassuring hand on Caleb's shoulder. "Beyond all chance of salvation, I am alive."

Seline frowned at that. "I'm not trying to discount what he—what *you*—did," she said, nodding to Caleb, "but as amazing, as brave as it was, courage won't open this door for us."

This time, it was Caleb who answered. "No, you're right. It won't. But, then, it wasn't courage that saw me through to the camp. It was hope. The gate will open." He looked around at all of them, his gaze finally settling on Aaron. "The gate *will* open."

"Of course it will," Aaron said with a confidence he didn't feel. *But it had better do it soon.*

CHAPTER THIRTY-ONE

"Forgive me, Majesty, but I must say again that this is...unwise."

Adina ignored the guard, pulling the bandage tight, barely containing her hiss of frustration as it was soaked through, almost instantly, with fresh blood. The man she tended had taken a deep cut to his thigh, and had been pulled back from the line of battle only moments ago, yet in those moments he had lost a shocking amount of blood, and his face looked pale, his skin shrunken. "Is...it...bad?"

Adina met the soldier's eyes, saw the pain and the fear lurking there and swallowed the lump in her throat. "You'll be okay," she said. "Everything will be okay." It wasn't the first lie she'd told, nor was it the first dying man she'd told it to, but it hurt as much as the first.

She rose from where she'd knelt beside the soldier, and saw that some of the blood that had pooled on the ground beneath him had soaked into her leather leggings, adding to the stains already marring the material. Proof, if proof was needed, of the lives the day had taken and with no end in sight. And what was more fitting than blood staining the garments of the queen who had led this man and those like him to their deaths?

Captain Marcus was watching her with a troubled gaze, the other three guards standing with him refusing to look at her, as if by not seeing the blood covering their queen's hands and clothes, they might somehow forget the horrid events of the last few hours.

She had taken the captain into her service as a guard, believing that his assistance when they'd arrived back in Perennia to deal with Grinner had proven him trustworthy, and she felt glad that she had, for he alone had the courage to meet her eyes, to question her. Courageous, but wrong for all that.

"I will not hide away in a tent when I could be of some help, Marcus," she said. "I will not ask others to die for me and refuse even to have the courage to witness their sacrifice. They deserve that much from me and more."

The guard captain nodded. "Of course, Queen Adina, and I...the men, we appreciate what it is that you do. It's only...it is dangerous, here. The few creatures that have managed to breach the line have been cut down quickly enough so far, but they *have* breached the line." He glanced around, taking a step closer and speaking in a whisper. "It would not do, Majesty, for the men to see their queen cut down. It would...it would not help their resolve."

"Then I suppose," Adina said, heading toward another of the wounded even now being dragged back from the line by two of his comrades, "that we will have to not let that happen, Captain. It is why you're here, after all. Isn't it?"

"Yes, Majesty," the man said. "And I and the rest of the guards will, of course, do whatever is within our power to keep you safe, will sacrifice our lives, if need be. But, Majesty...it must be said that these creatures we fight are beyond normal men, and should you remain out here, I cannot guarantee your safety."

Adina stopped and stared at the man. "I grew up, Marcus, in my father's court, surrounded by guards and men who had dedicated their lives not just to protecting my father, but all of his family as well. We had around us a castle, walls of stone to protect us against the world, yet still my father died. Still, my brother began to assassinate my siblings—tried to assassinate me as well. I survived that attempt, if only just, with the help of great allies. Yet still we find ourselves thrown into a war against a man that shouldn't exist at all."

She took a slow, deep breath, and shook her head. When she continued, her voice was low, quiet. "No matter how tall the battlements, no matter how thick the walls, they might still be broken, Captain. Even shields made by master smiths might be shattered. If my life has taught me anything, it's that the only guarantee in life is there are no guarantees."

The man's mouth worked, as if he might say something more, but he only nodded. "Of course, Majesty."

Still, Adina could see his thoughts lurking just under the surface of his expression clearly enough. "I will not make of myself an ornate sword in a wealthy merchant's home, Captain, to sit upon a mantle and be admired, yet never taken down for fear of damage. A tool ignored and held in too high regard to be of any use, even when it might prove helpful in some small way. I do not deserve it—no one does."

Adina watched the guard captain's face, and felt some sympathy for him. Despite her words, the man was obviously torn between his duty to protect her, and the deference and respect he believed she was owed. She sighed and started forward once more, heading to the wounded man even now being laid on the ground in a growing line of his fellows. The guard captain would just have to look after his own worries, for she had greater problems to attend to. She knelt beside the wounded man wordlessly, grabbing gut and a needle positioned at intervals for the healers' use, and began the work of closing the wound in the man's arm. This one, at least, would not prove fatal, unless infection should set in. Something to be thankful for—monsters they might be, but Kevlane's creatures rarely left a job undone.

As she worked, she thought again of the captain's words, both the ones he had spoken and those which he had left unsaid. There was truth there, a truth she could not ignore no matter how many times she tried to refuse it. If she fell, the army's morale would suffer a terrible blow, would grow weaker at a time when it needed every ounce of strength. But somewhere, among that battle, among those thousands fighting and dying, Aaron stood. And not just Aaron, but all of those she had come to call friends. How many still lived? Reports were scattered at best, and she'd dared not send a messenger that was sorely needed elsewhere to check on Aaron only for her own comfort. *And not just Aaron,* she thought again. Gryle, Leomin, Darrell and Sergeant Wendell. They were all out there, somewhere, scattered among the army.

For a time, once the fighting had begun, Adina *had* stayed in her tent, but soon her anxiety, her need to be doing *something,* had driven her from it. She had strapped on her sword before leaving—not missing the looks of anxiety shared by her guards as she did so—and then, despite Captain Marcus's protests, had stepped out into the day with no clear understanding of what she meant to do, only knowing that the air in the tent had felt as if it were growing thicker by the instant, so that she could barely breathe.

It was then that she had seen the lines of wounded behind the fighting lines, the healers doing what they could, but with so many getting hurt so quickly, they were not able to keep up and so, her thoughts on the others, but Aaron most of all, Adina had begun doing what she could to help. And despite the fact that many of those she worked on were strangers to her, in binding and cleaning their wounds, she found some release from the fear that had been growing in her, fear for Aaron, that she might never see him again. And so each soldier to which she ministered became the sellsword, the wounds she cleaned and bound and tended were *his* wounds, the blood that stained her, his blood, and the tears that she wept inwardly, those that threatened to crack the façade of calm and confidence that she maintained with an effort, were tears wept for him.

Adina cleared her throat, forcing down the tears that threatened to come back once more and saying a silent prayer to the gods to look after Aaron and all the other soldiers, to make the passing of those who sacrificed their lives to protect not just their city, but their country, as peaceful and painless as possible. She had just finished sewing up the man's wound and was reaching for a bandage when there was a chorus of shouts and the sound of fighting grew louder, more immediate, but she paid it little attention. The sounds of battle were all around her, after all, and stopping to listen to them would do nothing to help the man who lay on the ground in front of her. So she grabbed a long strip of white cloth from a nearby pile and began to wrap the man's wound.

She was still working when someone grabbed her arm and jerked her back. She cried out in surprise, stumbling and letting go of the bandage as something flashed in front of her. She turned to her right and saw that one of the swift creatures had somehow broken through the line, and the soldiers there were even now fending off several of its comrades. The creature was covered in cuts and blood, and it swayed uncertainly on its feet. A quick glance to her side showed her that it had been Captain Marcus who had pulled her away from the creature's strike, and the man let out a growl as he stepped in front of her, swinging his blade.

Despite its wounds, the creature reacted with a speed that—though slower than normal—was still faster than any man, and the momentum of its blow knocked Marcus's weapon out of his hands and sent it hurtling through the air. The creature followed up the parry with a swift lunge toward the captain, its sword leading.

Guided by instincts from her training with Captain Brandon Gant, Adina shouldered Marcus aside, barely managing to get her own blade up in time to block the strike.

Her arms shook with the force of the blow, but she was holding the blade in a two-handed grip, and managed to keep hold of it. Still, in her panic, she had stepped awkwardly, and, unable to pivot and use her body's momentum, her return strike was weak, and the creature easily blocked it, knocking it wide.

A frozen instant in time, then, as the creature raised its sword for a strike she would not be able to parry. But suddenly a length of steel erupted from the creature's chest in a shower of blood. A moment later, it collapsed, and Adina was left staring at the wounded man on whom she'd been working, the bandage that she had not managed to finish wrapping dangling from his arm. "I...thank you," she managed, surprised to still be alive.

The man bowed his head. "Of course, Majesty." Then he turned to Captain Marcus and the other guards staring at him with wide-eyes, as if he'd just risen from the dead. The soldier turned the blade and offered it, hilt first, to the captain. "Your sword, sir."

Marcus recovered his wits enough to give the man a grateful nod. "Thank you."

"No problem at all, sir." The man rolled the shoulder of his wounded arm, wincing as he looked around at the battle raging on all sides. "Well then. Guess I'd better get back to it." He bowed to Marcus then more deeply to Adina. "Captain. Majesty."

They watched him walk back into the line of soldiers, heading for the front once more before sharing a look in which passed a world of understanding. And when Adina moved to the next of the wounded, the captain followed her in silence.

CHAPTER THIRTY-TWO

They drove deep into the enemy ranks, the eleven Akalians creating the point of a spear, making use of what momentum they gained in their charge to stab deeper and deeper into the magi's creatures.

At the head of the spear, the Speaker's sword was a blur, cutting left and right as he and his brothers fought the battle for which they had trained their entire lives. All was chaos, the creatures themselves slow to react for all their speed, as if taken off-guard by the Akalian charge. Several were dead within moments.

But for all the Akalians' skill and dedication, the creatures they faced were not mere men, to be gripped with fear and break at the unexpected violence that had come upon them. Soon they began to fight back, and one Akalian fell with two blades impaling him, another following soon after.

Yet still the black-garbed men charged, not counting their losses, not this time, for they were all lost, had been since they had taken their first step onto the wall. And so they cut their way toward the gatehouse, moving not like separate people at all, but like one creature, a creature of one purpose, of one will.

The Speaker didn't know how long he fought, or how many of the abominations had fallen to his blade. His thoughts, in truth, were hardly on the battle at all, but on the family he had lost so long ago. With each strike of his blade, their forms became more distinct, and with each parry, they drew closer. He barely felt the cuts and wounds he received, for such hurts meant little in the face of the strange mixture of pain and pleasure the memories brought. His weariness, the ache in his muscles, too, meant nothing, for a man is never too tired to pull his loved ones close, to whisper in their ears that he is there, that he will always be there.

Eventually, he cut down another creature and saw that there was nothing between him and the gatehouse, save for a regular guardsman, his tremors at the immensity of the violence to which he had borne witness visible as he raised his sword. The Speaker paid him little mind, turning for the first time to look behind him.

Two of his brothers remained. Their black garments were torn and ripped in dozens of places, and everywhere their skin showed, so too did bloody cuts and wounds. One Akalian's left arm hung uselessly at his side, drenched in blood that still pumped from a deep gash on his bicep. Past them stood the remaining creatures, six in all. The ground was littered with the bodies of their comrades as well as several black-garbed forms, and the gap which the Akalian charge had created was even now filling, as the creatures moved to encircle them.

The Speaker met the eyes of his two brothers. Then they each nodded, and in those nods was a world of understanding. They had come to the end of things, to *their* end, and that was alright, was as it should be.

"I'll need a few minutes," the Speaker said, uttering the last words he would ever say to one of his brothers. The two men said nothing, only turned to face the army of creatures gathering at their backs.

Now that he had stopped, the Speaker began to feel the full weight of his wounds pressing down on him, felt his vision growing dim as the blood he'd lost took its toll, but he forced his feet onward, toward the waiting guard and the key hanging from his belt. There was little time left.

CHAPTER THIRTY-THREE

There was a loud, metallic creaking, and the western gate of the city begin to rise. At first, Aaron thought he must be imagining it, so convinced had he become that they would die here, standing before the wall of the city without ever having set foot inside. But the gasps from the others assured him that his mind wasn't playing tricks. The Akalians had done their work and now, finally, the western gate of Baresh was opening.

"Come on," he said to the others. "It's time."

The Virtue-bearers moved toward the gate, surrounded by the Ghosts. As the gate continued to rise, Aaron was able to make out more of the city beyond. What he saw first were the corpses. Dozens of them, belonging to the creatures and the Akalians both, and it was clear enough that there had been a slaughter. And among those corpses, stalking toward the open gate like some revenant returned from the land of the dead, some symbol to stand for all the pain and agony the day had wrought, was a man. His clothes had been black once, but no longer. Now, they were cut in so many places that they were barely clothes at all, and he was coated in blood, as if he had taken a bath in it. Yet for all that, the man made his way to the gate, and despite the distance that still separated them, Aaron recognized the Speaker of the Akalians.

Each of the man's steps seemed to take a monumental effort, yet still he moved forward until he stood beneath the gate itself. There, he stopped, and Aaron increased his pace, breaking into a sprint. In a few moments, Aaron and the others were on him, but by then the Speaker of the Akalians had fallen to one knee, his sword—stabbed into the ground—the only thing keeping him upright.

Now that he was closer, Aaron could see the full extent of the Speaker's wounds, and it was all he could do to keep from gasping at the sight of them. The others, though, were unable to repress their own shock and dismay, and he heard the sounds of it as they came to stand beside him. Aaron had seen much death in his life, far more than his share, and he had grown used to the look of it. It was not a friend, yet it was familiar, and he saw it now, in the Speaker's form where the man swayed on one knee, gripping his sword with both hands.

Slowly, as if each movement were a great trial, the Speaker raised his head, and for all his wounds, for all the terrible abuse his body had endured, his eyes, when they met Aaron's, were clear and lucid. "Aaron...Envelar," the man said.

"Speaker," Aaron said, surprised by the pang of sadness that stabbed at his heart. "You did it. You and your brothers did it."

The man glanced back at the corpses of the other Akalians where they lay scattered among their enemies before slowly turning back to Aaron. "Yes."

"Come on," Aaron said, offering the man a hand. "We'll get you a healer. There's got to be—"

"We both know there is not," the man said in a voice little more than a whisper, so quiet that the others—who had stopped a few feet behind Aaron—could not hear. There was no regret in the man's voice, no bitterness, only a calm clarity that somehow affected Aaron more than anything else could have. The Speaker met his eyes, and he must have recognized the sellsword's anguish, for he gave a small smile. "Do not despair, Aaron. It was always going to end thus, and—" He broke into a coughing fit, and the sellsword winced at the blood that spilled from the man's mouth.

"Speaker, I—"

The Akalian held up a trembling hand. "Forgive me, but there is little time. The great dark comes. When I die, you will receive the spirit of Aaron Caltriss, the Virtue of Will. He has told me as much. *Use* it, Aaron. Finish what we have begun, and do not let my brothers' sacrifice be in vain."

A Sellsword's Hope

Aaron swallowed hard, nodding. "Of course, Speaker. And...thank you. Without you and the other Akalians..." He trailed off, unsure of how to continue, but the Speaker smiled, taking Aaron's hand and gripping it with a surprising strength.

"The magi's evil has marred the face of the world for far too long. For too long, the world has had to live under the shadow of Caltriss's desperate choice, and Kevlane's betrayal. End it, Aaron. Put the magi to rest. Put them *all* to rest."

Aaron frowned. "I don't...I'm not sure what you mean, Speaker."

The man met his eyes, and in that moment he no longer looked like the leader of the Akalians, a man who had lived for hundreds of years and who had spent nearly all of his life in battle with the darkness always threatening to encroach on the world of the living. He looked, simply, like a man, one who had come to the end of his life and found that, despite everything, he was content.

"You will know, when the time comes. And please, when you remember me—remember me not as the Speaker of the Akalians, but as Raenclest, a man who did not always succeed in making the right decisions, but a man who always tried. Now," he said, "if you don't mind, Aaron, I would speak to my daughter."

"Of course," Aaron said, and he stepped away.

***

They all watched her to see what she would do, and for a moment, Seline only stood uncertainly. Her heart was hammering in her chest, and her throat was unaccountably dry. She was afraid. Afraid to step forward, feeling somehow that in doing so, she would be killing the man who knelt beneath the gate, watching her with eyes that held a world of emotion. Suddenly, she was no longer the sure, confident, independent woman she had tried to be for her entire life. All the years spent full of hate not just for the world but for everyone in it, fell away, and she was a child again. A frightened, unsure child.

Seline, you must hurry, the Virtue said into her mind. *For there is not much time.*

But what would she say? What *could* she say to this man whom she had never known? And why, if he was a stranger, did her chest ache at the sight of him here, breathing his last breaths? She'd stepped closer before she realized it. "F-father?"

At first, the black-clothed man didn't answer, and a new fear rose in her, a desperate, panicked thing. She had waited too long, had stood torn between her emotions for too long, and he had succumbed to his wounds. But then he took a slow, deep breath and met her eyes. "Daughter," he said. And in that simple word, whatever was left of the wall Seline had built around herself broke, and the tears began to pour from her eyes.

"I'm...I'm here."

"I am sorry that we did not have more time," he said. "I...I need you to know that I loved you and your mother—always. I wish...I wish things could have been different, between us. I would have...much liked. To be your father."

Seline fell to her knees in front of him, taking one of the man's hands in her own. "You *are* my father. But...surely there has to be *something* we can do," she said. "One of the healers..."

"Would be better served seeing to those who might still be saved," he said in a soft, comforting voice. "It's okay—in calling me 'Father,' you have given me a gift greater than any you could imagine. Now, you will be alright. You are strong, Seline. You get that from your mother. Always remember, though the world has its cruelties, it is not *all* cruel. There's goodness here. It does not beat its chest or scream to be heard, must be searched for to be found, but it *is* here." He smiled, glancing past her, and Seline followed his gaze to where Leomin watched, tears gliding silently down his face. "He is a good man. He cares for you."

Seline nodded and here, at least, she felt no compulsion to dissemble or hide her own feelings. "I care for him too."

"He knows. It is good that you know now, as well. I love you, daughter."

"And I you," she said, her voice wretched with a profound grief she had not felt for years, since her mother had died. "Father," she began, suddenly wanting to ask a thousand questions, but his shoulders slumped, his head lowered, and when the breath left his lungs, it did not come again.

Seline lowered her own head, and tears, hot and wet, poured down her face. She felt a hand on her shoulder and turned to see Leomin standing there. The Parnen said nothing, only watched her with eyes like windows in to her own soul, reflecting her own pain. Seline did not knock the hand away, as she would have done not so long ago, but took comfort in the understanding it offered. *Search for goodness.* "I will, Father," she whispered. "I will." She rose, and though she felt sad, she also felt lighter, buoyed up, for though her father had not been with her during her life, he had, in his final moments, taught her how to live. "Come," she said, taking in Leomin and the others, "let us finish this. While there is still time."

***

The desert wind howled like some great beast in the darkness, but not one out to hunt for prey, only one calling out its loneliness, a testament to all the living creatures of the world, those who walked their own paths of loneliness, forged and fashioned by their own hands. The sand was soft beneath his feet, and the night was neither too hot nor too cold.

The man walked a path through that lonely darkness, the swirling sands erasing his footsteps behind him. And as he walked, he began to pick out the faint glow of a light in the distance, so pale that it might not have existed at all. The sound of a woman's soft humming reached him. It was a familiar sound, one of comfort, of love given and love received. It was the sound of family.

The tent lay in the distance, outlined in the darkness by the light of a lantern within. It was as if there were nothing else in the world save the dark and the tent, the light and the humming. *What is this?* the man asked, his voice formless in that great void.

A gift, a voice answered, and the man turned to see another standing beside him where none had been before. The man's form was like shifting smoke, blurred and indistinct, but his eyes, and the smile he held—sad and overjoyed at once—were unmistakable.

A gift? For who?

For you, of course, the stranger said.

The man turned back to the tent where, inside, he could just make out the form of a woman and the small bundle she held in her arms.

Go and meet them, Raenclest. They wait for you. They have waited for you for a very long time.

And he did, traveling into that great darkness, toward the woman and the child. To his family.

CHAPTER THIRTY-FOUR

Aaron felt as if he was struck by something, and he grunted in surprise, staggering at the invisible force that threatened to knock him from his feet. *Co, what...*

Father? the Virtue asked.

I am here child, came the reply, the long-dead king's voice full of sadness.

Realization struck him then, and Aaron turned to the body of Raenclest, still kneeling by the city gate. Proof then, if any were needed, that the man was dead in truth, for his Virtue had left him. Aaron wondered at the implications of possessing two Virtues at once, but forced the thoughts—and more than a few worries—down. There would be time for them later. Assuming, of course, that there *was* a later.

"Come on," he said to the others. He turned, meaning to lead his party into the city, but had barely taken a step when a robed figure glided out into the street ahead of them.

"Tell me, Aaron Envelar. Did you really think it would be so easy?"

Aaron stared at the man standing a short distance away. He was thin and bald, and even in the poor light the moon provided, the sellsword could see the amusement dancing in the stranger's eyes. "Do I know you?"

"No, Aaron Envelar," the man said with a slow smile, "but I know you—as does my master. Did you really think we did not know of those *Akalians*? Did you really believe we would simply sit back and let you march into the city?" The man raised his hand, gesturing, and suddenly dozens of the swift creatures poured out of the alleyways to stand on either side of him.

One of the Ghosts shouted a warning, and Aaron spun to see at least twenty of the creatures gathering behind them, and bit back a curse. The closest of Perennia's soldiers, seeing what was happening, started toward the gate at a run, but moments later it slammed shut, blocking their way.

The bald man who was still watching him with that same small smile. "So I ask you again, Aaron Envelar, did you really believe it would be so easy?"

Aaron shrugged. "I'd hoped. Anyway, who the fuck are you?"

"My name is not important," the man answered, "but you may call me Caldwell."

"You're right—it's not important. You'll be dead in a few minutes anyway." Aaron started forward at that, the others following, and the bald man raised a finger.

"Ah, ah. What is your hurry, *General?* Do you think to save the army you have so foolishly brought to oppose a god? They are out there," he said, gesturing to the closed gate, "dying. Wondering, I suspect, why their leader has abandoned them. Or do you, perhaps," he continued, his grin widening, "believe those ships which even now approach the harbor might somehow save you? Sorry, but they won't. My master sees all things, knows all things. The moment you decided to oppose him, your fate—and the fate of those poor, hapless souls that follow you—was sealed. Still, it is not all bad. I have a gift for you, a *reacquaintance,* shall we call it, with one I believe you know."

He motioned again, and another figure stepped out from a nearby alleyway, coming to stand beside the bald man. Despite the deep scars on his face and limbs, Aaron recognized the figure as Savrin, the swordsman he had fought when he and the others had escaped from Baresh. But whatever the man had once been, he was that no longer—the mage had done his work, and the thing staring at Aaron with empty, dead eyes was no man at all, but a monster, a weapon crafted in a forge of despair and pain.

"Ah yes," the bald man said, "I can see you do recognize him. A special one, is he not?" He shrugged. "Still, not so special now, for my master has crafted many such recently. Not that it will matter to you, of course." He turned to the creatures. "Kill them."

CHAPTER THIRTY-FIVE

"Where are they, damnit?"

Balen turned from where he stood on the deck of the ship, his hands propped on its railing, to see Captain Festa pacing back and forth, his hands balled into fists at his sides. It was at least the fifth or sixth time the man had asked the question, yet still there was no answer. They were close to the port now, could make out the eastern side of the city of Baresh in the distance, but, so far at least, there was no sign of Baresh's navy. A navy that, Balen knew from his days as a smuggler aboard the Clandestine, was not insignificant.

"Maybe they left."

Balen winced as the captain spun on Urek who stood nearby. The man had spent the better part of the journey bent over the rail of the ship, puking his guts out, and even now there was a distinct green tinge to his skin, but he was speaking at least, so that was something. "Maybe they left?" Festa repeated.

The big man grunted, shrugging. "Well. They ain't here, that much's for sure. So yeah. Maybe they cut out—they knew we'd be marchin' on 'em soon enough, after all."

Festa stared at the man if he were the world's biggest fool, then with a huff stared back up at the crow's nest. "Any sign up there, Pater? And I swear by the gods, if you've fallen asleep again dreamin' about playin' hide the anchor with Benjy's sister, I'll throw you to the sharks and save the bastard the trouble!"

The bastard in question, Benjy, turned from where he was working the lines of the sail to scowl up at the crow's nest, and Balen winced, not missing the small, cruel grin on the captain's face.

"No sign of the enemy, Captain!" Pater shouted back with, what seemed to Balen, appropriate haste. "Only our own ships and the city, comin' on fast now."

"Like I said," Urek ventured. "Gone."

Festa paused in his pacing for a moment to glare at the man before resuming. The truth was, Balen shared the captain's anxiety. From what everyone said, Kevlane, was no fool. He had to know that Perennia had ships, after all, and he doubted it would be as easy as docking and unloading the troops they carried without being bothered. A nice idea, but a dangerous one. Even if the mage knew nothing of naval warfare, he had generals and commanders in the city who did, and it was too much to hope that the man would refuse to listen to any of their counsel.

He stared off into the darkness where, all around, he could see the lights of the rest of Perennia's fleet surrounding them. That alone gave him unease, for Balen was used to being aboard a smuggling ship, and he'd never thought to find himself in an army convoy bent on sieging a city. What's more, the closer they drew to Baresh, the more he felt like a man who had decided it would be a good idea to go swimming in the ocean with some raw, bloody meat strapped to him. Just because nothing had taken a bite out of him yet didn't mean nothing would, and it would serve him right when it did.

Festa stopped again, looking up at the crow's nest. "And what of the western gate?"

There was a hesitation, as Balen could envision Pater reaching for his spy glass, and he felt his own breath catch in his throat. Aaron had been confident the Akalians could get the gate open, but Balen wasn't so sure. It seemed to him that when a man started putting his trust in folks with the sort of reputation those bastards carried, then he was desperate indeed, so it was with no small relief that he listened to the lookout's reply.

"The gate's open, Cap!"

Balen let out the breath he'd been holding with a relieved sigh that was shared by the others—sailor and criminal alike—

standing on the deck with him. He was just starting to think that maybe this whole thing would work out, after all, when the lookout cried out again. "Hold that last, Cap. I...something's happening..." He trailed off, not finishing what he'd been about to say, but Balen felt his stomach turn at the unmistakable sound of confusion and more than a little fear that had been in the man's voice.

"Well, what's happening, damnit?" Festa called back, looking out toward the city as if somehow he could see past the harbor and the buildings. Then he turned, his gaze skimming the dark waters around them, but whatever had startled the lookout could not be made out from their place on the deck. "Is it the navy? Do you see them?"

"Not the navy, Cap," the man called back. "It's the gate it...it's—"

***

"—closing."

"*What?*" Brandon said, looking up from the command table.

"The western gate, Commander," the messenger said. "It's closing."

Brandon rushed to the tent flap, and gazed out in the distance, hoping, praying the man was wrong. But he wasn't. The western gate of the city, the means by which they had intended for their army to make it inside, was closing, leaving them surrounded on all sides and with no place to retreat. "*Shit,*" he growled, rounding on the messenger. "How many?"

"S-sir?"

Brandon fought to keep his patience past his growing dread. "How many made it inside, man?" he demanded. "How much of the army?"

The messenger recoiled, swallowing hard. "Um...sir, none of them."

"*None* of them?"

"Sir, General Envelar and his...squad made it through, along with the Ghosts but..."

"*Damn,*" Brandon hissed. That meant Aaron and the others were trapped on the inside of the city, without reinforcement, without help. *And make no mistake,* he thought, *you're just as trapped out here.* Brandon knew a fair amount about military tactics, had read enough of the histories of battles to understand their intricacies the way few others could, but it didn't take a military strategist to know what happened to an army surrounded with its back against a wall.

He stared out into the distance, as if he could somehow see the ships carrying troops to the eastern side of the city. He hoped they were having a better go of it; otherwise the war would be over before it had even properly began.

"Sir, your orders?"

The messenger's voice pulled him from his thoughts. "Orders?"

"Sir," the man ventured, obviously uncomfortable, "the gate was our best hope...with it gone. Perhaps, it would be better to retreat?"

Brandon grunted. "Retreat to where? Retreat *how?* There's nowhere to retreat *to,* lad. Not, at least, unless we can all grow wings, and that doesn't seem likely." He considered for a moment, then shook his head. "No, we won't retreat, not even if we could. Aaron and the others have made it into the city—the longer we can hold off Kevlane's army here, the better chance they have of making it to the mage and doing what needs doing." *A small chance, one in a thousand, if that, but better than nothing. Maybe.*

"Yes sir," the messenger said. "And...should I tell the queen?"

Tell her what? That her army is surrounded with no escape, that the gate has been closed, and her lover has been trapped on the inside with the other Virtue-bearers and practically no soldiers at all? "No, lad," Brandon said, taking a slow deep breath. "I'll tell her myself."

CHAPTER THIRTY-SIX

"Captain, what do we do?" one of the sailors asked, but if Festa heard, he gave no sign. Instead, he continued to pace the deck, slamming his fist repeatedly into his open palm, as if he might somehow beat the answer out of his own flesh.

Balen hoped he did, because he himself had no clue. They'd gone over the plan in detail, spent hours huddled over maps with Aaron and Brandon Gant explaining how it would go, but this part had not been in the plan. The gate was not supposed to close. And, judging from what Pater had shouted down, the vast majority of the army was still stuck on the outside of the city.

It was an eventuality that had, at least, been foreseen, and the answer to it had been the troops carried by Festa and the other ship captains. Yet the captain hesitated, frowning and continually glancing in the water as he paced as if somehow the enemy navy—still nowhere to be seen—might appear.

He was still pacing when a shout from the lookout in the crow's nest alerted them of two ships separating themselves from the group and rushing toward Baresh. They were intent, it seemed, on releasing their troops and rushing to the aid of the army, perhaps planning to open the gate once more.

Festa growled a curse. "That's Manerd and Goderd. What do those two fools think they're doing?" he demanded of no one in particular, and no one answered. Partly, of course, because given the captain's current mood, the first one to answer would no doubt find himself going for a swim, but mostly because what they were doing seemed obvious enough.

Balen watched the ships, hopeful and tense all at once. It seemed to him that everyone not just on Festa's ship, but on all the ships, held their breath. They were getting close, close enough that he began to feel sure that they would make it, after all, when the night was split by an earth-shattering *crack*. The ships were stopped as if they had rammed into a wall. Wood split and cracked, the sound of it tortured and thunderous, and the two vessels began to shift dangerously. Despite the distance, Balen could make out sailors running along the decks of the ships, could hear their screams and shouts as the two vessels floundered and began to sink.

"Damnit," Festa hissed. "The bastards have a harbor chain."

Sailors poured over the sides of the doomed vessels as they sank into the dark water and, amid the chaos, Balen saw what the captain meant. A thick chain, its links visible rising out of the water close to the docks on either side, had appeared in front of the ships. "Come on then," Festa said, "forward, but *slow!* We'll see if we can't save some of those poor basta—"

Suddenly, a *roar* echoed in the air, and Balen's eyes went wide at the unmistakable sound of cannon fire. The cannon ball struck one of the ships on the right side, and the ship pitched dangerously, taking on water.

"Captain," Pater yelled, "*enemy ships to starboard!*"

The warning was unnecessary, for everyone was already spinning to look off in the distance where ships were appearing on the horizon, a fleet of them. The enemy navy, it seemed, had finally decided to show itself.

The next several minutes were a flurry of activity as Festa and the other ships' captains turned to face this new threat. The ships nearest Baresh's navy began to engage, answering with cannon fire of their own, and Festa glowered at Urek. "Well," he said, "I guess they didn't leave, after all."

The big man nodded thoughtfully. "Still, there ain't all that many of 'em. Reckon we've got 'em licked at least two, maybe three to one, eh?"

"Sure," Festa said, "and how much help, do you suppose, will we be able to give to the army camped outside the gates when we're too busy fighting, eh?"

Urek grunted. "On account of the ships and that chain there?" he asked, jerking a thumb in the direction of where the remnants of the two unfortunate vessels floated on the water.

Festa opened his mouth, preparing, Balen suspected, to issue some scathing retort, and—all too aware that Urek and those standing behind him including the muscular woman, Beautiful, were criminals and not above killing a man, if they saw a need—he spoke first. "A boom chain, they call it."

Both men turned to glower at him, and Balen winced as their full attention fell on him. "You see, it keeps enemy ships from reaching the harbor," he said, gesturing uselessly at the floating remains of the two sunken ships. "They raise and lower it with a mechanism controlled by two boom houses." He scanned the docks, pointing out the towers to which the chain was clearly attached.

The big man studied the distant structures, rubbing his chin thoughtfully. "So, it seems to me that all we got to do is get over to them houses there, and drop this chain."

"Sure," Festa said, "and since you're performing miracles, why not fill the ship's hold up with coin? Not that we're likely to be able to spend it, the way things are going," he finished, muttering the last.

Urek turned and glanced at his companions, Beautiful, the hawk-nosed man Balen believed went by the name of Shadow, a youth who was shifting from foot to foot as if unable to remain still, and one more, a man with a perpetually sour expression as if the world had screwed him over plenty, and he was just waiting for it to inevitably happen again.

They all looked back at him, their expressions grim. The woman, Beautiful, nodded, followed by the hawk-nosed man, then the youth and, finally, the frowning man. "Well alright then," Urek said. He turned back to Festa. "If you've got a boat can get us on the shore without becomin' shark food, we'll take care of your chain for ya."

Festa barked something somewhere between a laugh and a growl. "Gods, man, I'm not asking you to do that. Anyway, it'd be suicide. There'll be guards inside the buildings, you know? Not that it'd matter much as the doors will be locked up tighter'n my wife when she's of a mind. No," he said, scowling back at the shore, "we'll figure something else out."

The big man waited a moment then said. "Well?"

"Well, *what?*" Festa demanded.

"Figure anything out yet?"

The captain's face began to grow a deep shade of red, and Balen spoke hurriedly. "Urek, I think what Captain Festa means to say is that it won't simply be a matter of knocking and asking to be let in—the guards stationed there will have the doors locked up tight, and they'll be reinforced. You couldn't break in, if you wanted to."

The big man grinned widely. "That sounds like a challenge, first mate. Anyway, you let us worry about that—we're criminals. Gettin' in places we ain't wanted is pretty much what we do. Now," he continued, turning back to Festa, "you got a boat we can borrow or not?"

***

"I still think this is a bad idea."

Urek grunted, and Balen noted his hand twitching on the oar he held, as if he were considering using it to knock the man overboard. "Shits, if it's such a bad idea, maybe you should have said as much back on the ship, instead of nodding along."

"I assumed we were all agreeing about how stupid of a plan it was," Shits grumbled, crossing his arms across his thin chest.

"It seems to me," Shadow said, glancing up from where he was picking at his fingernails with the tip of one of his knives, "that you just enjoy complaining. I would even go so far as to hazard a guess you knew exactly what you were agreeing to."

The other man's face shifted, as if he might laugh, and he managed a frown belied by the glimmer of amusement in his eyes. "Well, can't say as I rightly remember one way or the other. Either way, just because I'm a fool don't mean it ain't a shit plan. I reckon I can think of better ways to die than being hacked up by a bunch of city guardsmen. Like maybe havin' a fat whore try to smother me with her--"

Urek let out a warning hiss, stealing a glance at Beautiful where she sat on the other end of the rowboat. Balen stopped skulking long enough to follow the big man's gaze and breathed a sigh of relief when the woman seemed not to have noticed the thin man's comment. Her legs were crossed, her hands resting gently on one knee, something almost dainty about her posture. But Balen had seen the woman fight before, and he knew that the slightly whimsical expression she had would disappear fast enough if some unfortunate bastard managed to piss her off. But instead of growing angry, the woman continued to smile in the direction of the shore, like she was some noblewoman on a boat touring the waterways of the city instead of a criminal on a mission that meant almost certain death while, in the distance, the constant roar of cannon fire could be heard as ship after ship was sent to a watery grave.

As if the thought summoned it, a cannon ball, apparently missing its intended target, landed less than a dozen feet away from their rowboat, and water fountained out, forcing Urek to row desperately for several seconds lest they be capsized.

When he finally managed to get the small vessel under control, the crime boss and his crew all turned to look at each other, their expressions grim. Finally, the one named Shadow shrugged. "Must have been aiming for Shits."

The thin man scowled at that, but his expression broke, and he began to laugh. Soon they were all laughing, even Beautiful who had left off gazing at the distant shore when the cannon shot hit the water. All, that was, except for Balen. *They're all insane*, he thought miserably as their braying laughter boomed out into the darkness. *Gods, I'm doomed.*

He decided, then, that he should have fought harder when Captain Festa volunteered him to go on the journey, to make sure the thing was "done right." As if Balen had any idea what the mechanism that controlled a boom line even *looked* like. Well, he did, fine, but it would have been a simple enough thing for the criminals to figure out on their own, and he had told Festa as much, doing what he thought was—under the circumstances—an admirable job of keeping his voice from cracking as he focused on sounding reasonable.

The captain, though, had only grinned, as if he knew well enough the direction of Balen's thoughts, and had said every boat needed a sailor, even a skiff like the one they were currently on. Balen had still been trying to form a response to *that* particular bit of insanity when Urek and the others had stepped up, clapping him on the back, and the next thing he knew, he was on a boat heading toward certain death.

"So," he said, as much to interrupt the loud laughter of the others—the last thing they needed to do was draw any more attention to themselves—as to distract his racing heart. "You haven't told me what the plan is."

"It's shit," Shits said, using a finger to wipe the tears from his eyes. "Where you been at, sailor?"

"One more crack like that," Urek said, "and you can take the other boat, Shits."

"Other boat?" the man asked, frowning and looking around.

Urek grinned menacingly, and Shadow sighed. "There's no other boat, Shits. I believe what the boss is saying is he'll throw you overboard."

"Oh. Right. I knew that." The man started to say something else, but the crime boss raised a questioning eyebrow at him, and he subsided into sullen silence. Not nearly sullen enough, so far as Balen was concerned. If anything should put a man in a bad mood, it ought to be heading to his death on a boat full of lunatics.

"Anyway," Balen went on, deciding to try again before he started puking in fear. "How do you mean to get the boom house doors open?"

Urek grinned at him. "Now, see, the lad here's got that covered," he said, nodding to the small youth sitting beside Balen at the boat's center. "Why don't you tell him, Osirn, set the man at ease. Why, he looks like he's going to shit gold, he don't get an answer soon."

The youth nodded so vigorously that it was a wonder his head didn't come off his shoulders. "O-of course, Urek. You see, s-sir—"

"Balen, please," the first mate answered. *If we're going to die together, the least we can do is be on a first name basis.*

"R-r-right. Balen. Anyway, t-the way I f-figure it, the problem is, well, you know, that the doors are l-l-locked. Right?"

That's the first problem, but I reckon there's better odds it'll be the guardsmen with the swords that'll kill us before a door will. "Right."

"W-well. See. M-my plan is to u-u-unlock them."

Balen waited for the boy to continue, and several seconds passed before he realized he'd finished. He spun to the big man, giving him an incredulous look, and saw Urek grinning at him. Seeing that grin, Balen's fear turned into anger. "You've got to be fuckin' kiddin' me," he said. "That's the plan?"

The big man shrugged. "Seems like a good enough one to me, Balen. Best thing, in my experience, is to keep a plan simple. That way, there's less chances of the thing goin' sideways on ya."

"B-but that's not a plan at *all*," Balen sputtered, unable to help himself. "That's like saying the best way to beat another army is to just walk up and, gods, I don't know, kill them."

Urek nodded slowly, studying Balen carefully. "Seems to me that's just about the best way to get it done. You feeling alright, first mate?"

"Am I *feeling* alright?" Balen repeated, his eyes wide. He saw the other criminals watching him in expectation, genuinely waiting for his reply. Finally, he sighed, slumping back down in his seat. "I'm fine."

"Good," the big man said. "The gods know we've got a job ahead of us, and the last thing we need is for you to go acting crazy."

"Gods forbid," Balen muttered, not bothering to hide the bitterness in his voice and all too aware of the irony in the man's statement. An irony which, unless one of the gods decided to perform a miracle for poor old Balen, looked bound and determined to get him killed.

"Still," Urek said after a moment, "there's some sense to what you say, I'll admit that much. And, turns out, I might just have an idea."

"Thank the gods for that at least," Balen said, feeling a faint flare of hope in his chest. "So what should we do?"

"Well," the big man said, nodding slowly as if considering it, "you got me to thinkin' maybe there's a bit of the plan that we're leavin' out. Might be, we could make this thing a whole lot easier, help the chances we all walk away with all of our bits in their proper places."

"All of them?" Shadow said, his tone almost bored as he resumed picking at his nails with his knife. "That's too bad. We'd be doing the world a favor, if we misplaced Shits's face."

Urek grunted. "I imagine there's some whores'd thank us for it, but I don't think that'd be fair to the 'em—after all, at least with that mug of his, they all know what they're in for soon as he walks up."

"Anyway," Balen said, desperate to get the crime boss back on track, "you said there was a plan."

"Well," the big man said slowly, "I ain't tryin' to claim it's the best of one, but I figure it's worth a shot."

"So what is it?" Balen said, only just managing to repress the scream that threatened to come out.

"Well," Urek said, meeting his eyes and grinning widely, "I figure maybe we ought to knock first."

The boat erupted in laughter again at that, and Balen sank fully into his seat, thinking it wouldn't be such a bad thing if the next cannon ball didn't miss by quite so wide a margin.

***

The creatures came slowly, taking their time as they approached the ragged circle Aaron and the others had formed. In no hurry, and why should they be? The creatures outnumbered his group at least three to one. Even with the Virtues, the outcome seemed all but certain. "Stay close to me, kid," he said, pushing Caleb behind him. A useless gesture, but it was the only thing he could think to do. There were just too many, that was all, and that was even before he considered the one that still stood beside the bald man, the one who had once been Savrin, a talented, if arrogant, swordsman.

That one, he knew, was different from the others. Better. Aaron had seen him move before, with a speed that put even the other creatures around him to shame, and his strength had been enough to shatter Aaron's sword with one strike. The other creatures were fast, but at least they were weaker than their hulking counterparts, their limbs too long, too thin. The other, though, had all their strengths and none of their weaknesses. Had they faced him only, the thing would have been in question; never mind the other sixty or more creatures with him.

"What do we do, sir?" This from one of the Ghosts who glanced at Aaron from his own place in the impromptu circle. There was no fear in the man's voice, only the question. Which just went to show he was either a fool, or he believed in Aaron's ability to get him out of even this mess—in short, a fool.

Take as many with you as you can and die as best as you can. It was on the tip of his tongue, the words just about to leave his mouth, and he was trying to consider how best to make it to the bald man. If he was going to die, at least he would cut that one down, would give answer to the small smile that he still carried on his face. He'd actually gone so far as to open his mouth, to take a step forward, when another voice, a man's voice, spoke. But this one didn't come from any of those standing in the circle with him. Instead, it came from inside his own head.

Touch him.

Aaron recognized the voice as belonging to the long-dead king, the Aaron Caltriss for whom he had been named. *Touch him? Touch who?*

You know. His power is greater, true, but just because the weaknesses are not as obvious, it does not mean they are not there. Kevlane, in his hate, his arrogance, left the man more of himself than the others. It is this part that makes him greater than they, the part that still remembers what it is to be human.

Wait a minute, Aaron thought, *you're saying he's still a human? That he remembers* being *human?*

Yes, the king answered. *He remembers. He has only forgotten that he remembers. You need only remind him.*

And to do that, I have to touch him?

Yes.

So just manage to touch the fastest, strongest living creature on earth—one, I might point out, who seems all too intent on killing me—without somehow getting cut down in the process?

Yes.

"Well," Aaron muttered, "I guess I've got nothing better to do."

"Sir?" the Ghost asked, a confused expression on his face.

"Stay with me," Aaron said. "We drive as fast as we can, as hard as we can. Don't stop for anything. I need to touch that one." He pointed at the creature which had once been Savrin. He was at once relieved and shocked when no one asked a question, even so much as commented. Instead, they only watched him, confident he knew what to do. *Gods, I hope you're right.*

He glanced at Leomin and Seline, at Gryle and Tianya and Caleb. All friends, all here because of him. They nodded to show they understood. And so Aaron drew his sword and charged.

The creatures reacted immediately, rushing forward with blinding speed, but Aaron called on the power of his bond with Co, touching upon what little pieces of their humanity remained, so that he knew where the strikes would come from before they did. His sword lashed to one side, knocking wide a blade aimed at his throat. The creature stumbled, off-balance, but Aaron was already moving past, trusting one of the others to finish it.

And then they were in the thick of it. As he pushed his way forward, Aaron took what few opportunities presented themselves to steal glances at the creature who had once been Savrin and the bald man. The two hadn't moved, only stood, waiting, the bald man with a smile on his face, the creature with a blank, unreadable expression.

The Ghosts and Virtue-bearers fought well, following him and plunging deep into the waiting line of creatures. But for all their skill, for all their courage, they were outnumbered and surrounded, and soon the greater speed and numbers of the creatures began to tell as first one Ghost fell, then another. Aaron felt the deaths through his bond with the Virtue, felt them like some piece of him being ripped away, and he used the resulting anger to fuel his strikes.

A murderous rage consumed him as it had on other occasions with the Virtue of Compassion but, this time, it was different. This time, no matter how great the fires of his fury burned, still his will, strengthened by the Virtue of Will, was equal to the task of controlling it, of harnessing it. He took what gifts the fury offered—strength, motivation, speed, and left the rest. For the first time in what felt like a very long time, his anger was his, his to grow and tend and use. And so he did.

He stoked the blaze of his anger until it wasn't a flame at all, but a great onrushing river of white heat, one that could not be stopped by any foolish enough to stand in opposition to it. Here, were those who, if left unchecked, would destroy everything he loved, everything he held dear. The bald man, standing with that smirk on his face, hardly a man at all but a creature, a *thing* as surely as the rest of them, one who would live off the pain and agony of all of Telrear, one who would gorge himself on their loss. In Aaron's mind he became not a man at all, but an agent, a representative of all the evil in the world, one who owed an accounting.

The loss of his parents, the loss of Seline's father, the Speaker, Beth, and all the rest, he laid at the bald man's feet. This one, then, owed a great debt, and Aaron and those others with him would collect it. He was faster, stronger, his strikes cleaner, more sure than they had ever been. But through the dual powers of his bonds both with Co and Caltriss, Aaron spread that fury, that strength, to those around him, and they plowed their way through the creatures, striking them down as they charged forward of one purpose, of one shared will, and each of Aaron's companions that fell, sacrificing himself to that great purpose, only strengthened the resolve of the others.

He wasn't sure how long they fought, how many lay dead around them; he only knew that, when he risked another glance at the bald man, his smile was gone, replaced by an expression of disbelief mingled with anger. Then, Aaron sensed an attack coming, and jerked his attention back to the melee, throwing his sword up in time to block a strike that would have taken his head from his shoulders. Before he could counterattack, Gryle let out a growl and stepped forward, swinging a sword he had apparently found somewhere in a two-handed grip, like a lumberjack chopping at a tree. The attack was awkward, the man untrained, and the creature managed to get its own blade up in time. Not that it did it much good. Powered by the chamberlain's incredible strength, the sword sheared through the creature's blade without slowing, tearing into the creature and, when it fell to the ground, it did so in two separate, bloody pieces.

Suddenly, a furious shout rose over the din of the battle, "*Kill them!*" An instant later, Aaron found a lane opening in front of them as the fast creatures moved to the side, clearing the last two dozen feet between him and the bald man. Across this empty space, the creature who had once been Savrin met Aaron's eyes, and it drew its blade from where it was sheathed at its back so swiftly that it seemed to Aaron as if the length of steel had simply appeared there in its hands, as if by magic.

"I'll handle this, General Envelar!" one of the Ghosts shouted, stepping in front of him and charging the creature.

"*No don't—*" Aaron began, but before he could finish, the creature moved in a blur, charging forward, and an instant later the Ghost collapsed to the ground, dead. It studied Aaron over the corpse, watching him with the same unreadable expression which it always seemed to carry.

"Savrin," Aaron said. "You don't have to do this—we're not the ones responsible for what has happened to you. I'd help you, if I could."

The creature said nothing, and the bald man laughed. "Do you seek to reason with it?" He shook his head, sighing as if bored. "Aaron Envelar, what you see before you is no man but a slave, its mind, body, and soul dedicated to serving the will of my master. A weapon, nothing more. But a weapon that will do well enough for you and this *rabble.*"

Aaron saw motion to either side of him as the other Virtue-bearers came to stand with him. Seline, the short blades she held in each hand coated with blood. Gryle, his sword bent and twisted, even the carefully-forged steel no match for the power with which he used it. Tianya, her hand clasped over a wound in her arm, Caleb, holding a sword in two hands, the blade shaking with nervous tremors, but his eyes confident and sure and unafraid. And Leomin, a vaguely-surprised expression on his features, as if he hadn't expected to live this long.

The bald man laughed, looking at each of them in turn. "This is your great army then, is it? Still, I suspect my master will be pleased to find that you have been foolish enough to bring all of the Virtues to him." He shook his head and motioned to the creature that had once been Savrin. "Get it done quickly—there is still more work to be done tonight."

Though he could feel the creature's intent, knew the strike was coming, Aaron was only just quick enough to get his blade up in time. Still, the blow landed with such force, that he cried out in surprise as his sword was knocked from his grip, spinning away into the press of thin, fast creatures surrounding him and the others, a silent audience to their inevitable deaths.

"*Stop.*" The creature hesitated, its blade already raised for another attack, and Aaron followed its gaze to see Leomin stepping forward. The Parnen's expression was set, his jaw clamped tightly shut, and Aaron could feel the power of the man's Virtue coming off him in waves.

But if the creature was affected by the Parnen's efforts, it gave no sign. Instead, it cocked its head, studying him, then started toward him, raising its blade higher with the clear intent of cutting him down. Leomin's eyes widened in surprise, but he did not move, and his hands knotted into fists at his side as Aaron felt him redouble his efforts with the Virtue.

Still, the creature did not slow, and Aaron was about to step forward, weaponless, when another voice spoke. "Leave him alone!" Seline appeared in a blur, her crimson-coated blades moving faster than the eye could follow. At least, the normal eye. The creature seemed to have no great difficulty, its blade moving with incredible speed, blocking each strike, in a distracted, almost bored sort of way, its gaze remaining locked on the Parnen.

Finally, the woman stepped back, panting hard, and the creature's own blade flashed out. She moved both her blades up in front of her to block it, then let out a scream of surprise and pain as the force of its blow sent her flying backward where she struck one of the Ghosts, and they both collapsed to the ground.

Aaron watched her long enough to see that she—and the man she'd hit—were hurt but alive, painstakingly rising to their feet, then he turned back to the creature who had begun walking toward Leomin once more.

For his part, the Parnen had fallen to one knee, and his face was sallow and pale, his breath coming in ragged gasps as if he had just expended some monumental effort—an effort which, apparently, had had no effect. No time to wait then. "Sword," Aaron said, reaching out to the nearest Ghost who handed over his blade without comment.

Then, with a growl, he launched himself at the creature. It was fast, impossibly so, and even knowing from which direction its strikes would come, still Aaron barely managed to block them in time, launching counters of his own that the creature brushed aside with no more effort than a man might use to swat at an annoying fly. Only his bond and a lifetime spent training with the sword kept Aaron alive, but in less than two minutes he was exhausted, his muscles straining with the effort of keeping up with the creature's impossible pace. He tried to look for an opening to touch the creature, but it was too quick, far too quick. He was just beginning to realize that he was doomed when he saw movement out of the corner of his eye, accompanied by a shout of anger.

The creature's sword lashed out at the approaching figure, but Aaron anticipated the strike and brought his own blade up, stopping the blow with a jarring impact. A moment later, Gryle barreled into the creature. The creature's sword flew out of its hands at the impact, and it and the chamberlain tumbled to the ground in a heap. A second later, the creature had managed to get on top of the chamberlain, but Gryle had wrapped it in a tight hug, pinning its arms against its sides.

The two struggled, and Gryle hissed through gritted teeth as he the creature tried to break free of his hold. "*Hurry,*" the chamberlain grated desperately.

Aaron cursed and lunged forward, calling on his bond with the two Virtues as he did, and then his hand fell upon the creature's arm. The connection came with a terrible jolt, as if he had been struck by lightning, and he cried out in surprise. He felt the creature's emotions rush through him like a tidal wave. Strange, alien thoughts filled his head. There was hate there, a hate so powerful he had never felt its like, hate for itself, hate for the one who had made it and for all others, an ever-hungry, devouring hate that lusted to destroy everything and everyone.

The feeling was so strong that Aaron felt as if he would be consumed by it, but he gritted his teeth, desperately clinging to himself in a maelstrom threatening to tear him apart. Then, suddenly, that terrible sensation vanished, and all else disappeared, the people around him, the city street and the buildings crowding either side of it, all gone in an instant.

He found himself standing on a dark shore. There was no moon or sun, the world seeming to exist in a perpetual, twilight gloom. There was a great, *roaring* susurration that he felt in his bones, and Aaron spun to see dark, churning waters of an ocean rearing up as if alive. Suddenly, hundred-foot-tall waves were rushing toward him, as if eager to destroy this stranger who had dared intrude upon their world.

"No."

He turned and saw that another stood on the shore with him. Here, in this place of emotion and will, the long-dead king, Aaron Caltriss, did not appear in the misty, ephemeral form that he often did. Instead, he appeared as a man, a man of courage and strength who had stood against the darkness of the world. A man who had, for a time, beaten it.

"We will stand against it," the ancient king said. *"Together."*

"But how?" Aaron said. A great, terrible wind had risen, whipping at his clothes, and his words seemed to be snatched away, barely audible even to his own ears.

"No man is ever so given to the darkness that he might not be made to see the light. For all his Art, for all his power, that is one thing Boyce never understood," Caltriss said, gazing out at the approaching waves, at the storm clouds gathering overhead. *"He is hate, Aaron Envelar. He has been twisted into a creature of madness and pain, yet for all that, he is human still. You must remind him."*

"And how am I supposed to do that?" Aaron demanded.

The old king gave him a small smile. *"It takes only one light, Aaron Envelar, to stand against the darkness."* He turned back to the roiling waves. *"Only one."*

And then Aaron knew what he had to do. Yet he hesitated, gazing out into that roiling water. *Co?* he asked.

I am here, Aaron, the Virtue answered. *I will not leave you.*

He nodded, hesitating another moment. Then, Aaron Envelar took a slow, deep breath and stepped from the shore and into the waiting storm.

CHAPTER THIRTY-SEVEN

The row boat struck the shore a hundred feet from one of the boom houses. Or so Balen thought. There was no way to tell for sure, as a wall had been built on either side of the docks, and the stone edifice blocked the structures from view. The night was dark, but in the sporadic bursts of cannon fire and by the ruddy light of the torches they carried, Balen could make out soldiers patrolling the wall, and he was covered in sweat. Any moment, one of those soldiers would look down, would see Balen and the others in the small boat at the base of the wall, and that would be the end of it.

So far, the guards' attention seemed more focused on the sea battle in the distance, but that was little comfort. Even if none of the patrolling soldiers noticed him and the others, the wall was twenty feet at least, and it seemed to him that their mission might well fail before it had even truly begun.

If the others in the boat with him shared any of his own fears, they showed no sign, simply studying the wall—and the guards moving along its surface—with what looked, to Balen, at least, to be dangerously close to indifference. *At least they stopped laughing before we got close.* That was something, anyway, and he hadn't been able to suppress his audible sigh of relief when Urek had called for quiet.

"What now?" he whispered.

"Now we climb," Urek said, his tone business-like, almost bored. "Oh," he went on, as if it was an afterthought, "and we try not to die." He motioned to Shadow. "Get it done quiet and clean. If one of 'em raises an alarm, we're done."

"Aye aye, boss," the man said, putting the knife he'd been fiddling with between his teeth—a recipe, Balen figured, for a bad day—before stepping past him.

The first mate waited for the man to bring out a rope or a grapple, but he didn't. Instead, he simply reached out and, as if by magic, began scaling the wall, climbing it as easily as he would a ladder, moving as silently as a ghost.

Balen looked at Urek in surprise, but the big crime boss only shrugged. "A skill he's practiced climbin' into a few women's windows, I suspect."

Shadow reached the top of the wall but waited, stuck against it like some great bug, as one of the wall guards patrolled closer to him. As soon as the man drew even with him, the hawk-nosed man leapt upward, his arm flashing out. In another moment, the guard's corpse tumbled into the sea.

Balen stared in shock, then turned, sure that one of the other guards must have noticed, and saw one a short distance away that had just turned back on his patrol, heading in the other man's direction. *He'll see, gods, he'll see him.* But the hawk-nosed man had somehow managed to take the guard's sword before throwing him over, and now he was marching toward the other guard, in direct imitation of the dead man. So precise was his act that had Balen not witnessed the attack himself, he would have thought Shadow *was* the guard.

The approaching guard, too, seemed not to notice the difference. Not, at least, until he drew closer and froze. The water crashing against the harbor made it impossible for Balen to make out the man's words, but he didn't miss the defensiveness in his posture. A defensiveness that lasted for the second it took Shadow to lash out with the blade. Moments later the guard was following his dead comrade into the water.

Balen found that he was sweating, holding his breath, and he looked around the wall but saw no other guards close enough to worry about. Shadow apparently noticed it too, for he was soon lowering a rope down to those in the boat, fastening its other end to the wall. *Gods,* Balen thought. *Two men dead without even knowing what was happening. So fast...*

He nearly screamed as someone clapped him on the back, and he spun to see the crime boss grinning at him. "Relax, first mate. We're on your side."

For now, Balen thought, and gained little comfort from the thought. After all, as the big crime boss was only too keen to say—they *were* criminals, after all.

"Well," Urek grunted as he turned to Beautiful, "ladies first."

***

Balen was the last up the wall, and he was panting from the effort by the time he half-climbed, half-collapsed onto the stone with a grateful sigh.

"Stay low," Urek whispered, "don't want any of these bastards catchin' sight of us and wonderin' why there's five guards where there ought to be only two."

An order which Balen was all too happy to follow, as his breath was wheezing in his lungs—from fear as much as from exertion—and the muscles of his arms and legs felt weak. They waited, Balen's heart galloping in his chest, as Shadow untied the rope and hung it down the other side of the wall. Far too quickly, he was forced to follow the others as they climbed down.

"Well," the crime boss said once they were all crouched at the inside base of the wall. "That was easy enough. Now for the hard part."

Balen, whose feet had slipped nearly a dozen times on the water-soaked harbor wall and had felt sure each time he was going to follow the hapless guards into the shadowy depths, could have argued about how easy the climb had been, but he decided there was little point. He was here, after all, and it was far too late to turn back now.

"Alright, first mate," the crime boss said, turning to him. "Take point and lead us to this boom house of yours."

"Me?" Balen said. "On point?"

"Well sure," Urek said, grinning, "that way, if they've got archers posted, at least I know the first arrow won't hit me."

Sighing heavily, Balen started forward, the smiling criminals following.

***

Aaron stepped off the shore into the dark water, expecting to be swallowed by it. Instead, the water seemed to retreat before him, receding farther with each step he took. There was a lantern in his hand, though he had no understanding of how it came to be there. By its light, he watched the water gather around him, swirling and shifting as if it desperately wanted to consume him, yet seeming to be held back, somehow, as if pressing against an invisible wall. *It takes only one light,* he thought, the dead king's words repeating in his head, *to push back the darkness.*

He stepped tentatively, all too aware of the water gathering around him higher and higher as he walked, until looking up, he realized that he was surrounded on all sides by great towering walls of it, so high he could not make out the tops. Swallowing, he pressed on through the damp trail the separating waters left before him. He didn't know for how long he walked, but eventually the path he followed opened into a wide circle.

The man knelt on both knees, his bare back to Aaron. The sellsword could see the man was wracked with tremors, as if he was freezing. The stranger did not turn at Aaron's approach, and soon the sellsword was standing beside him. Savrin. But when the man turned to him, his eyes were not the dead, emotionless eyes of the creature he had become, but those of the man he had once been. "I...don't I know you?" the man asked.

"Yes," Aaron said. "We've met before."

The man nodded, turning away once more, and Aaron followed his gaze to a woman and a boy standing in the center of the circle formed by the surrounding water. He did not know them, but at the same time...he did. He was overcome with a love for them that he knew was not his own. "Your sister," Aaron said as realization struck. "Your nephew."

Something bothered Aaron about the two figures and, looking closer, he saw that neither moved. It was as if they weren't people at all, really, but paintings or sculptures.

They are his memories, Co said, her voice quiet and sad. *The small part of him that is human remembers them.*

"I cannot reach them," the man said, his words somewhere between a scream and a sob. "I've tried. But as much as I try...the waters will not let me. And...and I begin to forget."

Aaron frowned, and saw that even as he watched them, the figures grew slightly less distinct. The lines of their faces, the colors of their eyes blurring, so that he couldn't have said for certain what shade they were.

"It is always dark here," the man went on. "Always cold. I...I think..." He turned, gazing at Aaron with desperate eyes, his grief writ plain upon his face. "I think, maybe, I knew them. That I *should* know them. But...I forget." He heaved a heavy sigh and seemed to shrink on himself. "I...see things, sometimes. Feel things. There is a man...like me, but not me. I think...I think maybe I am evil."

Aaron found it hard to look at the man's tortured visage, and he felt a fresh wave of rage wash over him. Kevlane had stolen the man's body, had made of him a monster, but the greatest evil he had committed was in leaving enough of him to know what he was, to sense something of what he had become, and what he had lost.

"I have been alone for so long," the man said, and this time he didn't seem to be talking to Aaron at all. "I screamed, looking for help, begging for anyone to come, but no one did."

"I am here now." Aaron said, swallowing the lump, one of grief and anger, gathered in his throat. "Take my hand, Savrin," he said, offering his own.

"Savrin," the man said, as if tasting the word. "I...I think that was my name. Is it my name?"

"Yes," Aaron answered. "Now, come. I will lead you to them."

The man took his hand, and Aaron pulled him to his feet, starting forward. "B-but the waters," the man said. "They will come...they have drowned me, I think...I do not remember how many times."

"Not this time."

They had covered about half the distance toward the two figures when the man hesitated, resisting Aaron's pull. The sellsword saw the fear on the man's face, saw the tears trailing their way down his cheeks. He was shaking his head desperately. "I can't..." he said. "I can't remember. Pella...Larn...I can't."

"You must," Aaron said. "But you must do it on your own. I cannot force you, Savrin."

"T-then," the man said, turning to Aaron with a desperate hope in his eyes. "I can be with them, again?"

"One day," Aaron said. "But...now, I can give you the man who has taken you from them, Savrin. That much, at least, I can do."

The man frowned, as if confused. "Someone...did this to me?" He gazed out at one end of the circle, and Aaron followed his eyes to see a vague, shadowy figure forming there, indistinct and unsure. Slowly, it resolved itself into the unmistakable visage of the bald man who had ambushed him and the others in the street.

"Yes," Aaron said, frowning at the figure who stood as still as the woman and boy. "But do not be afraid, Savrin. What he can take from you, he has taken already. Now, you must take some of it back—you must remember. Now, come. They wait for you."

The man did not resist again, and Aaron led him to the center of the circle where waited his sister and his nephew, where waited, in truth, his humanity.

***

Aaron's eyes snapped open, and the world rushed back with force. The creature that had once been Savrin howled, the first sound he'd ever heard it make, and it tore its way free of the chamberlain's clutches, knocking Aaron's arm loose with such force that the sellsword stumbled and would have fallen, had Tianya not caught him. "What has happened?" she said, her voice a breathy, shocked whisper. "What did you do?"

"I helped him remember," Aaron said, as the thing that had once been Savrin rose to its feet. It turned to him, and he wasn't sure if he imagined the flash of knowledge, of understanding, he saw in its eyes, or if it was really there. "At least...I hope I did."

Aaron moved forward to help the chamberlain to his feet. The creature must have struck him a glancing blow during the struggles, for Gryle had one hand pressed against his bloody nose. "You alright?"

The chamberlain swallowed hard, breathing heavily, but nodded. "Better than can be expected." Aaron grunted, looking back to the creature as it turned to regard him and the others.

"*Well?*" Caldwell demanded in an angry hiss. "Finish them!"

The creature turned slowly, staring at the bald man, and for the first time Caldwell looked uncertain, afraid. The creature retrieved its sword from where it had fallen and started toward him with unhurried footsteps. One of the Ghosts moved forward, perhaps meaning to cut it down from behind, but Aaron grabbed the man's arm, halting him. "Wait," he whispered. "Just wait."

"Y-you have to do as I command!" the bald man said, watching the creature's inexorable approach with wide, terrified eyes. "In the name of Kevlane, your god, I command you to kill them!"

Yet still Savrin walked on, and Caldwell, frozen with either disbelief or fear, only stood there until the creature came upon him. Then, there was a blur of movement as Savrin unceremoniously drove his blade into the man's stomach.

Caldwell let out a scream of surprise and stared down at the blade impaling him in disbelief. "I-it can't be...i-it's impossible."

Savrin spoke then, in a voice that sounded harsh and tortured, as if each word was a great effort. "I...remember. I...told you...I would kill you."

"B-but it can't be," the bald man whimpered. "I-it...can't—"

His words were cut off as Savrin took a step back and, with a flash of his sword, cut the man's head from his shoulders. Then he turned back to stare at Aaron, and now the sellsword saw some of the man he had once been in his gaze. One of the Ghosts let out a shout, and Aaron spun, cursing as he saw yet more of the creatures coming out of the alleyways between them and the city gate.

Then there was someone at his shoulder, and he looked to see Savrin standing beside him, gazing around at the dozens of creatures surrounding them. "*Go,*" he said. "Finish what you have started. I will hold them...for as long as I can."

"Are you sure?" Aaron said, surprised at the emotions—anger, grief, sadness—that roiled in him.

"He wanted a monster," Savrin said without looking away from the creatures gathering around them, "and so I will give him one. Now, go...while there is still time."

Aaron turned to see the other Virtue-bearers and what remained of the Ghosts watching him. He had a moment of shock as he realized that only two of Perennia's elite troops remained standing. The rest lay dead, their bodies scattered among the corpses of Kevlane's creatures.

"Alright, you heard him," he said, forcing the words past the lump in his throat. "Let's finish this." And then they were running. The creatures tried to close in around them, but wherever they approached, Savrin was there, his blade flashing like lightning in the orange, ruddy glow of the street lanterns.

Soon they were past the mob of creatures, running through the streets, their breath rasping in the cold night air while the sounds of battle rang out behind them. They reached an intersection in the street, and Aaron turned to Caleb. "Which way?"

The youth's eyes were wide, and he was staring back at the battle going on behind them in a stunned sort of way.

"*Caleb,*" Aaron said again, louder this time, "which way?"

The youth jumped at the sound of his voice and turned to look at him. "Um…with the creature…how did you…"

Aaron saw the question in the eyes of the others, too. "Look," he said, "I'll tell you all about it later." *If we survive.* "But right now, we've got more important things to worry about." He glanced back at Savrin who moved in a blur, his sword lashing out and cutting down one creature after the other. "As good as he is, he won't last long, not against so many." And, of course, that wasn't even considering the army even now being slaughtered outside of Baresh's walls. An army of which many of Aaron's friends—not to mention the woman he had come to love—were a part.

"Right, sorry," the youth said, swallowing hard and forcing his eyes away from the bloody spectacle taking place near the gate. "This way."

CHAPTER THIRTY-EIGHT

Two guards stood in front of the boom house, their figures visible in the wavering orange light of the torches placed in brackets on either side of the structure. Urek paused and held up a hand, indicating for the others to stop. Now, with the wall blocking the harbor from view, Balen couldn't see the battle raging on the waters outside the port, but he could hear it well enough. Cannons roared in the darkness like angry gods, more often than not followed by the tortured wailing of wood as one ship or another was struck. The night sky was lit by intermittent flashes of light as the battle raged on, and Balen felt almost grateful to be here on the shore instead of among that battle.

"*What now?*" he whispered, suddenly feeling very exposed, never mind the fact that it was dark, and the place in which they'd stopped was well away from any of the torches placed intermittently along the length of the harbor wall.

In answer, Urek motioned toward the hawk-nosed man. "Keep it quiet, will ya?"

"Sure, boss," the man answered, and if he felt any of the anxiety that plagued Balen, his voice didn't reflect it.

Balen watched Shadow creep away in the direction of the chain house, seeming to vanish into the darkness, living up to his name. Swallowing hard, Balen watched the guards. Minutes passed, each dragging on until it felt like they'd been crouched against the wall for an eternity. Then one of the guards suddenly stumbled and collapsed to the ground with a knife jutting from his throat.

The other guard spun, starting to pull his sword, but a figure rose out of the darkness behind him and dragged a blade across his throat. Seconds later he lay dead beside his companion. "Alright then," Urek said, his voice as calm as if they were sitting in a tavern somewhere having a drink, "come on."

The others started forward, following the big man, and Balen stared after them, shocked by how quickly the two men had died, without ever even knowing what had happened to them. *Gods, let me remember never to piss that man off,* he thought.

By the time he arrived, the band of criminals had already dragged the two bodies out of the torchlight, and the youth, Osirn, was crouched in front of the door, with what looked to be small metal tools in his hands. "Ah, first mate," the big crime boss said with a grin, "I was beginning to think you got lost."

If only I was that lucky, Balen thought, looking around at the guards on the wall and those who patrolled the docks. "What now?"

"Now," the crime boss answered, "we let Osirn here do his work."

"And what if one of the guards sees us and raises the alarm?"

"Well," Urek said, scratching his chin as if thinking it over. "Then I imagine we'll die. Painfully, no doubt."

His grin did little to assuage Balen's fears, and the first mate cleared his throat in an effort to keep back the whimper gathering there. "And the guards on the inside?" There would be several, he didn't doubt. After all, only a fool would set up a harbor chain against an enemy navy and not make sure it was well-guarded. And as good as Shadow was, he wouldn't be able to sneak up on the men inside as he had the other two.

The crime boss nodded, frowning. "I been thinkin' about that. Interestin' fact; while I was studyin' on Baresh's army, I learned they don't let women into their ranks."

Balen was about to ask the man if now was really the best time for a military lesson, but a grunt from beside him made him turn to see the woman, Beautiful, frowning at the crime boss. But if Urek saw, he gave no sign, only studying Balen as if it were only the two of them there.

"Yeah, on account of, they say, women are too weak and not smart enough to be soldiers."

The woman hissed, and Balen noted the others stepping slowly away from her. Urek shrugged, as if unaware of the effect his words were causing on Beautiful. "Can't say as I understand it, myself. But accordin' to what I've heard, the army of Baresh looks at those things different. They figure women are good as little more than brood sows, poppin' out babies and all."

There was a metallic *click,* almost inaudible over the constant growl issuing from the giant woman's throat, and Balen swallowed hard, taking a step back himself. "Got it," Osirn said in a breathy, excited whisper.

Urek nodded and drew his sword, offering it to Beautiful without a word. The large woman snatched it from his hand, stepped past him, and slammed her foot into the door. There was a shout of surprise from inside the boom house as the door flew open, and then the woman charged inside. Balen stared in shock and recoiled as screams began to come from inside the building. Then he realized that the woman, however strong she was, was in there alone facing the gods alone knew how many guards. He started forward, but the crime boss grabbed his arm, halting him.

"I'd give her a minute or two, first mate," he said.

"But she might need help," Balen said.

There was a *crash* from inside, and Urek grunted in what might have been a laugh. "I don't think she'll be the one lookin' for help just now."

"Was that true, boss?" Shits asked. "About the army not takin' women, I mean?"

"How the fuck should I know?" Urek said.

After a minute or two, the sounds of fighting from inside trailed off, and the big man grunted. "Alright then. Let's go."

CHAPTER THIRTY-NINE

"Come on *my* ship?" Festa bellowed, swinging the chair leg he held with two hands. There was an audible *crack* as the stout length of wood struck the man in the jaw.

The enemy sailor stumbled back toward the deck's rail, and the captain's second strike sent him tumbling over the side and into the dark water below. "Get your own damn ship!" he bellowed after the man. Frowning, Festa spun in time to see the last of the enemy sailors either cut down or thrown overboard.

"Captain," a sailor asked, running up to him, "what are your orders?"

"Get that old grumpy bastard, Emer, up here to see to the wounded."

The sailor swallowed, his expression falling as if he'd just been given a death sentence. Aside from the captain himself, the ship's surgeon was the most feared man on the ship, but the man nodded and started away.

Festa studied the battle taking place on all sides as the Baresh navy engaged Perennia's. Perennia's had the greater numbers, but most of the ships making up their convoy were captained by smugglers used to running from fights, not military commanders. More than one ship had gone down to Baresh's trained fleet, carrying its sailors—and the soldiers in its hold—down into the dark abyss the Sea Goddess called home.

He'd just turned back to gaze at the shore when another sailor approached. "Do you think they'll succeed, Cap?" the man asked, and Festa could hear the fear in the man's voice.

They'd better, he thought. *If not, we're done, and the army with us.* But he said none of that, spinning on the man instead with a growl. "How the fuck should I know?" he demanded. "Now, get back to your damned job before I decide to feed the Sea Bitch one more fool."

The man swallowed, hurrying away, his shoulders hunched as if in expectation of being struck with something. And that was alright. Let the man focus on fearing his own captain instead of the doom that seemed more likely by the moment. Once the man was away, Festa turned back and studied the shoreline once more. *If you're goin' to do something, Balen, it had better be soon.*

***

The scene inside the boom house was one of unmitigated carnage. Blood was smeared on the floor and the walls, and bodies lay scattered like broken dolls, their limbs twisted at strange, impossible angles. Beautiful stood in the center of the room, covered in blood as if she'd bathed in the stuff, her chest heaving, her thick hands clasped into tight fists.

Balen felt the gorge rise in his throat and forced it down with a will, gagging. The woman spun at the sound, her eyes wild, a feral hunger dancing in them, and his breath caught.

"That was nicely done, Beautiful," Urek said.

"Women *can* fight," she said in a voice that was little more than a growl.

"Sure they can," the crime boss said in a soothing tone normally reserved for wounded animals or the insane. Which, Balen thought, fit well enough. "Of course they can. And I reckon you showed these lads that well enough."

The woman stared at him, her chest still heaving, and Balen tensed, half-expecting her to charge. Instead, she only sighed and some of the menace left her features as she looked at her hands. "I've ruined my nails," she said in a musing tone, as if she'd chipped one of them having tea instead of butchering what Balen thought—though he couldn't be sure as all of the guards' pieces weren't in their proper places—had been at least four men.

"A damn shame," Urek agreed, as if it were the most reasonable comment in the world. "But don't you worry—we'll get 'em done proper, when we make it back to Perennia."

She smiled widely at that, revealing what few teeth she had left. "Thank you, Urek."

"My pleasure," the big man said, then he cleared his throat and turned to Balen. "Well, first mate? What now?"

Balen realized they were all looking at him and, for a moment, he couldn't speak, unable to force words past the terrified lump in his throat. "Um...right." He turned to the mechanism in the center of the room—a large wheel made for two men to turn, so that they could lower and raise the harbor chain at will. The broken, battered form of one of the guards lay atop it.

"Sorry about that," Beautiful said, giving him an embarrassed look. "I can be...messy, sometimes." She hefted the body as if it weighed nothing and tossed it to the side of the room.

"Um...no problem," Balen said, pointedly avoiding her gaze. He reached for the handle, wincing at the blood covering it. "I'll need some help."

Urek nodded, stepping forward, and in a few minutes, they had lowered the harbor chain. "Alright then, time to go," Urek said.

They started for the door, but Balen hesitated. "Wait a minute, what's to stop the guards from raising it again, once we're gone?"

Urek grunted. "I've been thinkin' about that. Beautiful, you got any of that fire powder on you?"

"Of course," she said.

"Good," the big man said, pulling one of the torches from the wall. "I reckon I might just have an idea of how we can put it to some use."

A moment later, they were hurrying out of the boom house as the blaze grew behind them at an alarming rate. Balen stumbled out, coughing and waving his hands at the smoke already billowing from the burning structure in great clouds. His eyes were burning, and he could barely see. So it was that he bumped into Urek's back without noticing and grunted in surprise.

The others stood unmoving, and he followed their gazes to see what appeared to be at least twenty soldiers charging toward them. "W-what do we do?" he croaked.

Urek grunted. "We run."

***

"Captain, something's happening on the shore!"

Festa spun away from where he'd been studying the battle and, at first saw nothing. He was just about to ask Pater what he meant when one of the boom houses burst into flames. He breathed a heavy sigh of relief. The bastards actually did it. "Alright," Festa yelled, "the harbor chain's been dealt with, boys! Signal the rest of the fleet—it's time we got all these dirt feet off our boats!"

The signals were relayed and soon dozens of ships were racing toward the harbor, carrying their cargo of soldiers with them.

CHAPTER FORTY

Darrell parried the strike that the enemy soldier aimed at his head and countered, his own blade sliding underneath the man's helmet and into his throat. His opponent stumbled away, disappearing into the melee, and the swordmaster took the brief moment of respite to try to get his ragged breathing under control. They'd been fighting for what seemed like forever now—he'd long since last track of the time—and he thought he'd never been so exhausted.

His sword arm was weak, almost numb, and he bled from several minor cuts, made by blows that never should have landed, had he not been so tired. Still, the sun had only just began to rise, so he knew that, despite what his muscles claimed, they couldn't have been at it for more than a few hours, and he thanked the gods that he was still alive to see the new day—there had been several times, in the night, that he had not thought such a thing possible.

Yet for all his gratitude at still being alive, the sun's light was not wholly welcome, for it revealed the true extent of the staggering losses the army had suffered. Hundreds, no, thousands, lay dead. The lines of Perennia's army had grown noticeably thinner over the last hours, were growing thinner even now, and with no end in sight. For now they fought not just Kevlane's creatures, but Baresh's army as well, its soldiers spreading out and surrounding the besieged troops. Such a maneuver would have been dangerous considering the greater numbers of Perennia's army, had the creatures not been interspersed among the regular soldiers, causing death and destruction and creating gaps in the line everywhere they appeared.

Darrell felt a hand on his shoulder and turned to see another soldier stepping forward, relieving him. They had been set on regular rotations since the fighting began with the goal of keeping the freshest troops up front, but the truth was that the man replacing him looked as exhausted as the swordmaster felt. Darrell was too tired to speak, so he only nodded gratefully, shuffling through the line of defenders toward the army camp. His feet dragged, his legs weary beyond belief, and his journey back through the line was made all the more difficult by the muddy ground.

Darrell made his way to where the water was kept, unable to keep his eyes from the dead and dying scattered along the ground behind the line. He grabbed one of the skins and drank deeply, but the luke-warm liquid was unequal to the task of washing away the dust coating his throat. He was tempted to sit, to take a moment to recline in the grass before he went back to the front, but he resisted the urge. He knew that to do so would be folly, for his weary muscles would tighten into knots, and he doubted very much if he'd be able to get up again. So instead he only stood, stretching his aching muscles, and looking toward the western gate of Baresh which remained stubbornly closed.

Darrell was no general, but he had spent his life training with the blade, fighting one battle or another, and he knew that if the gate didn't open soon, it wouldn't matter. Nor was that his only worry, for Aaron and the others were somewhere inside the city. *Gods look after them,* he thought. The intention had been for the army to follow them inside, to assault the mage's castle and defeat him. But from what Darrell had heard, barely anyone had entered the city before the gate closed again. It seemed all too likely that Aaron and the others had already been cut down by whatever forces waited on the other side.

Don't think like that, he scolded himself. *You can't think like that.* "Besides," he said softly, "you've your own battle to fight."

So, he started back toward the line once more—he was old, and he was tired, and he was afraid. But he wasn't done. Not yet.

CHAPTER FORTY-ONE

No longer stuck outside the harbor, the ships rushed Baresh's port eagerly, docking wherever they could. Defenders waited there, their blades ready to meet the soldiers who poured out of the ships' holds. There were not many of them, as the mage, Kevlane, had focused the majority of his forces and his creatures against the army outside the city gates.

Still, even had there been thousands, the outcome would have most likely been the same. For Perennia's soldiers had spent the last hours in a battle at sea, listening to the sounds of cannon fire all around them and knowing that there was nothing they could do. At any moment, one of those cannon blasts might find the ship on which they stood and send them down to a watery grave.

They knew, too, that the army outside the city was hard-pressed, an army full of their comrades, their friends. So when the ships finally docked, the soldiers of Perennia rushed into the waiting defenders without hesitation, grateful to face their foes at last. They crashed into the enemy soldiers like a great wave, sweeping them aside under the force of their attack.

The thing was over in minutes, and Festa stepped off his ship and onto the shore feeling—as he always did when the water was no longer beneath him—like a man hopelessly out of his element. When he reached the docks, he found hundreds, thousands of soldiers watching him, waiting for what he would say. He cursed Aaron Envelar under his breath for making him the commander of the naval expedition. Oh, he knew ships well enough, but what in the name of the gods did he know about commanding soldiers?

"Sir?" one sailor asked. "What do we do now?"

Festa glanced at the man, then at those waiting eyes and grunted. "Thom is waitin' outside the city, along with all the rest of 'em. They been patient enough, I reckon. I figure it's about time we let 'em in."

There was a roar of approval at that, and then the soldiers were off, heading toward the western gate. *Just stay alive for a little while longer, you old fool,* Festa thought as he started after them. *We're comin' to get you.*

***

Aaron and the others followed Caleb through the city. From time to time, Tianya warned them away from one street or the other, using her heightened senses to avoid the majority of the city's troops and Kevlane's creatures.

As for the rest of Baresh's citizens, there didn't seem to be much chance of stumbling into them, for the streets and back alleys they traveled were deserted, the city's citizens apparently having decided they could do their shopping and other activities on a day when they were less likely to get killed.

Aaron should have been satisfied with how far they had come through the city without a fight, but he wasn't. Instead, his thoughts continually drifted back to the army outside the city gates. They'd been hard-pressed when he and the others had entered Baresh, and he thought it unlikely their situation had improved since. With the creatures and Baresh's own troops surrounding them on all sides, and nowhere to retreat, the question wasn't *if* the army would be defeated, only *when*.

They'll be alright, Aaron, Co said into his mind. *She will be alright.*

There was no reason to ask who she meant, for the Virtue could read his thoughts as easily as if he had spoken them aloud, and she would have known well the worry that had plagued him over the army and Adina's fate. Kevlane was a cruel, bitter creature, and Aaron knew that, should the army be defeated, he would show no mercy to the queen who had led it.

His only chance of saving Adina, of saving May and Darrell and all the others was for him and the others to make it to the castle as quickly as they could and somehow find a way to defeat an ancient mage who had lived for thousands of years. A mage whom Aaron had personally seen heal from wounds that should have killed him.

For all his power, Kevlane is just a man, a voice said, and this time it was not Co, but her father, Aaron Caltriss, who spoke. *He is a man with a man's failings, and he can be defeated.*

You can do this, Aaron, Co said. *You must have faith.*

Great, Aaron thought back as he followed the youth around a corner and into a back alley. *Since you both seem to know so much, any idea of how we can beat him?*

Silence at that, and he wasn't surprised. Apparently, they had no more idea of what he would do once he met the mage than he did himself. Of course, that was a problem that could wait until—and *if*—they reached the castle. So far, their trip had been safe enough, but the sun was rising, and they could no longer count on the darkness to hide their progress through the city.

Tianya hissed and held up a hand, stopping them, and as if his thoughts had conjured them, two of the fast creatures stepped out of the alley mouth he and the others had been heading toward, cutting them off. Frowning, Aaron turned to look behind them and saw two more of the figures standing there. "Well shit," he said. He considered using his ability as he had on Savrin, touching upon that part of the creatures which was still human, but quickly dismissed the idea. Doing so with Savrin had left Aaron exhausted, and if they made it to the castle, he would need all his strength to battle with Kevlane.

He glanced at Seline to see her blades already in her hands. She saw him looking at her and gave him a brusque nod.

He turned to the Parnen. "Leomin, keep the boy and Tianya safe."

Then, Aaron drew his own blade, stepping to face the creatures behind them as Seline and Gryle moved to the front. As if they'd only been waiting for their cue, the creatures suddenly blurred forward, their long blades flashing behind them. Aaron stepped to the side of the first creature's lunge, narrowly avoiding the blade that would have impaled him, then he lashed out with his own sword at the creature's throat. Any normal man would have been unable to dodge the blow, but the creature reacted instantly, leaning its head back so that the sword's tip passed within inches of its neck.

Which put its face right in line with Aaron's left hand as it came around in a fist. The strike took the creature in the jaw, and its bones—weakened from the mage's use of the Art—*crumpled* beneath Aaron's fist. It stumbled, off-balance, its jaw hanging askew at an unnatural angle, and Aaron sprang forward, his blade driving into its stomach and out its back in a crimson shower.

Through the power of his bond, he felt the creature's companion coming from behind. He tried to pull his blade free, but there was resistance, and he saw that the one he'd impaled had dropped its own sword and was grasping his blade with both hands. Growling, Aaron struggled against it, but it refused to let go, and he was forced to leap away from the strike. The creature didn't have time to pull its blow, and its sword cut deep into the neck of its companion, severing its head from its shoulders.

Unarmed, Aaron charged forward before the creature could turn, bulling into it with his shoulder and driving it into the alley wall. Aaron bent, trying to pull his blade free of the headless corpse, but the creature was on him in an instant, and he jumped away, narrowly avoiding its strike. As he did, one of his feet caught on the corpse, and he stumbled, nearly falling.

The creature didn't hesitate, rushing at him in a blur, and Aaron brought his hands up in what he knew would be a vain effort to defend himself. But before the creature could make it to him, a sword flashed out, striking it in the side with such force that it seemed to collapse around the blade before falling to the ground in a heap. Aaron followed the length of steel to see Bastion, the giant Ghost, standing over the creature's body.

"Thanks," he panted.

The Ghost nodded and saluted with a fist to his chest. "Of course, sir. I'm sure you would have had him in another second, only I knew that you said we were in a hurry so..."

Aaron grunted and glanced back to see that Seline and Gryle had already handled the other two, their unnatural speed no match for the Virtue-bearers' combined gifts. The others were watching him—Leomin with something that might have been amusement in his eyes. The bastard.

If he would've waited another moment, Co said, *I'm fairly certain we wouldn't be having this conversation right now.*

There was no arguing with that, and Aaron opened his mouth to say as much, but he never got the chance. Tianya stepped forward, her eyes wide. "There are soldiers coming. A lot of them."

Aaron frowned, realizing that, now that she mentioned it, he could hear the sound of booted feet down the other end of the alley. "A little bit more warning would have been nice," he hissed, reaching down to pick up his sword from where it lay on the cobbles.

"Sorry," Tianya snapped, "I was a little focused on those…" She gestured at the four corpses littering the alleyway. "Those *things.*"

Suddenly, soldiers poured into the alleyway from the opposite end, ten, twenty, and more coming every second. "*Shit.*"

"What do we do, sir?" This from one of the Ghosts. Aaron thought quickly. With the collective power from their bonds with their Virtues, he felt fairly confident he and the others could deal with the soldiers. The problem, of course, was that even if they managed it, the amount of noise such a fight would cause would draw all the troops in the city down on their heads. And there was another reason, one that wouldn't have bothered him at all a year ago but that now lodged itself in his thoughts, refusing to be moved.

These men might well be innocent, Co said, echoing his thoughts. *They almost certainly don't know that they fight for a monster.*

True. Not that such a thing would keep their blades from cutting down Aaron and the others. A sword wielded by a fool, as his old swordmaster had always been so fond of saying, was far more dangerous than one wielded by even the most skilled swordsman. Aaron concentrated, drawing on the power of the bond. He closed his eyes, and when he opened them again, he could see the magenta outlines of those men piling into the alley's far end. Dozens, near a hundred, but that wasn't the worst of it. The worst thing was that, as he turned to scan the city around them, he saw several other groups of equal or greater size moving to cut them off.

"We have to run," he said. "Now." The others didn't comment or complain, only followed him as he darted down the alleyway, the soldiers shouting and giving chase.

They came to an intersection, and Aaron halted. He glanced at Caleb and saw that the youth's eyes were wide and frightened as he looked back at the approaching soldiers. "Which way?"

The boy didn't answer at first, and Aaron was beginning to think he wouldn't, but he swallowed hard, seeming to master his fear. "T-that way," Caleb said, pointing a finger, and Aaron set off again, pulling on the youth's arm to get him running.

Aaron, Co said into his mind, *if you arrive at the castle with all the troops in the city following you...*

I know, damnit, I know, Aaron thought back. *If you've got a better idea, I'm listening.*

She didn't respond which, of course, was answer enough, and Aaron ran on. They would only have to hope that they put enough distance between them and the soldiers to somehow make it past the castle guards before being caught between the two groups. But hope, he knew, wasn't a plan—it was what a man did when a plan failed. Still, there was no help for it, so he ran on, leading the others down the city streets, the soldiers coming behind them.

They made their way toward the castle as best they could, but the soldiers were out in truth now, several groups of them hunting Aaron and the others, and more than once they were forced to take an alley or side street that led away from their goal to avoid their hunters. On such occasions, it was only the powers of their bonds with the Virtues that saved them, giving them sufficient warning of the enemy soldiers.

Still, Aaron didn't need the power of the bond to know the troops were cornering them, the net closing. Soon enough, they would be left with nowhere to go, nowhere to run. They would have to fight, a situation that was becoming less and less appealing with each new group of soldiers that joined the chase. Should they stop to fight, they would be surrounded in less than five minutes, their only means of escape a trail paved in blood.

But their situation, dire as it was, wasn't what bothered Aaron most. Instead, it was that while he and the others wasted time being chased through the city, Adina and the rest of Perennia's army was stuck outside of Baresh, surrounded and fighting a battle with only one possible outcome.

His thoughts were still focused on this when he turned down a side street, glancing behind him to make sure the others were following. He was just beginning to turn back when, suddenly, the ground seemed to vanish from beneath his feet, and he shouted in surprise as he fell *through* the street.

What the fu—he began, but he never had a chance to finish the thought. He fell for only a few seconds before striking hard stone, his head bouncing off it. He grunted in pain, rolling to the side on instinct in an attempt to avoid whatever trap had been set for him. He could see nothing, only darkness, and felt the ground come out from beneath him again as he rolled. Then hands were on him, pulling at him, tugging him back.

"Whoa there, fella," someone whispered harshly, "*that ain't the sort of bath you*—" The voice cut off and there was a shout of surprise from above them and another impact, then another. Aaron looked and saw, outlined in the early morning sun, a large square hole, the one he must have fallen through. Even as he watched, the others—who'd been following right on his heels—fell, apparently too close to stop before it was too late.

Aaron struggled against the hands holding him, but there were too many, far too many, and he was still trying to grasp the sword at his back when someone pulled it away from him. His eyes darted around him, trying to get some sense of his attackers, but in the weak light coming through the hole, their features were indistinct, and they could have been anyone. Any*thing*.

Damnit, Aaron thought furiously. The others had trusted him, had followed him, and he had led them directly into a trap. He'd been too focused on the soldiers in the city, too focused on trying to avoid being surrounded, to pay any attention to anyone *below* the streets. And who would have thought of such a thing anyway? Not that the thought was any comfort. They'd trusted him: Leomin, Adina, Brandon, and all the rest, and now it seemed that they had been fools to do so.

The thought made him angry, and he growled, giving his arm a sudden jerk and breaking free of the hands holding him. He brought his elbow back where he thought one of his attackers was and heard the satisfying *crunch* of someone's nose giving way under the force of the blow.

The man grunted a curse and stumbled away. Aaron took the opportunity to try to break free, but there were still too many, and soon both of his arms were caught and pinned fast. Then he was unceremoniously dragged to his feet and slammed against a wall.

"Son of a bitch," someone said, and judging by the wheezing sound of his words, it was the man he'd struck. "I think he broke my nose."

"Never mind your damned nose," another voice said in the darkness, and there was something almost familiar about it, though Aaron couldn't place it. "Just get that hatch closed and fast. Unless, that is, you'd prefer spendin' the night—and all the nights that follow it—in the dungeons. And that, I think we both know, would be the best possible outcome."

There was a grumble from nearby, but apparently the man listened to the unseen speaker, for in another moment the hole in the street vanished as if it had never been, taking with it what little light had made it through the hole and casting Aaron and the others into a darkness more complete than any he had experienced before, save for Tianya's world of madness.

"Aaron?" a scared voice said in the darkness, and he recognized it as Caleb.

"I'm...here," he growled, still struggling vainly against his captors, "just—"

"Shhh," someone hissed in a harsh whisper. "*Not another word—not unless you like the idea of your head decoratin' the castle walls.*"

Aaron frowned, but he stopped his struggling, figuring that if the men—whoever they were—had meant to kill him and the others, they would have been dead already. The others must have had the same thought, for in another moment all signs of struggling ceased and silence fell like a blanket.

At first, Aaron heard nothing, but soon he could make out the sounds of booted feet from above them. Footfalls, a lot of them, and muted shouts he couldn't make out, but he didn't need to hear them or see the owners of those footsteps to know what they were after. He tensed, ready to burst into action should the soldiers find—or be led—to them.

But whatever had hidden the hatch, it had apparently done so well enough the soldiers didn't notice, and within seconds the sounds of their footfalls and shouts began to recede as they continued down the alleyway in search of their prey. They waited until the soldiers could no longer be heard at all, then another minute passed, and another.

Finally, a voice spoke out of the darkness, that same familiar voice that Aaron couldn't quite place. "Well, that'll do for that lot, at least for now. Now, give us a light, won't ya, Fane? It's as dark as Salen's own black heart in here."

A moment later, Aaron heard the distinctive sound of a flint being struck, and torchlight blossomed in the darkness, its glow painfully bright. He couldn't see much in the shifting light, but he was able to make out what looked to be a dozen men standing around him and his companions who were pressed against the wall much like he was.

The strangers' clothes were little more than filthy rags, covered in dirt and other substances he thought he'd rather not identify, and all of them had a haggard, exhausted look, as if they hadn't slept or had a good meal in a long time. They blinked in the torchlight like owls or rats.

"Well, look here," said a figure who stepped out of the crowd to stand beside the man holding the torch. "If it ain't Aaron and Leomin."

"You...you know us?" the Parnen said, craning his neck as if he might see the figure better but unable to do much, as two men still held him pressed against the wall.

"Well, I'll say," the figure said. "Still, maybe it'd be more proper to say 'General Envelar,' eh? Or 'the possessor of the Virtue of Compassion,' while you, Leomin," the man continued, turning, "possess what I'm thinkin', likelier'n not, is the Virtue of Charisma."

The Parnen's eyes went wide at that, and his mouth worked as if he would speak, but no words came out. Aaron frowned. "Call us whatever you will, stranger. It doesn't make a damned difference to me, but if you aim to kill us get it done already. I'm getting bored."

"*Kill* you?" the figure said. "Well, why in the name of the gods would I do that?"

"Aaron," Gryle said from somewhere off to his left, "should I—"

"Just wait a minute, Chamberlain," Aaron said, his frown growing deeper. There was still something familiar about the stranger's tone, and not being able to place it was driving him crazy, like a rock a man found in his boot and couldn't get out no matter how he searched for it. "Go on, stranger. You were saying?"

The man sighed, stepping forward, so that Aaron could finally make out his features. A big man, tall and broad-shouldered, ears that were little more than lumps of flesh on the sides of his face, and a small paunch that said his fighting days, such as they had been, were long behind him. But the flesh on his face sagged, evidence, Aaron suspected, of a big man who hadn't had enough food of late to sustain his significant frame. "Stranger again, is it?" the man said. "I'll admit, I've looked better, and maybe I could do with a washin' or two, but you keep up this nonsense, and you're liable to hurt my feelings." He shook his head. "Give a man a place to stay, feed 'em proper, and then he acts like he don't know you from any other swingin' dick. Oh," he said, as if just having a thought. "That gets me thinkin'—how's that pretty woman of yours? Alright, I hope. The gods know the world's an ugly enough place; we ought to appreciate what little beauty we can find in it, when we can."

And then, suddenly, the pieces clicked in to place, and Aaron's eyes widened. "*Nathan?*" he said, shocked to find the innkeeper here and shocked, even more, to see how much weight he'd lost since he'd last seen him.

"There it is," the innkeeper said, nodding and flashing a grin. "And my feelin's are saved, for what that's worth."

"But what are you doing here?" Aaron said, confused. "Shit, for that matter where *is* here?"

Nathan grunted. "These here are the city sewers. King Eladen—gods watch and keep his soul—had 'em built years ago as a means of fighting a lot of the sickness runnin' rampant in the city. Particularly, o'course, in the poor quarter. Time was, there'd be crews sent down on a regular basis, patrollin' the tunnels and makin' sure all the shit was stayin' where it belonged, if you know what I mean."

Aaron saw they were standing in a sewer similar to the ones he had traveled in Avarest with Adina what felt like a lifetime ago. There was a wide culvert running through the center of the tunnel with a stone walkway on either side, where he and the others now stood. Staring at the tepid brown river running through the culvert, Aaron said a prayer of thanks to whatever god had made sure someone grabbed him and pulled him back from falling in when he'd first landed and tried to roll out of the way. What a hero he would have been then, drowning in a river of sewage.

"You said there was a time when crews were sent down to check on the sewers and maintain them. No longer?"

The innkeeper snorted, then paused to hock and spit into the river of filth flowing past. "Naw, not any longer. Since that bastard Belgarin took over, the crews have stopped bein' sent. I reckon he had more important things to worry about than keepin' the sewers clear and maintained—like sendin' the city's fools off to fight a war. And this new fella—whoever in the Fields *he* is—ain't seen his way to givin' a shit about it one way or the other neither. Though, to be fair," he continued, scowling, "it ought be said that he's made some other changes."

"New fella?" Aaron asked.

"Oh sure," the innkeeper said, winking. "I've learned a bit since you all been gone, since that day in the tavern when those *things* attacked us." He grunted. "Truth be told, most of it I'da been just as happy not knowin'. But then, I've always heard that a man's got to play the hand he's dealt, never mind if it's shit, and I been tryin' to do that the best way I know how."

"Wait a minute," Aaron said, "you mean...you've been down here since that day when we were attacked in your tavern?"

"Well sure," Nathan said. "Couldn't exactly go back, could I? Even if those damned creatures didn't show up and kill us for helpin' you, the inn was wrecked to shit, anyway. That big monster of a bastard saw to that when he knocked a hole in the damn wall."

Gods, Aaron thought, feeling a fresh wave of guilt. The innkeeper had done nothing to deserve it, but by staying in his tavern, by asking for his help, he had put the man at a great risk, had basically painted a target on his back for Kevlane and his creatures. "Shit, I'm sorry, Nathan. I never meant—"

The other man waved a hand, dismissing it. "Fields, I know that, Aaron. If I didn't, I'd say the odds'd be good I'd have let you take that bath you seemed so intent on, when you first got down here. Anyway, don't lose any sleep over it. I won't say I exactly planned on spendin' my vacation down in sewers smellin' of shit and worse, but then, the world's got a way of kickin' a man in the ass, just as soon as he starts figurin' he knows how his life's gonna go. That's just how things are, and there ain't nothin' you nor anybody else can say about it. And anyway, we been makin' due, and that's about the best any man can claim."

"*We*, you say," Leomin said. "Does that mean…forgive me, Nathan, but is young Janum okay?"

Aaron winced, realizing he'd forgotten all about the youth, the innkeeper's nephew who he'd been looking after for his sister, and he was relieved to see the big man grin. "Well, as full of piss and vinegar as any youth is, and a trial sent by the gods themselves, I can tell you that much. But he ain't got no holes in him he weren't born with, if that's what you're askin', Leomin. Still, I reckon he can tell you better'n I can."

The innkeeper turned and looked into the crowd and the youth stepped forward, clearly uncomfortable being the center of attention. His clothes were as filthy as the rest, but he didn't share the wasted, sickly look that Nathan and the others did. A testament, Aaron knew at once, to his uncle's attentions, for without asking he was certain the innkeeper had gone hungry more than once to see the lad was fed.

"Hi, Leomin," he said, studying his feet as if embarrassed. "Aaron." He nodded to each in turn, avoiding their eyes, and Nathan snorted.

"Don't let the lad fool you into thinkin' he's soft and shy. After all, he's the reason more than anythin' else why I've found myself in the unenviable position I'm in."

"It's good to see you well, Janum," Aaron said, and Leomin grinned, nodding his agreement. Then the sellsword frowned, turning back to the innkeeper. "Unenviable position? What do you mean?"

Nathan snorted, and now it was his time to avoid their gazes. "Well, it sounds so damn foolish to say out loud, I don't—"

"Uncle's the rebellion leader," Janum blurted, clearly excited to share the news.

Aaron's eyes went wide. "Rebellion leader, is it?" he asked, turning back to the innkeeper.

The man fidgeted, looking like a child caught doing something foolish. Then he heaved a sigh, finally meeting Aaron's eyes with obvious reluctance. "I guess you could call it that, though it sounds damn pretentious. Anyway," he went on, scowling at Janum, "the boy's stubborn, and he won't listen to reason even if it came up and slapped him on the head. Before long, I imagine he'll have folks callin' me Lord Nathan and bringin' me all manner of gifts." He snorted. "Shit and piss mostly, I suspect—the sewers ain't got a lot else to offer."

"There's a rebellion then? In the city?"

"I reckon you'd call it that," the innkeeper said. "Anyhow, suffice to say there's folks got tired of not bein' able to go out at night, of hearin' or seein' their friends and family caught by those, those *things* and whisked off to the gods alone know where. A man can only take so much of that, 'fore he has to make a stand. Never mind that we wouldn't pose no more trouble to 'em, if they caught us out, than an ant would to a man." He shrugged. "Still, we do what we can."

"Well, that's great," Leomin said excitedly. "If you've got a rebellion already, then maybe we can get something accomplished after all."

Aaron nodded slowly, thinking it over. "First of all," he said, glancing around at the strangers watching him, "I think you ought to know King Belgarin isn't alive anymore—hasn't been for some time now." He paused, expecting for someone to object. When no one did, he went on. "Anyway, the man now wearing his face is an ancient mage—Boyce Kevlane, in the stories." There were some gasps at that, but still no one argued. "He's been taking people off the streets—those who are stronger or faster than normal men—and turning them into monsters, an army of abominations to do his bidding."

The innkeeper considered that, rubbing his unshaven chin, and Aaron waited for him to tell him that he was a fool, that he was being ridiculous. He didn't though. Instead, he only grunted, and finally nodded. "Well, that settles that then."

The other dirty men nodded as if it made perfect sense, and Leomin frowned. "But...aren't you surprised?"

"Sure," Nathan said, "we're surprised, Leomin. But not too much. When good honest folk—or, at least, folk as honest as can be expected—start disappearin' off the street for no reason, when you see creatures out of nightmares roaming the night, then you know somethin's goin' on. And after learnin' what I did from you all the last time you visited and seein' the Virtues first-hand...well. When one fairy tale turns out to be true, I don't suppose it's so great a stretch to imagine another'n will also."

That made sense enough to Aaron, but there was something else troubling him. "So, Nathan, this rebellion of yours..."

The innkeeper winced. "Gods, but I hate that word. Makes us sound like warriors in shinin' armor battlin' against some evil tyrant, when the truth of the matter is we're more like rats nippin' at the tyrant's heels when he ain't lookin', liable to get squashed under foot if he takes it in mind, and with our own fool selves to blame." He saw Aaron about to say something else and raised a hand. "Alright, so we've done a few small things—nothin' big, understand. We heard of some folks we thought was gonna be taken, well, sometimes we can get there before those things can, get 'em out of the city while there's still time. And we been doin' what we can to spread the word around Baresh, let folks know what we're up against. My ma, gods bless and keep her, always said that knowledge was the key to power, and this time, I reckon she would have been right enough." He shrugged. "Small things like that, is all. Ain't none of us warriors, and even if we were, judging by what I've seen and heard, it wouldn't make no difference, not against such as those creatures."

Aaron nodded, suddenly getting a sinking suspicion he knew why he'd been feeling uneasy about the Parnen's excitement. "And this rebellion or, whatever you call it, how many have joined it?"

Nathan raised his hands to either side to indicate the bedraggled men standing with him. "You're lookin' at 'em."

"That...that's all?" Gryle said, then slapped a hand over his mouth, his face visibly coloring in the torchlight. "Forgive me, I..."

"Easy, friend," Nathan said, grinning, "ain't no offense at pointin' out a thing that's true. Sure, we ain't no army that might storm the castle gates. But we've done what we can. Anyway, you'd be surprised how hard it is to find recruits when all you can promise 'em is a stay in a sewer, rat flesh for dinner, and a death that, likely as not, will be mighty painful. Far as that goes—"

Nathan cut off as a man walked up out of the crowd and put his hand on the innkeeper's shoulder, whispering in his ear. The innkeeper listened, frowning as he did. "Right." He turned back to Aaron. "Here I am flappin' my gums like a fool with those soldiers out searchin'. Even here, in the sewers, you can't be too careful, and it's best not to stay in the same place for long. Those creatures of Kevlane's ain't the prettiest things, but they got some mighty keen ears on 'em. Somethin' we learned to our grief a while back. There used to be more of us than there are now. Anyway, come on—I'll show you where we been stayin'."

"Thing is, Nathan," Aaron said, "we're in a bit of a hurry."

"Oh?" the man asked grinning. "S'pose that's why you all were runnin' like Salen himself was after you."

"Right," the sellsword answered, thinking of the army camped outside Baresh. "Anyway, we don't have a lot of time. We have to get to the castle as quickly as we can."

The innkeeper nodded. "Mean to cut the snake's head off before he can bite anyone else, do you?"

"Something like that."

"Well, as to that, I might just have a way of helpin' you to get there without you havin' to get cut up into small pieces by the city guard." He glanced at Aaron, raising an eyebrow. "Or, if what I've seen is true, maybe cuttin' *them* up into small pieces. But even if you all manage to survive, such a fight will cost you more time than I'm thinkin' you want to spend."

"And you've got another way?"

The innkeeper winked. "Come on." He set off at a walk, Janum following and pausing to bow deeply to Leomin before hurrying after along with the rest of the rebellion.

"I believe he is right," Caleb said. "Should we take to the surface once more, we will almost certainly be forced to fight. I calculate the odds at twenty to one, based on the number of troops we've seen. Worse, of course, if they realize where we are heading, and it seems all too likely that they will soon, if they haven't already."

Aaron nodded. "Anyone else?" He looked at Gryle, but the chamberlain didn't seem to be paying attention at all. The heavy-set man was too busy staring in horror at the river of murky water in which unidentifiable debris floated, reminding Aaron that, though men may change, there is always some bit of them left behind when they do. For her part, Tianya only shrugged, and Seline turned to look at Leomin, a question in her eyes.

Bastion stepped forward from where he stood with the only other remaining Ghost, and Aaron had a moment of shame and anger at the reminder that only two of their number had made it this far, then bowed his head. "General, wherever you lead, we'll follow."

The other Ghost nodded, and Aaron grunted, swallowing the lump in his throat as he turned back to Leomin. The Parnen noticed everyone looking at him and fidgeted nervously. "I might echo young Bastion's sentiments, Aaron. Besides, as Caleb has so cleverly pointed out, our destination must appear obvious enough to those soldiers, and it would be no surprise if they chose to head to the castle instead and just wait for us there. I do not know what Nathan has in mind, but surely it can be no worse than what we already face."

"Alright then," Aaron nodded. "Let's go."

Nathan and the others waited a short distance ahead. As he and his companions followed the innkeeper through the sewers, Aaron fought to contain his impatience, begrudging each minute that passed.

They moved in silence, the only sound the murky water rushing past, and their soft, almost imperceptible footfalls on the stone walkway. They'd been traveling for about half an hour, and Aaron was just about ready to take their chances in the street when they came to an intersection where four waterways connected. The walkway was broader here, allowing them to stand in a semi-circle as Nathan raised his hands to either side like a man showing off his new castle. "Welcome to paradise."

"Paradise" consisted of a few dozen sleeping bags scattered haphazardly on all four of the corners of the intersection. Planks lay across each channel, granting access between the four corners, and here the sound of the onrushing water was so loud as to drown out nearly all other sounds.

There were a few modest tents among the sleeping bags, and scattered around them were small, contained fires at which sat a few older women and more than one child. Seeing the children's ragged clothes and dirt-smeared faces, Aaron felt a fresh wave of anger at Kevlane. The mage's evil had caused harm of which even he was unaware.

Nathan followed his gaze and stepped close, having to shout to be heard over the torrent. "I know what you're thinkin'—what kind of fool brings a kid to a place like this? But there wasn't any choice. Their parents were targeted, you see, and they had to be hidden." His face twisted with anger. "We didn't manage to save all the parents, but the kids were left orphaned with nowhere to go, so we took 'em in. We care for 'em the best we can. Not ideal, I know, but we didn't have a lot of other options."

"No," Aaron said, "not ideal. But you're doing a good thing. Now, Nathan, I don't mean to rush you, but you were saying something about having a way to get us to the castle without going into the streets?"

The innkeeper nodded. "That's right. Or, maybe it's more right to say that Willard knows a way."

"Willard?" Aaron asked. "Where is he?"

Nathan grinned. "Oh, you ought to know 'em. You two have already met, after all. Leastways," he shrugged, "after a fashion." He turned, cupping his hands to his mouth. *"Hey, Willard!"* he shouted. *"Come here a minute, would you?"*

A man from a nearby tent approached. As he drew closer, Aaron noted the rag—now coated in blood—the man held to his nose, as well as the scowl on his face. Aaron sighed. *Of course it would be him.*

The man drew close, eyeing Aaron warily as he did. "Yeah, boss?"

"These folks here are lookin' to get into the castle, Will. I thought maybe you'd be able to help 'em out with that."

"Maybe," the man grumbled, "if'n, that is, that one keeps his elbows to himself. I won't say it's the first time my nose has been broken, but that don't make it fun, neither."

Aaron winced. "Sorry about that. I didn't know who you were or what was going on. Still, I appreciate the offer, but how exactly are you going to be able to get us into the castle?"

"Won't be by my good looks, I can tell you that much," the man said. "Feels like my nose is about three times bigger'n usual."

"Oh, stop your grousin' will ya?" Nathan said. "He said he's sorry, didn't he?" He turned to Aaron. "You'll have to forgive Willard. The man loves to complain, and I imagine we'll all be hearin' about this one for weeks." He frowned. "Assumin', of course, any of us got weeks left. Anyway, you remember those teams I was tellin' you about, the ones that used to get sent down in the sewers?"

"Sure," Aaron said, nodding slowly, "to maintain them and make sure everything ran right."

"That's it," Nathan confirmed. "Well, Willard here used to supervise those teams—did it for years. Yeah, I reckon he knows just about every inch of these sewers—shit, it's thanks to him we didn't all end up gettin' lost down here in the first place."

"But it's been a while, hasn't it?" Aaron asked. "Are you sure you still know them as well as you once did?"

The man snorted, then cut off, closing his eyes and pressing his hand against his nose. "Look, fella. I know these sewers better than I know my wife—"

"—That much I don't doubt," Nathan interrupted, but if the man noticed he gave no sign.

"Shit, if this Kevlane you're talkin' about really is in the castle, well, I imagine I could damn near set you down in his lap, if you had a mind. Get you close enough to kiss him, if that's what you're lookin' for."

Or stick a blade in him, Aaron thought. Of course, if his past experiences fighting the mage were anything to go by, it would take a lot more than that to stop him. Still, he decided he would worry about that when the time came. He had to get there first. "That sounds good. But if these sewers were as widely used as you say they were, then surely there are others who know them, others who might have told Kevlane about them. For all we know, he might have guards stationed there even now."

"Sure," the man grumbled, "and maybe the rats'll get tired of bein' dinner and band together, form their own army and run us out of here. All I can tell you is that if those *things* ain't found us down here yet, it's on account of they ain't been lookin'. As for what's waitin' at the castle, well, that's your affair, ain't it? Now, do you want me to show you the way or not?"

Aaron raised an eyebrow, glancing at Nathan who gave him an apologetic look, shrugging. "And what will you do?" he asked.

The innkeeper smiled. "Oh, what we can, Aaron. We'll do what we can."

Aaron grunted, turning back to Willard. "Alright. Show us."

CHAPTER FORTY-TWO

The dead animal lay in the middle of the street. Balen thought it was a dog, but he couldn't be sure, as flies were swarming around the corpse in a thick cloud, obscuring most of it from view—a thing for which he was thankful. Still, enough of the beast was visible to make his gorge rise in his throat. Balen swallowed the sour saliva flooding his mouth and finally managed to pull his eyes away from the grizzly sight, focusing on the band of criminals walking the street with him instead.

They'd fled the guards at the port, Urek leading them into the city, down first one alleyway then another, seemingly at random. By the time they lost their pursuers, Balen's breath was coming in ragged gasps. Still, the crime boss refused to slow, pushing farther into the city. Balen followed, doing his best to ignore the increasingly painful stitch rising in his side.

Finally, just when Balen was beginning to think that being cut down with a sword might be preferable to forcing his exhausted body any further, Urek slowed their pace. The first mate suspected he was the reason for that as the band of criminals barely seemed winded at all. Between bouts of envy and annoyance, Balen consoled himself with the fact that running from guards was a regular activity for them and, so far as he was concerned, they could keep it.

In truth, he was just glad to have put some distance between themselves and the guards chasing them. Or, at least, he had been. Now, he wasn't so sure. Despite his exhaustion, Balen was beginning to notice his surroundings more. The dead dog—if it had *been* a dog—was the first of it, but now that he was no longer struggling just to breathe, he saw that the houses they passed were little more than crude shacks, and that wasn't all. The streets were empty, seemingly abandoned, yet he couldn't shake the feeling they were being watched.

Balen's unease grew, and he moved up to walk beside Urek. "I think something's wrong here," he said.

"Oh?" the crime boss asked, turning to him. "And what's that?"

Balen struggled to find the words to communicate the feeling of dread sitting in his stomach like a stone. For several seconds, nothing would come. Then, almost desperate, he said, "A dog. There was a dead dog back there."

"Sure," the big man said, nodding. "I saw it. What's your point?"

Balen was suddenly overcome with the feeling—the certainty—that they were being followed, that if he looked back, he would see someone or some*thing* following silently in their wake. The feeling was so strong that he spun, his breath catching in his throat, but there was nothing there. Only the street, and the sullen, menacing silence filling the air so thickly he thought he might choke. He licked his lips, turning back to the other man. "Well, I mean...shouldn't someone have picked it up, or...?" He trailed off, not sure how to finish.

Urek grunted what might have been a laugh. "Oh, they wouldn't do that, first mate," he said in a quiet voice. "That dog was put there for a reason. As a warning."

Balen didn't like the sound of that, not at all, and despite the coolness of the air, his forehead broke out in sweat. "Um...warning? A warning about what?"

"To not come this way," the other man said, as if it were obvious.

Balen felt a tingling between his shoulder blades and couldn't resist the urge to glance behind him again. Nothing. No one. Or, at least, if someone *was* there, they were staying well hidden. As soon as the thought occurred, he felt sure it must be true, and it did little to comfort him. After all, why would their followers need to hide? Try as he might, he couldn't think of a single answer to that question that didn't end in blood. "So..." He paused, glancing at the other criminals, but they were all looking ahead, their expressions stern, serious, but not scared. Or, if they felt any fear, they hid it better than he did. "So...why are we coming this way? And...so far as that goes, couldn't they have just put up a sign?"

Urek flashed his teeth at him in a humorless grin. "This is the poor quarter, first mate. Few enough are those here who can read and, even if they could, you have to admit, a dead animal has a certain...effect."

Balen swallowed. Oh, it had had an effect alright, there was no denying that. "I think...we should probably get out of here." He cleared his throat. "I mean, that is, they may need our help at the western gate."

The crime boss nodded solemnly. "Probably they do."

Balen waited, but the man offered nothing more, so he decided to try again, struggling to keep his voice from cracking with the fear building in him. "So...can we go then? Don't you think it would be wise to get out of here before whoever put that warning there finds us?"

Urek grunted, coming to an abrupt halt. "Too late for that, first mate. Been too late for a while now, I expect."

Balen was about to ask the man what he meant when a dozen men and women seemed to appear in the street in front of them, gliding silently to block their way. Their clothes were little more than rags, their faces haggard and weary, and they had an underfed, malnourished look. Yet, the swords and knives they held were more than sharp enough to get the job done. He spun, meaning to retreat down the street, only to find another group—this one larger than the first—standing behind them. Several of these held crossbows and looked as if they had the skill and inclination to use them.

The first mate reached for the knife at his belt, knowing it was useless but refusing to go down without a fight, but the big man caught his wrist in an iron grip and gave his head a single shake. "Wait, first mate," he said, his voice without emotion, his eyes never leaving the group in front of them. "I know they might not look like much, but this lot here's grown used to violence."

So Balen did. His hands sweating, his breathing uneven and shallow, he waited. A second later, one of the men stepped forward, motioning with a finger for him and the others to follow. "W-what does he want from us?"

The big man glanced at Balen. "Seems to me he wants us to follow him."

"R-right but...what do we do?"

Another humorless grin. "I'd say we follow."

They were led down the street in a grim procession, no one speaking, and Balen asked himself, not for the first time, why he'd ever set foot on shore. He was a sailor, by the gods, meant to be on the sea, and he couldn't help being surprised that this was how it would end. Out of all the dangers he'd fretted over in his life (many over the past few months) he'd never thought he'd be killed by criminals in a strange city for no reason other than a dead dog in the street.

He looked at his companions, and though none of them looked afraid, their expressions were all dark. Save, perhaps, for the one called Shadow, who was even now holding a knife in his hands, admiring the blade, a small smile on his face. Balen was overcome with a sudden urge to slap the man—not that he ever would, of course. There were more pleasant ways to die than that one, and he'd seen the hawk-nosed man at his work enough to know he'd stand little chance. But why were they all so damned *calm? Oh, you're a sailor alright, Balen Blunderfoot,* he thought despairingly, *and a fool to boot. Why else would you let yourself get caught up with this lot?*

They didn't have to wait long, and Balen was still trying to decide whether that was a good thing or not when he and the others were led to the front of a tavern. The group they'd been following went inside, and Balen and his companions were ushered in after them. The common room was packed with people, the noise almost a living thing as they all laughed and shouted and spoke, seeming to take no notice of Balen and the others, as if a group of people being forced into the tavern at the ends of swords was a common occurrence.

Then a man sitting near the back rose. He was an older man with short gray hair, and a patch over one eye. He was short, with a noticeable paunch, and wore clothes at least as unassuming as the rest. But the moment he stood, the commotion in the common room cut off immediately, and those who had been deep in conversation only seconds before turned on their stools and chairs to regard Balen and the others.

For a time, no one spoke, and the silence grew thicker and thicker, heavier, until Balen felt as if he would be crushed under the weight of it. Then the small old man walked toward them, several others rising from the crowd to flank him. "Interesting," the old man mused. "I heard there was a group of people traveling my streets, but at first, I didn't believe it. After all, who could be so foolish as to walk into a man's home uninvited?" He gave a smile that held no humor. "Surely, I have met many fools in my day, but few as foolish as that. Imagine my surprise, then, when I realize that they have indeed trespassed and, what's more, I recognize some of their number."

He came to stand in front of Urek, six men on either side now, blades in their hands. He studied the big man for several seconds. "Urek."

The big man nodded his head once, grimly. "Eyes."

The two men stared at each other silently, and Balen's breath caught in his throat. He nearly collapsed with relief when both men broke into wide grins and embraced. The old man stepped back after a moment, all sense of menace gone from him now. "Ah, but it's good to see you, lad."

"You too, sir."

The old man smiled, turning to look at Beautiful. "Ah, Beautiful, but you are as radiant as ever. You look as if you haven't aged a day since last I saw you."

The woman beamed at that, displaying what few teeth she still possessed. "As charming as ever, I see. Good to see you, Eyes."

The man grinned. "At my age, lady, I'm thankful to still be around to *be* seen." He turned to the hawk-nosed man and gave him a wink. "Shadow. Still playing with those knives, I see. Dangerous, that."

The hawk-nosed man looked up from where he'd been picking at his nails with one of his blades. "Almost criminal."

The old man laughed, a loud, bellowing laugh completely at odds with his small frame. Finally, he turned to Balen, Osirn, and Shits. "I don't think I know these others."

"Count yourself lucky," Urek grunted.

"My name is Eyes, gentlemen," he said, offering his hand to each in turn. He did so to Balen last, and the first mate took it, surprised by the strength of the man's grip.

"P-pleasure to meet you, Mr. Eyes."

The old man laughed again. "Just Eyes, that's all. First and last name both. Some...acquaintances of mine used to use the name to mock me, after I lost this one in a street fight," he said, jerking a thumb at the patch.

"Not that they're around to mock anyone anymore," Urek said.

Eyes shrugged. "Not unless someone finds a way to bring the dead back to life, at any rate. Regardless," he said, turning back to Balen, "I decided to keep the name. After all, eyes *see* don't they? And in my experience, there are few things more dangerous than a man who sees more than others."

"Except maybe a blade," Shadow offered.

"Oh, dear Shadow," the old man sighed, amused. "I see you are still of a singular mind—it is why I respect you so much. Still, what damage might such a blade do without vision to guide it, I wonder?"

The hawk-nosed man shrugged at that, and the mirth slowly left the old man's face as he turned back to Urek. "I heard about Hale. I'm sorry for that."

Urek cleared his throat, nodding. "Went down fightin' and took more than his share of the bastards with him."

"He would be glad of that, I think," the old man said. "Never mind the fact that the world is always ready to make more bastards. Now, why don't you tell me what's brought you to my door?"

"S-soldiers were chasing us," Balen blurted. "They—"

"Have been taken care of," the old man said, his eyes never leaving Urek. "Now, is this the only reason you have come here?"

Urek winced, hesitating, then finally sighed. "No. We need your help."

"At the gate, you mean," Eyes said, and the way he said it made it clear that it wasn't a question.

"Yes."

"We are criminals, Urek. Pick-pockets, thieves, muggers and, yes, sometimes murderers. But unlike you, we are not soldiers."

"I know."

"And yet, you would have us come anyway."

Urek nodded again. "Yes sir."

"Why?"

The big man frowned as if in thought, and it was several seconds before he spoke. "The boss believed in this fight, Eyes. And whether you know it or not, you're in it. You can't hide from what's coming—none of us can. Silent and the others have gone to fight the mage, Kevlane. He wears Belgarin's face and—"

The old man waved a hand. "I know all of this already, and from all I've heard of this Silent he is capable. But is he capable enough, Urek?"

Again, the big man took several seconds to answer, but slowly he nodded. "I believe so, Eyes."

The old man studied him for a time without speaking. Then, he shrugged. "Ah, why not? I grow bored sitting in this tavern. Besides," he said, frowning now, and with that simple expression the menace returned to him in a rush, and Balen felt a tingle of fear run up his spine. "This mage has gone too far. His creatures wander the darkness, calling it home where once it was ours, and many of those who go out to do their work never return. Good men and women have vanished, never to be heard from again. Yes, we will help you, Urek, and I will pray that your confidence in Silent is justified."

The big man let out a heavy breath and nodded. "As will I, Eyes."

CHAPTER FORTY-THREE

Wendell always thought he'd die in battle. Of course, he'd also always hoped he was wrong, hoped that instead he'd die underneath a particularly skilled whore, with a soft mattress below him and soft flesh above. There had even been one or two times—when he'd found himself with more coin in his pocket than normal—that the gods themselves couldn't have said he didn't give it a good go. But, so far at least, he hadn't managed it. And as the morning wore on, as the corpses piled higher on both sides, he grew more and more certain he wouldn't get another chance.

His sword arm ached, his legs felt as if someone had tied weights to them, and he'd long since lost count of the times he'd nearly been killed in the fighting. But he fought on, telling himself that if he was killed, at least he'd be able to take a rest.

An enemy soldier came at him out of the melee, and Wendell slung the mud he held in his left hand—easy enough to find, now that the ground beneath their feet had been trampled. The mud struck the man's face, and he recoiled. The sergeant took advantage of his surprise to lunge forward and stab him through the gut. The soldier blinked at him as if surprised, and Wendell winced.

"Sorry about that, fella."

The man's mouth worked, as if he would speak, but then he fell off the blade impaling him, collapsing to the ground amid the scattered corpses of friend and foe. Wendell was just reaching down for another handful of mud when a *roar* split the air, and he spun to see one of Kevlane's giant monstrosities appear out of the throng right in front of him. A thick shaft of wood impaled it through the stomach—one of the huge bolts Caleb had directed the city's smiths to fashion, along with massive wooden contraptions used to fire them—but the creature seemed oblivious of it.

Its inhuman gaze locked on Wendell, and the sergeant did the first thing that came to his mind: he threw the mud he held. It struck the creature in the chest, and the monstrosity paused to look down as if confused by his tactics, then it let out another roar and charged toward him in a half-shuffle, half-run, swinging one of its massive fists.

Wendell tried to move to the side, but his foot caught in the mud, and he stumbled, falling to his knees, the creature's blow sweeping over his head and missing him by inches. He saw his boot stuck deep in the mud and gave a tug, falling over in surprise when his foot came free, leaving the boot mired in the mud. He was still rising when impossibly large hands grabbed him, lifting him several feet off the ground with no apparent effort.

Wendell looked down to see the creature's cruel visage studying him. "And they say I'm ugly," he said. Then he kicked the creature as hard as he could in the face. Its nose smashed flat, but it didn't so much as stagger, so Wendell kicked again. Then again. He was just about to kick for the fourth time, when the creature let out another roar and suddenly he was sailing through the air.

He hit the ground hard, his head bouncing as he rolled until he finally came to a stop against one of the many corpses scattered around the ground. Groaning, Wendell blinked in a vain effort to clear his blurry vision and stared at the corpse's face, slack in death. "Tell me, friend," he hissed. "Just how bad is the afterlife?"

He—and the corpse—were suddenly cast in shadow, and he craned his head that suddenly felt like it was two sizes too big to see the creature looming over him, the wooden shaft still protruding from its stomach. Wendell tried to move, but his body felt battered, and his muscles wouldn't obey his commands. "Never mind," he wheezed to the corpse beside him as darkness closed around his vision. "Seems I'll find out soon enough."

A fog seemed to come over his eyes, so that when the creature bent down to pick him up, it was little more than a vague blur.

There was a shout from somewhere off to his left, and a metallic flash. Then darkness.

***

Hands were on his shoulders, shaking him with unmistakable urgency. "Alright, alright," he mumbled. "What's the hurry?" It seemed to Wendell the one good thing about being dead ought to be that a man no longer had to rush to get anywhere. After all, he'd already *gotten* there, hadn't he?

Still, the hands shook him, and he winced, opening his eyes. A blurry form hovered above him, and as his vision focused, it slowly resolved into an older man with scruff on his chin and cheeks from where he hadn't shaved.

"Where are all the women?" Wendell mumbled. Maybe he hadn't gone to sermons as often as he should have, but Wendell felt sure there'd been something about women, beautiful ones, waiting on the other side of death. "Those priests were damned liars," he said. "This ain't nothin' like what they promised."

"You're not dead," the man answered. "At least not yet. Now, come on. Get up."

Wendell didn't really see the point, but he let the man drag him to his feet. He remembered the last thing he'd seen before the darkness had taken him—the huge creature leaning over him—and he snorted. "Not dead. Well, I think I'd know, wouldn't I?"

He frowned then, looking over the man's shoulder at a massive body lying a few feet away. Its shoulders were impossibly wide, muscled to the point of grotesqueness, along with the rest of it, but the most striking thing about the body was that it was missing a head. He frowned at that. What kind of afterlife *was* this, anyway, when a man couldn't even count on having his head, when he got there?

"Apparently not," the stranger said, and Wendell turned back to look at him.

"Wait a minute, you're that sailor, fella, ain't you? Thom? The one as is in love with that fiery-haired woman, May?" He sighed. "Dead too, eh? Well, you've my sympathies, for what it's worth. I suppose ships got their own dangers."

The man's jaw flexed, as if maybe he had a bad tooth, and Wendell was just getting ready to tell him he ought to have that seen to when the man spoke again. "Yes, my name's Thom, but I'm not dead—neither of us are. I...well." He grunted. "I guess I saved you."

The sergeant frowned, looking at the massive corpse again. "That your work, is it?"

The man's face grew pale, but he nodded. "Guess so."

"Well, you were thorough, I'll give you that. Now, look, about this whole not being dead thing—"

"I can't believe it," the man said.

"Well," Wendell said, nodding, "they say denial's the first—"

"No, damnit," the man hissed, grabbing him by the shoulders and spinning him around, "*look.*"

Wendell did and, in the distance, he saw the western gate of the city opening. The gate was pretty far away, but he thought he could make out figures swarming onto the walls and out of the gate itself.

"Come on," the man said, "we need to get over there."

Wendell shrugged. "Why not? It ain't like we can die twice, is it?"

"Damnit," the man growled, "we're not dead, alright? Now, let's go."

"You go on ahead," Wendell said, scowling. "There's something I got to do first. Tell me, before you go, you ain't happened to seen a boot anywhere, have ya?"

***

"Captain Gant."

Brandon heard the club owner's voice, but only in a distracted sort of way. He was busy staring at the table before him, at the map spread out and the pieces representing the army scattered among it as if, by doing so, he might somehow create more troops out of thin air.

"Brandon."

"A moment, May," he said, rubbing his weary eyes as he tried to think of something to get them out of the mess they were in. It wouldn't be long now before they were overwhelmed—already the line had grown dangerously thin in places, and there weren't enough reinforcements left to fill the gaps. "The western side is hurting the most," he mused aloud, "maybe if—"

"*Brandon!*"

He started, finally pulling his gaze away from the map to see the club owner standing directly in front of him. "What is it, May? No offense, but I'm busy trying to keep us—"

He grunted in surprise as she took him by the shoulder, marching him to the front of the tent. "May, there's really no time to—"

"*Look*," she said, throwing the flap aside and thrusting her finger out.

Brandon followed the pointing finger to the western gate of the city, saw to his shock, that it was opening. "Spy glass," he snapped, holding his hand to the side, and a moment later one of the messengers thrust it into his hands.

Brandon looked through it and saw that it hadn't been his imagination after all—the gate *was* opening. And, what's more, he saw figures moving about on the battlements. Frowning, he swept his spyglass around until he saw a heavy-set man covered in furs. The man's face was red, and it looked like he was shouting something at those others scurrying around on the top of the walls. He realized with a start that the man was Captain Festa. "Well, I'll be damned," he breathed.

As he watched, those on the walls readied bows and began to shoot down into the mass of the enemy army and its creatures. Hope flared in his chest for the first time in hours, and he spun to look at the nearest messenger. "Go get the queen. And you others spread out—let the squad leaders know we're making for the city. Now."

CHAPTER FORTY-FOUR

It felt to Aaron as if they had been walking for days. The gloominess of the sewers, lit only by the ruddy glow of Willard's torch, seemed to stretch on and on forever. Talking had long since ceased as each focused on the task ahead of them. The only sounds were those of the murky river winding its way past and the annoyed squeaks of rats scurrying away at their approach.

Aaron knew he should say something, should try to keep their spirits up, but he found that he could think of no words that might comfort them. His thoughts were on what they intended to do, on the mission they had set themselves, and on Adina and the others who were counting on them to succeed. And with each step he took toward their goal, he felt a dread building in him, a thought that was quickly becoming a certainty. They would lose. How could they not? The mage had hundreds, if not thousands, of creatures at his command, and even if he didn't, what chance did they have against a man who had lived for thousands of years? Aaron himself had thrown the man from the top of a castle and even that hadn't been enough to kill him. It was an impossible task, a hopeless one. How were you supposed to kill a man who couldn't *be* killed?

He thought of Adina, wondered if he would ever see her again, or was it too late even now? Had the army already been defeated? Were he and the others racing toward an unwinnable battle to save a war already lost? He considered casting his Virtue out to the western side of the city but decided against it. For one, it was unlikely that the Virtue's power would reach so far and, besides, he knew he would need every ounce of strength he possessed when and *if* they reached the mage.

"Alright then," Willard said, coming to stop beside a ladder built into the stone wall. He turned back to Aaron and the others. "This'n here should take you up to the servants' quarters, built off of the castle but inside the walls."

"Is there no ladder to the castle itself?"

The man gave him a humorless grin. "Naw, there ain't. Seems the builders thought maybe it'd be too convenient, havin' a ladder leadin' right up into the castle. You know," he said, eyeing the sellsword, "in case anyone got it in mind to say, I don't know, assassinate the king."

Aaron sighed. Not surprising, really, but that meant they'd have to make it from the servants' quarters to the castle in broad daylight. It was too much to hope that all the castle guards had decided to take the day off. "Alright, thanks."

The man grunted. "You want to thank me, maybe next time try keepin' your elbows to yourself." He started down the tunnels then paused, looking back. "Good luck to you all. If there's ever a man needed killin', I reckon that bastard up there is it." And with that, he left.

Aaron looked at the others. "Look, we've no way of knowing what's waiting up there. For all we know, Kevlane knows all about the sewers and has a trap set and ready for us on the other side of that hatch. If any of you wants to turn back, now's the time to do it."

He met each of their eyes in turn and felt a mixture of relief and regret when no one spoke. "Alright then. Let's go."

CHAPTER FORTY-FIVE

All along the battlefield, the soldiers of Perennia's army, many of whom had long since resigned themselves to death, stared at the western gate of Baresh as it opened as if witnessing a miracle. For the first time since the battle started, they began to hope.

They were still weary, even the luckiest of them sporting minor wounds. Their limbs still felt leaden, yet for all that, for all that they had endured in the last hours, they felt a renewed excitement, and men and women who had thought themselves too tired to do more than stand and watch their deaths come found they had some strength left, after all. Those who could fight did, the army line forming into a semi-circle surrounding the gate as the wounded went first into the city. Those who could walk did so, but those who needed help found it at the hands of the soldiers, sailors, and more than a few criminals, who rushed from the gate to their aid. Hands once used to pick locks or strip a man's valuables from his pockets were now used to carry those who needed help to safety.

May watched the proceedings with something like awe, thinking that such a moment must surely stand as proof that the world was not completely damned, after all. When faced with the worst, men and women, strangers, might band together to help one another.

"It's a wonder, isn't it?"

Captain Gant stood beside her, studying the withdrawal. "Yes," May said. "I wish only that it had not cost so much." She looked around at all those forms lying still and unmoving within the circle of the army's retreat. Was Thom among them? He'd been fine, last she heard, but that had been before the retreat had been sounded, and she'd been busily coordinating with the captain and squad leaders on what supplies were left them. Only now that the retreat was well and truly underway did she have time to think about it, and she felt a cold shiver run up her spine. What chance did an old sailor have when so many trained soldiers had died? "So many dead," she said in a voice barely more than a whisper. "For nothing."

"Not for nothing." She turned to see Adina arriving with several flustered, exhausted guards. The queen's clothes were stained with dried blood. She, too, looked weary, and her eyes reflected the hours she'd spent seeing to the wounded, many of whom were beyond hope. Yet, for all that, there was something almost triumphant in her face. "Not for nothing, May," she said again.

The club owner only nodded, not trusting herself to speak as she scanned the steady procession of wounded being taken into the city, searching for a certain stubborn old man with more courage than sense.

"We will find him, May," Adina said, discerning the direction of May's thoughts.

Yes, May thought, *but will we find him alive?* And, of course, there wasn't just Thom to think about, but Silent, too, and all the others. She felt a wave of shame at that, for while she fretted over Thom, Aaron and the others were inside the city. Despite the fear she must be feeling, the queen was trying to comfort her.

"Queen Adina," one of her guards said, "it's time we got you into the city."

"We have gone over this already, Captain Marcus," Adina said. "I will not go into the city until the wounded have been seen to."

The man nodded. "Yes, Majesty, but the last of the wounded are being led into the city now."

"He's right, Majesty," Brandon said. "All that can be done for them has been—there is nothing more you can do here. It's time."

Adina gazed out at the fields, at the dead lying scattered about it, and a tear trickled down her face. That, and only that. Then, she seemed to gather herself and nodded. "Very well." She turned to the club owner. "Will you walk with me?"

May smiled, impressed not for the first time by the other woman's compassion and not just that, for if the past hours had shown her anything, it was the strength, the courage that buoyed up that compassion, the foundation upon which it had been built. "Majesty," she said, "I would be honored."

CHAPTER FORTY-SIX

Leomin watched the others climb the ladder and disappear into the darkness above.

I don't like this, Leomin, Aliandra said into his mind, and he was forced to agree with the Virtue. They were in the sewers of a hostile city, planning to do battle with a mage out of legend. Leomin had been a smuggler for years, and had often been in danger, but he had always run *away* from it, not toward it. Still, there was no choice, and he knew it, so he took a deep breath and smiled at Seline before following the others up the ladder with a confidence he didn't feel.

The room he climbed into was completely dark, and someone grunted as he bumped into them. "Where are we?"

"Tianya?" Aaron asked from somewhere off to Leomin's left.

"It appears to be a small garderobe," the woman answered, no doubt calling on her bond with the Virtue of Perception to make out their surroundings clearly. "There's a door here."

Leomin himself could see nothing, but he heard the click of the latch well enough, and he followed the others out into a big room, wincing as his eyes protested at the bright sunlight pouring into the room from several windows. Simple cots were lined up along the room's length, reminding him of the troops' barracks back in Perennia.

"The servants' quarters," Gryle said, nodding.

None of the beds were occupied, and Leomin was just about to say a quick prayer of thanks for their luck when the door at the end of the room opened and four guards wielding crossbows stalked inside, their weapons pointed at Leomin and the others. A fifth figure followed them inside, and Leomin blinked in surprise as he recognized the newcomer.

The woman was wearing a blue silk dress, and she smiled upon seeing them, as if some suspicion had been confirmed. "*Maladine?*" Leomin blurted.

The representative of the Golden Oars bank smiled warmly, nodding her head at him as if to cede a point. "Just so," she said. "And how are your royal mother and father doing, I wonder?"

Leomin frowned, at first not realizing what she meant, then he recalled the cover story he'd given the last time they'd come to the city, when he was plying the woman for information. "Um...they are...well. Thank you for asking."

"Well, that's good," the woman said, giving him a knowing smile. Then she looked around at the group, mock concern on her face. "And where is dear Servant? I do hope nothing untoward has happened to him."

Leomin cleared his throat, trying to formulate some response, but she beat him to it, waving a hand. "Never mind, dear Leomin. I won't force you to squirm any longer. I have learned a few things, since our last...shall we say, *meeting*. As pleasant and diverting as it was,"—she winked—"I must admit it left me with a few questions, ones which, upon waking to find myself alone and you long gone, I have since endeavored to answer."

Leomin felt his face flush, and was all too aware of the arched look Seline was giving him. "I...do forgive me for that, madam. I assure you, it wasn't by choice. Business matters, I'm afraid, demanded my attention."

"Indeed," she said. "The business, I imagine, of escaping the city before the guards found you." Leomin's breath caught in his throat at that, but she wasn't done. "Oh, don't look so surprised, Leomin." She grinned mischievously. "Or should I say, 'Captain?' You see, a woman of my profession knows well the importance of information, the value of it, and it was not so very difficult to link the Parnen who escaped the city with the one who had shown me such a pleasant night. Both, after all, had bells in their hair." She frowned as if disappointed, staring at his long braided hair. "Not now, though, and that is a shame. I did so love the look of them."

Leomin risked a glance at Seline's scowl before turning back to the woman, "Yes, well, forgive me but…"

"Enough," Aaron said, and Leomin breathed a heavy sigh of relief, thankful as everyone present turned to look at the sellsword. "Fine, you know who Leomin is, and we know who you are. Now, what do you want?"

"Ah," she said, "and this must be General Envelar. Oh yes, I have heard of you—I doubt there are any in Baresh who haven't now. Still," she said, giving a pouty look, "I would have thought you'd be taller."

Leomin saw Seline reaching for the blades at her side, and the representative of the Golden Oars held up an admonishing finger. "I wouldn't do that, if I were you. You're fast, I know, but even I doubt that you are fast enough to stop so many crossbow bolts at once—particularly when they come from both sides."

As if they'd only been waiting their cue, four more crossbowmen piled into the room from the other side. Leomin swallowed, glancing back at Seline to see her hands drop, a silent snarl on her face.

"Ah, such anger," Maladine said to Seline. "Why, I do believe if these men weren't with me, you'd like to tear me limb from limb. Is that simply frustration at being caught, I wonder, or something more?" She glanced between Leomin and Seline, her smile widening. "Ah, I *see*. My, Leomin, but you do stay busy, don't you?"

"Is there a point to any of this?" Aaron demanded.

The woman sighed. "Very well, I see my audience grows weary. Yes, Aaron Envelar, there is a point. You see, I know of these sewers, just as I know many of Baresh's other secrets. As I believe I've mentioned, I make it my business to know such things. So, when I heard there were a group of fugitives in the city who had somehow managed to evade several groups of guards…" She paused, shrugging. "Well, it was no great leap to guess that the rebellion—such as it is—saw fit to help you."

She laughed at the look of surprise on their faces. "Oh yes, I know of the rebellion. Just as I know of these sewers, and of the Virtues you all carry. Just as I know that you have come to kill the king."

"Yes, we have," Aaron said. "Now, if you're done talking, why don't you do whatever you intend, but I warn you that we will not surrender. There's an army outside the city counting on us."

The woman raised an eyebrow. "It seems you've spent too long in the sewers, General. The army is no longer outside the city but within it, the gate closed behind them and nearly all of Baresh's forces caught outside." She shrugged. "Still, judging from what I've learned of the creatures' strengths, I do not doubt that they will find a way through the gate sooner rather than later. And as for what I intend, well, isn't it obvious? I intend to help you."

Leomin grunted in surprise, his own shock mirrored in the expressions of the others. "H-help us?" he said. "But...why?"

Maladine shrugged. "Does it really matter? Very well, if you must have an answer, then let us say simply that chaos is bad for business, and I am a woman who prides herself on doing what is good for her business."

Leomin frowned, studying her. "But that's not the real reason—or, at least, not the only one."

A hardness came into her eyes then, and she shook her head slowly. "No, it isn't, but it is the only one I will give you. Now, will you accept my help or not? I can get you into the castle—the guards are used to seeing me there, and will think nothing of it should I add a few more bodyguards to my own retinue. Otherwise..." She shrugged again. "I suppose you can take your chances on your own, but I would not wager on you setting foot inside the castle, not with as many guards as are now patrolling the grounds."

Leomin felt a hand on his shoulder and barely managed to hold back a scream before turning to see Aaron watching him. "Well?" the sellsword asked. "You know her better than any of us. What do you think?"

Leomin cleared his throat, pointedly avoiding Seline's glare. "I...for what it is worth, Aaron, I do not believe she is lying."

The sellsword nodded slowly. "Good enough for me." He turned back to the woman. "Alright, we'll take your help, and you have our thanks."

She clapped her hands together softly. "Oh, now isn't this fine? And who knows?" she said, glancing at Leomin. "Perhaps we will have an opportunity to...renew our acquaintance."

Leomin swallowed hard, unable to get any words out past the lump in his throat, and the woman giggled before motioning to the guards. "Come. This way."

The others followed her, but Seline took his arm, and reluctantly he looked up to meet her gaze. "We *will* talk about this," she said. "Later."

"O-of course," Leomin answered, but she was already walking after the others. He watched her go, heaved a heavy sigh, and followed.

CHAPTER FORTY-SEVEN

Guard Captain Marcus knew he should be relieved. After all, they had made it into the city—for some time there, it had looked like they never would, and that Perennia's army would be crushed outside. Yet, what he felt more than anything was not relief, but fear. Fear not for himself, but for his charge, Queen Adina, who now crouched by one of the wounded lining the street, ministering to the man's wounds and murmuring soft, reassuring words. Those nearest watched her in awe, as did her patient, clearly amazed to see their queen tending to the army's wounded personally. Marcus, too, was amazed by it, but he wished she would take a break.

Though the queen hadn't uttered a single complaint, he knew she was tired. The army's healers had taken breaks in the long hours spent outside the walls, but she had not, moving from one wounded soldier to the next with an urgency that was humbling, always smiling and doing her best to comfort those she tended. But for all that, Marcus could see her exhaustion—he saw it in the way she moved, but, more than anything, he saw it in her eyes.

He resisted the urge to ask her to rest, for he knew she would only refuse and, besides, there was no denying the effect her presence had on the troops' morale. Even those suffering from wounds straightened their backs when she came near, and for a moment, the pain seemed to leave their faces, replaced by admiration and, Marcus believed, hope.

So instead of asking her to stop, he busied himself scanning the nearby alleyways. Though the western gate opening had saved the army, Marcus reminded himself that they were within an enemy city now. Any moment, soldiers might come rushing down one of the side streets to attack them and, if they did, it would be his job—and the job of those guards standing near him—to keep the queen safe.

"She really does care for them, doesn't she?"

Marcus's nerves were stretched so tightly that he nearly screamed at the unexpected voice, and he spun, his fingers tightening around his sword hilt. But instead of the enemy soldier he'd half-imagined, he recognized the man standing beside him. At first, he couldn't place him, then his eyes went wide as he realized that the newcomer was General Yalleck, the commander of Avarest's armies. He bowed his head. "General Yalleck."

The older man gave him a small smile. "That is my name. And yours, guardsman?"

Marcus cleared his throat. "It's uh...that is, I'm Marcus, sir."

The general inclined his head. "A pleasure. But...my question?"

Marcus frowned, confused. "Sir?"

"Queen Adina," the general prompted, turning back to study the queen as she went about her work. "She seems to care for her people."

"Yes sir," Marcus managed, surprised by how quickly his life had changed. Only weeks ago, he'd been the guard captain of a city gate; now he served as one of the queen's personal bodyguards and was speaking to a general who commanded one of the world's greatest armies. "She does."

Yalleck nodded thoughtfully. "Still, I suppose it could be only a show. Other rulers have done as much in the past, pretending to care for their people only to secure their support. A man might be left to wonder if such was the case here."

"Forgive me, General," Marcus said, "but such a man would be a fool."

The general turned to him, raising his eyebrows in surprise at the feeling in Marcus's voice. "Oh?"

"Yes. General, I've watched the queen for these last hours as she's ministered to the wounded and the dying. I've watched her try to save those who could not be saved. I've seen her stand up from men and women who died despite her efforts, and each time I've seen her take invisible wounds of her own. Yet, she moves to the next without hesitation, doing what she can, oblivious of her own pain, or the danger she puts herself in. No," he said, meeting the other man's eyes, "it is not a show, General. It is simply who she is."

Yalleck studied him for several seconds, then turned back to watch Adina, deep in thought. He seemed to come to some sort of decision, and he turned back to Marcus with a small smile. "Thank you, guardsman." He started away but had only taken a step before he turned back. "And guardsman?"

"General?"

"Keep her safe. I think that, should we win the day, Telrear could do little better than have one such as she lead us into the future."

***

"May, I told you, I'm fine," Thom said wearily. He sat with his back propped against the inside of Baresh's wall, along with hundreds of other soldiers, the nearest of whom were finding the strength—despite their obvious exhaustion—to grin as the woman fussed over him.

"Fine?" she said. "*Fine?*" She shook her head, holding up his arm to display a long, shallow cut across it, as if he hadn't noticed it well enough already. "Does *this* look fine to you, Thom?" She scowled, looking around them. "And just where *is* that damned healer, anyway? She said she'd be here way before now."

"Probably seeing to someone who actually needs it, May." He sighed. "Look, it's nearly stopped bleeding, and it was never deep anyway."

"As if it needs to be deep to get *infected,*" May said, shaking her head. "I'm going to go find her—you just stay here. Don't you move."

Moving was the last thing on Thom's mind just then as his weary body soaked up the brief moment of respite while the fresher troops from the ships manned the battlements, shooting arrows down at the enemy army now forced to lay siege to their own walls. Still, the woman kept studying him, so he nodded. "I'll be right here, May."

"You'd better be, Thom," she said, narrowing her gaze. "Now, I'll be right back."

With that, she was gone, stomping through the crowd of resting soldiers who pointedly avoided her gaze as she swept past. Thom didn't envy the healer, when May found her.

"Well, why ain't I surprised to find you lazin' about when there's work needs doin'?"

And there was Festa walking up. The captain was covered in thick furs as he always was in the north, but Thom didn't miss the cuts and tears in them, nor the splatters of what appeared to be fresh blood covering them. "Captain," he said, surprised by how glad he was to see the man alive and well.

He started to rise, but Festa held out a hand, forestalling him. "Don't you get up on my account," the captain said, grinning. "I don't mean to find myself on that she-devil's bad side, she comes back and sees you standin' up with no one but me to blame."

"I'm fine, Captain. Just tired, is all."

The man grunted. "Well now, that's what you get for playin' at bein' a soldier ain't it?" He shook his head slowly. "A man your age. Still, I'm glad to see you made it through so far—the gods know it's a pain in the ass trainin' a first mate, and I don't aim to do it again anytime soon."

Thom grinned, knowing the relief in the man's voice for what it was. "And what of you? Aren't you needed to command the troops?"

Festa snorted, sitting down heavily beside Thom. "Captain Gant, General Yalleck and the Queen got that one handled well enough, and it's just as well. I'm a sailor, Thom. I don't know nothin' about battles and defendin' walls. I'll leave that to them, and gladly."

Thom laughed. "Still, from what I hear you did a fine job, bringing the lads all the way through the city and fightin' the enemy as you did. Might be you missed your callin', Cap."

The other man frowned. "Much more talk like that, first mate, and I'll make sure the healers got some real work to do on you when they get here, you hear me?"

Thom nodded, but he couldn't keep the smile from his face. "Yes, sir."

"Anyhow," Festa said, rubbing at his chin, "it'll be good to have you back on the ship. Blunderfoot's a good enough sort, but he's a jumpy bastard. Why, I can't so much as pull out a chair to have a seat without him cringing like a child scared of the bogeyman."

I imagine that's because, if you're touching a chair, it's better than even odds you're getting ready to throw it at someone, Thom thought, but he only nodded. "How is Balen, anyway?"

Festa frowned. "Can't say as I know for sure. Him and those criminals got the harbor chain down—if it weren't for them we never would have been able to dock—but I ain't seen 'em since."

Before Thom could respond, there was a loud *screech* of tortured metal, and he spun to look in the direction of the gate. On the gate's other side, he could make out one of the giant creatures. The thing had at least a dozen crossbow bolts protruding from its chest and arms, but it hardly seemed to notice, and the sound he'd heard was it using its incredible strength to force the gate open.

Thom rose, hurrying toward the gate to offer what help he could, and he heard Festa shouting at the nearby troops from behind him. Wherever Balen and the others were, they would have to see to themselves for now—Thom and those with him had their own problems.

CHAPTER FORTY-EIGHT

Kevlane stood gazing out of the castle window, watching the battle at the western gate with eyes capable of seeing farther than any man's, one of the many gifts of the Virtue of Adaptability. One of the many benefits of being a god. And had someone been there to see him, they would have noted eyes that didn't belong to any human at all, but ones that had been shaped and formed by his bond, mimicking the superior sight of a bird of prey.

Yet for all his power, for all their utility, his eyes could do nothing to change that which they viewed, and the ancient mage's hands knotted into fists at his sides, his nails digging into palms until blood began to drip onto the castle floor. His army—his glorious, unstoppable army—was somehow trapped outside the city. Oh, they would get in sooner or later, but being outmaneuvered, made a fool of, made anger boil within him. Envelar would pay. They would *all* pay.

There was a knock at the door, and Kevlane snarled. He had left specific instructions to not be disturbed, and who would *dare* defy such strictures? *If that is you, Caldwell, I will show you the true nature of my wrath.* He had sent the advisor, along with a complement of his experiments, to see to the situation at the gate; whatever had happened, the man had clearly failed. The only consolation was that this failure would be his last. Kevlane would see to it.

"Enter," he growled.

The man who stepped through the door wore the clothes of a clerk, and he was bent nearly double, his eyes staring at the ground as if afraid to meet his ruler's gaze. "*Look* at me," Kevlane demanded in a hiss.

The man did, slowly, and he let out a gasp when he saw the mage standing there. Kevlane frowned at the man's reaction, then realized that this one did not know his true identity, and had thought to find King Belgarin within the room. Now, though, Kevlane did not wear the king's face but his own, and his eyes were not that of a man's at all, but of an eagle. He closed his eyes, calling on the bond, and suppressed the wince of pain as his eyes readjusted, becoming his own once more. When he looked up again, the man had fallen to his knees, his face pale as he studied Kevlane with an expression of abject terror.

"Well?" Kevlane demanded. "What do you want?"

"I-I-I c-came to tell you, S-Sire," the man said, his voice a whimper. "M-Madam Caulia of the G-Golden Oars waits in your audience chamber."

Kevlane frowned, stalking toward the man. "You disturbed me for that?"

The man swallowed, recoiling. "S-she would not leave, S-Sire. She insisted on you meeting her."

Kevlane stared down at the clerk. "She *insisted?*"

"Y-yes, M-Majesty."

The mage studied the man for several seconds, the only sound that of the blood dripping from his hands onto the stone floor. "And what of Caldwell?"

"T-there has been no word, Majesty."

"Very well," Kevlane said after a moment. "I will meet with Maladine Caulia, and she will regret her presumption."

"O-of course, Majesty," the man said, backing toward the door, still on his hands and knees. "I'll let her know—"

"Oh, that's quite alright," Kevlane said, baring his teeth in a grin. "I'll let her know myself. Tell me, Clerk. Have you ever wondered what it would feel like to fly?"

"M-Majesty?" the man asked in a confused tone, finally daring to meet Kevlane's eyes.

Without a word, the mage lifted the man even as his muscles grew with the power of his bond and, with a bellow of rage, hurled him at the window. The glass shattered as the clerk's body plowed through it, and Kevlane stood there, listening to his screams of terror until they dwindled away into nothing. Then he headed for the door and Maladine Caulia, promising himself the woman would suffer for her presumption.

CHAPTER FORTY-NINE

Thom arrived at the gate with dozens of other soldiers, all of them staring in horror as another of the giant creatures joined its companion, heaving against the massive iron gate. Crossbow bolts and arrows stuck out of them in dozens of places, but they went on about their task, their unnatural muscles straining against the barrier between them and Perennia's beleaguered forces.

They'd raised it to the height of a normal man's chest when several soldiers rushed the creatures, perhaps meaning to kill them while they were occupied with the gate, but one of the fast creatures appeared then, its long, slender blade sweeping under the slowly rising gate in a blur and cutting the men down.

Thom gritted his teeth, glancing to either side of him to see soldiers lined up in a semi-circle around the gate, waiting to throw themselves at the creatures. *Gods, we're all dead. May was right—I should have stayed on the damn ship.*

"Out of the way!"

The voice sounded familiar, and Thom and those standing with him spun to see a group of people running toward them. He grunted in surprise as he recognized Balen among them, a crossbow in his hands to match those of the dozens of others with him. Thom didn't waste time, pushing the soldiers nearest him. "You heard him, move it!"

In seconds, the path between Balen's group and the gate was clear, and bolts flashed out of the crossbows, dozens of them, burying themselves in the two monstrosities beside the other quarrels already protruding from their bodies. Thom hurried to Balen. "Glad to see you alive, Blunderfoot."

The first mate handed his crossbow off to another man and stepped to the side of the street with Thom. "Glad to be alive, Thom. It's been a real shit day so far, I can tell you that."

Thom nodded. "It ain't lookin' like it's gonna get any better. Those crossbows ain't gonna work. We've tried it."

"Not like this you haven't."

They both turned, and Thom frowned at an unfamiliar older man with a patch over one eye. "Do I know you?"

"Thom," Balen said, speaking fast, "this is Eyes. He uh...well, he runs the uh..."

"I'm a criminal," the old man said, smiling. "Pleasure to meet you. Anyway, as I was saying, those quarrels are different from those your troops have been using."

Thom frowned, studying the creatures who were still steadily raising the gate inch by inch. "They look the same to me."

"Well, they are, in fact," Eyes said. "Except, of course, these are coated in poison."

"Poison?" Thom said. "Gods, man, why would you have quarrels coated in..." He trailed off.

The old man gave him a vulpine grin. "That's right. Criminals."

Before Thom could answer, there was a loud *crash,* and they turned to see one of the behemoths collapse, toppling like a massive tree. The second strained, its body shaking now that it was taking the weight of the gate alone, then its unnatural muscles gave out, and it fell, the iron spikes on the gate impaling it as it slammed closed.

"Damn," Thom said, looking back at the older man. "Nice arrows."

"So they were," Eyes agreed. Thom frowned, and the old man nodded. "Yes. That was the last of them. The next time they come, I suppose we'll have to do things the hard way."

CHAPTER FIFTY

The anxiety of Aaron's companions was clear in their tense postures and carefully-controlled expressions as they waited for the mage to arrive in the audience room. Aaron, was nervous to, but what he felt more than anything else was shame at bringing them here. A ship captain, a chamberlain, a child, a woman who had just lost her father, and another who had only just recovered from nearly dying. And the Ghosts—Bastion and the other whose name he thought was Clyde, the only two remaining of Perennia's elite troops. They were here because of him, had suffered because of him, and if they found their death here, in this place, it would be *him* who had led them to it.

They chose to come, Aaron. Co said. *You know that. Would you now hold yourself responsible for their choice and steal from them the value of their sacrifice? Is that not the same theft of honor of which you accused Tianya, not so very long ago?*

Aaron sighed. *You're right, Firefly.*

Maladine Caulia had departed shortly after showing them to the audience chamber, telling Aaron and the others she would see them once it was finished. She'd said the words confidently enough, but he hadn't missed the speed with which she'd retreated, taking her guards with her, and the truth was, he couldn't blame her.

Still, he stood as confidently as he could, all too aware that the others were stealing nervous glances at him. For his part, his gaze remained on the door the mage would come through. Assuming, of course, that Maladine had been honest and that there weren't, even now, an army of the mage's creatures rushing toward them, intent on cutting them down.

The thought wouldn't leave him, and before he knew it, he'd called on the power of his bond with Co. Not much, but enough to see the auras of those within the castle walls—a soft magenta for the regular guards and servants of the castle. But there were other auras, more than he would have liked, weak and barely there at all. Those, he knew, belonged to Kevlane's creatures, those poor souls on whom he had worked his dark Art.

And, among all of these, there was one other: a dark, twisted aura that was uncomfortable to look upon. The mage, then. A man who had lived for thousands of years, who was responsible for untold deaths, Aaron's parents among them. A man, if man he still was, who healed from any wound, who could shape his body and appearance to whatever was needed, who wielded untold power. And he was coming straight for them.

His frown deepened as he noticed two others accompanying the mage, their auras marking them as normal castle guards. They were walking down the hall now, moving toward the audience chamber.

"Aaron," Tianya said, opening her eyes from where she'd been concentrating on her own gift and turning to Aaron, a panicked look on her face, "he's not alone."

He nodded grimly, drawing the blade at his back. "I know. Seline, watch the left of the door. Bastion, Clyde, the right." He paused, looking at each of the others in turn. "This is why we came here. To finish this. So let's finish it."

They all nodded, and then there was no time left for worries or fears, for the door was opening. Kevlane walked in wearing Belgarin's face. "Maladine," the mage was saying even before he was through the door, "how dare you—" He cut off, and Aaron was rewarded with a look of shock on the man's features, one enhanced when a moment later, the two guards following him let out grunts of pain and surprise as Seline and Bastion brought the handles of their weapons down on their heads, knocking them unconscious.

The mage glanced to either side of him, then looked up at Aaron and the others standing there, and slowly his surprise faded, replaced by a smile that looked more like a snarl. "Aaron Envelar. You have come."

Aaron shrugged. "We have unfinished business."

"So we do," the mage said, walking slowly into the room, apparently unconcerned with the fact that he was alone and surrounded by his enemies. "So we do." He shook his head, still smiling. "I must confess, I had not thought you would be so foolish as to come here, to my place of power."

Aaron gave the man a smile of his own. "I've been known to be foolish from time to time."

"And these others," Kevlane went on, studying Aaron's companions. "All Virtue-bearers, I see—I can feel it." He laughed. "And have you all come, then, to give me what is rightfully mine? To bow in worship to your god?"

"I've never been much good at bowing," Aaron said.

The mage cocked his head, studying them. "Then I will show you how. Do you truly think you have any chance at victory? Even now, your forces at the western gate are dying. Did you really believe—"

Whatever he'd been about to say was lost in Gryle's roar as the chamberlain stepped out from where he'd been standing behind the door, swinging the chair he held. Powered by the man's Virtue-enhanced strength, the blow struck the mage in the back with a *crash*. The chair itself shattered into splinters at the impact, and the mage hurtled across the room to slam into the far wall, crashing through the stone. Aaron blinked, stunned, as part of the wall gave way, falling on top of the man, and in seconds he was buried in rubble. Gryle had a confused, surprised look on his face, as if he couldn't believe what he'd just done. He still held the shattered remnants of the chair in his hands. The chamberlain saw Aaron watching him, and his face turned red before he finally shrugged.

Aaron and the others turned to stare at the pile of rubble in silent disbelief as Seline and the two Ghosts came to stand with them once more. A cloud of dust slowly settled, but nothing else stirred. *Could it really be that easy?* Aaron thought, but the small surge of hope vanished a second later when the stones began to tremble. Then there was a savage, bestial growl, and Aaron and his companions were forced to cover their eyes as the mage burst free in a shower of stone and debris.

Kevlane's neck hung at an impossible angle, and his back was twisted strangely. The bones of his arms and legs had torn through the skin in several places, but he was standing just the same, and even as Aaron and the others watched, his body began to reknit itself, his neck straightening with a sickening *pop*, his body twisting as his spine shifted back to where it belonged. "You *dare*," he snarled in a voice that barely sounded human at all, "to strike your *god?*" He took a step toward them, the bones protruding from his body snapping into place as he did, his flesh mending itself.

He started to take another step, but something flashed past Aaron in a blur, and the mage staggered as one of Seline's knives embedded itself in his chest. The mage looked down at the blade in disgust, then pulled it free in a spurt of blood. "*Enough,*" he hissed. "You cannot defeat me. Now, give me the Virtues, and I will make your deaths quick. They are killing you anyway. You know that, don't you?" His gaze swept Aaron and the others, his lips spreading in a too-wide grin at the obvious look of understanding on their faces. "The power the Virtues contain is too much for any mortal to hold. You feel it, don't you? Like poison coursing through your veins?"

His gaze settled on Caleb, and his grin widened. Aaron's saw that the youth's face was pale, his expression sickly. "What of you, little one?" the mage ventured. "Would you like for me to take your pain away? I can, you know. The Virtues are, after all, my children. Do you understand the price of such knowledge as you carry? The mind grows, young one, and the body weakens. Soon, you will be a shriveled thing, and others will scream when they look upon you. Unless you give it to me now. I can save you from what it would do to you—from the monster you would become."

Caleb's mouth worked and, at first, nothing came out. Then, his back seemed to straighten, and he met the mage's eyes. "Go to the Fields."

Kevlane snarled, and the hand holding the knife flashed forward, impossibly fast. "*Look ou—*" Aaron began, but it was too late. The blade flew through the air, directly at Caleb, but suddenly Tianya was there, stepping in front of him, and the blade buried itself in her chest. She gasped, falling to her knees, and Caleb screamed.

"No!" Aaron shouted in anger and disbelief. He had fought the mage before, but he had never been so fast.

"Oh yes, Aaron Envelar," Kevlane said, grinning, "my creations are not alone in the gifts the Art has given them. Since last we met, I have...improved myself."

Aaron rushed to the woman's side, catching her before she fell. "I...saw him—" she started, then paused, coughing up blood. "About to...throw. I'm...sorry, Aaron...that I could not help more."

"Sorry?" Aaron said, shocked at the fury and grief roiling in him. "Why would you be sorry? Now, don't talk like that, everything's going to be—"

"It's...okay, Aaron," she managed, and she went limp in his hands, and he fell to his knees, still cradling her in his arms. She gave him a small, almost imperceptible smile. "Really...it's...okay. I will see them again. The Tenders." Her gaze grew unfocused then, and her smile widened. "My friends." Then her eyes closed, and the breath left her body and did not return.

Aaron stared at her in shock. *So fast,* he thought wildly. One moment, the woman had been alive. The next, she was dead and gone, all her hopes and dreams turned to nothing but ash. A life that had taken years to fashion, made from the experiences and the choices of her past, snuffed out in a second. His jaw clenched, Aaron laid her down gently on the floor.

When he rose, he did so with fury coursing through his veins, and he spun on the mage, the handle of his sword clenched in a white-knuckled grip. "You bastard," he growled.

He charged then, bellowing in rage, his sword leading. The mage moved impossibly fast, dodging the first strikes, but Aaron called on his bond with Co. As he'd discovered months earlier, the power of the bond was muted against another Virtue-bearer, yet still it gave him some sense of the mage's movements, and his sword caught the man more than once, digging a bloody furrow across one of his arms, a leg.

Kevlane lost his balance when the blade severed the muscle of his leg, and he staggered. Aaron took the opportunity to lunge forward, impaling the man with his blade. He tried to pull the blade free, but it was suddenly stuck fast, the mage's flesh reforming over it. Kevlane gave him a grin, then swung a hand. Aaron managed to move to the side, avoiding being struck in the face, but the blow crashed into his shoulder with shocking force, and his hand was ripped away from the sword's handle as he went flying, crashing into the wall. He felt a rib crack, and he cried out in pain, falling to his hands and knees.

"So easily is the great Aaron Envelar bested."

Groaning, Aaron raised his head to see Kevlane walking toward him slowly, pulling the sword from his stomach as he did. Bastion and Clyde gave a shout and charged the mage from behind. "*Wait,*" Aaron tried to yell, but the words came out in little more than a rasping whisper, and it was too late in any case.

Bastion swung his sword at the mage's back in an overhanded strike, but the mage sidestepped it easily, his eyes never leaving Aaron's as he swung his arm behind him. The blow connected with the young giant's shoulder, and he was hurtled back to slam against the wall. His head struck the stone, and he slumped to the ground, unconscious.

The second Ghost, Clyde, was only seconds behind, but before he could reach the mage Kevlane turned, throwing his arm up in his attacker's direction. Suddenly, his arm changed, growing by several feet and turning into little more than a spike, impaling the Ghost. Clyde stared down at the limb protruding from his chest with a vaguely surprised, confused look, before collapsing to the ground in a pool of blood.

A moment later, Kevlane's arm looked normal again, the only evidence of its change the torn sleeve of his robe. He sighed, looking back at Aaron. "Such frail things, you mortals."

"*Bastard,*" Aaron croaked, staring at Clyde's unmoving form, and Tianya's not far away. Both now dead and with himself to blame. With a growl, he rose to his feet, doing his best to ignore the sharp pain from his wounded rib. "I'll kill you for that."

The mage grinned. "You cannot kill a god, Aaron Envelar. You can only suffer his wrath."

The others started forward, toward Kevlane, Aaron's fury at the deaths of his friends mirrored in their expressions—then, the door was thrown open. They all paused, looking to the door to see dozens of Kevlane's creatures pouring into the audience room. "Oh gods," Aaron breathed.

"That's right," Kevlane said, his grin widening. "Did you really believe you would be able to come into *my* castle and defeat me? And did you, in your foolishness, think Savrin was the only one of his kind? Your friends will die here, and you will be able to do nothing but watch. And once they have died, I will see to the others who assault the city's western gate. Your woman is there, is she not? Oh, but I will bring such suffering upon her that you will wish to tear out your own eyes, having seen it. She will die, Aaron Envelar. All of those you have come to love will die and only then, only when you are nothing but a weeping, despairing wretch, will I end your life."

Aaron felt the fury build in him, fury borne of his bond with the Virtue and of himself, rising and rising until it seemed as if it would consume all that he was, all that he had ever been, replacing it only with an unquenchable blaze that would devour everything in its path.

Aaron, a voice said into his mind, *you must not. You cannot beat him, not like this, you—*

But Aaron wasn't listening. There was nothing but the anger now, *he* was the anger, and with a shout of rage, he charged.

***

Leomin watched, stunned, as Aaron rushed at the mage, rolling and retrieving his sword before continuing to charge, his blade weaving a net of steel. Yet, for all his skill and speed, the mage was faster, and what wounds the sellsword managed to inflict healed practically instantly. He looked back to where the creatures were surrounding him and the others. Two dozen, at least.

Leomin reached out to them gently with his charisma Virtue and saw, as he'd suspected he would, that though there might be enough of their humanity left to remember their training, there wasn't enough for him to exercise the power of his Virtue. *What am I doing here?* But he knew the answer well enough. He glanced to the side where Seline held a blade in either hand, her lip curled into a silent snarl. He loved her. It wasn't an easy thing for him to admit, even to himself, but it was true anyway. He loved her, and now they were both going to die.

He'd spent years jumping from one bed to another, from one woman to another, and now that he had finally found one that meant more to him than just a night's entertainment, he was going to die. *She* was going to die, and there was nothing he could do to protect her, nothing he could do to save her or anyone else. Leomin had always prided himself on his ability to find satisfaction in even the darkest of circumstances; he was a man who smiled and laughed often, so different, in so many ways, than the rest of his subdued, quiet people, yet a product of them nonetheless. His life, he knew, his outlook on the world, was a rebellion against the cold, pale way in which most of his people lived. Yet, this had always seemed a rebellion worth fighting, one that, in the end, he was destined to win. He did not think so now, and for the first time since he was a child, taken into the care of the priestesses, Leomin the Parnen felt despair.

I am sorry, Leomin, Aliandra said into his mind. *For so much...I am sorry.*

As am I, Aliandra, he thought back as he drew the sword he'd been given. It felt strange in his hands. Wrong. He had been called many things in his day: Leomin the Scoundrel. Leomin the Bold. The Clever, the Fool. But Leomin the Warrior? No, that he was not, and the blade he held seemed to know it. "Seline," he said in a whisper, turning to her. "I just...I want to tell you...I—"

"No," she said in a tight, desperate voice. "No, Leomin." Her eyes met his, and he saw tears gathering there, felt his own heart cry out in answer. "You can tell me whatever it is you want to say," she continued, "but...after."

Leomin swallowed the lump in his throat and nodded. "Very well, my lady." And with that, he turned back to the creatures and his death. *I love you,* he finished.

***

Caleb's hands shook with fear, and the blade he held—a small but sharp knife Seline had given him—nearly fell from his sweaty grasp. It was not fear of pain or hurt that grew within him, robbing him of his strength, for in his short life, he had known much pain, much hurt—his mother had seen to that. Instead, this fear was one of failure, a fear that, no matter how hard he tried, it would not be enough, could *never* be enough.

We only do what we can, young one, Palendesh said, and there was a deep, abiding sadness in the Virtue's voice.

And if it isn't enough?

You ask for an objective answer to a subjective question, Caleb. Whether or not your contribution is "enough" is not based on the outcome, but on your own view of that contribution. The glory comes not from victory but the attempt.

Which is to say we'll die. As Tianya did. The thought made tears well in his eyes. He had tried so hard to save her, *had* saved her, yet she had died anyway and for nothing.

Not for nothing. Never that. And all who live will die, Caleb. It is a contract made as soon as we enter the world, one signed without our consent. Still, do not despair, not yet. We might still have a few surprises for these abominations. Now, concentrate. See them, young one.

"I'm *already* looking at them," Caleb said in a harsh whisper, and Gryle put a hand on his shoulder in what was no doubt meant to be a comforting gesture. Caleb gave him a smile—a weak, frail thing, but the best of which he was capable.

I did not say to "look," the Virtue answered, taking on the tone of an annoyed tutor. *I said to "see."*

Caleb let out a heavy sigh, peering at the creatures once more as they surrounded him and the others. Then, suddenly, something seemed to click in his mind. He watched the creatures moving, and in their movements, he saw puzzles, riddles and, what's more, he saw their answers. A slight shifting of a leg, an imperceptible tilt of the hip, to carry them in the direction they would go—the direction they *must* go.

Very good, the Virtue said. *All of nature—men included—abide by laws, young one, and it is only the ignorant who believe in randomness, in chance. The rules are there—they always have been. It is only for us to see them, to understand them. And, understanding them, to use them to our advantage.*

But they're too fast, Caleb thought back, doubtful and scared of the small bit of hope flickering inside him. He had seen their speed before, after all, when they had fought the creature at the gate, and he had been little more than a blur of light and shadow.

They are fast, the Virtue agreed, *yet even they cannot move as fast as you can think. Tornadoes, lightning strikes, these are fast, yet even they might be avoided, if one only knows how.*

Avoided, Caleb thought, *but not defeated.* Still, the blade seemed to fit better in his grip than it had. Suddenly three creatures charged forward, and Caleb's mind studied them with a speed of thought he had never felt before. *Three. Seline rushing forward to meet the first one. The second going for Gryle. That left the third, rushing at him now.* His mind caught details, processing them faster than he would have thought possible. *Sword held in left hand. Eleven steps would bring him within striking range.*

And based on the angle of the sword, which telegraphed the sweep of it, he knew well what shape that attack would take. The thing was fast, as he'd known it would be. And that's what he counted on. The moment before he judged the creature would strike, Caleb leapt to the side, in the direction of the one charging Gryle. His attacker's sword chased him, reacting as he had known it would. Normally, Palendesh was right—the mind was always faster than the body—but Kevlane's creatures had little mind left, and so the blade chased Caleb who rolled past its comrade, and the sword took Gryle's attacker in the side.

Guided by the creature's speed and strength, the blade bit deep, and Gryle's attacker was nearly severed in two before it collapsed to the ground. Caleb rolled to a stop, spinning in time to see the chamberlain's eyes go wide in surprise, even as he stepped forward and brought the chair he'd grabbed down on Caleb's attacker as it tried to free its blade from its comrade. There was a *crunch* as the creature's body broke beneath the chamberlain's blow like a stack of kindling, and Caleb turned away in time to see Seline meeting her own opponent head-on.

They moved in a blur, their strikes so fast that even Caleb's Virtue-enhanced mind had difficulty following them. Seline was faster than Kevlane's creation, yet its prodigious strength meant that she had to dodge rather than parry, and when she finally buried her blades in the creature's neck, ending its life, Caleb saw that she was panting and sweating heavily, her eyes wild around the edges. He also saw, with surprise, that there was a streak of gray in her hair, one that had not been there before.

Some small, rational part of his mind acknowledged that, though Kevlane was a monster, he wasn't wrong. The Virtues *were* killing him and the others. And the more they used the powers of their bonds, the quicker that death came. It was not the Virtues' fault, no more than it was the fault of a rock when, caught in a land slide, it crushed some unsuspecting victim, but that didn't change the truth of it.

You can leave them, you know.

A voice in his head, not Palendesh's, not this time, but the other, as if Caleb's thoughts had summoned him. *They will lose—surely, you must see that much, at least.* There was no emotion, no inflection in the voice, as if the speaker didn't feel one way or the other about what he said, and was only stating an obvious truth.

You don't know that, Caleb thought back, shaking his head furiously, as if the simple gesture might banish the voice, but it did not.

Don't I? the voice, *his* voice, responded. *Look around you, boy. Use the knowledge you have and see.*

Caleb did so, reluctantly. Aaron was battling with Kevlane, and though the sellsword fought with more skill and fury than he had ever seen, inflicting wounds on the mage despite his greater speed, it didn't seem to matter, for each wound healed instantly as if it had never been. Caleb turned away, pointedly avoiding Tianya's body, to see Seline panting, standing over her opponent's corpse. No sooner had he turned to her than he picked out one of the creatures preparing to rush forward, but not toward the woman. "Leomin, watch out!"

The creature moved in a blur, racing toward Leomin, its sword raised. Seline noticed as well, and suddenly she appeared beside the Parnen, knocking him aside and bringing her blades up in time to parry. But for all her speed, the creature's attack was driven by a strength no mortal could hope to match. Seline screamed in shock and pain as she was thrown backward, tumbling across the ground until she finally struck the wall and lay still.

With a shout of anger, Leomin stepped forward, driving his sword into the creature's heart. The creature's body tensed in shock and surprise, and when the Parnen pulled the sword free it fell dead at his feet.

You see? the voice asked. *One is dead, yet what difference does it make? There are more, too many more. To stay is to die—there is nothing you can do to help them. But with your gift, you might find a way out. A small chance, but better than none.*

Caleb rubbed at his head furiously. "No," he whispered, "I won't leave them. I won't."

Then you will die

"Then I'll die," he growled, turning to face the remaining creatures.

***

Anger burned through Aaron, a living, hungry beast, and his sword flashed left and right, the power of his bond anticipating the mage's attacks. Yet even as he fought, he knew he would lose, for the strength his anger had given him was not limitless, while the mage's ability to heal from the wounds he inflicted seemed to be.

He saw Seline hit the wall, saw her fall limply to the floor, unconscious, and despair threatened to overcome him. Tianya dead, and Seline out of the fight. That only left Gryle, Caleb, and Leomin to face the dozens of remaining attackers. Not enough. Not nearly enough.

Aaron renewed his efforts, driving forward and plunging his sword into the mage's stomach. Kevlane grunted as the blade went in, but a moment later the sound turned to a slow laugh, and before Aaron could retract the blade, the mage grabbed him by the shoulders, lifting him from the ground effortlessly and carrying him backward to slam him against the wall. Aaron's wounded rib screamed in protest even as fresh agony roiled through his back at the impact. When the mage let him go, he collapsed to the ground, wheezing.

Kevlane took a step back and grinned as he pulled Aaron's sword free of his chest and tossed it aside. "Do you see, Aaron Envelar?" the mage said. "Do you see what you have brought on yourself and those you love?" He pointed to the three remaining Virtue-bearers, surrounded by his creatures. "They will die, and they will do so in pain, and in their last breaths, they will curse you for bringing their deaths upon them."

Aaron growled, trying to rise, but his battered muscles refused to obey his commands. "I'll...kill...you," he hissed.

"Oh?" the mage asked, laughing. "And how will you do that, I wonder? It seems to me you cannot even stand."

Despair settled over Aaron then, pouring over him and quenching the fire of rage, sweeping away hope in its wild torrent. He had failed. And because of his failure they were all going to die. Leomin, with his easy laugh—he was not laughing now. Gryle, the chamberlain who had been practically scared of his own shadow when they first met. Now, he had found his courage and, in finding it, he would die. As would Darrell and May, Adina and all the rest. They had counted on him, trusted him. And he had failed. Even with the power of the Virtues of Compassion and Will, he was not enough. He had never been enough, and he had been a fool to think otherwise, a fool to think one person could make a difference.

You're wrong, a voice said into his mind, and he recognized it as that of Aaron Caltriss, the long-dead king. *Even a single stone might start an avalanche. You can be that stone, Aaron. You must be, for there is no other.*

But how? Aaron thought back, desperately.

A question I asked myself when the barbarian kings marched on my city. It is for this reason we began the spell, Aaron Envelar, the incantation that ultimately created the Virtues.

"But what difference does that make?" Aaron demanded. "The spell failed."

"Wait," Kevlane said, and Aaron looked up to see the mage frowning. "Who...who are you talking to?"

A moment later, the ghostly apparition of Aaron Caltriss appeared standing beside the sellsword, and Kevlane gasped, backing away with wide eyes. "N-no," he said. "I-it can't be. Y-you're dead."

The long-dead king gave a small, sad smile. "Not dead, Boyce. Not truly. Now, please, hear me. You were a good man once. You can be that man again. Even now, it is not too late."

"I-it's not possible," Kevlane said, and there was no mistaking the fear in his voice. "You died. I *saw* you die."

Caltriss went on as if Kevlane hadn't spoken. "You have suffered, Boyce, and for that I am sorry. You have let your grief and anger make of you a vile thing. But it is not too late to save yourself. You must only choose to do so—none can go so far into the darkness that they cannot be brought again into the light."

The mage began laughing then, a loud, shrieking laugh that echoed with madness. "I am not who I once was," he said, his voice a harsh whisper.

"No, you're not," the king agreed. He stepped forward, reaching out a misty hand to the mage. "Will you stand with me, Boyce? One final time?"

Kevlane stared at the offered hand as if it were a viper baring its fangs, his eyes wide, his mouth working as if he would speak but couldn't manage the words. Then, a hardness came into his face, madness dancing in his eyes. "*No,*" he grated. "*No!* They must die for what they did to me. They must all die!" He was screaming now. "And even you cannot stop it! I am the ruler here now, not you. It is I who have the power."

A profound sadness came over Caltriss's face, and he nodded slowly, turning to Aaron. "Finish it, Aaron Envelar."

"Finish *what*?" Aaron gasped, from where he had fallen to his knees, the pain making it difficult to talk.

"You know," Caltriss said. "The spell—it was begun, but never finished. The Virtues exist, Aaron Envelar; they need only someone with the *will* to guide them, to bring them together." And with that, the form of Aaron Caltriss vanished into mist.

"N-no," Kevlane said, his voice screeching, "that isn't possible! You can't—"

Understanding bloomed in Aaron's mind, and a small smile came to his face. "But I can." The Virtues had been fashioned by the Art, but they had been made by the power of Will, the will of Aaron Caltriss, a man who had wanted nothing but to defend his people. They had been separate for thousands of years, alone, waiting only for someone with the will to bring them together once more.

Aaron, Co said, sounding afraid, *you know what it will do? The Virtues...we should never have been created at all. Don't you see? The virtues my father strove for are nothing without the striving. They are only great because of the struggles and challenges we face to attain them. Without that...Aaron, you have seen the darker side of the Virtues, what they are capable of. To have them all, at once...it will kill you.*

A blade that cut he who wielded it just as it did he who it was wielded against. That, Aaron understood. "It's okay, Firefly," he said. "It's okay." One death to save thousands, to save hundreds of thousands. It was an easy trade to make.

He rose to his feet, the pain of his battered body still there, but no match for his will. He raised his hands to the side, calling on the power of Aaron Caltriss's will, of his *own* will. At once, he felt the Virtues, not just as they now were, but as the people they had been, with their own hopes, their own dreams, now only shells of themselves, hollowed out and broken. He felt them, and he called to them. And they answered.

Power rushed into him, and a sound like a thunderclap tore through the air. Aaron screamed as the Virtues answered the call, as his body filled with their gift, their curse, and he fell to his knees, shaking from the storm raging inside him. Then, as quickly as it had begun, it was done. And when he rose a second time, he was not just Aaron Envelar, not anymore. He was an old man, Palendesh, a seeker of wisdom, of knowledge. He was Davin, "Dav" to his mother, a young man, eager and hungry to use his power, with a fast tongue and faster feet. And he was Evelyn, the daughter of Aaron Caltriss, who wanted only to protect, to save. He was compassion, and he was strength. He was speed and charisma, and intelligence, and perception and he was the will to guide them all. The spell was finally complete.

"Almost," he said, and those others, so long lost and left abandoned, spoke with him. He studied the mage in front of him, and Kevlane backed away, his hands in front of him.

"N-no," he growled, "you will not have it. The Virtue is *mine*, they will *all* be mine. *Kill them!*" he screamed. "*Kill them all!*"

Something struck his consciousness, and he did not have to turn to look where the others stood. Instead, he felt the movement of the creatures, understood it in an instant, as if each of their steps, each raising of a sword, was a part of the carefully choreographed motions of a play, one he had seen a thousand times. One which he knew each part of, one which he understood better even than its actors. He knew. He understood. And then he moved.

***

Caleb watched the creatures, waiting for his death to come, then suddenly, the air *cracked* with a sound like a thunderclap. Someone screamed then abruptly went silent, and he spun to see Aaron rising from where he'd fallen, saw Kevlane backing away from him, his face pale, his eyes wide.

It has been a pleasure to know you, young Caleb. Truly, an honor.

Caleb frowned. *Palendesh?*

The spell, lad. It finishes. I am called, and I must answer. It is finished. Finally. There was relief in the Virtue's voice, and Caleb was still trying to understand what he meant when something happened. He felt a tug, as if someone had grabbed his shirt and pulled him forward, and he staggered into Gryle who had also stumbled. He and the chamberlain and Leomin were staring at each other, confused, when they heard Kevlane's voice.

"Kill them! Kill them all!"

The creatures started toward them, but before they could reach Caleb and the others something was among them, a streak of movement, nothing more. Yet everywhere it moved, it left the creatures dead in its wake, and Caleb gasped as he watched them fall like wheat before a farmer's scythe.

In seconds, it was done, and Aaron Envelar stood among dozens of corpses. His chest rose and fell evenly, as if he hadn't just killed dozens of Kevlane's strongest creations, and if the hurts he had suffered earlier pained him, he showed no sign. But it was his eyes that captivated Caleb the most. They were alive with colors, a storm of them: blue and yellow and magenta and gray, all shifting in his irises like storm clouds.

Without a word, he walked past Caleb and the others, toward Kevlane who was trembling, his hands clenched into fists at his side, his face contorted with rage and insane hate. "It's *impossible!*" he screamed. "You can't, I—I am a *god!*"

"No, Kevlane," Aaron said, and it seemed to Caleb that a chorus of voices spoke with him. "You're not a god, but a man who has made of himself a monster. You are not ready for the power which you carry. No one is." And with that, the sellsword reached out his empty hand to Kevlane, his fingers extended.

The mage screamed, stumbling as if something had been ripped from him, and Caleb thought that he knew all too well what it was. He turned, with the others, to stare at the sellsword in awe.

***

Aaron felt the Virtue of Adaptation as it entered him along with the others. His body thrummed with power, and he felt invincible. Yet, at the same time, he knew the power of the Virtues was killing him, tearing him apart, for no man could possess such strength.

Aaron! Co's voice, speaking among a horde of others, yelling, her voice sounding weak and frail in the storm raging inside him. *You have to let it go—you have to let us go!*

But hers was not the only voice in his mind, not any longer. There were others—Melan, the Virtue of Strength, twisted by an insane rage; the Virtue of Adaptation, bent and perverted over thousands of years spent in the mage's possession. Their voices, too, echoed in his mind, as did the others. A chorus of voices, and in that chorus, a promise. Of power. Enough power to protect those he loved but more than that—enough power to shape the world to his will.

And so Aaron hesitated. Yes, the Virtues would kill him, eventually. But, then, all men died, didn't they? And with the gifts the Virtues offered, there was no telling what he might accomplish, what he might become. Kevlane had thought himself a god, but Aaron would be a god in truth, and with the Virtue of Adaptation able to heal his body, counteracting much of the side effects of the Virtues, there was no telling how long he might live.

Aaron, listen to me—

But he didn't. The storm of power roiling through him was too tempting, too seductive in its possibilities. He could be anything. Anyone. With such power, he could make of the world what he would. The gods had screwed it all up, made a place in which people suffered and died, but it wasn't too late. He could fix it. He could fix *all* of it. No more squabbling kings and queens leading thousands to their deaths. No more children walking down the stairs to see their parents dead. He would be the king, for all the world. He would be their god.

Aaron, please...

He would do what those before him couldn't—what even Aaron Caltriss could not. He would become a god and, in so doing, he would save the world. He took a step toward Kevlane, and the air hummed with the combined powers of the Virtues roiling through him. He was unaware of the feral snarl on his face, or the way his iridescent eyes danced with a fury that could only be borne of madness.

He took another step, his sword held in a white-knuckled grip, but, suddenly the world seemed to *shift*, and he froze as he realized that he was no longer in the audience room of the castle. Instead, he stood in a circular parapet. In the center of the room was a table upon which a man lay, and the sellsword recognized him as Aaron Caltriss.

Forming a circle around the king were seven men and women of various ages. They were knelt, their heads down, and they chanted something under their breath, words Aaron could not make out, and what little he heard sounded strange, alien to his ears.

Beside the table, closer than the others, stood another man. Aaron recognized this one, too, and he snarled, preparing to launch himself forward. The mage's hands were raised above his head, and the air in the room seemed to crackle with energy. Some small bit of Aaron's mind registered distant sounds of combat—screams, the faint clashing of steel. Distant, but coming closer. And then, suddenly, he knew where he was, *when* he was. Here, now, was that dire moment in which the spell had taken place, in which the Virtues had been born. There, standing beside the prone Caltriss, stood Kevlane, the ancient mage who had caused so much suffering, so much death. There was a hunger on the mage's face that hinted at the monster he would become.

The storm of emotions within Aaron reached a crescendo, and with an animalistic scream he charged forward, his sword leading. The blade cut the air, swift and true, but when it reached the mage, it went through him as if he were made of smoke, and Aaron stumbled, nearly losing his feet.

He spun, frowning, and saw one of the kneeling figures, a young girl, no more than sixteen, seventeen perhaps, raise her head to study him. Her mouth still moved, chanting the alien words, but her eyes watched him. She rose slowly to her feet and walked toward him. But strangely, as she did, another version of her remained kneeling, chanting the words while the other approached him.

"You've come," the young woman said. "I was not sure you would...that I could bring you here."

Realization struck Aaron like a hammer blow, and his breath caught in his throat. "Wait...*Co?*"

She gave a small smile at that. "Not here—not yet. Here, I am only Evelyn, daughter of Aaron Caltriss, and one of those chosen to participate in this great folly."

Aaron was vaguely aware of the chanting in the room beginning to rise in pitch, growing slowly louder, but he was too focused on the woman standing before him to pay it much attention. "I don't understand. Why did you bring me here? I was just about to kill Kevlane...I was going to fix it."

The girl cocked her head, studying him. "The world, you mean?"

"Yes."

She nodded slowly, her gaze taking in Kevlane and her prone father, a sadness in her eyes. "Others have set out to do the same. In the end, they all failed."

"But I won't," Aaron said. "With the power I have now..." He trailed off.

"They do not fail for want of power, Aaron. They fail, more often than not, because of it. Wishing to change the world is a good thing, an admirable thing, but such desires are much like the Virtues themselves, a blade likely to turn in one's hand, and many who set out to be heroes become tyrants instead. And the greater their power, the more suffering they leave in their wake."

Aaron opened his mouth to protest but paused when she held up a hand to silence him. "Wait," she said. "Watch."

Aaron gritted his teeth in frustration, but he did as she asked, following her gaze to the circle of the mages. At first, nothing seemed to change. Their chanting continued, and from somewhere in the distance, the sounds of fighting grew louder, closer. Then one of the kneeling figures, an old, wizened man who Aaron somehow knew was Palendesh, raised his head, and there was unmistakable fear in his wide eyes as he gazed about him. Yet his mouth continued to work, continued to chant the words, as if even in his fear, he could not stop what had begun.

The kneeling Evelyn raised her head next, and the fear in her eyes matched the old man's. Their gazes met, and a dark realization seemed to pass between them. "We begin to understand," the Evelyn standing beside him said, her voice full of sadness.

"Understand what?" Aaron demanded, having to raise his voice to be heard over the chanting growing louder by the second.

"The spell was tainted," the woman answered, and he could see silent tears gliding down her face. As she spoke, more of the seven began to raise their heads, one that Aaron knew to be Melan, later to become the Virtue of Strength, trembling, blood leaking from the corners of his mouth where he had bitten the inside of his cheek.

A phantom wind suddenly rose in the enclosed room, snatching at Aaron's clothes, as if it wanted to carry him away, to banish him from this place, this time. "*What do you mean 'tainted'?*" he yelled past the roar of air.

"Perhaps," she said, and though she spoke in normal volume, somehow he could still hear her words clearly over the high-pitched chanting and rush of wind, "it always was. Perhaps, there was some failing in our Shaping or perhaps, even then, the one who guided us," she paused, turning to look at Kevlane, "was twisted by his own desires. Either way, the spell was tainted, and we begin to understand that."

"Then why didn't you stop?" Aaron asked.

She smiled sadly, turning back to him once more. "Some roads, once they are started down, cannot be abandoned until you reach the other side. This is one such road."

Colored mist began to gather above each mage's head in a thickening cloud despite the driving gusts. Aaron noted that the colors were the same as those Virtues the mages would become. Movement caught his eye, and he saw Aaron Caltriss raising his head from where he lay, his gaze meeting his daughter's where she knelt. Neither spoke, perhaps because they could not, but still an understanding passed between them, communicated from her terrified expression to her father's, and he nodded one short nod, giving her a sad smile, his eyes full of unquestioned love and regret.

"He knows," Aaron breathed.

"Yes."

Kevlane began to wave his hands and arms in a series of intricate, precise gestures, and the colored clouds began to drift toward Aaron Caltriss. All the while, the king's eyes never left his daughter's, and though she continued to chant, Aaron could see tears running down the young woman's face, could see her terrible, wretched grief writ plain on her features.

The clouds of mist gathered above Caltriss and slowly began to seep into his body, almost tentatively. The wind grew stronger, howling through the chamber, and it was all Aaron could do to keep his balance as he watched the dead king. Caltriss's body tensed, his back arching as the Virtues entered him. His form was wracked with tremors as he struggled against some mysterious force, his muscles trembling as if under great strain. Then, his eyes finally left his daughter, and his mouth opened in a silent scream. Abruptly, the mists exploded out of him in a shower of color, vanishing into the air, and Caltriss slumped onto the table. He turned to regard his daughter, a world of meaning in his gaze, then, slowly, his eyes closed. They did not open again.

Aaron stared at the dead king, stunned. "He...he *made* the spell fail."

"Yes," the woman said, her voice low, little more than a whisper.

"But...*why?*"

"Because, Aaron Envelar," she said, meeting his eyes, "my father, in those last moments, knew the truth of the Virtues, knew their great cost. For power always has a cost, and this one was that, eventually, he would have become a terror more horrible than any of those he sought to protect his people against. And so, instead, he chose death."

Aaron's mouth worked and, for a time, he could find no words. Then, slowly, he turned to her. "What would you have me do?"

"We are tired, Aaron," she said, gesturing to the other mages. Kevlane stood in the center of the circle as if frozen, studying Caltriss with a look of triumph and hunger on his face, as if he had not yet realized the spell's failure, did not yet understand that, in the end, Caltriss had denied the power it would have given him, power no man should possess.

But the other mages had all lifted their heads and turned to stare at Aaron, and in those gazes he saw the exhaustion of which she spoke, a weariness beyond what any mortal should have to endure. "We are so tired. We have waited, have been waiting, for so very long, reliving this moment over and over. We are the Virtues, but we are also our memories, our pain, a pain that has endured for thousands of years. I would have you end it. I would have you let us rest."

Aaron blinked, surprised by the sadness welling up inside him. "Co—Evelyn, I..."

"I know, Aaron," she said, placing a hand on his shoulder. "I know. You will do well, and you will finish what you have started. The people will be safe, and it will be because of you. It has truly been a pleasure to know you, sellsword. I will miss you."

Aaron cleared his throat. "And I you, Firefly. But...how? How do I do it?"

"It's easy," she said, a small smile on her face. "Resting is easy, Aaron. You just have to close your eyes."

He looked around once more to the other mages studying him with naked hope and nodded slowly, surprised by the depths of sadness he felt. "Goodbye, Evelyn."

"Goodbye, Aaron."

"Do you regret it?" he asked, the words coming from him without him realizing they would. "Choosing me?"

She smiled widely this time. "Of course not. After all, you made me laugh."

Aaron swallowed past the lump in his throat, giving her a smile in return.

Then he closed his eyes.

***

The mage stood before him, his face a mask of fear and anger. *"What have you done?"* he hissed.

They were gone, all of them. Aaron knew it, felt it, an absence where Co had been, where all the others had been. For better or worse, he was only himself now, he and no other. "I did what I had to do," he said, walking toward Kevlane, "what Aaron Caltriss tried to do thousands of years ago. The Virtues should not exist, Kevlane. They should never have existed."

"Y-you *fool!*" Kevlane screamed. "Y-you could have been a *god.*"

"I'm a man, Kevlane," Aaron said, suddenly very tired. "And that's more than enough."

The blade plunged into the mage's chest, questing for his heart and finding it, and Kevlane gasped, staring down at the steel impaling him, at his death, in disbelief. "Now rest, mage," Aaron said, and there was no anger in his voice, no fury, only an abiding sadness. "It's easy, you know. All you have to do is close your eyes."

Kevlane opened his mouth as if he would speak, but no words came, and a moment later he stumbled off the blade, collapsing to the ground. Aaron watched him, watched his body twitch feebly as it learned the truth. Then, the mage let out one final breath. His eyes closed for the last time. And he rested.

***

Those stationed at the western gate would speak of that battle in years to come. Sailors would regale their shipmates with the tale, soldiers would speak of it in the barracks in hushed tones, and even hardened criminals would whisper of it, as if to speak any louder would somehow sully the past, would strip the moment of its grandeur.

As the body of Kevlane fell to the ground in Baresh's castle, so, too, did the abominations he had created. For they had been invested with his Art, his will, and when the mage breathed his final breath, they collapsed. They had made it through the gates, and the last half hour had been one of bloody struggle. Men and women slowly rose from where they'd been, seconds from death, to look at the bodies of their attackers scattered about the ground like so many puppets with their strings cut.

No longer supported by their eerie allies, the remaining army of Baresh found itself vastly outnumbered. A surrender was negotiated, overseen by Captain Brandon Gant. And then it was over. The cheers began slowly at first, tentative, uncertain. But soon they rose, higher and higher, and for all their losses, for all their suffering, the wounded and the well cheered alike. For it was over. The sun shone high in the sky, chasing away the shadows. The night had gone, and the day had begun in truth.

CHAPTER FIFTY-ONE

It was slow going as Aaron and his remaining companions left the castle. Bastion and Seline had finally roused, but their feet were uncertain beneath them, and the others had to help them along. Here and there, castle guards watched them pass, but they said nothing, nor did they move to block their way. They only watched the procession: a young boy; a Parnen over whose shoulder was draped the arm of a dazed woman; an overweight chamberlain on whose face swam a thousand different emotions, none of them fear, helping a young giant. And behind them all, a sellsword, a man who once had cared only for the coin in his pocket. A man who had once held the incorrect belief that surviving was the same thing as living.

They made their way through the castle, heading toward the entrance, a silence following them. But this silence was not one of regret but of understanding, and if there *was* sadness then it was a knowing kind, the same one might feel watching the leaves turn orange and brown in autumn, knowing that a new season was upon them. And in their silence they each, in their own way, said goodbye to the season that had passed and, together, shared the knowledge of its passing.

Someone shouted his name, and Aaron looked up to see Nathan running toward him, accompanied by his nephew, Janum. "Aaron," the innkeeper panted, coming to stand in front of him and the others, his hands resting on his knees as he gathered his breath. "You're okay. But," he added, looking around, "not all of you."

"No," Aaron agreed. "Not all of us."

Nathan nodded somberly. "I'm sorry for that, truly. And...Kevlane?"

"Dead."

The innkeeper breathed a heavy sigh of relief. "Well, that's good at least. I had thought as much, of course from what's happened, but—"

"What's happened?"

The big man waved a hand. "I'll explain everything soon but...Aaron, they're waiting for you. For all of you."

The sellsword frowned at that. "Who's waiting?"

The innkeeper raised his eyebrows as if surprised by the question. "Well...everyone."

Aaron and the others shared a troubled glance then followed Nathan out of the front gate of the castle. They blinked in the sunlight, shading their eyes like men and women who had spent months in darkness. *And, in so many ways,* Aaron thought, *we have.*

Soon, his eyes grew accustomed to the brightness. He heard someone—he believed Caleb—gasp, and the once Virtue-bearers froze together on the castle steps as they saw what waited for them.

Thousands of people crowded the castle courtyard, spilling out into the street, so many that Aaron could not see, even from his place on the top of the steps, where the crowd ended. It was as if it stretched on into eternity, as if every person not just in the city, but in the world had gathered together.

"Aaron," Gryle said from beside him, "what...what do we do?"

Aaron was just about to say that he didn't know when, suddenly, there was movement among the crowd. At first, it was hard, staring at that mass, to figure out what was happening. Then a shock of surprise ran through him as each and every one of those gathered fell to a knee, bowing their heads. At a loss for words, Aaron looked at the others beside him, saw his own disbelief mirrored in their expressions.

Suddenly, part of the crowd began to separate, forming an avenue, through which several figures approached. Aaron felt a relief greater than any he'd felt before when he saw Adina there.

And not just her, but Captain Gant, and May. Darrell and Balen, Thom and Wendell, and all the rest. Even Urek and his band of criminals. They were bruised, battered, and clearly exhausted. But they were alive.

It was in that moment that Aaron realized he'd resigned himself to never seeing them again, any of them.

Thank you, Co, he thought, *for everything.*

Adina and the others approached, all of them smiling and laughing, and Aaron felt as if he were in a dream, one he might wake from at any second.

But then Adina was there, pulling him into an embrace. Her lips were on his, and it was no dream after all. "Oh, Aaron," she said, "thank the gods that you're okay." She took in the others with her gaze. "That you're all okay."

She stepped away then, and Aaron surveyed the crowd once more, feeling as if something was expected of him. "Adina…why are all these people here? What do they want from me?"

She smiled, holding his hand in hers, and turned to study the crowd with him. "They don't want anything from you, Aaron. You've already given it to them."

"What?"

She laughed. "Don't you know? You—all of you—you've given them the best gift anybody can have. Hope, Aaron. You've given them hope."

And despite his exhaustion, despite all he had been through in the last few hours, he found himself smiling. "Hope," he repeated, glancing to either side to see that the others were also smiling. "Now, that's a fine thing."

CHAPTER FIFTY-TWO

Aaron fought back a yawn as he walked down the castle corridor. At the end of the hall, two guards waited. When he approached, the smaller of the two dropped down onto one knee, bowing his head.

"Oh, get up, you bastard."

Wendell rose, grinning widely. "Forgive me for sayin' so, Sire, but I ain't sure that's the way a king ought to talk."

Aaron grunted, glancing at the other guard, Bastion. The giant soldier's wide grin vanished when he did, and he pointedly avoided Aaron's gaze. "Tell me, Bastion, if I asked you to throw this bastard out of a window, what would you say?"

Bastion laughed. "I'd say that Sergea—forgive me, *Captain* Wendell still owes me some coin from last night's card game. It'd be a shame if something happened to him before he was able to pay me back." His smile widened, and he met Aaron's eyes. "Majesty."

Aaron sighed, shaking his head. "Gods, but I've got to look into finding some guards who are mute. At least then, I wouldn't have to listen to all of this 'Majesty' and 'Sire' shit all the time."

Wendell snorted. "Yeah, must be tough, being a king. You've our sympathies, Sire."

Aaron's scowl seemed to have little effect, so he sighed instead. "And Queen Adina?"

"Waiting for you, Majesty."

"Alright, I'll see you bastards at the dinner tonight. And Wendell?"

"Majesty?"

"No waving your boot at people this time, alright?"

The scarred man finally looked chastised at that. "Of course, Sire."

Aaron grinned and walked on. He paused to glance in a room he passed to see Gryle standing beside an easel on which had been placed a large parchment. The chamberlain—now a tutor—was in the middle of a lecture on proper etiquette during a formal dinner while his two pupils—Beth's grandson Michael, and Caleb—moved toy soldiers around on the table where they sat. After so much had happened, it felt good to Aaron that some things, at least, were back to normal.

Gryle, noticing his pupils' distraction, cleared his throat. "Caleb, what are your thoughts on the conflict in the western reaches under the reign of King Altes and its causes?"

The boy glanced up from where he'd been placing a toy soldier to attack one of Michael's. "Forgive me, Gryle, do you refer to Altes or Altes the Second, his son? Mostly, the original conflict was due to economic concerns, primarily revolving around a lack of taxes being collected from the nobles of the western reach, but it was resolved, at least for a time, before King Altes the Second took control after his father's passing. The second rising of the conflict was due more to—"

"Very good," Gryle interrupted, and Aaron couldn't help but laugh at the mixture of exasperation and pleasure in the chamberlain's eyes. Gryle let out a squeak of surprise when he noticed Aaron for the first time, dropping the quill he held. It rolled under the desk beside the easel, but the chamberlain didn't seem to notice. "Majesty, forgive me, I didn't see you there."

"No problem at all, Gryle," Aaron said. "And we've been over this—call me Aaron. We nearly died together a dozen times; I'm pretty sure it's acceptable."

The chamberlain frowned in thought. "Forgive me, Majesty, but I would have to check the proper precedents. Though, if I'm being honest, I'm not quite sure...perhaps Elastra's *Treatise on Decorum and Propriety*." He rubbed at his chin. "I think, perhaps, there's something there."

Aaron sighed. "Never mind, Gryle. Carry on."

"Of course, Sire." The chamberlain looked around on the floor, trying to find the quill he'd dropped, and distractedly grabbed the solid oak desk, lifting it with one hand before retrieving the quill and setting the massive desk back down again. He resumed his lecture, apparently unaware of the impossible feat of strength he'd just performed.

Well, Aaron thought, *at least some things are back to normal.* The Virtues may have been gone for months now, but some of the effects they'd had on their bearers still lingered. The exact extent of the changes was unknown, but that he—and those others—*had* changed, was not in doubt. After all, what but the Virtue of Strength's insanity would have convinced him to accept the position as King of Telrear? But, of course, he knew. The reason—*his* reason—waited for him even now, so he gave the two grinning youths a wink and walked on.

He found her standing in the doorway, as he'd known she would be, staring into the small room. She turned at his approach and gave him a smile as he walked up to her, taking her hand. "Wife," he said.

"Husband."

"Remind me to have Captain Wendell flogged," he said quietly. "The man's been even more insufferable than usual since he became captain of the castle guard."

"Of course," she said, grinning and speaking in a low whisper. "This time, let's hope something won't come up to keep the captain from getting his just punishment. You know, like it has the last dozen times you were going to have him flogged."

Aaron gave her a smile of his own, unable to help himself. "The others are still coming for the dinner?"

"May and Thom for sure," she said, "and if his letters are any indication, I expect Festa will be glad to have the two of them off his ship for a time." Her eyes danced with amusement. "Apparently, Thom has become quite the lay about since May started sailing with them."

Aaron grinned. "It'll be good to see them both. And the others?"

"Balen will be here," she said, "as will General Gant, of course, and Urek and his crew. As for Leomin and Seline…" She rolled her eyes. "Who knows."

"They haven't responded to the letter?"

"Oh, they responded," Adina said. "After a fashion. A boy from the inn where they're staying brought the letter—apparently, they couldn't be bothered to leave their rooms."

Aaron laughed quietly, then followed his wife's gaze as she looked into the room once more, at the slatted crib, and the small bundle asleep within it. "She's sleeping better," Adina said.

"Thank the gods for that," he replied. "Maybe that means we'll be able to get some sleep ourselves. I seem to remember enjoying it."

She grinned and, as if his words had been a cue, suddenly the baby stirred, her eyes opening slowly to stare at her parents standing in the doorway. She grinned, cooing, and crawled toward them, frowning when she fetched up against the wooden slats of the crib. Then, an intense look of concentration on her face, she reached out one pudgy hand and with what seemed to be no effort at all, tore off several of the oak slats. In another moment, she was crawling across the floor to them, and Aaron and Adina shared a sigh. After all, it wasn't the first crib they had gone through, and he didn't imagine it would be the last. Adina hurried into the room, scooping the now-smiling baby up from the ground.

Aaron leaned against the door frame, watching as Adina spun the baby in circles, her laughter and the little girl's filling the room. Soon, they were both on the floor, the queen of Telrear making frightened noises as she crawled across the room, fleeing from the giggling baby chasing her. It didn't take long for the baby to catch her mother—it never did—and soon she was climbing on top of her, pulling her hair.

Adina turned to look at Aaron, raising an eyebrow. "What sort of king are you, that you'll let your wife suffer in battle with this, this *tyrant?*" she said, pausing as a very familiar—and largely unwelcome—sound came from the baby, and Adina and Aaron stared at her with wide eyes. Finally, when it was finished, Adina cleared her throat. "I seem to recall it being your turn."

Aaron winced, doing his best not to breathe through his nose. "I'd love to, of course," he said, "but the thing is, I've been talking to

Gryle and Wendell, and since I'm the king I'm not sure that it would be proper to..." He trailed off at Adina's scowl and sighed.

Then, taking a deep breath, Aaron Envelar, once sellsword and now king, ventured into his daughter's room to do battle. And, this time, at least, his sword was nowhere to be seen, and his opponent waited for him with outstretched arms, her large, child's eyes dancing with laughter.

"Come on then, Evelyn," he said, taking his daughter from his wife. "Let's go see Uncle Wendell."

THE END OF THE SEVEN VIRTUES

BY JACOB PEPPERS

To stay up to date on the next release and hear about other awesome promotions and free giveaways, **sign up to my mailing list.** For a limited time, you will also receive a FREE copy of *The Silent Blade,* the prequel to The Seven Virtues, when you sign up!

Go to *jacobpeppersauthor.com* to claim your rewards now!

And now, Dear Reader, we have come to the end of The Seven Virtues. It was a long journey, I know, but one I hope you enjoyed.

If you did enjoy *A Sellsword's Hope*, I'd really appreciate you taking a moment to leave an honest review—as any author can tell you, they are a big help.

If you want to reach out, you can email me at JacobPeppersauthor@gmail.com or visit jacobpeppersauthor.com. You can also follow me at Facebook or on Twitter.

I can't wait to hear from you!

Note from the Author

Well, dear reader, we have come to the end of The Seven Virtues. The great evil has been met, has been conquered, and the threat Kevlane posed is finally defeated. So celebrate, if you wish. After all, it was a long road that brought us here, wasn't it? A long, tiring path, full of twists and turns that sometimes carried us deep into places of shadow, where light is but a passing memory, quickly forgotten.

Yet, for all that, we have arrived, have come to a place where, finally, we might be allowed to catch our breath. So celebrate, and I will celebrate with you. And do not be ashamed, if the tears you shed are not wholly happy ones. After all, we made it, but not all those who set out on this adventure with us were so fortunate. Those, like Beth, like Raenclest, and Hale, and so many others, who were lost along the way who, as our road took us in to shadow, we found missing when once again we arrived into the light.

Still, we might be comforted in the knowledge that, without them, without their sacrifice, we would have never come to be here in this place of…I will not say peace, for such a state is all-too temporary in the living and only the fallen might truly claim it. Instead, I will say a place of rest, a place to reflect, to mourn and to grieve and, yes, to celebrate. For no matter how many were lost, it could have been so much worse, couldn't it?

Aaron and Adina, Wendell and Gryle and all the others, they wait for us up ahead in the castle. Shield your eyes from the morning sun and peer into the distance—there, do you see it? The white walls of Perennia, shining in the morning sun despite the blood still staining them, and why not? Hope, after all, is never wholly clean, is it?

I know you must be eager to be off, but why don't you sit with me here, on this fallen tree, and rest your weary feet for a time? We will visit Aaron and the others, of course, but I suspect we will not stay overly long. After all, there are other paths to explore for we, wanderers, and, as ever, one world, one story is not enough to sate the hunger we share.

We will need to gather our strength for a time, and I feel that we have earned that. But let us not tarry too long. After all, there are other stories, other dramas playing out in different places, different worlds. I have heard of one such, in my travelings, and a name, spoken in whispers, The Son of the Morning. Soon, I will go there and lend what help I can, and perhaps you should come as well. For though this part of the story might be finished, ours is not, and we have many adventures ahead of us. There is joy, somewhere down the road, awe and laughter and, yes, grief, but why not? It is all of a part, just one more step on the trail, one more leg of the journey.

So rest now, and when you are ready, we will leave this place and journey on to another. And do not worry about Aaron, about Adina and all the others. Kevlane might be defeated, his creations finally put to rest, but as for our sellsword? Our princess? Well…Even I don't know where all of our paths might lead, but, if you ask me, their story might not yet be finished.

Thank you so much for going on this journey with me. I hope you enjoyed meeting Aaron, Adina, and all the others. They were a pleasure to write. As always, I want to give a special thanks to the beta readers and editors for all their input and efforts in helping me to make this series the best it could be. They are a wonderful group of people who I cannot thank enough.

It's a funny thing, finishing such a long series. On the one hand, I find myself sad to be leaving the characters in The Seven Virtues behind (I confess that I have a particular fondness for Wendell). On the other hand, I'm excited for what's to come, and I look forward to once more stepping into the world of The Nightfall Wars and catching up with Alesh, with Katherine and Rion, and their companions. I think their story has gone unspoken for too long, and it's past time I told it.

So stick with me. True, this story might be done (only time will tell) but there are thousands of others out there waiting for us.

How about we find them together?

Jacob Peppers

About the Author

Jacob Peppers lives in Georgia with his wife, his son, Gabriel, and their three dogs. He is an avid reader and writer and when he's not exploring the worlds of others, he's creating his own. His short fiction has been published in various markets, and his short story, "The Lies of Autumn," was a finalist for the 2013 Eric Hoffer Award for Short Prose. He is the author of the bestselling series, The Seven Virtues, as well as The Nightfall Wars, and The Essence Chronicles.

Printed in Great Britain
by Amazon